"…a masterfully written tale that immerses readers in a journey
of faith, perseverance, and the undeniable power of God's hand in our lives.
From the opening pages, the story captivates with its rich characters and
intricate plot involving the interplay between darkness and light, Angels
and humans, and God and His world, offering a profound reminder that
even in life's darkest moments, hope and redemption are never out of reach.
I was drawn into Koontz's narrative which challenged me to reflect on the
question: What does it truly mean to trust God's plan, even when it defies all
understanding? Kim Koontz doesn't just tell a story—she invites readers to
embark on a transformative experience. *The Catalyst, Book One: The Waiting*
will leave you pondering your own journey of faith and how God uses even
the most unlikely circumstances to accomplish His divine purposes.
This is a must-read for those who long to be inspired and reminded
of the beauty of walking in obedience to God's call."

—Matthew Dowling, Pastor and Hospital Chaplain

"A riveting, genre-crossing work, *The Catalyst, Book One: The Waiting*
gives readers a glimpse into Great Depression-era America with an
engrossing narrative. Historians and history enthusiasts alike will
appreciate the on-point and nuanced details of life in this era.
All readers will appreciate the storytelling. Truly a type of novel
all its own, and a fresh take on historical fiction."

—Luke Pickelman, M.A., J.D., Professor of History
at Northwestern Michigan College

"When I started reading *The Catalyst*, from the first chapter, I was hooked!
Characters you love and hate. This story will bring God into your life
even if your faith is nonexistent and for those who are believers,
your faith will be strengthened. I highly recommend this book!"

—Adrianne Croket, Marketing Specialist for Visiting Angels Dearborn

"Kimberly Koontz masterfully crafts an immersive portrayal of small-
town America on the brink of the Great Depression. Her vivid storytelling
introduces a gripping narrative where a team of warrior angels gathers

to confront the impending forces of darkness in a high-stakes battle for humanity's soul. This novel seamlessly blends historical ambiance with fantastical elements, creating a thought-provoking and thoroughly engaging experience for readers."

—Jay Jahnke, Senior Supply Chain Manager

THE CATALYST

~ BOOK ONE ~
THE WAITING

KIM KOONTZ

M·P·P
www.MissionPointPress.com

Mission Point Press

Published by Mission Point Press
www.MissionPointPress.com

Cover illustration: Jeff Bane
Book design: Deirdre Wait

Hardcover ISBN 13: 978-1-965278-38-3
Paperback ISBN 13: 978-1-965278-39-0

LCCN: 2025900803

Printed in the United States of America

This book was a marvelous journey, a true test in perseverance and meticulous scrutiny—not only in historical study of an era I hadn't lived through, but also in the disciplines of equestrian show jumping. The story nested in my imagination for over a year, which was effortless to actually write, but researching the details of everyday life in the early 1900s was a joyful challenge. I endured hours of internet searches and historical reference-checking to capture the essence of this period in time and fell madly in love with the era—and yes, even the struggles and inconveniences of doing it all by hand.

The combination of writing about two worlds—one heavenly, the other earthly—provided an unexplored canvas to let my imagination connect with these polar opposite realities in a way that made sense. We, mere mortals, acknowledge the existence of life ever after, but I don't think it is realized that we are not alone in this basecamp for life's battles that we call earth.

Angels, I do believe, are as real as any one of us, and the exploration of how they might shape our human existence is absolutely fascinating, and it gave me great satisfaction to create this story with the influence of such celestial helpers in mind.

For my readers who choose to experience *The Catalyst*, I hope you take something from the story that is special for you. This story isn't just for horse lovers, history buffs, or devout believers; it has something for everyone—and I believe it was meant to carry a message.

Whether you are deeply rooted in faith, recently planted, or still a seedling in a Styrofoam cup—no matter your religion or faith belief, I hope this book uplifts you and strengthens your heart.

Kindly,
Kim Koontz

For God, the one who gave me an imagination.

THE CATALYST:
Book One – The Waiting
Playlist

1. "Wild Angels" – Martina McBride

2. "When You Come Back Down" – Nickel Creek

3. "Jesus And John Wayne" – Gaither, Alabama, The Oak Ridge Boys

4. "Take Me Out to the Ballgame" – Champs United

5. "Fly Over States" – Jason Aldean

6. "The Fire Within" – Jennifer Thomas, The Rogue Pianist

7. "Angels Among Us" – Alabama

8. "Hard Fought Hallelujah" – Brandon Lake, Jelly Roll

9. "Fire & Brimstone" – Brantley Gilbert, Jamey Johnson, Alison Krauss

10. "The Horse Nobody Could Ride" – Joey + Rory

THE CATALYST

Nine angels stood shoulder to shoulder as rolling clouds, tinged with dark hues of purple and orange, surged toward them. Battle-scarred warriors sharpened by fire, they had endured their time of testing on earth. Adorned with medals symbolizing the trials they had faced in their mortal lives, they stood together, unwavering in their faith.

Each had been given a unique gift and power to intervene in the human experience. Called by their Heavenly Father as His elite soldiers, they accepted their assignments graciously, waiting for the arrival of the last warrior to unite them for one final mission.

1

In September 1926, one week after his fourteenth birthday, Benjamin William Paulie sat along a cart path used for bringing supplies to the stables owned by Charles and Claire Collins. Two farmhands, including his father, Samuel, opened large gates, allowing carts carrying riding gear and equipment to pass through. After the gates closed and the men began their duties, Ben would often sketch and daydream, imagining himself guiding his horse over railed fences, seated atop colorful fabric, with shimmering tassels caressing his legs.

As the horses approached the gate, his father whistled—a secret code to let Ben know the horses were coming. When he heard it, he moved to stand at the narrow gap between the fence posts where he could see the parade of bridled noses, reins draped along their manes. Most strutted past the fence, paying little attention to anything beyond the gate, but the last horse always stopped at the gap in the fence. Ben could hear the handler's mumblings, voicing their frustration in colorful language as they pulled the horse forward.

His father's workday ended at four o'clock, just as the sun began to settle beyond a row of tall trees. Brushing the dirt from his pants, Ben tucked the drawing pad under his arm and ran over to greet him. As they walked home, he held his father's calloused hand, swinging their clasped fingers in the air. They talked about airplanes and fishing, but mostly they talked about horses. Ben's imagination seemed limitless, and he carried himself with a free-spirited curiosity about the world that entertained his father, asking lots of questions about the horses, often without pausing for an answer before asking another.

Samuel didn't have all the answers and tried redirecting Ben's attention to other subjects, like toolmaking and practical skills such as blacksmithing and lumbering, but all Ben wanted to talk about was the horses. A pragmatic man, Samuel focused on practical concerns, like whether the hunting season would yield enough to carry them through the long winter, the ache in his lower back from years of hard labor, and the unsettling signs that the body he and his family depended on in his thirties might not be as resilient in his forties and beyond. But more than anything, he enjoyed thinking about his wife, Emily, and their children.

Jonathan, their oldest, was finishing school and was interested in construction, architecture, and joining the Navy. As a young boy, he would haul boxes, building blocks, and scraps of wood, spending entire days constructing make-believe cities. Samuel spent many weekend mornings sipping his coffee and admiring the detail and craftsmanship of the project that Jonathan had spread out on the living room floor the night before.

Margaret, their daughter, was already studying to be a nurse, an interest that began by applying bandages to teddy bears and offering medical advice to pretend patients. She had a gentle personality, calm, and investigative.

Ben, the youngest of the siblings, had struggled in school. His teachers observed that his limited social development caused difficulties in the classroom and advised that he continue his studies at home, where he could feel more comfortable and less distracted. Samuel and Emily knew early on that he was different. As a young child, he was slow to develop his speech and didn't socialize with other kids, which made school even more troublesome. Teachers often assigned him chores like cleaning chalkboards, erasers, and assisting in gathering supplies for art projects—anything to keep him busy and occupied—dismissing him from group activities. Over time, he became more withdrawn and disengaged. Rather than forcing him to be in an environment where he wasn't thriving, they decided to allow him to learn and develop at his own pace, outside the classroom.

Ben's time on the farm while his father worked gradually increased. After countless instances of Ben disappearing into the backyard and reappearing at the farm with torn pant legs and poison sumac rashes from running through thick brush, his parents were persuaded to let him accompany Samuel to work most days.

In the evenings, they gathered around the table for supper. Jonathan and Margaret talked about their day at school, Samuel and Emily discussed news and chores that needed tending to, and Ben drew pictures. After the meal, Emily and Margaret cleaned the dishes and prepared lunches for the next day, while Ben sat at the table and sketched. Once the evening chores were done, they all huddled around the radio or a puzzle.

One late September morning, Samuel gave Emily a kiss on the cheek and walked outside, waiting for Jonathan and Margaret to gather their books. Fall was on their heels, and coming off the summer heat, the brisk autumn morning felt refreshing. Ben pushed off the newel post at the base of the landing to catch up, throwing his pack over his shoulder and hurried for the door.

Emily held the door ajar as Ben rushed past, shooing away a fly that had squeezed through a hole in the screen. She made a mental note to remind Samuel to fix the rickety hinge before the cold set in and the winter winds tore it off the frame. Clouds rolled quickly across the sky as she hugged her shawl tightly around her shoulders, fighting the chill, and watched her family walk down the driveway—three growing taller every day, and one getting shorter, likely from years of manual labor that had bent his posture closer to the ground. She felt proud of them.

When they reached the end of the driveway, Samuel looked up at the sky as ominous clouds began swirling toward town. "Be careful," he said, stopping Jonathan and Margaret. "Farmers are harvesting, churning up a lot of dust, and the wind is already picking up."

Margaret tightened the scarf under her chin, bumping Jonathan with her elbow. "Let's go, we have school pictures today and I don't want messy hair!"

They hurried more than usual as bursts of wind clipped at their backsides.

"We're going to get there before the second bell," Jonathan said, feeling the gusts push him forward.

"Maybe for once in your life, you'll be on time."

Samuel and Ben had a longer walk and were against the wind, squinting to keep the blowing dust out of their eyes. By the time they reached the farm, the wind had gained strength, bending tree branches and sending loose debris tumbling along the ground at their feet. The windmill in front of the farmhouse spun rapidly, and the rope fastened to the flag smacked against the pole in a frenzied spiral. Samuel noticed one of the handlers struggling to secure a gate snapped off the pin with such force that it broke the hinges. The sky, which had looked aggravated earlier, now appeared furious. Wind whipped dust into Ben's eyes as he heard voices calling from the barn, though he couldn't make out the words. Ben turned around, using his back to block the wind, and saw a giant tail stretching longer and bending toward the ground. Frozen, he tugged at his father's shirt sleeve, pointing to the sky.

Samuel's jaw dropped as he watched the tornado approach. Locking a firm grip on Ben's arm, Samuel pushed against the wind toward the gate, shielding his vision in the crook of his elbow. He knew Ben was small enough to squeeze through the opening between the gate and fence post, and even though the route outside the fence would be longer, it was the farthest from equipment and objects that could be tossed into the wind.

Ben's small frame trembled as he looked around in horror, the world growing darker and louder with each passing moment. Samuel tightened his grip on Ben's shoulders to steady him, straining to speak as the wind pressed harder against his face. "Run all the way to the barn by the hillside. In the back, there's a small door under the hay shoot. Get inside and hide until I come for you—go now!" he said, positioning him sideways through the opening. He gave him a hard shove, then urged him to start running.

Looking down the fence line, Ben saw the horses gallop across the fields, zigzagging with the shifting wind. He sprinted as fast as he could but shielding his face from debris made it difficult to keep his eyes open, and the wind pushed him sideways. Samuel watched until Ben's silhouette faded into the dust-filled air, then made his way to a storage barn behind the farmhouse. As Samuel pushed through the wind, his footing gave way, and he tumbled to the ground. Pain surged through his entire body; his vision blurred as a pulsating throb inside his head made him nauseous. Unable to regain his footing and struggling to breathe, he crawled through the mud toward the small barn. Finding a sturdy post, he fought to balance on his knees on the slippery ground and he braced himself against it to stand.

Ben felt a flicker of relief as the paddock came into view—just a little farther, and he would be there. Just as he passed it, he heard a deafening crack. Looking over his shoulder, he saw a door flipping end over end, tumbling across his path. As he raced toward the next building, the wind shifted direction, pushing him forward. He saw the barn up ahead, sitting on a stone foundation with two massive wooden doors on one side and a buggy ramp at the front entrance. He pushed the latch on the small door upward and quickly slipped inside. Sitting against the stone wall, he wrapped his arms around his knees and prayed. The wind tore violently at the roof, and the sounds of shifting, cracking, and splintering wood made him press his back against the jagged edges of the stone in fear. He thought about his mother, alone in the house, and how scared she must be. And Margaret and Jonathan in the small schoolhouse. And his father. His hands trembled as he swept rolling tears from his cheeks, and he wondered: Where did the horses go?

*   *   *

Charles held up a lantern, slowly opening the basement hatch. The house was dark, and the walls seemed to sway and stretch with eerie tension. As he passed the study, he saw the big oak through the window, its branches arched as if invisible ropes were pulling them to the ground. Holding the lantern out in front of him, he saw someone standing before the storage barn door—the same door that Samuel had worked on just yesterday. As he leaned toward the window, squinting out at the dark figure, an explosion rocked the house. Charles managed to shield his eyes with his arm just in time before he was showered in splintered wood and glass; his grip on the lantern faltered, sending it tumbling across the floor planks until it came to rest at the foot of a sturdy, iron horse-shaped doorstop. Straining to look out the window—now a gaping hole filled with jagged glass—he saw Samuel lying on the ground. Maneuvering through the kitchen, Charles felt his way along the countertop, taking unsteady steps toward the door. When he pushed against it, a gust of wind snatched it from his grip, sending it toppling across the ground. Stepping off the porch, he quickened his pace. "Samuel!" he yelled into the roar of the storm, drawing in deep breaths. His voice, normally loud and baritone, sounded soft and lost against the howling wind.

As Samuel pressed his fingers to his temples, desperate to stop the throbbing in his head, he heard shouts coming from a silhouette that emerged out of the darkness. Even through the storm, Samuel recognized Charles's voice calling to him. Mustering his strength, he hoisted himself onto his heels and pushed off the ground. Just then, Samuel saw a large object slicing through the air. It was a blade from the windmill which had graced the farm with its rhythmic rotations for years, but now it spun loose, hurtling in their direction. He leapt forward, launching himself into Charles's side, sending him to the ground. A split second later, something heavy drove into his back, throwing him face down into the mud, and the pain that coursed through him disappeared.

Minutes later, a calmness fell over the fields. The winds subsided, branches hung in limp surrender, and the grounds fell silent. Boards and beams that had fought and lost against the relentless punishment stood as tattered testaments to the brutality of nature.

Carl, a horse trainer, lifted a plank that held the barn door shut and stepped out. The destruction stunned him, and he called out to the others behind him. The paddock was toppled, reduced to a pile of splintered planks teetering in a heap. Shreds of fabric, glass, tires, and a cart seat were tossed about like a handful of dice. A horse trailer lay on its side in an open field, its tires still spinning. The farmhouse roof was badly damaged; its windows were shattered, and entire sections of siding were ripped from the rafters.

One of the farmhands, Elliot, stepped out behind Carl. "God in heaven," he whispered. "Can you believe this?"

Carl walked to the farmhouse to check on Claire and Charles, tossing boards and broken pieces of pottery from his path, while Paul, the head granger, and Elliot surveyed the property.

"Paul!" Elliot called. "Look over there, on the ground!"

They ran as fast as they could, rushing to Charles's side as he kneeled over Samuel with his hand on his chest, rocking back and forth in desperate prayer.

*   *   *

Ben sat huddled next to the barn's stone wall, brushing a spider off his pant leg, when he heard gravel rustling and hushed voices outside the door. Paul cleared a branch from the small door and pushed on the door hatch. Ben looked over at the men, hands still clasped around his knees, shaking and teary-eyed, "Is my father with you, is he coming to take me home soon?"

Stepping forward, Paul kneeled in front of him. "There's been an accident, Ben. Come with us, we will make sure to get you home safe."

"But… my father, he said to wait here, that he would come get me and we would go together."

Elliot reached down and helped him to his feet, brushing hay and dirt from his clothes. Ben saw concern and sadness weigh heavily upon their faces and his stomach sank. Elliot took his hand, "We will take you, all of us together."

Ben's eyes widened as they maneuvered through debris. Large trees were uprooted, fencing cracked and splintered, toppled over like wooden dominoes. A sharp grinding noise caught their attention: the rotator from the windmill had wedged itself into a window frame. The spinning cylinder scraped against the aluminum sill, making an eerie screeching sound. It saddened Ben to see the windmill's destruction; he had spent hours hypnotized by its rhythmic rotations. A large mound of lumber, posts, and beams lay in a heap where the paddock once stood.

A loud crack echoed from the tree line and a horse trotted over the hillside. "I wasn't expecting to see that one back," Paul said, "was kind of hoping he would have kept running."

Looking around Carl's bulky frame, Ben could see the horse was laboring as it crossed over the field. It was the horse he sketched many times. "Mr. Elliot," he said, looking up at him, "am I going to see my father now?"

2

EMILY CLUTCHED HER HANDKERCHIEF TIGHTLY as friends lined up to pay their respects and offer condolences. Charles and Claire were waiting at the end to greet the family. The line slowly shortened as folks made their way off the grounds; the grief and trauma on Emily's face nearly broke Claire's heart, and she rushed forward and hugged her tightly.

Ben watched her as she talked with his mother. At the farm, while his father worked, he occasionally saw her coming and going, wearing fancy clothes and large hats and returning with all sorts of packages. Her dresses were always perfectly pressed and covered in flowery designs, but he had never seen her this close before. She looked friendly, her face fair except for a sprinkling of freckles across her nose and cheeks. Emily dried her eyes with her handkerchief and then took Margaret's hand, motioning for him and Jonathan to follow them to the black car waiting to take them home.

As they pulled up to the house, Emily caught a glimpse of Samuel's worn overalls pinned to the clothesline. After exiting the car and thanking Pastor John for the ride, the family silently entered the house. A heaviness settled over her as she walked through the door. *The house feels different,* she thought; quiet and hollow. Ben lay on his parents' bed, holding his father's fishing pole close to his chest—a Shakespeare with a Level Wind Reel. On the bedside table was a picture of the two of them during a fishing trip, their catch dangling from the line.

Looking up at the ceiling, he listened to voices downstairs and car doors opening and closing. Pulling himself off the bed, he peeked out the curtains and saw Mr. and Mrs. Collins' car and Elliot's truck. He gave the rod a final glance, propped it in the corner and went downstairs. Rounding the landing, he saw Mr. Collins standing in front of his drawings, which hung from a wire above the entryway. Mr. Collins was looking intently at a drawing he had sketched after supper just days ago. Ben had drawn this particular horse many times, and this image captured it looking out of the gap in the fence, its eyes a steely charcoal color.

Ben walked quietly down the steps, passing behind him and turned toward the kitchen.

"Young Benjamin," Charles called.

"Yes sir."

"Are you the hand behind this masterpiece?" he asked, turning from Ben to the sketch and then back again. "Impressive, young man. You are quite talented."

"Thank you, sir," he said quietly.

"I'm not a betting man, but I reckon you have a fondness for these animals."

"Yes sir, I do."

"And this one here?" he inquired, pointing to the drawing he had been studying.

"I like that horse, sir. Does he have a name?"

"I've heard him called many things, but none that young ears should hear. He's a bit temperamental and somewhat uninterested in the routine of training, but he will make a decent cart horse if nothing else."

Ben looked down at his socks, circling one foot in front of the other. "How much does a horse cost?"

Pinching his chin, Charles considered the motive behind the question. "If he does the job I bought him for, about two thousand dollars. If he doesn't, then I guess whatever the feed cost for the last two months," he chuckled.

People began to gather in the kitchen, arranging trays of food and stirring pitchers of lemonade and iced tea. Ben took a seat at the table, sliding his hands along the smooth tablecloth, looking around at the crowd of people. Jonathan was at the opposite corner of the table picking at the last bite of his sandwich. Through the screen door, he could see Margaret pulling dandelions, bunching them into a bouquet.

Charles spoke quietly with Ben's mother in the corner, and whatever he said made her smile. Resting his head in the bend of his arm, he caught a waft of perfume that tickled his nose; it was familiar, reminding him of church. When he lifted his head, a plump figure passed by holding a white dish with yellow oven mitts.

"Gladys, so lovely to see you," Claire said. Gladys put the casserole on the counter and the three women embraced before beginning to talk quietly.

Closing his eyes, Ben was comforted by whispering voices and wonderful smells filling the kitchen. Charles found Elliot and Paul standing in the living room, admiring the mounted bass that hung above the wood burner.

"Now that's a catch," Charles said.

"Caught it last fall on a day trip to Indian Springs," Paul said. "It was the first cast of the day; we didn't catch another. Hard to believe we won't have any more trips together."

Slowly backing away, Charles dropped into a chair.

"Charles, you alright?" Elliot asked.

Slouching forward, he held his face in his hands, shaking his head. Unable to hold his emotions back, the grief and guilt bubbled up and he began to weep. "If I would have just stayed inside, he would have had no reason to push me out of the way, no reason to be taken from his family."

The women walked into the room, deeply disheartened to see such a strong and resilient man overcome with emotion. He stared at the floor, wiping away his tears, when a pair of flat black shoes rounded at the toes and heavily worn past the leather came into view.

"Samuel would not have acted as he did in that moment if he didn't have a reason. Even if we don't know what that was, we must honor it," Emily said, reaching for his hand as everyone huddled around to pray.

When the gathering ended, Paul and Elliot waited outside for Charles to give them instructions for the next morning. "Might not be a bad idea if we stop by Bernie's. We can start haulin' lumber," Elliot said.

"I wouldn't be so quick to think he's gonna rebuild," Paul said.

Elliot looked at him with surprise. "You think he's fixin' to sell?"

"I think we should prepare ourselves for the possibility. Here he comes now."

Charles helped Claire into the car, noticing Paul and Elliot waiting by the truck, and thought it best to give them time away from the farm. "Give it a day or two boys. I reckon we all need some rest from the hell that knocked us on our keesters."

"Maybe you're right," Elliot said, watching him walk away. "Maybe he ain't puttin' it back together."

Later that evening, as he looked out over the bruised landscape, Charles reflected on better times when visitors lined the fences, hoping for a glimpse of his prized racehorses. All his life, he'd never quit on anything—never let the tough times break his dreams. For as long as his heart still beat, he still had hope. All of life's knockdowns, blind spots, and surprises only made him more resilient. To him, that was life, and he kept that fire in his belly alive, sitting there a bit longer just feeling it burn. "I am not down!" he scorned, looking into the dusky sky, pushing his fists into the air. "We will get back up. We will all get back up!"

Red-faced and trembling, he held his hands up to the heavens, steadied his quivering lip, then punched his hands into his trouser pockets. He strode purposefully across the moonlit ground, and his mind was already on the many duties the dawn would bring. *I'll call Bernie to get an order of lumber going, Paul and Elliot can take inventory, we can rebuild what we can and let the rest work itself out.* The internal chatter of his thoughts quieted as he spotted the horse standing between the gate and the edge of the cart path. He took two more steps, then stopped, watching it linger, fixated on the ground. He remembered watching Ben sketching his drawings in that exact spot for hours and found it curious why the horse—now free from the confines of the enclosure—was standing there.

When Charles returned to the house, Claire was in her chair with a canister of glue, holding pieces of a pottery dish over her lap table. She briefly glanced up at him before quickly returning her attention to the fragments in her hands. "Maybe this is a sign that we should start something new—something beyond this way of life that has been so very good to us and begin thinking about what could be around the corner."

Leaning against the doorframe, Charles looked up at the tarp loosely covering a drafty void where the stained-glass window had been. A thick layer of canvas covering the kitchen window popped loose from a nail, filling the basin with leaves and debris. Walking over with a heavy sigh, he could see the silhouette of the horse through the canvas.

"There is still magic here, Claire. We may have been taken by surprise, but our roots are here—this is our home. Waking up each morning next to you, in this house, on this land, gives me so much happiness. Through our years of marriage, we have faced many challenges, yet we have always found our way through the bends and overcome them. I know it looks bad—and I'm scared and doubtful too—but would we be happy somewhere else?"

Setting the lap table aside, she was startled when a cabinet door popped loose from its hinge, swinging pitifully in the background. The floppy door exemplified their current situation, and they began to laugh, easing the heavy burden of brokenness they felt. She removed her glasses, wiping away a few happy tears, cherishing his passion and determination, which could turn the most dreadful circumstances into possibilities.

The next morning, sunlight streamed brighter than ever, unfiltered by the trees whose branches now lay splintered across the ground. Uncurling from her slumber, Claire stretched and glanced over to Charles's side of the bed. It was empty. Propping herself up on her elbows, she looked around the room. The closet door was ajar and a hanger had been pulled askew—she was certain that spot was reserved for his work flannel. In an open drawer, there was a disheveled mop of socks, as if he'd been digging for a particular pair. Pulling on her robe, she shivered when her bare feet touched the cold floor. Reaching the bottom of the stairs, she heard a rustling sound coming from the porch. To her surprise, Elliot was there, fastening a mail slot from scraps of wood and aluminum.

"Mornin', Mrs. C!"

"Good morning, Elliot. Have you seen Charles? He was carrying on last night about a horse and Benjamin and all sorts of ideas before rushing off to bed. He seems to have left early this morning in his work clothes."

"Well, I did pass him on my way back from Bernie's; he left a note pinned to my wiper blade for an order of lumber."

"What items?"

Elliot reached into his shirt pocket and handed her a piece of paper torn from the frayed edges of a brown paper bag. "Looks like he was in a hurry if this was his idea of writin' material."

Scanning the list, there was one item marked with a star that piqued her curiosity—a small pair of boots, size seven.

Elliot looked perplexed as well. "I don't know any more than that Mrs. C. Your guess is as good as mine."

*　　*　　*

As Emily shuffled through the kitchen, she gazed out the window and caught sight of Samuel's tool bag hanging from a hook on the shed outside. A wave of uncertainty swirled through her clouded mind. What now? How would she manage alone? The loneliness was suffocating. She buried her face in her hands, quietly sobbing in spurts and sniffles, and reached for a handkerchief from the pocket of her nightgown to dam the flood of tears. The sound of light tapping on the screen door roused her out of languor, and she smoothed her tangled hair with her hand.

"Hello, good morning," Charles said. "I am so sorry for the unannounced visit—I can return another time."

"Not at all," she replied, "please, that's not necessary. I presume I will have lots of these moments. Catching me between them might be as rare as catching a shooting star. So please, come inside."

When he opened the door, the squeaky hinge finally gave way, dropping the door to ground level where it teetered on the top step. He grabbed onto both sides, looking at Emily awkwardly through the screen as he held it against him. "This wasn't the greeting I was hoping for this morning," he said, feeling clumsy and intrusive, but was relieved when a small grin flashed across Emily's lips. The lift to her spirits surprised her as much as it did Charles. "At least this will not bother us anymore," he said, propping the fractured door against the house. "I will bring some tools and repair it properly."

"I honestly wouldn't know what to do without that creaky old door, it's become such an annoying comfort. I guess I just accepted it as part of the kitchen's charm."

"How about we try for a little less charm, and we get you a new hinge."

"Yes, we could give that a try," she said. "Can I make you a cup of coffee? I have some brewing, it's just about ready."

"Please. I left quite early and missed my morning kick-in-the-pants."

"Wonderful. Please sit down—I'll join you in a moment."

Pulling out a chair, he noticed the stack of drawings on the table, little windows into Ben's inner world of fantasy. "Someone has been drawing again I see."

"Yes, that is all he does; he dreams and draws." Emily sighed, her mind wandering as she prepared the coffee. "I worry about the kind of structure and support I can provide for him now. As his mother, all I do is worry—that is what mothers are good at. Samuel had a way of going about life with unwavering discipline, keeping our lives in balance. I just don't know how to recreate that... But enough of my complaining. What brings you by, Mr. Collins? Is it to offer a much-needed word of encouragement, or to break my door," she said with a kindly grin.

"Please, call me Charles or Charlie—anything but Mr. Collins. I don't know how to propose this without sounding meddling, but as you know, Samuel's father and I had history. He asked me to hire Samuel when he was just a youngin, and I watched him grow into the man he became: dedicated, hardworking. I thought of him as a son. Although I never told him that directly, I hope he knew that I did. What I'm trying to say is that I think of your family as my family, and I feel there is something remarkable about Benjamin. One cannot deny he is enraptured with horses, and well... I have horses.

"I would like to invite him to spend some time at the farm, Emily. We can teach him useful skills and offer him some work; nothing too hard, but something to build his confidence and give him an opportunity to learn new things—only if you approve of course. And I would like to give him a horse. The one in all his drawings. He's a good horse, would make for easy training if he ever wants to ride. He's slower than molasses in November, so he won't be too hard to handle."

Emily set a mug on the counter and glanced at Charles, a hint of nervousness in her eyes. "He doesn't know anything about these animals. He's small, not strong like Samuel and Jonathan. How do we know he won't get hurt?"

"I reckon we don't for sure, but what is the harm in letting him find out? I have trained many young riders in my day. I'm not saying he will want to become a rider, but self-discovery is worth the risk, and I truly believe he has something to discover. Yesterday I saw the horse standing unharnessed, at the very spot where Benjamin would wait and sketch, day after day. It is simply an observation, but I believe they would become fast friends, and maybe a friend is what he needs."

*　　*　　*

Paul pulled in the drive, and seeing Elliot and Claire standing in the yard, he grabbed the post digger and a roll of rope from the seat before stepping out of the truck. "Morning, getting an early start?" he said sarcastically, looking at his watch as the hour hand nudged past eight. "Morning Mrs. C."

Playing along, Elliot pointed to the blue sky. "Weather delay."

A drift of cool morning air fluttered the bottom hem of Claire's robe, giving her goose bumps on her arms. "I'll leave you to your work then, and once I get dressed, I'll come find you. You can put this old woman to work!"

Elliot followed Paul down the path, feeling somewhat overwhelmed: Every building had some degree of damage. Roofs were missing shingles. The hay trolley assembly on the main barn had detached from the pulley and landed on the grain wagon, splitting it apart in the middle. Paul pulled a notepad from his jacket and took the pencil from behind his ear and began making a list of supplies. Elliot took the last swig from his thermos and set it on the overturned wagon, bracing it between wheel spokes. Hearing a distant rumble, he turned and saw a slow-moving cloud of dust trailing behind a truck with bold white lettering painted on the door that read "D&M Seed and Building." It couldn't have been anyone but Daniel McDonald, the nephew of Charles's good friend Earl Crampton, who was expanding the family's seed business into construction. Daniel was young and capable, with a knack for fixing anything broken, from floor to rafter and everything in between. Elliot counted more trucks following behind him and clapped his hands, waving his hat in the air.

"Grab your gear boys!" Daniel said, directing the men to the barn with an overexaggerated arm motion like he was leading troops into battle.

Paul was relieved to see the group of men sling tool pouches over their shoulders, carrying rope and ladders. Seeing so many familiar faces pitch in to help rebuild made the situation feel more bearable.

"Y'all definitely took the brunt of it. Almost seems like it came down straight over this place," Daniel said, looking out over the property. "Darn good thing it left us something that'll hold a nail."

"Much obliged, Daniel," Paul said. "We ain't too sure what we got to work with; haven't seen everything yet."

Daniel turned to his crew to make introductions. "Y'all know these guys," he said, pointing to Dale and Denny. "And this here's Pete, Thomas, David, and Tim. And you know Clay and JT from last year's lumber clearing."

"Sure do appreciate it fellas," Elliot said with excited energy.

"Anything to help," Daniel answered, looking over at Paul. "Alright boss, what's the show?"

The men huddled around Paul as he opened his notepad and licked the tip of his thumb, flipping the first page over. "I took down some supplies we need; Bernie has most of it in stock," he said, tearing the page from the binding and handing it to Dale. "I think the main barn is the most critical, and we lost the hay trolley. The entire assembly will need rebuilt: windows, doors, roofing, and fences all need some type of repair. Let's start with what we can salvage and stabilize the framework. Elliot will tend to the horses. But approach everything with caution: Just because it's still standing doesn't mean it won't fall on your head, so look up and check joists and beams. It's likely there was some shifting, so do a safety check first." Looking back over the list, he heard the cadence of footsteps and noticed a rather awkward expression on some of their faces.

Claire walked into the huddle, outfitted in a pair of overalls that veered quite sharply from her traditional style of pressed flower dresses with neat pleats and sashes. Paul lost his train of thought when she boldly stepped in beside him, sporting a wide-brimmed sun hat with a fishing lure embedded in the brim, adding what she perceived to be an outdoorsy, rugged effect. There was a bulge from the front pocket of her overalls and Paul couldn't help but stare.

"I brought treats," she said, pulling a rolled paper bag from the pocket of the denim one-piece. "Brownies. These should put a pep in our step!"

"Thank you, Mrs. C," Paul said, reaching for the bag.

Now empty handed, she tucked her arms through the bib, noticing their darting glances and accidental eye contact that was quickly deflected to the sky or the ground.

"Mrs. C," Paul said, "wouldn't you feel more comfortable, say, maybe—"

"Paul, I have known you since you were knee-high to a goat. I bandaged your knees, made soup when you were sick, put calamine lotion on your elbow when you got your first bee sting on my porch. But hear this: The woman standing in front of you can help with more than just cuts and bruises. Now you look in your little notepad of things to do and you give me a job that is useful, or I will find one myself."

The men were taken aback by her confidence and determination. She tapped her foot, waiting expectantly for her assignment. She couldn't be sure, but she thought the two gentlemen standing in front of her took a tiny step backward.

Scanning his notepad with the tip of the pencil, Paul marked a check next to the last item: the hay trolley. "You'll need a strong grip to help draw the hoist, so we'll put those batter stirrers of yours to good use."

"Brownie batter biceps," she said, flexing her upper arm muscle. Some of the men loosened up a bit, chuckling as they buckled their tool belts. She looked around searching for something to carry, picked up a wrench that was left behind, and proudly dropped it inside her pouch.

With four horses returned to the stables, Elliot went to the back barn to cut more lead rope. It looked to be in good shape, suffering only a fraction of the damage compared to others. Looking along the corners of the roof, he heard labored breathing. When he turned the corner, he found a horse lying just a few yards away, in pain from a tear along the hoof wall in its hind leg. Kneeling beside him, he brushed the horse's neck, slowly moving down the spine and working his way to the hindquarters, pressing the other joints to find any other areas of pain. He suspected the injury happened during the storm and couldn't imagine the horse being able to stand on it for more than a few hours. Giving it a smooth stroke along the mane, he left to find help.

He spotted Daniel and Denny carrying a piece of lumber to the paddock and ran over. "We'll need a vet back here—let Mrs. C know," Elliot said, pointing to the back of the barn.

"She's… well… she's hoisting the hay trolly. We just finished getting her up there," Daniel mumbled, realizing how ridiculous that sounded. Elliot just stood there looking confused. "Paul is heading to get more rope; you can probably still catch him."

Sliding a box of tools across the seat, Paul saw Elliot jogging up the drive and rested his arms over the doorframe.

"We need Vet Taylor, got a horse down with a torn hoof wall. It looks bad; found him by the barn in the back, probably been there for a couple days," Elliot said, propping his arms on his hips and breathing heavily.

"I'll stop there first then. Be back shortly with more lumber."

∗   ∗   ∗

Returning his mug to the sink, Charles looked over at the shabby door, then turned back to Emily. "Could I bother you for a piece of scrap paper and a pencil? I want to take a few measurements of this door before I go."

Rubbing sleep from his eyes, Ben shuffled worn slippers across the floor, surprised to see Mr. Collins in the kitchen. He didn't recognize him right away in his work clothes.

Charles stepped back into the kitchen and unlocked the tape measure, sending it whipping back into place before snapping to a stop. "Good morning, Benjamin."

"Good morning, sir."

Turning around quickly, Charles heard a series of cracks followed by a loud thud and excused himself to investigate. A thick branch had snapped off a maple, shattering a small window and knocking several rows of stacked wood out of alignment. Surveying the mess, he was surprised to find Benjamin standing alongside him.

"What made it fall Mr. Collins?"

"Likely the storm weakened some limbs. It's a big break; lucky it broke when everyone was inside—a branch that size could hurt someone."

Emily stood on the back stoop, "I'll get dressed and clean it up."

"Not necessary," Charles said. "Benjamin and I can tackle this, right?"

"We can put them back, Momma. I can help him."

Ben grabbed hold of a large piece, grimacing and struggling to lift it.

"Working men don't wear slippers," Charles said. "How about you change clothes and eat breakfast first. I will come back with some parts to repair the door, and then we can stack the wood. How does that sound?"

"Yes sir Mr. Collins, I'll be ready."

On his way to town, Charles saw Paul coming toward him and slowed to a stop. "Afternoon Paul, where you headed?"

"Doc Taylor's. Elliot found an injured horse by the back barn that needs to get looked at. Then I'll be picking up some lumber."

"How bad is it?"

"Elliot said it looks bad. Caught me just before I left."

"I'll be there as soon as I can," Charles said, hoping it wasn't the horse he saw last night in the field.

*　　*　　*

Hearing the bell clap against the door panel, Bernie looked up from his crossword puzzle and stood up to stretch, sliding the short wooden stepladder aside.

"Charlie, good to see you, my friend. Surprised it took you this long."

"The farm isn't on my list today, Bernie. I need a door hinge and some heavy screen, got a busted door to fix first."

"I got what you need, be right 'round." Bernie moved through the store like a steady breeze: He knew every nut, bolt, and blade from how it sounded or felt in his hand. He'd lost sight in his left eye when he was eleven and had limited vision in his right, but you wouldn't notice unless he told you.

Bernie looked at the measurements, handed the paper back, and disappeared into the aisles lined with wood crates and small containers. The store was a maze of tools and various equipment from floor to rafter. Folks could ask him for anything, and he'd have it pulled before they could pour a cup of coffee, which he kept brewing over hot coals all day.

He came around the counter with the parts, puffing on a cigar which over the years had made his voice sound like gravel under a steel sled. "How's the homestead comin' along? Heard the storm hit it pretty good. Wish I could help, but you don't want a half-blind man with a saw blade."

"We have our work cut out for us, that's for sure, but anything is possible Bernie. We'll be back on our feet in no time."

"Amen, my friend," he said, rolling up a paper bag and biting off a piece of twine, wrapping it around the screen. "You're all set—no charge."

*   *   *

Paul gave the crooked sign a tap to center it as he walked through the door of Vet Taylor's office. "Paul!" Margie called from behind the counter, setting a small mason jar aside she'd been filling with cotton balls. Her round face lit up, walking over to him with her arms open. "Oh, look at you! You get more handsome every time I see you!"

He felt his face flush when she grabbed him, rocking his broad shoulders back and forth, pulling him over to accommodate her short stature. He grinned through the embarrassment when she gave his rosy-coated cheeks a soft pinch. She had always ignored the biological fact that he was now a grown man; in her eyes, he would always be eight years old with a box turtle in a shoebox standing at the counter on his tiptoes.

"My dear, you're so skinny, are you hungry? We have some sandwich fixings in the back—I'll whip one up for you."

"I'm ok, don't go through the trouble. I need to speak to Tom, is he around?"

"No trouble at all," she said, hurrying around the counter to a cabinet, taking out a loaf of sandwich bread and shouting for Tom through a frosted glass window.

Through it, Paul could see a slow-moving shadow, and with a quick tug, out came Tom Taylor with an apple in his mouth. He took it out with one hand and gave Paul a handshake with the other. "Paul, good to see you, what brings you by young man? Got a turtle behind your back?" Tom joked, giving him a friendly bump with his forearm.

"We got an injured horse. Any chance you've got the time to take a look at him?"

Margie was already checking the appointment book, looking at the clock on the wall. "You have exactly one hour, better get going now."

"I'll gather some supplies," Tom said, and rushed back to his office, tossing the apple core into a trash bucket. "What kind of injury?" he asked, darting from corner to corner in his office.

"Might have a tear to the hoof wall," Paul answered, watching his shadowy silhouette moving about through the glass.

Tom stuck his head through the door. He had a strange head piece with a large round lamp mounted to an elastic band centered at his forehead and bifocal eyeglasses. "That's bothersome, Paul," he said, before continuing to rummage around. A moment later, Tom rushed out the door, his arms filled with equipment that rattled together and a black bag slung across his side.

"Thanks Ms. Margie," Paul said, holding up the bagged lunch she set on the counter.

"You are welcome, my dear. Good luck!" she said, waving goodbye with a feather duster in her hand.

*　　*　　*

Elliot nipped at his fingernail, watching Tom examine the horse.

"The good news is, it's not an injury to the coronet band. The bad news is that it looks to be inflamed, likely caused by a serious infection, and the internal structure of the hind leg might be severely compromised. This is an injury that is difficult to treat. It requires complete immobilization, and even then, the prognosis is uncertain."

"Suppose we should put him down?"

Tom took off his glasses and wiped the sweat from his forehead. "Might be premature to make that call right now, but my experience says it could very well happen. Sorry to say."

Elliot drove his boot into the dirt, spitting a corner of his thumbnail at the ground, wishing he had found the horse sooner.

"Not looking like good news," Paul said, walking up to the scene.

"Tom says he's got an infection and unless we keep him from standing on it, it likely won't heal. Might have to put him down."

Taking a small vial from his bag, Tom held it up and gave it a shake. "We will know by morning. This is a strong antiseptic, and if the swelling subsides overnight it might head off lameness, but if the swelling persists to the knee joint, then he'll need to be put down. It must be extremely painful, and you can see the protrusion from the inflammation," he said, pointing to the bulge above the coronet.

They watched as he prepared to apply the ointment. "If he flexes, that's a good sign, it means nerve damage can be ruled out. Even though the bottle is small, it packs a punch. I made it from juniper extract."

After the application, they watched closely for a jerk or a twitch, but there was no reaction.

"He didn't feel a thing," Tom said. "Not a good sign at all fellas. But that's all we can do for now—it will either work or it won't."

*   *   *

Ben was sitting on the front porch step when Charles returned with the door parts. He chuckled at the boy when he stood up, wearing a woven sack for a tool pouch and boots that had separated from the soles, exposing the worn thread from his socks when he walked.

In the bathroom, Emily paused at the mirror. The lines on her face seemed to have multiplied in the past few days. While focusing her eyes on her reflection, she noticed an odd distortion in her vision. A half-moon shaped sphere seemed to flash, causing her eyesight to diminish. She blinked repeatedly, trying to correct her focus, but couldn't get the blurry orb to go away and walked into her bedroom, using the dresser for balance. The room felt like it tilted, and a spinning sensation made her lean forward to grip the edge. Her palms began to slip slowly over the surface, and she collapsed onto the floor, knocking over a jewelry box.

Hearing the thud, Jonathan rushed around the corner. "Mother, are you alright?" he said, kneeling beside her and picking up jewelry that had toppled out of the box.

Trying to sit up, she propped her weight onto her elbows, feeling numbness on her left side. "I'm fine honey. I'm fine, really—I just lost my balance. Clumsy I know." He helped her sit up and she rested her back against the dresser, trying to bend her knee. "Don't mind me: I haven't had anything to eat yet and just got a little lightheaded, nothing to worry about."

"Here, let me help you off the floor," he said, positioning himself at her back to lift her up.

"I'll get up in a moment. Now go—you don't want to be late for school."

Margaret overheard the commotion and went to the door. "Momma, are you alright? Let me pick this up for you."

"I'll clean it up, it's my mess. Now off you go! I'll be on my feet in a minute."

"Alright, but please be careful, Mother," Jonathan said. Though still apprehensive about leaving, he went along with her request, thinking she was more embarrassed than anything else.

Emily sat up, massaging her thigh, but hardly felt anything, only a small twinge of pressure as she pushed down on her kneecap. Pressing along her shin toward her ankle, the sensation grew even weaker. After a few minutes, she pulled her knees up toward her chest and pressed down, noticing a strange tingling in her left leg.

*　　*　　*

"Hold this in place, just like this," Charles instructed, pulling the mesh across the door. "Always measure twice, it saves another trip to the hardware store."

Ben held the screen over the hole in the door, while Charles tacked it into place. The sleeve of Charles's shirt brushed his cheek, and the scent of pine and spice cakes filled his nose, reminding him of Christmas, or sitting in the woods with a warm cup of eggnog with cinnamon sticks. He liked it, and it made him feel a little hungry.

With a couple of turns from his screwdriver, the door had a new screen, and the squeaky hinge was fixed. "Let's try it out," he said, stepping out onto the stoop.

Ben reached for the shiny latch and pulled the door open. "It works Mr. Collins!"

Charles gripped the frame, watching the hinge glide effortlessly along the track in a quiet, easy stroke, and examined the screen at the corners. "Our work here is done. Now let's gather that wood."

Emily brought a knife to the table, picked an apple from the fruit basket, and began peeling. She turned the apple along the angled blade, not able to get a grip on the handle, and instead of carving one long strip, she had to reposition the blade repeatedly. She had done this countless times before, but today her control was sporadic and shaky. She put the apple down and held up her hand, spreading her fingers apart, then brought them together, noticing they moved involuntarily in twitches.

Ben stood atop a large log, rolling the soles of his worn boots over the surface, while Charles looked around. "Let's gather the scattered wood first, then we'll stack it by the shed and secure it with some rail ties that your father…" Charles bit back the rest of his words in awkward silence, not sure what to say.

"It's ok Mr. Collins; you can talk about my father."

"I was very close to your father, and I want to remember him and talk about him often to keep his memory near, but I don't want to cause you sadness, does that make sense?"

"I understand," he said, jumping off the log.

"Alright then, let's start stacking. I'll pick up the larger pieces, you grab the smaller ones."

Ben held a few pieces, waiting for Charles to finish the bottom row, then dropped the small pieces into the gaps. "I'm still a little sad I don't have my father anymore."

"You will always have a father. He didn't leave you, he just took another form."

Tugging on his ear, Ben tilted his head to the side. "Like a caterpillar?"

"A little like that," Charles said, smiling softly. "People have something inside of them called a spirit: it's inside all of us—you have one too. And when people pass on, when they die, their spirit leaves their body, which is just skin and bones, and their spirit lives on forever in a great and loving place called Heaven. In Heaven, they live with our heavenly father, God, and his son, Jesus. Your father is living Benjamin, and his home has no fences. He's in a beautiful place and you will see him again someday."

Ben smiled, "I talk to him all the time, and I talk to God and Jesus every night before bed."

"That's good, I'm sure you have plenty to say," Charles said, standing up and brushing dirt from his pant leg. Ben kept talking as they worked, sharing stories about his father and how he would sit on the stoop, watching him and Jonathan chop firewood and tinker in the shed. "I know he was good at fixing things. Maybe I could help you fix broken things, and I could see my friend again."

"Your friend, who is this friend?"

"Well, it isn't a person friend," Ben said. "You know him Mr. Charles. You liked my drawings of him, the one my mother hung on the wall, remember?"

"I do, I sure do. Horses make great friends."

Stretching his lower back, Charles admired the neat stack along the shed. "We done good Benjamin. It's time for me to head back to the farm now, but what do you say I pick you up in the morning if it's fine with your mother, and you can say hello to your friend?"

"You mean it?"

"Of course I mean it."

3
The Angels

Joshua rolled a cigar between his fingers, exhaling perfect circular rings, laying his cards on the table with a snap, stretching back in his chair and lacing his hands behind his head.

"Show off," Sarah said, watching the smoke rings expand and drift in Gabe's direction.

"It's like he has x-ray vision, beats me every single time," Gabe said in frustration, fanning the air and throwing his cards down in defeat.

"God didn't gift me with that superpower," Joshua said, stroking the fletching on his arrow. "That went to Jacob."

Moments later, a brilliant white glow illuminated the large doors that hung on gold hinges. Soft strands of light glistened against the marble that adorned three pillars in the center of their chamber, ornate chandeliers engraved with gold angels with wings of silver reflected beautiful specks of colored hues around the room. Soft swaths of silk fabric hung from crystal hooks along the mosaic ceiling tiles.

"Here He comes," Gabe said. "Sarah just came back from an assignment, so it's between the three of us. Quick—rock, paper, scissors, boys."

They stood in a line shoulder to shoulder and bowed their heads, feeling the warmth from the brilliant light that filled the room, so bright they couldn't look up from the tips of their boots.

Jacob felt His presence, and his eyes soon rested on two feet in leather sandals marked by scars on the tops of them. He felt Jesus's hand fall on his shoulder and an incredible peace and supernatural strength coursed through him. It was the most pleasant, comforting sensation he had ever felt. His hair was smooth and flowed in thick, wavy strands that fell just above His shoulders, and His complexion was a soft brown that shimmered like fine sand. His eyes sparkled, illuminated by shades of amber.

Jesus leaned into him, and Jacob closed his eyes, seeing the events unfold: He saw the storm, Samuel's death, Benjamin, and the horse. He saw it all, then the image disappeared. He opened his eyes to where Jesus had been standing; only a warm glow lingered for a moment from behind the door, then faded.

"Giddy up, cowboy," Joshua said, not letting an opportunity go by without cracking an animal-themed joke at Jacob's expense. Most times, he had a comeback ready, but right now, he wasn't in the mood for jokes. He felt the burden Charles carried, and it was a heavy one.

"Best out of three when you get back from talking to the animals," Gabe said, flipping a token in the air with his thumb.

Jacob pulled his hat off the tree post. "You're just jealous. All you can do is break stuff."

"When are you going to throw that nasty hat away and get something decent?"

"Never. It has style—something you wouldn't understand."

"Style? Does style smell bad and attract flies? Oh, no—those are horses. Horses attract flies, which is what you're going to go talk to," Gabe said, chuckling.

"Good day gentlemen," Jacob said, swiping the brim of his cap, "and lady."

"Go get 'em tiger," Sarah shouted before he closed the door, hearing their laughs from the other side.

*　　*　　*

Paul and Elliot pulled up a section of fence line to secure the grazing pasture as the sun dipped below the trees, then walked over to the main barn to help with any cleanup before nightfall.

Claire rinsed her hands under a spigot as the group of men gathered their gear. "Boys, this old crow is going to climb into her nest. I'm plumb tuckered out."

"We're turning in as well. See y'all in the morning!" Denny said.

"Should we call it a night?" Elliot asked, bending his head over, shaking the dust from his hair.

"You go ahead, I'm going to sharpen a few saw blades before heading out," Paul said.

Elliot put his hat back on and shrugged. "Ok, let's go sharpen."

Listening to Elliot's boots scuffing along the ground behind him started to aggravate Paul. "You mind picking up those sleds of yours, your legs ain't that heavy."

"Wow, look at that!" Elliot said, pointing to the setting sun. Paul looked up at the wave of orange and blue with purple edges as a warm haze of fluorescent light flooded the sky beyond the clouds.

"That means good weather tomorrow."

"He's getting back late," Elliot said, as the light from Charles's headlamps shone across the field ahead.

"He's been preoccupied."

"With what?"

"Saving the world, if I had to guess."

Elliot was good at reading Paul's body language and emotions, or lack thereof, and knew when to let things be, so he kept his mouth shut and plodded along.

As they got closer to the barn, Elliot's pace dragged to a crawl. "You that tired?" Paul said, waiting for him to catch back up, but Elliot just stopped, standing there with his hands in his pockets, staring up at the horizon. "What are you looking at now? Let's move it if you're going to help, I want to get this done before dark."

"Doesn't it look like somethin' out of a space picture? I swear it keeps gettin' brighter."

"Yeah, I guess, it's bright and strange."

"I haven't seen them colors in the sky in all my years walkin' these fields, have you?"

"I reckon not," Paul said, pausing to allow him this indulgence, realizing that sometimes he forgot how young Elliot was. He was still a kid in lots of ways.

*　*　*

Angel Jacob

Jacob looked over his shoulder as he left, admiring the view. The picturesque grand lodge, clad in beveled stone and tigerwood, stood in a bath of warm light. The beauty of the wood amazed him; the colors of the grain became richer as the centuries passed, reminding him of thick maple syrup or a golden honey glaze. The structure was surrounded by tall trees with a walking path connecting the other lodges and a communal fire pit in the center. It was home and he loved it. He walked through a field sprinkled with wildflowers and patches of shrubs and small trees with juniper berries, always ripe for picking. They were his favorite. The angels always walked along the same path when they were sent on assignment, and no matter how much they ate along the way, the trees always had fresh fruit and berries. The temperature was always constant—never cold nor hot—and everyone and everything was vibrant and beautiful. It was common to cross paths with lions and bears, and he always stopped to share a morsel of jerky he kept tucked inside his jacket pocket for them. Small children laughed and frolicked with all sorts of wildlife, never to be harmed. Only love existed here. No pain, sadness, sickness, or disease. No addictions, guilt, shame, or remorse—only peace and happiness, every day and for all eternity.

The rich colors of the landscape gradually dulled as he neared the ledge. The thick blades of grass became sparse, the fruit-filled trees and bushes grew further apart, and the ground cover cooled underfoot, becoming mostly dirt and clay. He grabbed a double handful from the last juniper berry tree and looked out over the edge. The clouds thinned, exposing the earthly realm. He could see the round sphere sitting beyond the dark shadows of blue and turquoise. The air turned crisp and the wind picked up, gathering dust and debris around his boots. Leaning over the edge, he held his arms out, feeling the current underneath as the visions he was shown reentered his mind. He understood the bond humans can experience with an animal, and the future of this young boy and a horse was to be charted. The angels could not see the entirety of the lives they touched and could not predict the outcome of their assignments. They had a job to do—that is all they knew.

He closed his eyes; the tips of his fingers and palms began to tingle. He stepped to the very edge where the dirt blended into a shiny silver stream of light, reflecting off the green and golden hues behind him. Leaning over, he fell into a tunnel of white billowy clouds. The lightness of his body was pleasant; he felt buoyant yet nimble. In Heaven, nothing in his body ever ached. He was a perfect balance of muscle and bone, light on his feet and brimming with limitless energy—even during slumber. As he neared earth, his body felt heavier, and the heat in his palms intensified.

As the stream carried him, details in the world below began to come into view. Bluish tones became oceans with whitecaps cresting and breaking on the surface. Dull browns became deserts, and rivers cut through mountainous land. As he descended further, he saw the roofs of houses and cars traveling along the roads and over bridges. He saw a plot of land surrounded by long stretches of fence, with neatly plowed crops lining the soil. A large farmhouse stood near the roadside, flanked by several small buildings and two large red barns with many stables and spacious enclosures. But despite the tranquility of this farmstead, signs of terrible destruction were visible. Trees were uprooted, one of the structures lay collapsed, and what looked to be a windmill lay in a heap of mangled wood and metal. He noticed two men walking between buildings as he hovered over the farm. The light circling him began to fade and soften as it delivered him to the ground just behind the barn.

Paul was losing patience waiting for Elliot to pull his head out of the stars. "You done gawking yet? We need to finish up before it gets any darker."

"Alright, but man was that neat lookin'. How many blades need sharpenin'?"

"Not sure. Four or five I figure."

"We should check on the horse to see if Tom's handiwork has done any good."

"We could, but I'd be surprised if he's still alive. I've never seen berry juice heal a wound like that. His chances aren't good—I'm thinking we'll find a dead horse."

"Can we check first, then sharpen?"

"I suppose we could."

*　　*　　*

Jacob took a deep breath, filling his lungs with the crisp air, taking in the smells, and picking up the scent of juniper berries. Odd, he thought, bringing his hands to his nose. He walked along the backside of the barn, looking at the trees. Taking a few more steps, he saw the horse lying in a patch of grass just beyond the barn. Kneeling beside its body, he saw the bandage around the hoof and pulled a fig sprout out of the loose layers of gauze and drew it across his nose. The elixir was bitter. "Juniper extract," he whispered. He ran his hand over the horse's leg: it was cold and stiff— he figured it must have died in the early morning hours. The nose was dry, and the eyes were closed tight, starting to crack and wrinkle. The knee joint was noticeably swollen, and dried puss had crusted beneath the bandage. He unwrapped the gauze, balling it up in his hand. There was a deep laceration that had severed a tendon. Most likely the nerve damage had prevented the horse from being able to feel anything in the leg, hindering it from being able to bear any weight on it. Yet in the vision, he'd seen the horse standing in the field for hours.

He shook his hands out, feeling the warmth under his skin intensify. Drops of perspiration ran down his back between his shoulder blades as he held his hands out with his palms up, letting the heat radiate to his fingertips. His hands turned a bold shade of red, so vibrant they were almost translucent, and placed them around the entire joint, holding them to the cold skin, letting the heat penetrate the bone. He tightened his grip, adjusting his fingers to cover the wound until he felt the skin under his grip warm and the coarse hair begin to soften under his fingers. The lacerated skin became loose and pliable, and he massaged the edges together until the open wound was closed. The blisters from infection began to shrink and tendons and ligaments fused together in strands of moist muscle fibers. Releasing his grip, he moved further up the leg to the knee joint, feeling fragments of bone splintered beneath the skin. Pressing into the joint, he let the heat and oxygen from his breathing bake into the area. Sweat from his face fell onto the stiff hairs, reviving the rich honey tones in the color. He drew his hands over the belly and placed them in the center, feeling bubbles and vibrations as the organs came to life. He put both palms over its eyes and felt the tickling of its eyelashes brush against his fingers.

"Good boy," he whispered. The ears began to twitch, and a loud forceful snort escaped from the base of the neck and out through its nose. He looked over its body, now very much alive. Pulling a handful of juniper berries from his pocket, he popped some in his mouth, then cupped the rest in his hand and squeezed, letting the berries liquify. Dabbing his finger into the purple residue, he applied it along the coarse hair on its forehead.

*   *   *

"Walk faster," Paul said, "the sky is getting dark. Now we'll have to mess around with lanterns."

"I'm hurrying," Elliot said, jogging up a few paces.

Two loud pops and cracks echoed through the air. "Was that you?" Paul asked.

"No, how would I make that sound? We're on dirt."

Putting a finger to his lips, Paul directed Elliot out into the grass while he continued along the side of the barn where they'd heard the sound. As Elliot crouched down and moved out into the clearing, he was stunned by what he saw, rubbing his eyes to take a second look. There, standing behind the barn, was the horse.

Pawing at the ground, it reared upward, kicking its front legs and whinnying loudly.

Paul reached for the blade that hung from his toolbelt.

"What are you doing, why are you reachin' for that?"

"Look at it, it's gone crazy!"

"Put that away; he's alive! It's a miracle!"

He released his grip from the knife, cautiously watching the horse while Elliot clapped and stomped around in circles, awestruck by the miraculous healing.

The horse reared up again, batting at the air. "Go, get a lead!" Paul yelled, "calm him the hell down!"

Elliot put his hat back on and held it onto his head as he hurried along the side of the barn. At that moment, the strange and wonderful orange light lit up the horizon again, glistening and swirling in the sky just beyond the trees before quickly fading. The horse calmed, its outbursts fading into soft sighs and gentle whinnies.

"What in this world is goin' on tonight," Elliot said.

"I have no idea, but that ain't the same horse: look at the markings on his head."

Elliot approached slowly with his hands open, careful not to spook him. "Easy, it's ok, easy," he repeated until he was close enough to examine the marking. He touched the hair over the strange diamond-shape, rubbing the tackiness between his fingers. "Smells like juniper berry," he said, licking the tip of his finger. "That's juniper alright, but no idea how it got there." He ran his hands over the area of the leg that was wounded. "Can't tell it was ever injured, there's not even a scab. Whatever Tom put in that vial sure worked like a charm."

"I'll stop by there in the morning, ask if he can look him over," Paul said, still bewildered and a little skeptical.

4

THE FOLLOWING MORNING...

Charles drummed his thumbs on the wheel, energized by the unusually warm October morning.

Ben was waiting for him on the porch, and as Charles turned into the driveway, he tugged the front door open. "Mother, Mr. Charles is here, I'm going now," he said, yanking the door closed and running down the steps.

"Good morning, Benjamin. Ready for a day at the farm?"

"I am, sir. I ate all my flapjacks."

"I can see that," Charles said, reaching over to wipe a smudge of syrup from his chin, "and ate them in a hurry I see."

*　　*　　*

Approaching Bernie's shop, Elliot noticed the sign was flipped to "closed." Peering through the window, he saw Bernie perched on his ladder rolling cigars, and he tapped on the door. Bernie slowly got up and tucked the roll behind his ear, stretching to loosen the kinks in his back, and unlocked the door.

"Mornin' Bernie, gettin' an early start today!"

Bernie pulled his pocket watch from his overalls, holding it out to check the time. "Not today, boy. Early is when the moon is brighter than the sun." Elliot topped off his thermos, taking a few sips as he watched Bernie separate tobacco buds and spit into his tin. "How's Paulie boy?"

"Grouchier than ever."

Bernie shook his head and chuckled. "Takes life too seriously. Even as a youngin, other boys be lookin' for trouble or gals, he'd be organizin' boxes 'round here, workin' harder than a mule." He propped his arms on the counter and pointed to a picture on the wall by the door. "That's the boy right there, with his pappy and me. We all went fishin'—wasn't such a sour face back then, got worse after his pappy died. Grew up too fast I reckon."

Elliot looked at the picture as if seeing it for the first time. It'd hung there ever since he could remember, but he'd never really seen it until now. The happy, round-faced boy gazed up adoringly at his father, with Bernie sitting on the other side. He couldn't remember the last time he saw Paul smile.

"Must be workin' hard today, too. That's good. Young men like yourselves are built for hard work; it's old folks like me that get to sit around all day," he said, spitting into the tin and wiping the residue from his chin. "Cough gets worse every day. Might be the black coffee, might be the cigars; I ain't givin' 'em up, no matter what Frank says."

Elliot snickered. "Nah Bern, you'll live forever. Guys like you are too stubborn to die."

"What we pickin' today?"

"Here's the list. We got some barn repairs ahead of us too, might be adding to it."

Wiping his forehead with a shop rag, Bernie put his glasses on and scanned the list. "These here are high-dollar items, and I got a customer comin' by today for the same gear—paying cash. That's better than credit, and I could use a box of England's, down to my last three. I'll fill it this time, but you tell Charlie it needs paid up, been two months now. Let's see what we got in the back."

They sifted through old boxes, dust swirling through the air as they swatted away the cobwebs. Elliot reached for a saddle hidden behind a milk crate. The stitching was coming apart, and a small hole marred the back of the seat, but it was better than nothing, and he brought it over to Bernie. "Found this old relic."

Looking over the saddle, he felt the edges of the stitching. "Damned mice got to it; those bastards chew through everything."

"Still has some life in it," Elliot said.

Bernie brought over a tattered box for the bridles and harnesses, which weren't in any better shape. "All second, third, and fourth hand, but should get y'all by for now."

*   *   *

Paul was working on a gate latch when Elliot walked up and dropped the saddle at his feet. "Where did you find that crusty thing?"

"Charles hasn't been keepin' up with the tab, so Bernie had to find leftovers. Said some fancy customer is coming in today for the new stuff, and he needs the cash for a box of cigars."

"Him and those damn cigars," Paul mumbled, shutting the gate to test the locking mechanism.

"Should we tell Charles about the account?"

"I reckon he already knows. It's really going to hit him once he sees that mangled piece of cowhide. Now give me a hand right quick setting a post."

"Where should I put this?" Elliot asked, pointing at the saddle.

"Leave it—ain't worth the sweat to carry it."

Elliot's eyes lit up when he noticed Claire walking by with a pitcher of sweet tea. "I could use some of that!" he said, wiping his brow. "Is that the boy over there, standing next to Charles?"

"Looks to be," Paul said, stopping to wait for Carl who was just a few paces behind them. "What's he doing here? He needs to be in school, not doing farmwork. He doesn't know a lick about horses."

Elliot shrugged. "Maybe he's fixin' to teach him, show him what we do 'round here."

"He ain't like other kids," Carl said, overhearing their conversation. "He don't learn that good. Sam didn't know what to do with him; this was the only place he wanted to be."

"Sam ain't here no more, so the kid should be doing what kids do," Paul argued, "getting proper schooling and doing things with kids his own age. He can't be a regular kid hanging around here with us all day."

Carl scratched his head in frustration. "That's what I'm tryin' to tell ya: He ain't no regular kid. Teachers kept him out of school—he has problems learnin' things. Sam told me about it. They tried keeping him in school, but he just didn't catch on—always got distracted. Eventually they gave up, figured he could learn some other way."

"I basically grew up here," Elliot said, glancing over at Paul, "and I turned out alright."

"That remains to be seen," Paul said.

"Maybe this is the best place for him right now. It'll be good for him," Carl said.

Paul unclipped his cap from his belt loop and slapped it onto his head. "School is the best place for him."

Watching him walk away, Carl leaned in. "He needs a woman—he's starting to get grumpy in his old age. And here comes Tom, probably here to check on the horse."

"It was the strangest night last night—you wouldn't believe me even if I told you about it," Elliot said. "I don't think Tom will believe it either."

Elliot gulped down a cup of tea while Tom greeted Charles, then eagerly caught up to him as he headed for the barn. "It's the darndest thing, Tom. That horse doesn't even have a limp and the swelling is gone. It just don't seem possible! How can berry juice do that?"

"Juniper extract is a potent anti-inflammatory, helps with swelling and kills every kind of bacteria I ever heard of… I even sanitize my equipment with it."

Listening to his simple explanation, Elliot still felt perplexed. "But that wound was deep—it would have left a scar at least. I ran my hand along the leg: no sign of even a scratch!"

Tom considered the mystery of it but believed in the power of nature's medicine. "The oils in the berry are healing for the skin, too. Softens it right up!"

"He's tied up in the back here. Looks like Mr. C and the boy are down there with him."

"He's standing pretty good!" Tom said, looking at the horse from a distance. "Looks like he's enjoying some company, too."

"You come to check him over doc?" Charles asked. "Seems to be doing right well; whatever you did, it worked, my friend."

"Look here," Elliot said, dropping to his knee and rubbing his hand along the hind leg. "Not even a callus!"

"I must admit, it is unbelievable how quickly it healed. This is just miraculous," Tom said, leaning in to look at the marking on its forehead. "Looks like he may have rolled in it—got a little on his head there. I'm afraid that might be there to stay."

"Gives him character," Charles said. "He isn't winning a beauty contest, that's for sure."

*   *   *

Bernie gulped his late-afternoon coffee, accidentally swallowing some grounds that tickled his throat. He was coughing so hard he didn't hear the door swing open. When he looked up, a tall, well-groomed man stood in front of him. Bernie pretended not to notice the man wrinkling his nose as he glared at his spit tin on the counter. His hair was dark and slicked back over his ears. He wore a pressed collared shirt and pin-striped tie under a blazer and pleated black slacks.

"Ain't from around here, are ya, fella?" Bernie asked.

"I believe we spoke earlier about some riding gear."

"You must be the Yankee—don't remember the name though."

"Clint Larson. Bought twenty-five acres off route 25, not too far from here, just down the road from a horse farm. Looked to be an impressive establishment at one time. Now it's just old and broken down."

Something about the man's demeanor unsettled Bernie, and he took his smugness for a passive insult, noticing the haughty smirk and the way his eyes scanned the store in distaste. "Townsfolk usually know who's buyin' what around here; seems you slipped in under the dark of night," he said, puffing on a cigar. "That farm belongs to the Collinses, longtime friends, been here for as long as I have—least the house has. Charlie built it up from nothin', made a good livin' there. Was a fine horse man with a keen eye for talent. Had a good run in the Kentucky Derby back in the day."

Clint raised a brow and smirked, visibly unimpressed with Bernie's reverence.

"Twenty-five acres is a good plot of land. What are you fixin' to do with it?"

"Saddlery to start, eventually expanding into the equestrian market. Now, can you show me the gear I requested?"

Resting his cigar in the cradle, he shuffled around the corner. "I keep the good stuff down this aisle here," he said, pointing to four Vela saddles hanging on a rack. "Yellow-pine built, no warping, rawhide wrapped—best saddle around in my opinion. Harnesses are on the beadboard at the end of the aisle here."

Clint rubbed his chin, admiring the detailed craftsmanship in the basket weaved designs. "I'll take it all."

On his way to the counter, Bernie stopped to admire the Red Packard Twin 6 Roadster parked outside. A young boy, dressed in heavy layers, tossed a wrapper to the ground and leaned against the door. He thought about asking him how he would like it if he emptied his ashtray on the floor of that fancy car but thought better of it.

"Lazy kid," Clint murmured, looking out the window while pulling bills from his money clip. A moment later, the boy walked through to the door. Clint drummed his fingers, impatiently waiting for the box, then pointed to the counter. The boy gathered it in his arms, grunting while struggling to balance the weight, then hurried out the door.

Bernie waited until they pulled away before opening the door and picking up the wrapper. He turned it over, noticing the shiny blue label that read, "Nutty Bar – Rockwood Confections, New York City," and tossed it into the waste bucket.

*　　*　　*

Jack stared out the window at a strange and unfamiliar landscape. As the fields passed, he thought about his friends and how many games of baseball he'd missed. The sun was high overhead, about the time his grandfather would stop for lunch. To console himself, he unwrapped another chocolate bar.

"I know this move is difficult for you, but it's for the best. I can make a lot of money in a place like this," Clint said, furrowing his brow as they passed by the Collins' farm. "Look at that place. If this is what these people call a training yard, I'm going to take this whole county by storm."

Jack listened to his father talk about money and his lofty ideas with feigned interest. Looking over at the farm, he saw a boy that looked to be his age walking a large brown horse. He saw lots of other people around: They were on the roof of the house and carts were being pulled into a long stable. He could make out some of the men talking and laughing as they worked. The sound filled him with sadness as he thought about his grandfather and friends in the city, longing for the comfort of having them close by. He brought the bar to his mouth for another bite, when his father reached over, ripping it from his hand.

"I better not catch you with another damn candy bar, boy, you hear me," Clint said, red-faced, and glaring at him in anger. He crumpled the bar in his fist and threw it out the window.

Jack massaged his hand, grimacing at the pain he felt in his fingers.

"You better shape up, boy, or you'll find out how hard your life can get. Quit sulking around feeling sorry for yourself."

When they got home, Clint slammed the door and carried the box to the pole barn. Jack looked down at his hand, slowly bending his fingers and rubbing at the swollen knuckle. A tear fell down his cheek and he batted it away, wishing a giant fire would burn the whole place down so he could move back home. As he watched his father cross the yard and go inside, he discreetly pulled another chocolate from his jacket and walked toward the porch. He heard his father shouting, then heard a loud thud and what sounded like glass breaking. An awful feeling rose from his stomach, imagining what was happening to his mother. He looked down the road in one direction, then the other, seeing nothing but long stretches of open fields.

*　　*　　*

Facing the bathroom mirror, Emily felt another tremor in her hand. She wiggled her fingers back and forth and reached for her comb when she heard a knock. "Margaret, Jonathan," she called. "Will you see who's at the door?"

Margaret placed the nursing magazine on her bed and headed for the stairs, picking up a Navy flyer that was sitting on top of the newel post. "Mother, Jonathan is looking at Navy stuff again," she said, and hurried down the stairs.

"Hello my dear!" Gladys said cheerfully. "You get more beautiful every time I see you, child."

"Good morning, Miss Gladys! Please come in—my mother is upstairs, but she's on her way down."

"I baked it this morning," Gladys said, handing her a casserole dish. "Bacon, spinach, and egg breakfast casserole. It's utterly delightful!"

Margaret lifted it to her nose and inhaled deeply. "Thank you! You always make the most delicious dishes."

"Feeding people makes me feel useful, dear. When you get up in years, it gets harder to feel that way, trust me."

Setting the casserole on the counter, Margaret peeked under the lid. "Would you like a slice, Miss Gladys?"

"Lord sakes, child. Do you see this caboose?" she said, patting the backside of her hips. "I taste test enough."

"Good morning, Gladys," Emily greeted as she came down the stairs. "So nice to see you."

"How are you feeling today, Momma?" Gladys said, embracing her in a hug.

"I'm feeling quite well, some days more than others." Emily's nose caught wind of the casserole, immediately perking her up. "What smells so divine?"

"Sit, sit," Gladys ushered, pulling out a chair. "Have a bite. Tell me what you think—I used a new vanilla."

"It's delicious!" Margaret said, already sampling a morsel.

"Child, you're a growing girl, you'd say that about week-old potatoes."

Emily picked up the fork, and her hand trembled, so she set it down quickly, unable to steady it. Across the table, Margaret was reading an article at the bottom of Jonathan's Navy flyer.

"What are you reading?"

"This is Jonathan's, it's a flyer for the Navy, he took it from Dillard's café. There's an advertisement on the back for a nursing program!"

"Frank and Millie's daughter is a nurse," Gladys said. "She just got a job in Des Moines, works at a clinic—such a sweet girl. Why, Millie told me just the other day, she met a nice boy, studying to be a doctor! It's a fine profession, missy."

Margaret picked up her plate and walked to the sink, holding the flyer in her hand. "And the uniform is so white and fitted, look at her hat, too," she said, showing it to Gladys.

"Yes, my dear, it's a fine uniform. But you better eat more of my casseroles if you want to fill it out like that young lady," she said, giving her a wink.

"I'm off to meet some girls from class at the library, Momma. I'll be back before supper," Margaret said, her face lightly flushed.

Sitting across from Emily, Gladys folded her hands on top of the table, pushing her glasses to the bridge of her nose. "When did that start?"

Emily stirred in her seat, hoping she hadn't noticed. "A few days ago. It must be nerves—honestly, it just must be," she said, though she sounded unconvinced of it herself.

Pushing back from the table, Gladys brought her hands down to her thighs with a slap. "That may be so my dear, but I am taking you to Frank. You can't be twitching like that, all unsteady. Let's go."

"Really, Gladys, I'd rather not. It will likely pass, it's only been a few days."

"The shakes aren't something to delay, my dear."

"I can't pay him," Emily said quietly. "I don't have money for a doctor's visit."

"My Morty, God rest his soul, left me enough for today and tomorrow. Now get your shoes."

*   *   *

As Frank examined Emily, he noticed weakness on her left side and significant instability during the neurological test. He rolled a stool over, pulling a silver cylinder from his coat pocket. "Look straight ahead for me," he said, holding the light up to her eyes. "Now squeeze my hand as hard as you can." Emily squeezed. "Now the other." She squeezed again. "Now push against both hands." Emily anxiously watched as he checked off boxes on a form in his notebook. "I would like to run a full blood panel," he said, looking up from his notes. "I'll send in Millie to draw it, you just sit here and relax as best you can. I know this is scary, but we will take care of you—we'll get to the reason behind this," he said, giving her a reassuring pat on the knee.

Millie peeked around the corner. "Hello Mrs. Paulie, nice to see you." Millie's voice was soft and calm. "This is the easy part: all you need to do is stay still."

Gladys looked up from the ball of yarn, resting the needle on her lap when Frank came around the corner. "We're going to run some blood tests, but I have concerns. She is showing some neurological deficits, and I have some reservations about sending her home today. Does she have anyone to look after her?"

"Frank, I have nothing going on other than this pathetic attempt at knitting a scarf and a dying tomato plant at home. I can keep an eye on her, don't you worry about that."

"Good. I'll know more once we get the results from the bloodwork. For now, just take her home and have her rest."

*　　*　　*

Paul emptied the bottle of saddle soap onto a rag and began working it into the leather seat of the raggedy saddle, listening to Elliot whistle while he cut sheets of sandpaper. "What bizarre tune are you humming? Haven't heard that one before."

"I don't know it good yet, but I listened to *The Lost World* and the opening music kinda stuck."

Paul chuckled as he scrubbed. "Large lizards with big teeth, not my idea of a good story."

"Do you believe there were large lizards roamin' 'round before people?"

"I believe what the Bible says: God created man in his image, and last I checked, God didn't look like a giant lizard."

"You need to let your imagination run a little, among other things, like finding you a nice girl—someone to soften you up before you turn into a sour old wretch."

"Too late for that."

Elliot cut the last piece of sandpaper, dropping it on the stack. "That's the last of it, but lookin' at it, doesn't seem like enough to finish that fencing tomorrow."

"I need another bottle of soap anyway. I'll drive over to the store and grab a bail or two while I'm there; Charles is expecting the horses tomorrow."

"Take your time, and if you happen to cross paths with a lady while you're out, stop and ask her on a date."

Paul stuffed the dirty rag in his pocket, handing him the clean one. "Two to three layers, topside and underneath."

Elliot picked up the bottle, tapping out the last bit of liquid onto the rag and started swiping, whistling, and humming as he worked out the grime.

5

Bernie tussled with a box, his shoulders sore after battling the last stubborn staple, which wrenched his back something awful. Feeling another coughing fit coming on, he tensed, bracing himself against the shelving. Barely able to catch his breath between the violent contractions that squeezed his ribs, he dropped his head on his arm and gripped the shelving, watching blood pool at his feet. His heel slipped and he collapsed against the wall. Reaching out for the coil of hose, the metal spindle snapped, sending hoses and heavy tools showering down onto his head and shoulders.

Paul was reaching for the door when he heard the clang of metal on the floor. Rushing inside, he called out, looking down each aisle. "Bernie, Bernie!" Turning the corner, he saw the tops of his shoes and rushed over, untangling the hose from his legs and arm. Bernie's eyes were clenched shut and his hands gripped his stomach, shaking in a relentless siege of contractions that sent a steady stream of blood down the side of his mouth and onto the floor.

The amount of blood he was losing sent Paul into a panic. He tore at his shirt buttons, balling the clump of fabric and holding it under Bernie's mouth to catch the blood. "We have to get to the hospital!" he said, his whole body shaking with fear. He moved between the wall and Bernie's back to lift him up when he heard the bell smack against the door. "Over here!" he shouted. "Down here, hurry, we need help!"

Denny ran through the store, sliding around the corner. "Go get Patrick, we need to get him to the hospital!" Denny saw the blood on the floor and his eyes went wide. "Go!" Paul shouted.

As the minutes ticked by, Paul stayed at Bernie's side, keeping him upright to ensure his airway stayed open. Time slowed to a crawl and Paul grew more agitated and restless, listening as Bernie's breath became shallow and more labored with every passing moment. Desperate for help, he checked the time on Bernie's pocket watch. Unable to wait any longer, he got in position to try and lift him off the ground when he heard gravel crunching and a loud engine. Moments later, the door opened, and Patrick and Peter Kincaid rushed toward him carrying two large poles connected by a heavy piece of canvas.

Hoisting Bernie onto the cradle, the men silently carried him to the ambulance. Peter loosened a belt and a seat dropped beside the stretcher. "We'll meet you at the hospital," Patrick said, hurrying to the side of the ambulance and jumping in.

Paul gripped the wheel tightly, swatting tears from his cheeks as he followed the speeding ambulance toward the hospital. His truck rocked and swayed over the uneven road as vehicles veered off to the side and a traffic cop waved them over the train station crossing. Paul took a sharp turn at the hospital entrance, pulling along the crosswalk, leaving the door open and the engine running. The ambulance came to a stop just up ahead and Patrick's door swung open.

"I'm so sorry. We lost him just before reaching town."

"No, no!" he shouted, pounding on the side of the box, yanking at the handles. "Open the door, get him inside!"

Patrick pulled him back, letting Peter push the back door open, holding a cloth to his mouth as he climbed out. "He stopped breathing shortly after we left the store. I'm sorry Paul."

Paul pressed his hands to his eyes and wept.

*　　*　　*

Walking alongside Juniper, Ben watched the toes of his boots hit the tall blades of grass, unaware of how close he was to the roadside. The horse began to slow, yanking up on the lead. Ben coaxed him forward, tugging gently, but he jerked again with a snort of air, this time shaking his head from side to side and pawing at the ground. He gave the lead another tug but was startled when he heard a voice behind the line of trees. Turning, he spotted a figure standing on the other side of the brush.

"Hello?" Ben's shaky voice cracked, waiting for a response.

Juniper tugged on the lead, but Ben didn't move. He could tell the person wasn't much taller than he was. For a moment, he thought it might be Jonathan but dismissed the idea—Jonathan would have just walked up to him. He started to feel a twinge of fear and called out again, his voice unsteady. "Hello? Who's there?"

The trees were thinner at the bottom, and he could see the tips of bright-colored sneakers.

The figure finally stepped out from around the last tree. It was a boy, and his clothes were different than other kids he had seen in school. He wore a baseball cap pulled down just above his bushy eyebrows.

Ben relaxed, happy to see someone his own age, but the boy looked angry. He didn't say anything; he just glared at him.

Juniper pulled back on the lead, as if trying to pull him away.

The boy stood there, a frown framing the corners of his mouth. "You gonna just stand there with that dumb look on your face kid?"

"Are you retarded like that ugly horse you got?" Jack snapped back.

Ben looked at the ground, afraid to look at him, and took a step backward.

"You're a retard, aren't you? You don't even talk, do you, you retard!" Jack scooped up a handful of rocks, shaking them in his hand. "Run you chicken!" he yelled, throwing a stone. "Run, you retard, run!"

Ben winced and felt a smack on the back of his head. Another rock hit his ear, causing him to feel sick to his stomach, and he dropped to his knees, covering his head.

*　　*　　*

Satisfied with the pop of color in the mangled old saddle, Elliot tossed the rag aside and shook his wrists. When he walked outside for some fresh air, he heard what sounded like shouting, and saw Ben fall to the ground and a boy standing by the tree line.

Jack turned his head and saw a man running across the field toward him. He dropped the rocks. "I'll see you again, retard boy," and disappeared behind the trees, running down the ditch line.

Brushing the dirt from his knees, Ben got to his feet and looked back toward the road.

"He's long gone," Elliot said, breathing heavily. "Took off over the hill up there."

"You know that boy?"

Ben shook his head, wincing when he touched his ear.

"Those rocks scraped it up pretty good," Elliot said, looking at Ben's ear before turning back toward the road, watching a figure dart along the ditch, zigzagging through the high weeds. "Let's getcha on up to the house, Mrs. C will have somethin' for that."

*　　*　　*

"I ate too much," Charles said, resting against the back of the chair and rubbing his belly.

"I'm sure you did, but you've been working hard, builds up an appetite," Claire said, clearing the table. On her way to the sink, she looked out the window. "Here comes Ben. I'll make another plate."

Feeling the fullness of his stomach, Charles groaned as he got up from the table and stepped out onto the porch.

Elliot had a hand on Ben's shoulder as he followed him up the steps. "Afraid he got mixed up in a squabble; took a good licking from a boy that came up on him from the road up ahead."

"A squabble?" Charles repeated, looking out over the hill, "what over?"

"That's what I'd like to know, but by the time I got there, the boy had taken off down the ditch."

Charles looked over the cut on Ben's ear. "Go inside, let the Mrs. take a look." Once Ben was inside, he walked off the porch and joined Elliot. "Guess we got some new friendly neighbors."

"I reckon it wasn't Ben's doin'—he ain't the type of kid that goes 'round lookin' for trouble."

"Sure isn't," Charles agreed, waving Carl over.

"Look there," Elliot said, pointing up the road at a fast-approaching truck.

"What in tarnation is this commotion about? Seems to be the day for the unexpected," Charles said.

Denny's truck skidded along the gravel to a stop. He popped the door open and ran over to them, giving them the hard news about Bernie. Charles hurried inside to tell Claire, while Carl and Elliot left together for the hospital. Soon after, Charles followed.

After Paul watched Patrick and Peter carry Bernie's body through a side entrance, he was ushered inside by a nurse holding a clipboard. She greeted him empathetically and led him into a small office. She spoke softly, offering him a coffee or tea, but her words were just another voice in his head as he replayed the last hour over in his mind. Two doctors hurried down the hallway, meeting Patrick outside the door. The nurse excused herself, leaving the clipboard on a small table beside him. He listened to their whispers, glanced down at the paper, and quickly looked away.

Moments later, she returned, reached into her pocket, and put a pen on the clipboard. "I'm so sorry for your loss. I know this is a very difficult process. I'll be right outside when you're finished." As soon as the door closed, he wept again.

Patrick stood outside the hospital doors, stubbing out a cigarette when Charles, Elliot, and Carl arrived. "Paul's with the nurse, having a real hard time with it."

"Hard time?" Charles asked, feeling a knot form in his throat.

Elliot looked at Carl, then back at Patrick. "You ain't sayin' he…"

Patrick nodded and lowered his head, reaching for another smoke. "Sorry to say; it all happened so fast."

*   *   *

On the way home from the hospital, Carl noticed their new neighbors already had lumber stacked alongside a pole barn and three more heaps further up the drive. A large wooden sign with "Larson Acres" painted on it was propped against a large tree. Driving slowly past the house, he saw a young boy pulling down a tree branch that was just out of his reach and a tall dark-haired man standing at the top of the steps. The scene sent a rolling chill down his spine.

Elliot gazed out the car window through glassy eyes as Charles pulled into the farm and cut the engine. "I reckon I should prep the stalls for the new horses comin' in, and I need to close up the equipment shed."

"Not today," Charles said. "I think we could all use some time to process this. Best to take the next couple days and just work through it as best we can, keeping an eye on Paul."

"You sure 'bout that? We ain't that far ahead around here yet, and we got them horses arrivin' in the mornin'."

"I'm sure, Elliot. This was a hefty blow for all of us, and the farm chores can wait a little while. Would you mind giving Ben a ride home? I think I need to take a walk around, and we should probably explain that ear to his mother."

6

The next morning, Paul found a note on his door from Fred Comer, the town attorney. He opened the letter, scanned down the page, then folded it up and tucked it back inside the envelope.

Taking a different route to town to avoid driving by the store, he pulled into a parking spot in front of Fred's place, a small brick building in the center of the town's square next to the barber shop. He felt disconnected, as if he was watching everything from a distance. People walked along the sidewalk in front of him, kids gathered around an ice cream truck, anxiously waiting for their turn at the window. Watching people go about their daily lives made him feel like a ghost. Leaning over the wheel, he rested his chin on his arm, looking through the windshield at three men sitting on a bench next to the barber shop pole enjoying the day. So much activity and life all around him, yet he felt dead inside; numb to the world around him, hypnotized by the rotation of red and blue stripes. One of the men on the bench stood up and lit a cigar. The earthy aroma of oakmoss pulled Paul out of his stupor and he walked over to the door, thumping the brass door ring against the knocker plate. A plump man wearing a sport coat that looked to be a couple sizes too small stood in front of him.

"Nice to see you, Paul, although I wish it was under more pleasant circumstances," Fred said, stretching out his hand. "Please come in. Can I get you anything?"

"I could use a glass of water if it's not any trouble."

"Of course not, come inside and have a seat over there, I'll be right back."

He walked over to a chair beside a large desk. A framed certificate hung lopsided on the wall and the air was saturated by stale smoke. It was a familiar smell, reminding him of wintry nights when he would sit by the woodstove listening to Bernie tell old stories.

The desk was littered with papers, and a Bible that was earmarked and stuffed with page markers sat on the corner next to a phone. Other than Mr. Collins and the Millers, not too many people were well off enough to afford phones, and it boggled his mind that you could hear someone through a box on the wall.

Fred came around the corner and handed him the glass.

"Thank you. It's been a long morning."

"I reckon it has. I'm sure you're plum tired," Fred said, pulling his glasses to the end of his nose and looking over the top of the frame.

"It hasn't quite settled in yet."

Fred pulled an envelope from the drawer and adjusted his glasses. "I understand, took weeks after my pappy passed for me to stop hearing him shuffle in through that door." Lifting the flap, he pressed the sides together and gave it a shake. A small silver key dropped onto the desk. He pushed his chair back, pulled the tight-fitting jacket over his belly, and opened a cabinet door, taking a small tin box from the shelf and set it on the desk in front of Paul. "I'll give you some time—be back shortly."

Paul waited until Fred left the room, then unlocked the box and took out a letter dated two days prior:

Dear Paulie Boy,

I knew this day was comin', Heaven's got one more cowboy. It gave me joy to watch you become a man and I'm proud of you. Hard workin' as you are stubborn. I know them horses were never your brand of liquor, so go make your own life now. Deed is in the box. Sell it, burn it down, or keep it open. If you keep it, make sure the coffee is hot and buy seed one month before the ground thaws. What I got here should be enough to get you by. Spend it on a good-looking woman and raise a family. Don't be a grumpy old fool like me.

My love. Bernie

Paul wiped his eyes and pressed the bridge of his nose between his fingers, not noticing Fred entering the room.

"He came in two days ago. He was in bad shape but didn't want you to know how bad, I guess. We went over all the details—I was here when he wrote that. The deed to the store is in there, as is the deed to the house and property and a cash note from the bank. He had all monetary assets transferred into your name."

"Wish I had known how bad it was. Should have made time to check in more than I did."

"You know as well as I do he wouldn't have told you. Men like him never do. But I'm afraid this won't be the toughest part of your day. Chuck wants to see you."

*   *   *

Clutching his watch and squinting against the morning sun, Charles paced in front of the barn, watching a dust cloud blow across the road a quarter mile out. By the time he reached the front gate, the six-horse carriage had almost reached him, two American Thoroughbreds anchored by loose leads walking behind it. As they drew closer, he got a better look at the horses and was impressed by their size. At two and a half years old, they looked to be every bit of seventeen hands.

"Fine morning," Charles greeted. "I trust the ride down went well?"

"Morning, Mr. Collins; it sure was a mighty fine ride. I'm George Sutton, the driver here is Stuart Mady."

"Good to meet you fellas. I was expecting Sawyer—he couldn't make the trip?"

"Afraid not," George said. "The horses that aren't being sold for training are getting auctioned this week, and Sawyer is handling those affairs."

"Getting out of the racing business?"

"Times are tough and getting even tougher. It was a choice to feed the horses or feed the family. Real hard times. Big industrial plants around our parts are shutting their doors, economy is drying up, and even the small-town stores are struggling to stay alive. Folks leaving the cities to find work out west. Surprised you keep running in these parts."

His words triggered a feeling of insecurity and doubt that Charles fought to ignore. "Well, I must say, these are some beautiful horses."

George pulled a piece of paper from his back pocket. "This is from Sawyer—certificates I believe. And the bill of sale for one thousand twenty-five dollars was agreed on?"

"They look to be worth every penny," Charles said, handing him an envelope.

"Thank you, sir. Heard you started training horses about the same time Sawyer did?"

"That's right, we just didn't grow as fast. Kept it small, no more than eight to ten kept on the grounds."

"Might we pull around? They could use some water before the journey back to Boone," Stuart asked.

"Of course, the well is behind the barn here, and that's my trainer up ahead, Carl Ebbers, been in the business longer than I have."

"Fine-looking Thoroughbreds," Carl said. "I would say you made a good investment, haven't seen hindquarters like these in a while. Bet they're quick off the line. Let's hope they run as good as they look."

"These here were the last to be sold," George said. "Sawyer was holding out, hoping things would improve before deciding to sell 'em. It was a tough decision for sure."

"We could sure use some contenders here—it's been a long stretch since we had any to get excited over," Carl said. "Ain't that right Charles."

"That's the truth fellas," he sighed. "We've been struggling for talent, but by the looks of them, maybe our woes are coming to an end."

"You hear about Sid Pemberton's horse, Rushmore?" George asked. "He's been quite the runner this year—took the Preakness Stakes race, heard he cleared about thirty thousand."

Carl looked over at Charles, expecting his face to turn bright red and smoke to come out of his ears.

"I heard about it," Charles said coolly, turning his attention to Elliot, who was walking the horses over. "Here they come now. It sure has been nice talking with you gentlemen, we won't hold you up."

Elliot helped Stuart hook the horses up to the carriage before taking the Thoroughbreds to the stable.

"Good luck to you," George said, extending his hand for a shake. "Hoping to hear some good news on the circuit."

"Give Sawyer my best," Charles said. With that, George climbed into the seat and Stuart snapped the reins, sending the carriage forward with jolt.

"You sure did bite your tongue when he mentioned Sid. You sure it's still in one piece?" Carl said with a chuckle.

"Hurts like the dickens."

*   *   *

Chuck Grover was stacking chairs when Paul arrived. "Paul, glad to see you… my sincere condolences. Bernie was a good man, and boy did he think the world of you. Let's go inside—we'll go over the details."

Paul felt at ease in the quiet building, listening to two women whisper by a stained-glass window in the corner next to a staircase. Large rugs covered sections of the floor and flowery vases sat in the center of little round tables. Chuck led him past the lobby to an office that was packed from end to end with bookcases. Three books set atop the shelves stood out to him: *Cremation Practices*, *Choosing a Site for the Sleeping*, and *Rest Assured*. A large basket of wood samples arranged on plywood boards covered the desk. The silence in the room was remarkable. Birds were fluttering just outside the window, but Paul heard nothing other than his own breath. He took a seat, patiently waiting for Chuck to finish reading the note he was holding.

Chuck slid the piece of paper back into the drawer and pushed it shut, then sat down slowly, stretched out his legs, and folded his hands over his chest. "Bernie has entrusted us with his burial wishes, and I would like to present some options." Pulling the first sample from the basket, he placed it in front of Paul. "This is a simple encasing made of pine—lightweight, not cloth covered. He asked for a natural grave, no liner, but I must respectfully disagree with Bernie's instructions. You see, Bernie gave me a large credit account to start this business, discounting the lumber at a fraction of the price—and that doesn't even scratch the surface."

Paul listened, but felt Chuck was really conversing with his conscience, so he stayed silent.

Chuck rose from the chair, flipping all the samples like dominoes until he uncovered the last one. When he lifted it, Paul could see it was much heavier than the first, as his forearm and biceps flexed when he lifted it over the desk. "This is what I have for Bernie: mature glazed cherry mahogany, full liner with brass finishes."

Paul concluded that his decision was final when he returned to the chair and folded his hands on the desk. "I'll pay whatever the cost, Mr. Grover. He left more than enough to cover this."

"I will not accept payment. This is already settled, and I won't be able to hear him grumble about it either. Does he have a suit?"

*　　*　　*

Standing at the door of Bernie's house, Paul hesitated, holding the key to the lock before going inside. He inhaled deeply; the air still held the aroma of sweet cherries. Ripe tomatoes sat along the counter under the window and fresh cut firewood was nestled in a basket by the wood burner.

He walked from room to room, listening to the birds chirp in the black walnut trees and the slow tick of his pocket watch. The house felt frozen in time, like a museum exhibit. The bed was small and tidy, one blanket, one pillow. A bedside table with an oil lamp was in the corner, a small dish that held some spare change sitting atop it. His pants were folded on top of the dresser and a few shirts hung in the closet. Two pairs of shoes—one pair for church, the other for work—sat nearby. The only embellishment was a corner stand holding several framed pictures of his family. Paul picked up one of the frames, the photo barely visible from years baking in the sun. It was Bernie as a young man with his parents and siblings. Next to it was a picture of him and Chuck Grover standing in front of a freshly painted sign for "Grover's Corners," the same sign sitting there now. Another picture was him carrying a piece of lumber, one clasp of his overalls undone. He looked happy, waving at whoever was behind the lens. One picture, sitting in the middle, was a boy, strawberry blond hair, holding up a fishing rod with a catfish dangling from the hook, seated on his father's lap, Bernie standing behind them with his hand on his father's shoulder. He closed his eyes and could almost feel the rod in his hand.

He found a brown shirt that buttoned up the middle, then sorted through his socks, selecting a dark brown pair and placed them on the bed. In the closet he found one pair of pressed pants and at least six pairs of overalls; the denim was worn so thin that it felt like Indian silk and the fabric around the buttoned hooking was frayed and separated. *No wonder he wore these all the time*, he thought, pulling the pressed pants off the hanger. Laying the shirt next to the pants, he tried to visualize Bernie dressed in them, but something didn't seem right. He looked over at the pictures again. In every picture except for one, Bernie was in his overalls, so he left the clothes on the bed, grabbed the socks, and pulled a pair off a hanger.

Chuck looked out his office window to see Paul walking up with a pair of overalls slung over his arm and couldn't help but smile. "I had an inkling you would come back with these."

"What can I say, it's what he would've picked."

"His plot will be prepared tomorrow in time for the service on Saturday. I can show you where if you like."

"I appreciate that Mr. Grover, but I should get to work, see you Saturday."

7

Sitting on an overturned bucket, Ben watched as Elliot examined two stalls. The dirt was damp, and the barn had a funny smell with layers of dust coating the beams. Natural light peeked through narrow gaps between the walls and roof. There were no shiny bronze hooks or gentle breezes like the big barn by the farmhouse. The ground didn't smell of cedar and wasn't soft underfoot. Elliot surveyed the stalls and some empty crates and storage bins, backing away from a corner swatting at cobwebs. "We've got our work cut out for ourselves, but this is his new home for now," he said, grabbing two rakes and a pitchfork. "You take this one, we'll make a pile in the center here."

Ben took the rake and stood at the first stall, looking at the dry, crusty layers of straw.

"Start in the back corners, and once you hit wood, keep raking backwards and push it out," Elliot said. "Watch how I get it pulled up and just do what I do."

Ben watched him move the straw, digging with the fork first and kicking the heavy piles with his boots. Then he stepped into the adjacent stall, dodging clusters of webbing that were hanging close to his head as he listened to Elliot hum and whistle, enjoying the happy tune as they worked. Every now and then, Elliot would sing the words out loud, "take me out to the crowd, buy me some peanuts and cracker jacks…"

"What is a cracker jack Mr. Elliot?"

Elliot straightened up in surprise, resting the rake against the wall and grabbing hold of the bars separating the stalls. "You ain't never had a cracker jack?!"

Ben shook his head.

"What about baseball, you ever play?"

He shook his head again.

"Jiminy—I figured being a boy and all, you'd know plenty about it. I got two mitts I keep in the shed; when we break for a bite, we'll play a game of catch. Baseball is the greatest game in the whole entire world! People cheer in rows of seats that wrap 'round the whole field!"

After the stalls were cleaned, Ben walked over to the horse and began stroking its neck, rubbing his finger over the odd marking on the forehead.

"That's somethin', ain't it?" Elliot said, leaning on his rake. "Doc Taylor said juniper berry left that mark—stained the hair right down to his skin. You thought of a name for him?"

"I like Juniper, sounds like the planet."

"Juniper is a fine name, I like it!"

"How do you spell it?"

"J-U-N-I-P-E-R," Elliot said, sounding out each letter.

"Can you show me how to write it?"

Looking around for a stick, Elliot cracked a twig in half about the size of a pencil and brushed at the dirt until he had a smooth canvas. "Here, I'll show you," he said, sitting cross-legged on the ground, carving each letter in the dirt. "Now you try."

Ben reached for the stick and dropped down beside him, focusing on the sound of each letter. When he finished it, he drew his finger across, underlining the letters.

"Spelling was hard for me, too. There's a bunch of words I still don't know how to spell. How 'bout we learn one new word a day, and after we finish up with feed, we'll go get them mitts."

"I would like that," Ben said, admiring the letters.

*　　*　　*

Looking around the tool shed for the post digger, Carl brushed against the worn saddle, crinkling his nose at the mangy condition and thumbing over the hole in the seat. The leather was freshly polished, making the chestnut brown hue look rich and vibrant. Walking across the field, he saw Charles fixated on a large flatbed roaring down the road, hauling huge planks of cedar.

"That's the third load this morning… you know where it's going?"

"I know where it's going," Carl said, "and who lives there. Drove by yesterday on my way home from the hospital. There's a sign going up, says "Larson Acres," got a horse's head engraved in the center of it. Daniel said he's bought over two hundred yards of lumber and has an order for fifty more. Came in from upstate New York, said he was a chilly fella, real quiet, too. Just paid in cash and left."

"He's in the horse business?"

"Don't know, but by the sign out by the lumber, he sure looks to be."

Charles looked out over the hill. "Let's keep our eyes and ears open— I'm sure we'll find out soon enough. I better head over to the barn, Henry and Albert came by to look the Thoroughbreds over."

"Place looks great Charles," Henry said, looking around the farm. "You've done a nice job putting it back together."

"It hasn't been easy," Charles said, taking in the view of the refurbished farm. "The barn took on most of the damage, but we made some upgrades in the repair process—put in some benches, extra storage, even added some venting. There's some storage in the back corner, use it as you need. Pasture's groomed, saddles and bridles are in these benches here if you want to ride today."

"We'll start with a warm-up and see how they fare; once we find out which one is faster, I'll let you know the one I'll be riding."

Albert scoffed. "We'll see about that old timer."

*   *   *

Ben pushed the straw into the corners of the stall, pressing it to the ground. "Mr. Elliot, can I put some of the soft pieces down for him?"

"The soft pieces are pine shavings, they cost more, so we keep that for the money horses."

"What is a money horse?"

"The ones that get trained to race other horses; when they win, they bring in money to keep us all workin'."

Ben reached into his pocket, pulled out four wheat pennies, and brought them over to Elliot.

"How much can he have for these?" he asked, dropping them into Elliot's hand.

Elliot looked at him and smiled. "*Whew-wee*, why I reckon that would cover a nice layer of that soft stuff. Tell you what: How 'bout you keep these three and we put one in the bank to buy some more. Deal?"

"Deal!"

"Alright, let's get some supplies. We can hang a feed pail if we find some rope and nails." They walked out of the barn, running into Charles as he rounded the corner.

"How's it going back here?"

Elliot flipped the penny in the air, catching it on the way down and plopped it into Charles's hand.

"What's this for?"

"This here young man would like to pay for some shavings to make the bed a little softer for the horse, sir, and he was hoping that would cover it."

Charles looked at the penny and winked at Ben, "I would say it will cover it just fine." He looked around the barn, setting his hands on his hips. "You boys have been working hard I see. It's looking good!"

"Yes sir," Elliot said, "he's a hard worker, learnin' how we do things 'round here."

"Mighty good," Charles said with a nod, walking over to Juniper. The horse slowly meandered over until its head fell under his open hand. He rubbed the horse's forehead, watching Elliot and Ben walk across the field.

As they crossed the field, Ben was captivated by two men wearing small black helmets on horseback bobbing up and down, rising off their saddles and sitting back down again. One man was moving his horse in wide curving turns, while the other trotted along the fence line. "Do they work here, too?"

"Them? Those're the jockeys, Albert and Henry, been racin' for Mr. C ever since I was your age, and probably before that. Real fine riders. Henry raced the Kentucky Derby twice and took a second-place win at the Belmont last year. I reckon they're gettin' a feel for how the new stock ride. If you wanna do good for yourself, be a jockey: That's where the money is."

Elliot opened the door of the shed, sliding his hand through the center of a spool of rope until it rested in the crook of his elbow. He moved quickly, fastening a tool bag around his waist, anchoring a hammer through the loop, and grabbing a pouch with a few patches on it, giving it a shake. "Got the nails," Elliot said, then reached into a crate, grabbed two baseball mitts, tucked them under his arm, and palmed a small white leather-stitched ball. "We got everything we need," he said, pulling a mitt over his hand and smacking at the webbing. "Here, put this one on your hand, it's a bit smaller than mine."

Ben wiggled his fingers into the mitt and gave the pocket a smack.

"Feels strange at first, but you get used to it; just remember to squeeze it shut when you catch the ball, like this," he said, dropping the ball into the glove and squeezing his hand around it. "Nothin' like it."

Elliot talked about baseball the entire walk back to the barn. Ben didn't understand most of what he was saying, but he enjoyed listening to him and imagining the plays Elliot would act out as they walked, pretending to scoop up a ground ball and tag out a runner. When they reached the barn, Elliot noticed a wheelbarrow sitting near the entrance, chock full of cedar shavings with the wheat penny sitting on top of the handle. "Looks like this load is on the house," he said, dropping the penny into Ben's palm.

"For this job, you'll want this," Elliot said, handing him a small, curved shovel. "This will hold the shavings better, gives you better control, and the pieces won't fall out."

*　　*　　*

Standing at the kitchen sink, washing the residue from the shavings off his hands, Charles looked out the window, feeling the farm was coming alive once more. Carl was leading the yearlings out of the barn for the student riders, Albert and Henry were in the pasture, and there was a fresh pie settling on the sill. Grabbing an apple from the fruit basket, he sat down to read the paper, shaking it out to scan the front page. The good feeling quickly faded when he read the headline at the bottom of the page, "New York Native Settles in Greenfield." The article read:

> Mr. Clint Larson, son-in-law of well-known New York Confectioner Henry Rockwood, owner and founder of Rockwood Confections located in New York City, leaves the sweet family business to bring custom saddlery to the Midwest. The Post's reporter Sam Kepper interviewed Mr. Larson, telling the Post that he sees an opportunity to explore new markets here in the Midwest, not only making fine saddlery but may potentially make an expansion into equestrian racing.

The story continued but Charles abruptly closed the paper. Claire came around the corner to find him stewing as he pushed his chair against the table with a heavy hand.

"Everything alright? You look a bit tense."

He picked up the paper, sending the apple rolling down the length of the table before toppling over the edge and across the floor. "Just sat down for a snack and a story—read this!" he said, slapping at the article with his finger.

She reached for the paper, read the article, then folded it up and calmly set it back down on the table. "Would you like some eggs?"

"Eggs? Doesn't that article concern you? This man just shows up in our town, obviously with a load of family money, and now he wants a piece of what we have! Doesn't that rattle you?"

"Not in the least," she said, tying an apron around her waist. "So, he wants to make some saddles. Why are you letting that bother you?"

"Did you not read the rest of it? He's jumping into horse racing, too!"

"Darling, he probably spent most of his adult life in the shadows of that candy company, reached middle age, and decided to try something different. He'll pull some leather, stretch a few hides, and learn that saddlery is hard work. Honestly, I see him running back to the comforts of the high life in New York once he gets a taste of it. Answer me this: How long have you been training horses?"

Picking up the apple, he rubbed it against his pant leg. "Thirty-two years!"

"Exactly, thirty-two years. It took thirty-two years to get where we are. You've got good men that work for you, trust you, and you have built a reputation over time. The success we have had is because of your talent and love for racing. Anyone who comes along looking to scratch an itch in this business is in for a rude awakening: It takes more than money in the bank sweetheart."

"With the amount of lumber I've seen coming through, it sure looks like he means business. You can make saddles out of a shed—he's fixing to build an operation!"

"He could build the Queen's castle. Doesn't mean much, only that he better have plenty of nails."

Wadding up the paper, he tossed it in the bucket with the apple core, kissed her on the cheek, and walked to the door.

"Would you like me to fix you a sandwich?"

"Not feeling hungry anymore," he said, stepping out onto the porch.

8

GLADYS SAT IN THE CAR, looking up at the drawn curtains of Emily's bedroom window. Part of her was relieved to know she was getting rest, but another part was more concerned and disheartened. Taking the casserole off the seat, she went up to the door, where Margaret surprised her. "Shouldn't you be in school dear?"

"I'm looking after Momma; she's not feeling well."

"You don't look too wide-eyed yourself. You look tired."

Margaret straightened her hair, tucking it behind her ears. "She had a restless night. I overheard her tossing and turning and couldn't fall asleep."

"Brush your hair, splash a little water on your pretty face. You're not that late. I can drive you, then I'll come back and tend to her."

"I couldn't ask you to do that Miss Gladys."

"You didn't ask me, and it's not up for discussion. Now go—nurses are smart people, and you won't get smarter by skipping school. Hop to it!"

Margaret hurried up the stairs to the bathroom while Gladys took the dish to the kitchen, filling the room with comforting smells of cheese and sausage that warmed her nose. Rummaging for plates, she heard stomps and thumps coming back down the stairs.

"I'm ready!" Margaret said, hopping around the corner on one foot, fastening the ankle clasp on her shoe.

"Have you had anything to eat?"

"No ma'am."

"That won't do, brains need fuel." She drew a slice onto a saucer and pulled a fork from the drawer. "Here, eat on the way—no time for proper manners. If it's saucy, use your sleeve. Where's Jonathan?"

"He already left; he walked Ben to the farm before going to school. Momma was still asleep when they got up, so they went about their day."

"Isn't that just like a man," Gladys laughed, pulling on her shawl and ushering Margaret out the door, devouring the slice. "You should take the time to taste it dear."

She finished the last bite, audibly enjoying the flavor as she spoke with her mouth full. "This is so good Miss Gladys, thank you."

"It's nice that Ben is still enjoying time on the farm, must be hard on him though."

"He's been much happier—he doesn't cling to me as much anymore. Mr. Collins gave him a horse. Well, I don't know if he gave him the horse, but he's letting Ben care for it."

"My, that was nice of him. Mr. Collins is a warmhearted man, a crown jewel around here, that's for sure. When I was a little girl, I dreamed of having a horse, but I got Morty instead," she said, laughing.

Margaret leaned back, happy that the rumbling in her stomach had quieted, and caressed the warm leather seat. "This is much nicer than walking."

Gladys pulled up to the schoolhouse and patted her on the leg. "Have a good day dear, and don't forget to learn something."

*　　*　　*

Emily lifted her head, feeling like the room was spinning, and listened for any sound in the house. The brightness of the sun against the curtains surprised her—it had been a long time since she'd slept in this late. Her body ached from deep within and a sheen of sweat had left her uncomfortably damp. Rolling to her side, she tried focusing on the family photograph sitting on the bedside table. The faces that had been so clear only days before were now blurry silhouettes, and she strained to bring them into focus. A whooshing sound settled between her ears and a sharp pain stabbed at her temples. Outside, she heard a car door close and the front door open. She tried calling out, but the pain gripped her, forcing her into silence. All she could do was listen as footsteps drew closer to her door. She felt helpless.

"Emily, you awake dear? It's Gladys."

"Yes," she said, her voice strained and breathy.

Gladys pushed on the door just enough to peek around the corner. "Margaret said you've been out for a spell." As she approached her bedside, she saw the sheen of sweat on her face and quickly reached over to feel the top of her arm. "My oh my you're warm, can I get you some water?"

She brought a hand to her throat, grimacing at the pain when she tried to speak.

"I'll fetch a glass of water and dry linens."

When Gladys closed the door, Emily pushed the top cover down below her waist. The fever had caused her to soak through the sheets and dampen the mattress. The back of her arm ached, sending waves of scorching heat pulsating to the bone, and she felt a raised blister that was sensitive to the touch.

Gladys returned quickly, setting the tray on the bedside table, and leaned over to help Emily as she struggled to prop herself onto the pillow. Noticing the blistered sore, Gladys gasped.

"That must hurt like the dickens!"

"I don't remember how it happened."

Looking around the room, Gladys found a thin stack of linens and a blanket hanging on a drying rack in the corner. "That'll do. Now let's get you up and I'll change your bedding."

Swinging her legs around, she tugged her nightgown over her knees.

"Here, hold onto my arm."

Steadying herself, she tried not to lean too much of her weight to one side.

"Don't worry about me, dear, there's a lot of meat on these bones."

When they reached the doorway, Emily released her grip, clinging to the wall for support until she reached the bathroom. As her nightgown fell from her shoulder, Gladys noticed another blister, similar in size to the one on her arm. It was then that Gladys knew this was more serious than the typical sour stomach. "I'll leave this door cracked in case you need me."

Emily looked at her reflection and waited until she heard Gladys's footsteps leave the hallway before pulling her nightgown down, turning her shoulder to the mirror. The top layer of skin was translucent, like a clear bubble covering the bright red flesh underneath, and her thighs were webbed with dark purple veins. A sudden pain in her temples caused her to moan and cry out in distress.

Hearing her groans, Gladys opened the door, catching her before she lost her balance. Seeing her pale skin covered in sores and veins worried her as she pulled a clean nightgown over her body and helped her back into bed. "You need to eat a little something."

Emily shook her head. "It hurts to swallow."

"You're going to need some nourishment. I'll be right back to fetch you some herbs and peaches from my house; you just rest and get some sleep."

*   *   *

When Paul pulled into the driveway, Charles was walking around the porch with his head down and his hands folded behind his back. He was nearly at the steps by the time Charles looked up from the ground.

"I didn't expect you back so soon. Wanted you to get a break, take a few days off, fully paid—we've got this place covered."

"I appreciate that, but I'd rather be working instead of sitting around with my thoughts."

Charles reached over, putting a hand on his shoulder. "I'm not sure what our plans are going forward with supplies… Bernie was so important to this operation, I feel lost without him."

"I can review our order history. I would like to retain the discount on raw materials—I believe he got five percent on bulk goods and another five percent on consumables. Might be a tough negotiation, but he kept those records year after year, so it's possible. We can also use them to identify seasonal patterns and create forecasting to maximize cost savings. I can go through the receipts. We shouldn't miss a step if I capture everything."

Charles raised his eyebrows, impressed by Paul's business acumen. "That's good Paul, obviously you've got a head for numbers. But I don't want you jumping back so soon—still think some time away might do you some good. Maybe take a fishing trip upstate to the lake, let the emotions sort themselves out."

"He gave me the store," Paul blurted out. "And nine thousand dollars on top of that. I own the property surrounding the store, including sixty acres of farmland. That could be cultivated for hay, corn, and barley—a lot of what we pay high dollar for. Figure if we start planting right away, we could save a bundle on feed, up to sixty or seventy percent if it goes well."

"You have much to think about, lots of good options. Business owner, farmer, farmhand… why don't you consider letting the last one go. You've been a bigger help around here than I could ever hope for, but with all your new responsibilities, it might be a weight around your ankle."

"This has been my life, and Elliot needs me here, too. He's not ready to manage it all on his own yet—he can't even remember how to tie a square knot."

"He's training up some help, and I think he's enjoying the companionship. You're the cornerstone of this place, the one with all the answers: the box, glue, and cutter. But now, you can drop your own seeds in the ground, shape and mold your own future. Hearing what you're saying, you could help the farm in much bigger ways, not just here, but other folks too. You're a hardworking, smart man, and I'm proud of you—now is the time to spread your wings."

*   *   *

Turning the pie in the window, Claire watched Charles and Paul walk toward the barn. As she raised the lid on the waste bucket and saw the crinkled newspaper, an idea came to her. After checking herself in the mirror, she untied her apron, slid the pie off the sill, and slipped out the side door to the car. Balancing the pie in one hand, she tugged on the door handle with the other.

"Careful, Claire, let me take that off your hands," Carl said, bringing the pie across his nose. "Smells delicious."

"Just came out of the oven, and I'm taking it to our new neighbors. Charles seems to believe a family of goblins moved to our town and I'm hoping to prove him wrong."

"I'm not sure this is a good idea," Carl said, suddenly not as hungry. "Maybe you should talk this through with Charles first."

"Horse feathers. Now, are you going to hand me that pie and crank the engine, or do I have to get my sleeves dirty?"

Carl obliged and held the door open. Claire situated herself, placing the pie on her lap and checking her lipstick in a compact mirror. "I'm excited to meet the lady of the house. Maybe we can have tea and enjoy sitting on the porch—you know, like I do with Grace and Bernice. Also, did you know they're from New York City? How exquisite! I can't wait to hear stories about life in the big city!"

He kept his opinion to himself, not wanting to spoil her lofty assumptions, however misguided. When he pulled into the drive, two men carrying a crate stopped what they were doing and set the box down.

"Why are we stopping so far away?" she asked, reaching for the door, but was stopped by Carl's arm reaching across her. "Stay here while I check things out first."

"Goodness me, you're as jumpy as Charles! What's gotten into you two?"

One of the men walked away, while the other one lit a cigar and leaned up against the doorframe.

"You lost?" the man said, his face cloaked behind a cloud of thick smoke.

"I know my way pretty good around here," Carl said, agitated by the inflection in the man's voice.

The man's eyes narrowed on him as he took another draw from the cigar. Carl watched his eyes shift, looking over his shoulder as he saw Claire approach from behind him.

"Hello, I'm Claire Collins, my husband and I own the farm up the road. We heard you and your family are new to town, and I wanted to offer a welcome pie to the lady of the house. Might she be home?"

Sensing her kind gesture wasn't welcomed, Carl grew even more uncomfortable and cautious.

The man leaned back against the doorframe, exhaling a puff that drifted downwind in her direction.

"And you are?" she asked, witholding passing any judgment on first impressions.

"Clint Larson."

"Pleasure to meet you Mr. Larson, this is Carl Ebbers." Clint didn't offer a handshake, just stood against the doorframe, obviously annoyed by the interruption.

"We'll let you get back to work," Carl said, extending his arm out to Claire, suggesting they be on their way.

Clint spat at the ground and curled his lips around the cigar.

"Before we go, I would like to meet the lady of the house, your… wife, perhaps? It was my intention to give her this pie."

"She isn't here. Went into town, won't be back for hours," he said, leaning over to spit at the ground again, closer to Carl's boot this time.

"Some other time then," Claire said, disturbed by his cool and inhospitable demeanor.

Following her down the driveway, Carl felt like he had just gotten out of a mud bath. "Wretch," he murmured under his breath. As they passed the porch, he noticed the front door cracked open and a woman in a blue dress standing off to the side, barely visible. The figure backed away slowly before closing it.

"I understand some folks frown upon unannounced visitors, but around here, we like to get to know one another. It might not be the big city way of doing things, but it sure is in this town," Claire said.

In a hurry to leave, he helped her inside the car and quickly shut the door.

"Fiddle-dee-dee, you know, he didn't even tell me her name. Don't you find that odd?"

"Everything about that man is odd. I wouldn't ponder it too much."

*   *   *

Ben and Elliot stepped out of the stall, covered in cedar shavings and straw, shaking the pieces from their clothes and hair.

"Looks like you replaced me already," Paul said as he walked in, looking at the mitts sitting on the bench. "Haven't seen these in a while."

"After asking a dozen times, I gave up on you," Elliot said.

Paul smirked, knowing he was right, and pulled a mitt on. "I've got a little time now."

"Now you're talkin'!" Elliot said, swiping the other mitt off the bench.

Walking to the edge of the grass, Ben sat cross-legged, spinning a piece of straw between his fingers and listening to the ball snap against their mitts. They joked and laughed, tossing back and forth. He watched their expressions change, becoming animated and more relaxed. And for the first time, he saw Paul smile. They continued to throw until noontime, laughing and talking about the good ole days. Elliot threw a high one into the air; when Paul caught it, he held onto it, rolling it over in his hands, tucking the mitt under his arm as he walked over to Elliot. They talked quietly for a few minutes, then Paul dropped the ball into Elliot's glove.

"Take my spot," Paul said, turning to Ben and holding the glove out.

Tossing the straw aside, he ran over.

"Elliot will teach you how to catch, he learned from the best."

Wiggling his fingers, he pulled the mitt over his hand and gave it a couple smacks.

"Stand here, and I'll go back over there," Elliot said, jogging back to his spot. When he turned around, Paul was walking away, looking back over his shoulder with a wave.

9

Jack Larson sat in the back row of the classroom, his gaze fixed on his desk. He only glanced up when the teacher called on him to stand, introducing him to the class in a way that made his cheeks burn with embarrassment. When the bell rang for lunch, he pulled a sack from under his desk and set it on top, ignoring the other kids falling into line by the door.

"Jack," Miss Higgins said, standing beside his desk, "we eat outside when the weather permits. Please gather your lunch and join the others."

He snatched the bag off his desk in a tight fist, looking out the window at the kids laughing and sitting on a large, quilted blanket.

Miss Higgins waited by the door, waving him outside. "Quickly, lunch time has started."

He turned the corner with his head down, pulling from her hand as she reached for his shoulder. He passed a row of jackets and sweaters hanging on hooks by the door that led to the schoolyard.

Miss Higgins called to him. "Hang your jacket, Jack, it's warm outside. You can put it back on when we finish eating." He looked up disdainfully at the crowded hooks, pushed the door open, and walked over to a tree, away from the circle. He sat with his back to the large trunk and pulled out a peanut butter sandwich, ignoring his classmates. Spontaneously, he pulled up his sleeve to avoid staining it with jam, but in doing so exposed deep scratches on his arm. He quickly tugged his sleeve back down to cover up the scars, scanning his classmates' faces to see if anyone was watching. Satisfied it'd gone unnoticed, he continued eating, unaware that Miss Higgins was looking on from the corner of the yard.

*   *   *

Millie sat at the counter, sifting through files when Gladys came into the office, standing on the doormat, clutching her pocketbook against her bosom.

"Hello?" Millie said, leaning over the counter.

Gladys stepped forward, her usually cheery demeanor now subdued by concern. After observing they were alone, she whispered to Millie, "I'm afraid Emily is not well. I will need to call on Frank to see her."

"We were afraid of that. Frank is on a call; let me check his calendar. It's going to be difficult to see her today, but tomorrow might—"

Gladys interrupted. "It must be today. Please Millie, I wouldn't be so bold if I didn't have great concern."

Pulling a folder from a tray, Millie scanned a sheet of paper. "Her test results came back showing low levels of antibodies."

"What does that mean, low antibodies?"

"Typically, we see that code when a breach of immunity is present. It can signal progressive disease or in some cases, infection. Frank noted visible sensory delays in her legs, significant tremors in the left hand, neurological deficits, and her vision test was troublesome. I don't mean to frighten you, but Frank's notes combined with the test results are worrisome." She reached for Gladys's hand, "Let's pray."

"Father in Heaven, we pray for our sister in Christ, give us knowledge and help us along this assessment. Give us strength, and faith to help Emily and to provide comfort and healing. Let us remember you are in control; your ways are not our ways, and your thoughts are higher than our thoughts, in Jesus's name we pray, amen."

They were still holding hands with their heads down when Frank came around the corner. "Oh, this doesn't look good."

"We were hoping you could pay Emily a visit today if you can manage it."

"Earl Crampton cancelled this afternoon. I have time."

"Here are the results," Millie said, handing him the folder. Alarmed to see the antibody results, he scanned his notes from the neurological exam and blood pressure reading. Along with the vision and neuro report, everything pointed to a compromised immune system. He flipped to the next page and read the words *probable diphtheria consult.* "I need to see her immediately. Gladys, if you wouldn't mind my driving, I'd like to ask you some questions on the way."

"I told her I was running an errand; this is going to take her by surprise."

"You did the right thing: your concern might save her life." As they started for town, Frank was overcome with feelings of inadequacy. If it was indeed diphtheria, he had no prior experience treating such a dangerous illness. "Could you describe the marks on her skin?"

"Very red, and the top layer of skin looks almost clear, like a blister. But the area underneath looks raw. Absolutely dreadful!"

"Is there any noticeable difference between them in size or shape?"

"Not that I could see, and I changed her nightgown—I would have noticed."

Frank gathered his bag and followed Gladys upstairs to Emily's room. She tapped on the door, opening it a crack, and peeked around the corner. "Emily," she whispered. "I brought Frank Miller with me, he's here to look you over."

Emily turned her head, squinting at the light. Her hairline was damp from fever and her complexion was pale, contrasting with the bluish hue around her lips and darkened skin under her eyes. Gladys stood at the foot of the bed as Frank assessed her, and even though he maintained his composure with a gentle tone, she could sense overwhelming concern.

"Help me lift her forward, I want to get a look at the lesions." Gladys held Emily's shoulders while he held a thick lens over the area. "Keep her steady, I need to get a skin sample." He tapped the tweezers into a vial, lifted the bifocals off his forehead, and removed his gloves. "She will likely be too weak to get out of bed, and I would advise that she stay in this room, limiting contact with others as much as possible until I can rule out some causes. Let's get back quickly, I'll need to test the samples."

*　　*　　*

Taking the key from the envelope, Paul unlocked the door. The scent of Bernie's last cigar still hung in the air and a full canister of coffee was on the counter. He unscrewed the bottom of the cylinder and started shaking the grounds into the trash pail, uncovering a shiny blue wrapper that caught his eye. Pulling the wrapper taut, "Rockwood Confections Inc., New York" was printed in bold white lettering on the label. He ran his hand along the counter, his eyes catching a cigar stub sitting in the tray next to the till. A receipt for Larson Acres was on top of the bank deposit: a sale for saddles, bridles, and three bits, totaling three hundred forty-five dollars. The receipt was sparsely completed—even the box for the house number was left blank, a highly unusual occurrence for detail-oriented Bernie, especially when it came to newcomers. Either Larson didn't want anyone to know his house number or Bernie just wanted him out the door. Under the till he found Bernie's crossword and an order form he was working on. After scanning the items, he went to the back room. Thick webbing blanketed the rafters, and most windows were cracked. A mouse scurried under shelving, countless unmarked boxes stacked in every corner, covering most of the floor. Looking around the room, he felt ashamed that he hadn't spent more time helping to keep things in order.

Across from the storage room was a small door, the window yellowed from years of accumulating dust and a doorknob that wobbled in his grip. Inside, books and photographs lined the shelves: One had uniformed men standing against a tree with rifles and horses, a paper clipping reading, "Civil War Era Begins." He picked up another picture of Bernie with three other men holding a wooden sign with the words: "Union Army." On the wall, encased in a box, was a flag with circular stars. He moved from picture to picture, touching the remnants of Bernie's life, lifting the strap of a military satchel hanging from a hook behind the door. Inside, a fighting blade and a canteen rested in the side pouch. He took a seat at the desk, rummaging through drawers until he found order records to reference and rolled them up. On his way out, he lifted the latch on the glass case, tucking the flag under his arm.

Outside, Clint stepped out of his car, lit a cigarette, and headed inside.

The bell clapped against the door when Paul came around the counter; Clint stood there glowering at him with a lit cigarette hanging from his lips. "Store's closed, you must have missed the sign."

He glanced at the flag under Paul's arm, removed his cigarette, and tapped the stem, sending a ball of ash to the floor before looking at his watch. "Closed? It's three o'clock in the afternoon. How can it be closed—somebody die?"

Paul took a few steps toward him, looking him in the eyes. "I said we're closed; the reason isn't any of your business. Now, we can stand here and talk about it, but it'll be a very short conversation."

He smirked behind a puff of smoke, tugged on the hem of his jacket, and tipped the brim of his hat.

Paul locked the door, glancing out of the corner of his eye at the New York plate on Clint's car before getting into his truck and heading into town.

Distracted from the tense interaction, Paul drove past the entrance into Grover's place and veered off the road in front of the main house. Chuck's wife, Gretta, kneeled at the edge of the porch.

"Paul, is that you?" she asked, wiping her forehead with the back of her hand, clutching a bouquet of chickweed and nutsedge in the other.

"Yes, it's me. Good afternoon Mrs. Grover."

Gretta struggled to her feet, her skin flushed, brushing off her clothes and straightening her hair. She may have been a married woman, but Paul's rugged appearance could cause the most devoted wife to swoon.

"What's that in your hand?" she asked, pulling off a gardening glove.

"I was about to ask you the same thing."

"Oh, these? I swear, they sprout up overnight. I'm so sorry to hear about Bernie; Chuck's been moping around all day, even snubbed his nose at steak and eggs this morning. You want me to find him for you?"

"Not necessary, I just wanted to drop this off for the ceremony."

"It would be my pleasure. Wait here and let me rinse off; I don't want to smudge."

After a minute or two, Gretta sashayed down the steps, drying her hands by fanning them in the air, hoping the lavender scent would carry, standing rather close to him as she admired the embroidery. "It's absolutely lovely," she said, trailing a finger across the silky threads and leaning forward to examine the stitching, "such impressive craftsmanship."

Feeling his personal space invaded, he took a step back, handing the flag out to her. "I best get back to my day."

Gretta took the flag and fluttered her eyelashes. "We'll see you tomorrow," she said, watching him walk away.

*   *   *

Frank and Gladys returned to his office. After a quick goodbye, Frank hurried inside to make a phone call to his fellow practitioner and colleague, Mort Stanton, while Millie busied herself straightening leisure magazines in the lobby.

"I'm afraid I need to make an overnight trip," he said, placing bottles on the counter. "I asked Mort to test these samples—there's no time to waste."

On the drive back to Emily's house, Gladys sang hymns, quieting her spirit with thoughts of God's goodness and grace, resting in her knowledge of the word, and feeling some peace as she drew on her faith. She thought about Margaret, so hopeful of her future on the cusp of the nursing program, and Jonathan, just a few weeks away from his departure for the Navy. And then she thought about Benjamin, so quiet and timid. With the school day ending in a few hours, she thought it best to tend to Emily and have a talk with the children when they arrived.

10

JUNIPER STOOD TIED TO A post near the barn, sniffing the air. A gust of wind traveled over a row of trees, bending the branches. His footing shifted and he yanked at the lead with a high-pitched whinny. Another stiff wind whistled through the woods, cracking a limb. He paced and pawed at the ground, putting tension on the lead as he backed up.

Hearing a whinny, Ben and Elliot quickly filled their pails, quickening their steps toward the barn. Another stiff breeze took Elliot's hat off his head, and he ran ahead to catch it. Ben hurried to follow him, spilling feed from the pails rocking at his sides. A loud crack coming from the tree line caused Juniper to rear up, pulling against the lead even harder, this time bending the post.

"Somethin' spooked him," Elliot said, setting the pail down, "the branches must be weakened from the storm." He took his hat off and gently rolled his free hand forward, his voice calm and steady. "Easy boy, easy," he repeated, trying to pacify his agitation. He untied the lead and its neck relaxed forward, nickering as Ben stroked its forehead. "Those branches snappin' and poppin' most likely scared him, he might be a little skittish for a while." He poured some water out of his thermos onto a rag and slapped it on the back of his neck to cool down. "Now, I'll show you how to groom him."

Ben set his pails aside, excited for another lesson.

Elliot grabbed two buckets from the barn and walked to the water tub, dipping one pail in and handing it to Ben. He took the other pail and filled it halfway, swirling the white sudsy liquid around. "This one has some soap added to it." He moved a brush down Juniper's back and along his sides and back over his mane. "You want to brush him real good to knock the dirt off before you take the sponge to him."

Ben worked the other side, following what Elliot was doing and helping to rinse the suds off.

"Now we pick," Elliot said, shaking the water from his hands. "You want to tie him off, just in case he gets jumpy and backs away when you lift his leg up." He stood with his body next to Juniper's front leg, explaining to him where to position his body. "Now run your hand down his leg like this; when you get to the fetlock here, give the hair a tug." Juniper kept his leg firmly on the ground. "See, he's being stubborn, so now, give this area a pinch," and he pressed together the soft tendon area and Juniper raised his foot. "Sometimes it just takes some proddin', but stand up straight, don't slouch in case he kicks."

Ben's eyes got wide when Elliot pulled a tool from his belt. "Don't worry, this is easy once you get the hang of it, but you got to know what's what on the hoof, so come closer and get a good look."

Ben was apprehensive, keeping some distance between them.

"There's the frog, sole, colleterial groove, and the wall," Elliot said, taking the hook and pressing into the frog, picking out the compacted dirt.

Ben covered his eyes and grimaced.

"Don't go closin' your eyes, now. This don't hurt him, and if you don't keep 'em clean, he could get the thrush."

Ben hesitantly separated his fingers, peeking through while keeping one hand pressed over his face.

Elliot started scraping again, picking around the hoof until the big chunks of dirt fell out, then took a small brush from the other side of his belt and moved it back and forth, sloughing out the smaller pieces. "You need to be the one to put his foot down—lets him know you're in charge or else he'll drop his foot anytime he fancies. Now you give it a try."

Ben slowly dropped his hand, bringing his thumb to his mouth, chewing nervously at his nail.

"Can't be doin' that on this job, you never know what you might be chewin' on."

With a sour face, he pulled his finger out of his mouth quickly and rubbed it against his shirt.

"Go ahead, I'll talk you along."

When Ben moved his hand down the leg to the fetlock, Juniper lifted his foot.

"That's how it's done!" Elliot said, watching him shake as he cradled the leg awkwardly. "You're doin' good, real good; now start pickin' 'round the triangle."

He held the pick gently, slowly dragging it along the surface, nervously glancing over at Elliot every few seconds to gauge how he was doing.

"Apply more pressure, you gotta get in there. Don't be afraid, he doesn't feel it."

He pressed into the area, loosening the dirt, gaining more confidence as pieces fell to the ground.

"Now take the other end of the pick and run it over the wall."

Ben concentrated on his movements, careful to stay along the groove.

Elliot watched him scuff the hoof and lower Juniper's leg, grinning so wide Elliot could see his teeth. By the time he cleaned the last hoof, his apprehension was gone. "Mighty fine job," Elliot said, pulling out the mitt tucked in the back of his waistband.

*   *   *

Tossing the ball into the air, Elliot called out, "Go on, Ben! Further down!" He picked a spot in the grass, waving Ben further down the yard, grinning as the boy shuffled into position.

Judging his distance from Elliot, Ben felt uneasy about making the throw, taking a few small steps back.

"Take one bigger step back—it's good, you can do this!"

Looking toward the road, then back to Elliot, he reluctantly took one more step backward, not as big as Elliot encouraged.

Elliot gave him an affirming nod, palmed the ball, and drew back, throwing a high one, giving Ben more time to get under it.

Ben watched the ball soar into the air, squinting against the bright sun. It arced down toward him, and with a satisfying thud, landed squarely in his mitt. He quickly squeezed it shut. Looking at the ball in the pocket, he held it up in triumph, then threw it back, nearly making it without a bounce.

As they tossed, a dust plume folded over the road; wheels clattered, and quiet voices became louder as the school wagon got closer.

Elliot pretended to be winding up a pitch in a World Series game, raising his glove over his head, turning his hips, and leaned forward like he was staring down the batter. Ben got nervous, thinking he was really going to let it fly. He tensed up, but Elliot faked him out, lobbing another soft toss.

Ben froze, and by the time he reacted, the ball dropped in front of him and rolled through his legs. Laughing burst out from behind him. When he turned to chase the ball, two boys were pointing at him. The boy on the end stood up and looked down at his feet, mocking him. Ben looked at the other kids, all whispering to each other and snickering. The boy at the end of the bench kept laughing, but his eyes weren't joyful—it was the torment and embarrassment he took pleasure in. Ben recognized the brightly colored sneakers and suddenly felt queasy. His stomach immediately lurched—before he even realized what was happening, he was hunched over vomiting, heaving up chunks that coated his boots. As the wagon passed by, the laughing intensified; some of the kids looked away, some pinched their noses and covered their mouths in disgust. Elliot dropped his mitt and ran over, putting a hand on his back and staring angrily at the boys who were poking fun.

"I'm sorry," Ben said, stepping away from his vomit.

"Ain't nothin' to be sorry for," Elliot said. "True story: Dallas Macy was a pitcher for the Seminoles.' Just before he pitched a no-hitter in the 1914 World Series, he went behind the dugout and tossed his eggs, but you know what he did after that?"

Licking the sour saliva from his teeth, Ben looked at him curiously. "What did he do?"

"He went out to the mound and struck out three batters in a row! Wanna know what the other team did that was laughin' at him?"

Spitting on the ground, Ben looked up with his hands on his knees, waiting for the rest of the story.

"They lost," Elliot said with a grin, handing him his mitt.

*　　*　　*

Charles came down the porch, searching his pockets for the car key. "You ready, son?" he said, giving Ben a gentle pat on the shoulder. "Your mother expects you home in time for supper."

"Monday, we'll get you up on that horse, let you get a feel for it," Elliot said.

"I'd like that," Ben said, wiping the toe of his boot across the grass.

Charles cranked the engine, looking up to give Ben a grin. "You're becoming quite the helping hand around here, doing all sorts of things a good farmhand knows how to do: cleaning stalls, grooming, learning to pick… that's a tough job, I'm proud of you!"

Grinning, Ben looked down at the mitt.

Charles crinkled his nose, searching the floor for something. "What's that awful stench?"

Tucking his shoulders together, Ben lifted one boot, putting it on top of the other to try and hide the smell.

"What in tarnation is that?"

"I got sick in the yard Mr. Collins," he said quietly.

Looking over with concern, Charles pressed his foot on the brake. "Are you feeling better?"

"I am. We were playing catch and some kids made fun of me when it went through my legs, then my stomach started to hurt. It got on my boots."

"Look here Ben," Charles said, motioning for him to look up. "Hold your head up. One day they'll learn a tough lesson, but just in case they're what I like to call 'doddypolls,' it might be best to show you a few tricks."

"Tricks, like magic?"

Charles chuckled, "Nah, the kind of tricks that give boys like that something to think about before picking on someone—like one hefty knuckle sandwich," then rolled his fingers into a fist, made a "bop" sound with his mouth, and gave Ben a sly wink.

Ben's eyes widened, looking at his hand and curling his fingers, imitating Charles with lukewarm confidence.

"I almost forgot," Charles said, reaching into his shirt pocket and pulling out a crisp dollar bill and one shiny quarter, "you earned this today."

Ben opened his hand and looked at the money, turning the dollar over, rubbing the paper between his fingers.

"I still have the first dollar I ever made: I was eight years old, carried milk buckets on a dairy farm. Took me one week to make that much."

"I'll keep this one sir—I'll keep it for sure!"

*   *   *

Margaret waited for Jonathan outside the schoolhouse, swatting at a fly that circled her hair.

"Looks like the poor girl is attracting flies," Ellie said, standing next to two of her friends who were giggling and pointing down at Margaret's shoes.

She looked down at her untied lace, frayed at the end. The cinch buckle had long since worn away, leaving the knotted fabric teased up at the end like a ball of matted hair.

Walking up beside her, Jonathan stared at the three girls as they pointed and laughed. "You wait," he said. "Ten years from now, they'll be old hunchbacked maids with warts on their faces."

"I do hope you're right," Margaret said, tucking her books under her arm and laughing quietly.

"Better fix that first," he said, looking down at her shoes, "you don't want to fall face first into the ground and give them something more to laugh about."

On their walk home, after the conversation about school had winded down, Jonathan blurted out what was on both their minds. "You worried about Momma? You think it's just the blues after losing Father?"

"At first, I did. I noticed her shaking a lot and figured it was just nerves and the worry of it all, but it's been getting much worse. The other day at the sink, she dropped a plate, just doing dishes."

"Yeah, I think you're right… I started to get concerned when she fell in her room—remember? She told us she just lost her balance, but I knew something was wrong."

Cutting across the field, Margaret noticed someone in the yard. "Isn't that Miss Gladys?"

"I think so, but why is she hanging our laundry?"

"She gave me a ride to school this morning—maybe Momma's still in bed."

Gladys clipped a pin over the corner of a bedsheet and noticed them walking up the road, working a little faster to finish the bundle before they reached the house.

"You two look even smarter today," she said, trying her best to hold up the corners of her mouth in a half-hearted smile.

"Is she still in bed?" Margaret asked with concern.

With a deep sigh, she let her fake smile fade. "She is. The fever isn't letting up. Let's go inside and I'll tell you what we know, how's that sound?" In her mind, she knew exactly how it sounded: positively dreadful.

Pulling an apron from a kitchen hook, she tied it around her waist and portioned slices of applesauce cake. The smells coated the room in cinnamon and vanilla.

Jonathan lifted his head from the crook of his elbow to inhale the aroma, watching Gladys carry saucers with silky apple glaze drizzling down the edges of spongy cake, pooling around the porcelain saucers as thick as marmalade.

"Margaret, would you be a dear and fetch some plates and forks."

"Yes ma'am," she said, jumping from her chair to have a taste.

Jonathan reached for the fork, hovering over his portion.

"Wait, wait," Gladys said, humored by his excitement, "let's not act like wild wolves! I know you were raised to wait until everyone had their serving before filling your cheeks," she said, looking over her glasses.

She pulled out a chair and picked at the apple topping with her fork, but suddenly lost her appetite, setting her fork down and folding her hands in her lap.

Jonathan pulled a finger across his plate to get the last drizzle of glaze and brought his finger to his mouth when a swift kick to the shin from Margaret's shoe got his attention.

"Ouch, what did you do that for?"

Scowling at him, she moved her eyes over to Gladys.

"I'm afraid your mother is quite ill, but we need to carry on for the time being until she recuperates. She's going to need a lot of rest and a lot of help, so I'm counting on you both to do your share. It might only be for a few days, but it might be longer, we just don't know yet."

"What is she ill with?" Jonathan asked.

"I don't think they know yet; Frank Miller stopped by today and is doing additional testing. It shouldn't be long until we know something more."

"Can we see her?" Margaret asked.

"Of course you can, and it's going to be important to check in on her regularly. I have been trying to get her to eat and drink, but she's not quite ready. I'm fixing to try again after our snack."

"I suppose I could stay with her," Margaret said. "Jonathan can get my school lessons and I can do the work here."

"Absolutely not. I'll see to it that you both get off to school and I'll take care of her during the day—you shouldn't be missing class."

"What about Ben? He'll need someone to stay with him, too. We can't expect you to look after him and our mother," Margaret said.

"Young lady, this is not a burden, and not up for discussion. I'm truly grateful that I can help. Now, if you have studies, get to it now while I check in on your mother."

"Can I come?" Margaret asked.

"You sure can. Why don't you fill a pitcher of water, and we'll see if we can get her to drink a little, but after that, it's time for studies. Jonathan, you may have one more slice, I can see your mouth watering from here."

Pushing the chairs back from the table and heading for the stairs, they heard footsteps on the porch. The knob jiggled and spun, and the door flew open. Ben ran inside waving the dollar in the air for everyone to see. "Margaret, look! Look what I earned today!"

Holding his hat in his hands, Charles stepped inside expecting to greet Emily.

"That's wonderful!" she said, giggling as she watched him disappear into the kitchen.

Charles stood in the entryway, taking notice of the pitcher Margaret was holding and the cup and saucer in Gladys's hands.

"Charles, so good to see you again. I would offer a handshake, but I'm quite full at the moment," Gladys said.

"Can I give you a hand?" he asked.

"Not necessary, we have a short walk."

"Where's Momma?" Ben asked excitedly, "I want to show her my dollar!"

"She's probably sleeping, we're going to check on her now."

"I'll come with you; this will make her happy!" he said, turning for the stairs.

"Honey, why don't you stay down here until we check in on her," Gladys said, "she might need…" but her suggestion fell on deaf ears: he was already on the landing, banging his boots up the stairs.

Charles could see the tension on her face, following his footsteps with her eyes.

Ben tapped on the bedroom door, calling out to her, then knocked a little louder. "Momma, you awake? I want to show you what I made today… Momma?"

"I'll be right back," Gladys said, hurrying up the steps with Margaret following close behind.

"Margaret," Charles said softly, "is your mother sick?"

She nodded, trying hard to be strong, forcing a smile that didn't quite reach her eyes. "She's been sleeping a lot."

Jonathan came around the corner when he overheard commotion and rushed up the stairs.

"Ben, I need those pillows there," Gladys directed, pointing to two that were laying on the floor beside the bed. "Margaret, I need a cool washcloth, and Jonathan, roll up that blanket there."

As they moved about, Gladys put her hands on Emily's shoulders, trying to soothe the tremors. Her eyes were completely closed, and her breathing was shallow. Gladys pulled back the bedding and cupped her hand over her mouth, alarmed by the deep purple coloring on her legs and feet.

"Margaret, please grab a few more blankets; check the line, I believe I hung two this morning, they might be dry."

"I can get them," Charles said, startled into action.

"Thank you, Charles," Gladys said, feeling relieved that he was there.

Jonathan and Ben stood close to each other, frightened by their mother's lack of response. Tears began rolling down Margaret's cheeks as she rummaged through shelves for a washcloth.

Emily moaned, letting her head fall to the side, struggling to turn her head against the pain and stiffness she felt.

"Mother, it's us, can you see us?" Margaret pleaded.

The only response was coarse, labored breaths. Finally, Emily strained in the direction of their voices, her mouth trembling as she tried to speak. She swallowed—the pain that followed took her breath away and she gasped, wincing in pain.

"Momma?" Ben whispered, leaning closer to her face, "we're here beside you."

Returning with a blanket over his arm and visibly unsettled by her condition, Charles clenched his hat tightly. "We need to alert Frank. He needs to see her now."

"He's on a train out of town," Gladys said, "he looked in on her earlier, took some samples for testing… might not return until Sunday."

"Then we need to see Millie—she can tell us what to do."

11

Paul made the turn heading out of town, passing Emily Paulie's house. He saw Charles's car pull out of the driveway, bumping and rocking as it sped onto the road, Charles quickly gaining speed as he turned toward town. Paul found it odd, but continued to the farm, seeing Elliot waiting in the driveway.

"Didn't expect you back here today," Elliot said.

"Wanted you to have this supply list before Monday. Add anything I missed; you might need to take feed inventory."

"Thanks. How you feelin' 'bout tomorrow?"

Paul pushed his shoulders back and released a pop of tension.

Elliot pulled a small leather notepad from his back pocket and handed it to him. "Here, I've been meaning to give this to you."

Paul turned it over in his hand. The well-worn leather binding felt soft to the touch. "What is it?"

"Just some Bible verses I wrote down—a few of my favorites. I find reading them from time to time helps settle my mind," he said softly.

"I suppose if God can settle *your* mind, then mine won't take half the time."

Shaking his head, Elliot hoped he would eventually take a look, even if it was just out of boredom.

*　　*　　*

That night, Millie was winding down after a long day, having made herself comfortable in her living room chair and pulled a blanket over her lap to fight off the early autumn chill. She reached for her copy of *Medicine Daily* and began flipping to the recipe pages when an article caught her eye. Her attention was grabbed by a bulleted list of symptoms with the headline: "Strangling Angel - What to Look For: A Rise in Diphtheria Cases." She pulled her finger down the list of symptoms: skin lesions, neurological complications, swollen lymph nodes, swallowing and breathing difficulties in advanced stages. Continuing down the list, she recalled Emily's exam results and the urgency in Frank's phone call to Mort. Curious about the contagion factor, she lifted the blanket and hurried to scour medical journals in the den when she heard a knock at the door. Another round of knocking came before she could get to the door. Peeking through the window curtain, she saw Charles wrap his coat tighter around his shoulders.

"Has Frank left already?" he said, out of breath and skipping any pleasantries.

"The train left about twenty minutes ago. I expect him back by Saturday evening, possibly Sunday—why?"

"I'm afraid Emily is very ill, and from what I saw, we aren't likely to save her if we wait till Saturday. Are you able to see her? I think she needs to go to the hospital."

"Come inside," she said, holding the door open and waving him through. "I think I have a hunch what this might be, but I need to look through the den. Can you give me a few minutes?"

"I'll wait," he said, taking his hat off and stepping inside.

"Actually, if you can help me look for something, it might save some time."

Millie opened the den's large oak doors and stepped into the dimly lit nook. Books and magazines lined the walls in tall bookcases; crates held stacks of journals and newspaper clippings. Charles marveled at a row of mason jars along the top shelf of a bookcase, each jar filled with various collections of herbs, roots, and berries.

"Over here, in this section," she called.

They faced an overwhelmingly crowded row of medical journals sandwiched between bookends. "Somewhere in these journals is a column on diphtheria remedies, and if we can find it, we may be able to do some further research."

Turning to look at her, Charles's brow furrowed, and his eyes were wide with panic. "Diphtheria?"

"I can't be sure," Millie said, taking one dusty journal out and scanning its cover, "but right before you arrived, I read an exhaustive list of symptoms in my medical magazine and I'm afraid she has most all of them." She put the journal back and looked at Charles with concern. "If she indeed has diphtheria, then she will soon begin to have respiratory difficulty as the disease reaches the advanced stages."

Charles took a few steps back, looking off into the distance like he had seen a ghost.

"Are you alright? You look befuddled."

He looked at her grimly. "She has that, too."

Millie removed her glasses, pulling them over her hairline, and began frantically thumbing along the printed bindings. "Let's move briskly— she may not have much time."

*   *   *

Clint stumbled through the door of his house, knocking over the umbrella stand and losing hold of his flask, sending it clattering to the ground. "Damn it, who left this in the middle of the floor!"

Jack heard his belligerent father shouting curse words and covered his ears. With a sudden chill, he felt the vibrations of his father's footsteps under his chair come to an abrupt stop just behind him. Jack lowered his hands and dropped his pencil. Clint reached down, grabbing hold of the pencil in his fist and brought it down hard against the surface of the table, snapping it in half before throwing the pieces onto the floor.

"Pick it up! Then go in there and clean up that mess," Clint mumbled through his words, his rancid breath heavy with the stench of liquor. "Next time you'll learn to leave it where you found it!"

Jack's eyes never left his notebook. He pretended he was somewhere else, waiting for the smell of whisky to dissipate before eventually reaching for his broken pencil. He pushed the splintered ends together then dropped them into the book and snapped it shut. He walked out of the kitchen, pausing at the corner of the hallway to listen to the mumbled curse words fade into incoherent grumblings as his father staggered up the stairs. Walking to the door, he focused on the staircase, not where he was walking, overlooking a sliver of glass from a broken vase which pierced the bottom of his foot. Jack instinctively clamped his hand over his mouth, stifling a yelp of pain, not wanting his father to come back down the stairs. Hopping around with his knee raised, he set the umbrella stand upright and grabbed his sneakers to avoid getting blood on the floor.

Swatting away the tears welling up from the pain in his foot, he carefully gathered the glass shards and carried them to the trash bucket. He tiptoed upstairs to the bathroom, found a bandage, and tended to the cut. Heading back down the stairs, he paused at the bathroom door when he heard the soft, muffled cries of his mother. The first time he'd heard her like that, it scared him, and that fear had fueled a desperate desire to protect her. But as the years went by, his fear turned to sadness. He had given up on being able to fix anything; all he had left was a dim hope that something would just happen. Maybe his father would have an accident, or they would lose all their money and have to move back to New York. But over time even that light was snuffed out, and a suffocating acceptance settled in. He pulled his ear from the door when he heard his father in the bedroom. A shiver ran over his body at the thought of being caught, and he quietly stepped away from the door, avoiding the creaky floorboards and scurrying down the stairs as quietly as he could manage.

*   *   *

Gladys glanced around the room at the worried faces staring back at her, waiting for Charles and Millie to come back down the stairs. Her anxiety became unbearable. Her feet tapped relentlessly on the floor, and her fingers drummed nervously. Finally, she was unable to sit still any longer, and she started to get up just as the sound of the door opening got her attention. Millie and Charles came down the stairs, all eyes fixated on them for answers.

"Might we speak privately?" Millie asked.

Wiping the sweat from her palms on her skirt, Gladys followed them into the kitchen.

"She has a rather severe respiratory infection," Millie said. "It's difficult for her to breathe and it could cause complications if not treated immediately. The hospital is more equipped than we are; I'm afraid she will need a lot of care in the coming days."

"Good heavens, I sure hope it isn't the influenza," Gladys said. "My Morty had a bout with that, took him months to recover."

"I'm concerned it could be something much worse," Millie whispered.

Reaching for her collar, Gladys tugged at the fabric to relieve the sudden tightness.

"I have a concern, going by certain symptoms she is presenting, that it may be diphtheria."

"Oh my!" Gladys said, putting her hands to her lips.

"I cannot say for sure—we will obviously know more after the test results come back. But I do want to raise the possibility that this could be something serious. I will return tomorrow with an update; Frank should be back by sundown."

Gladys took a seat between Jonathan and Margaret, looking at their dreary faces. "It's been decided that your mother will need to be in the hospital for her recovery. We will stay at my house, that way I can get along a little easier."

"We've never stayed away from home before," Jonathan said, "but I suppose it would be fine."

Margaret hesitated, looking over at Ben, concerned about the adjustment with his being in an unfamiliar place.

"Can I still go to the farm?"

"Of course you can, I'll take you there myself if need be." Gladys said. "I know it will be different, but it's only for a short spell; I have plenty of room and being in my own kitchen will set me right. I'll wait here—go pack a few small cases with necessities and we'll get settled for the night, I'm sure you will be back in a few days."

*   *   *

Claire pulled the kitchen curtain aside as the sun settled on the horizon, saturating the room in warmth. Checking the time, she slid the golden rolls out of the oven, brushing butter over their crusty surfaces before putting them back inside. As she closed the oven door, the front door opened. Charles kicked off his boots and hung his jacket on the hook, breathing in the sweet smell, letting it ease his emotions.

"You look like the world just followed you home."

He walked slowly toward her with weariness in his eyes. "Sorry I'm late for supper. Emily was taken to the hospital. She is very sick, and we're not sure what is wrong… but after doing some research, Millie is worried it could be diphtheria."

"Diphtheria? Oh, dear Lord, I sure hope she is wrong. I read an article many years ago about an English princess that fell ill—such a tragedy. I always thought of it as a childhood illness."

"I'm afraid not," Charles said, shaking his head. "Millie spoke about a rise in cases, just recently even. It pains me to see what those children have gone through; let's pray for better news tomorrow."

*   *   *

Paul rolled a towel, pulling it around his shoulders as water droplets trickled down his chest and soaked into the towel tucked around his waist. Blinded by the setting sun shining through the window, he closed his eyes, feeling the warmth on his skin as the tension melted from his body. Feeling too tired to prepare a meal, he grabbed a can of vegetable soup from the cupboard and a handful of Oreos, using Elliot's notebook to hold the stacked cookies. Thinking about the upcoming ceremony hurt his heart, and suddenly he was lost in thought. What was the point of this life? *We're here for a blink, then we're gone*, he thought. Where do we go when it's over? He pondered these questions while popping the last cookie in his mouth and brushing the crumbs from the notebook. The leather was soft and grainy, and he liked the way it felt in his hand. Turning it over, he examined the binding, opening it from the middle and fanning the pages. A shiny ribbon uncurled from the cover and the words on the first page read:

To my friend Paul,
    Let these words be a light onto your path. God is good my friend,
go see. —Elliot

Leave it to Elliot to lay a crumb trail, he thought as he turned the page. Each paragraph began with a name he recognized from Bernie talking about Bible scriptures. He flipped through the pages quickly, noticing every page was written on except the last page. He read the words: *for your favorites*. Paul sat back in the chair, curious enough to read more.

He read through several scriptures until the room grew too dark to see without lighting the lamp. He stretched his arms over his head with a yawn, set the notebook down, and went to bed. Lying on his back, he felt a strange peace. Normally, he drifted into sleep with his mind clouded by thoughts of the next morning's chores. Tonight, however, he felt an inner stillness and fell asleep pondering some of the writings from Elliot's notebook.

*   *   *

By the time Gladys and the children arrived, exhaustion from the day had set in, and they walked sluggishly, each holding a small suitcase. The driveway was long, lined with mature trees and sprinkled with wildflowers that released a sweet perfume. Margaret looked around the yard, amazed by all the rows of greenery along the red brick walkway to the front porch. Each row was planted in perfectly straight lines and marked by wooden stakes adorned with hand-painted pictures of vegetables. Jonathan's eyes bulged at the size of the pole barn, and he could see two cars and a tractor parked inside.

Swinging his suitcase by the squeaky handle, Ben climbed the porch steps, looking at the fashionably arranged furniture with bright colored cushions tied in neat bows.

Gladys opened the door, waiting patiently as Ben looked around the porch. He set his suitcase down, gazing at hanging flower baskets and a bright red bird feeder.

"My cardinals love to perch on that feeder," Gladys said, "must be their favorite color."

Jonathan and Margaret stepped inside, looking up at the high, vaulted ceiling. A wide staircase led up to the second floor, with a brass railing wrapped around a loft. Gladys hurried about lighting oil lamps and candles. The furniture was bright, and the windows were large, framed with pastel curtains tied with silky ropes that looped neatly around silver eye hooks. "Here, each of you take a lamp and I will give you a tour before we get some shut-eye; I want you to know where things are in case you need them."

They walked in a line from room to room, amazed by the fixtures and all the plants and flowers arranged in large bouquets. Jonathan liked the room she called the study: it had tall bookcases, a desk with a globe on top, and a wood-burning stove.

Margaret marveled at the kitchen, where glass jars of canned vegetables and jellies gleamed from a large pantry shelf and dozens of herbs and small plants lined the window ledge.

"Now for the good part," Gladys announced, "let's go upstairs and you can get settled for the night—all our dogs are tired."

They each grabbed their cases and followed her upstairs, gliding their hands along the smooth banister with large newel post caps, finding it strange that the steps were so quiet. The hardwood framed a long rug with rich colors, making the house feel cozy and warm.

She stopped at a spacious bedroom with one large bed and a smaller bed in the corner by a window. They set their cases down and began to walk around. There were two dressers in each corner and a chest at the foot of the bed covered with a yellow blanket and fluffy white pillows.

"Since I'm the oldest, can I have the big bed?" Jonathan asked.

Margaret sat down on the mattress, pushing into the soft fabric. "I sat on it first—looks like you two can argue over the smaller one."

"There's plenty of rooms for each of you," Gladys said.

"Really, we each get our own?" Margaret said.

"Why yes, and Margaret, there's a freshly painted room just down the hall. You might like that one: the color is splendid in the daytime."

She led them to a bedroom in the middle of the hallway and pushed the door open. The room was creamy taupe with blue curtains and large animals printed on the borders of the wallpaper. The bed was framed with a head and footboard, and a comfortable looking stuffed bear slouched against the bed pillow. "Ben, I was thinking you might be comfortable in this room; I take no offense if you want to stow the bear, he's been sitting there for quite some time."

Ben's eyes were wide as he stepped inside. Walking over to the fluffy bear, he felt the softness as he sunk his fingers into its fur. He looked at the animals on the border and saw several horses next to some cows and chickens. "I like this one, I like the animals."

"Alrighty Miss Margaret, now it's your turn." Gladys walked her to the end of the hall where moonlight from a small window shone down on a round table with a potted plant in the center.

Grinning, she stepped inside. The pale-yellow walls were soothing, and the bedding was a light green with ivory ruffles along the bottom with matching pillow shams. A large oval mirror framed a dresser, and a desk was tucked in the corner under a window; there was even a powder table with a delicate table-top mirror and an antique brush and comb set.

"It was a bugger to paint the door trim; I missed a spot on the ceiling there, but you have to look closely to notice."

"I love it, Miss Gladys."

"That's good child, I'm glad it will be comfortable for you. I know it's not home, but it'll do in a pinch."

Jonathan and Ben stood at the door, happy they got the rooms that were less girly.

"I know this is an adjustment, but please make the rooms as you like until we can get you back home, and don't be shy if you need anything.

Speak up! Last I checked I couldn't read minds." Gladys began to walk back to her bedroom, pleased to see that her guests were comfortable with their rooms. "I'll most likely be in the garden before you get up, I'm making pot roast tomorrow and need to pick some fresh herbs. Have a peaceful sleep and don't worry, your mother will be right as rain soon."

The three of them stood in Margaret's room. "I like my room," Ben said, "but yours is good too."

Margaret smiled and laid back on the bed. "You think we'll be here long?"

Jonathan shrugged. "Probably not, Miss Gladys says she will be better soon. And Momma doesn't have to worry about us, she can just rest and get better."

"I miss her," Ben said sadly, "I want to see her."

Margaret sat up, "Don't worry, Ben, it won't be long."

*   *   *

Millie followed two night nurses to Emily's bedside, which was separate from the others and guarded with a curtain. She pulled a pencil and paper from her satchel and made some notes, listening to Emily's labored breathing until another nurse walked over, giving her a startle. Her tabard dress was frayed at the bottom hem that reached the floor, unlike the other nurses with calf-length dresses. Her high-collared shirt was billowy at the shoulders with a tight-fitting buckled belt snug around her waist. She wore a triangular bonnet, and Millie noticed a faded bloodstain on her hip that stood out against her white apron. She assumed she was older, although her face was plump and youthful. Millie didn't recognize her, though she didn't know everyone who tended the night shift.

"The strangling angel is upon her," the nurse said in a whisper.

"My apologies," Millie said, setting her paper on her lap, "did you say strangling angel?"

The nurse lifted a hand to her throat, touching it gently; her eyes were fixed just over the bed, looking at the wall. "It has come to take her air:

seven days at most to get the antitoxin. The horse can help if you're quick about it."

Tugging at her ear, Millie tried collecting her thoughts. "I have only heard of one administration of a horse-drawn serum in my time in medicine, and it ended horrifically as a result of tetanus," Millie said, bending over to show her a list of laboratories she kept with her. "I do know of a place, somewhere around Chicago I believe, that was performing rather groundbreaking studies on large animals, producing mass quantities of serums. Do you know anything about it?"

One of the night nurses walked up beside her. "I'm sorry Millie, I stepped away for a minute, what were you asking?"

Looking up at her, Millie turned to the spot where the other nurse had been standing—she was gone. "My, she moves quickly. I was speaking to another nurse, she was right here—I wanted to ask her some questions."

The night nurse looked confused as she glanced around the room. "Priscilla is in the next room folding laundry. We're the only nurses here tonight."

Confusion set in, leaving Millie questioning her own sanity. "Would you excuse me, please, I need to stretch my legs."

Peeking around the doorframe, she looked down the long hallway from left to right: there was only one door to the laundry hall. Still bewildered, she returned to the bedside. She would think more on this later; right now, she had to focus on Emily. "This looks to be diphtheria, would you agree?"

"Sadly, I would have to agree with you."

"Do you know if anyone here has any experience with horses producing antitoxin? Is there a lab known by the hospital perhaps?"

"Possibly a city hospital, but advanced therapies such as those come with risks."

"Yes, I agree somewhat, although we've had some great victories over disease by crossing that line between risk and reward."

The nurse didn't seem too interested in her words and let Millie know it would be best if she gathered her belongings and returned in the morning.

"We will try to get some fluids in her system and give her some barbital for sleep. The doctor will make rounds later tonight."

"Thank you," Millie said, picking up her satchel and following her to the hallway. "Have you ever personally treated anyone with diphtheria?"

"Once, a five-year-old boy. Sadly, we lost him. Back in my grandmother's time, they called it the Strangling Angel."

Goose bumps quickly covered Millie's skin, and she rubbed her arms to shake the chill, looking over her shoulder for the nurse that had disappeared into thin air.

12

PAUL ROUSED HIMSELF FROM SLEEP with a deep yawn. Gauging the amount of sunlight hitting the wall, he figured it to be half past six o'clock, and was quite surprised when he picked up Bernie's pocket watch to see it was nearly seven. He couldn't remember the last time he slept well into the morning hours, even in the winter months. A shiver rippled through his shoulders when his bare feet touched the wood floor. The change of season was fast approaching, and a bowl of hot oatmeal sounded good after an early turn-in and a light supper. Through the window by his chair, he saw the front of Elliot's truck and Carl sitting on the backside of the bed with fishing poles leaning against the quarter panel. He rubbed his eyes, combed his hair through his fingers, and grabbed a bucket of water.

"Mornin'!" Carl hollered, lifting his thermos cup, "Thought we might head to the river and catch some trout, if we're lucky. Grab your pole!"

Paul squinted at the sun, wishing he could start the day with a soak, but accepted the invitation and went to the shed to put on waders and grab his tackle.

The ride to the river was silent, but Paul didn't mind—he was simply grateful to be among friends. When they arrived, they readied their poles and baited the hooks. Standing alongside the riverbank, the only sound was the current flowing over rocks and a beaver dam.

Elliot resisted the urge to talk, giving Paul space to think and just enjoy the morning.

Snapping his pole above the water, Carl drew in his line, reeling in a twelve-inch trout.

"Good catch!" Elliot said, pulling up the live well. "That's a biggin'—we're eatin' good tonight!"

"That's probably the last of 'em today," Paul said, looking up toward the sun. "It's gonna be a hot one."

Propping their rods over their shoulders, they made their way along the river, listening to the swish of water and fish tails flapping against the bucket.

"Can't remember the last time we caught a brown that big," Elliot said, "but somethin' told me today would be a good day of fishin'."

"You let us know when you get that feelin' about duck huntin'," Carl said.

*　*　*

The sun broke over the treetops as Chuck unfolded the last chair and brought it into line with the others. He stepped back, eyeing the rows to ensure each had an even number. The smell of damp pine and freshly tilled dirt was a delightful combination, depending on what side of the grass you were on. He placed five chairs at the head of the grave, checked the ground webbing for equal spacing, and surveyed the grounds, watching squirrels scurry among the leaves. This time of year, the air took its time to warm, and he fastened his top shirt button for the first time all season.

Gretta had put out baskets of wildflowers and cut back a few low-lying branches he'd meant to take care of. Satisfied that everything looked to be in order, he headed up to the house to put his suit out and get some coffee.

*　*　*

Unsettled after a restless night, Millie shuffled to the kitchen, thumbing through a stack of address cards for Mort's office number. She lifted the mouthpiece from the phone box and turned the crank.

"AT&T Trans Western Electric, this is Mertle, who can I ring for you?"

"Good morning, Mertle, this is Millie Miller. I would like Dr. Morton Stanton, Englewood, Illinois please, EW.7104-7."

"My pleasure. I have four calls ahead, just a moment."

Spinning the address card in circles, she waited for the connection, anxious to share her findings with Frank.

"Hello Mrs. Miller, I can ring him for you now, have a blessed day."

Pressing her ear to the box, she heard the transfer click and the operator dialing through. A short ring sounded, followed by a gruff voice.

"This is Dr. Stanton speaking."

"Yes, hello Dr. Stanton, this is Millie Miller. I have a message for my husband Frank, might he be there with you?"

"Hello Millie; Frank left for the train early this morning from Dearborn Station."

She strained to hear clearly through the pops and crackles of static. "I'm sorry, did you say my husband is on the train?"

His voice faded out and the light on the phone box began blinking.

"Doctor, are you there, can you hear me?"

His voice became clearer, but every few words or so were cut short— she thought she heard him say the word "toxin."

"Doctor, our connection is broken; did you say something about a toxin?"

The connection cleared for a moment, enough for him to speak clearly. "Frank is carrying the antitoxin."

"Sir, what is it for?"

Holding the receiver closer to her ear, she heard him say, "diphtheria," before his voice dissipated into heavy static.

Millie hung the mouthpiece and spun out of her chair, grabbing her shawl.

*　　*　　*

Standing between two large oak trees, Chuck picked up the flag Gretta had placed in one of the flower baskets and set it on the chair meant for Paul. He straightened his collar and watched Bernie's friends and family make their way down the path.

Pastor John was at the front of the line, followed by Fred Comer walking beside Daniel and Denny. The Kincaid brothers and Earl and Bernice Crampton were further down the path. Carl, Elliot, and Paul walked with Charles and Claire, followed by many others from church; he couldn't remember a ceremony with so many mourners.

"Afternoon Chuck," Pastor John said, reaching out to shake his hand.

"Good to see you John, although it's better to see you in church."

"I agree," John said, clutching his Bible. "Bernie was a man of God. I trust that he's in a better place than any of us."

Welcoming everyone with a warm smile, Chuck directed people to their seats and walked forward to greet Paul. "I set a chair aside for you in the front."

Paul grabbed it and slid it closer to the end of the row next to Elliot. He sat, staring blankly at the mahogany wood casket sparkling against the sun, the brass finishes illuminated against the rich color of the flag draped over the center. *An impressive work of craftsmanship*, he thought, chuckling quietly as he heard Bernie's voice in his head say, "put me in the damn dirt in a pine box with a box of England's."

Pastor John opened his Bible. "Hello friends and loved ones; welcome. Our hearts are heavy today as we say goodbye, for now, to our dear friend. Bernie meant so much to the folks of our fine town: always willing to help all of us, a faithful member of the church, and the kind of man that is difficult to put into words. Each of us knew him in a special way: Some of us trusted him to know exactly what tool would get a job done, some of us depended on him for our afternoon coffee break, and some were blessed to hear him sing in church, but everyone knew him as a friend. He was a fine carpenter in his younger days and a darn good fisherman. And one of us knew him as a father," he said, giving Paul a respectful nod. After reading Psalm twenty-three, he closed the Bible, holding it tight to his chest. "We know he's in the house of the Lord, may we all have comfort in that knowing."

Feeling Elliot's hand on the back of his shoulder, Paul was overcome by emotion, tears running down his face as he looked up for the first time. The deep pain in his eyes was felt by everyone. After a moment, his tears ceased, and he stood up next to Carl and Elliot and walked over to the stirrups. Chuck, Daniel, and Earl joined them to lower the casket into the ground.

After the ceremony concluded, Carl and Elliot stayed behind, waiting for Paul as he took a few minutes of solitude by the grave. John handed him the flag and put his arm on his shoulder. "It would be great to see you at church sometime."

He returned the gesture, thanking him for the words, and gave Elliot a nudge when he saw Gretta walking over.

Reaching for Gretta's hand, Chuck held her close, watching as everyone walked back down the path. "This is the hardest part," he sighed, "the moments after, when folks carry on, leaving one behind."

"What will happen to the store?" she asked.

"Paul's fixing to run it, at least that's what I hear, and if I know Paul, he'll be open for business come Monday."

"Is that right," Gretta said.

"Carl seems to think so, and I hope he does; Paul's a sharp young man—a serious fella, but sharper than my axe blade."

"Wait," Elliot said, waving to Paul and Carl, "here comes Mrs. C."

Her hair was in a high bun and her pastel dress was covered in a flowery pattern of green and yellow. All the hard work on the farm left a little slack in the fabric around her hips. "Boys, I've made some refreshments and would like you to come to the farm; thought it would be nice for us to be together. Everyone is heading there now."

Elliot's eyes lit up; Carl rubbed his belly. "Don't need to ask me twice."

Paul looked around as the trail of cars sat in a line. It wasn't how he wanted to spend the afternoon, but he couldn't decline. Claire could ask him to rope the moon, and he would give it his best effort. She reached for his hand, instantly making him blush and fidget awkwardly. "You're joining us aren't you, Paul? I don't want you to be alone today."

"I'll be there."

"Good; we'll see you at the house then."

"This is great!" Elliot said, "we can all be together, telling stories of good ole Bern."

Lacking the same enthusiasm, Paul looked at him with annoyance until his smile faded. Elliot stifled his excitement, but he knew that deep down, Paul appreciated the gesture and even drew comfort from it, even if he'd never admit it.

*   *   *

Margie held the leg of a large white dog while Tom drew the last stitch when the bell clambered against the front door. "Be right with you," she called from the exam room. Millie stood at the counter, observing a homely looking woman wearing a pair of shaded glasses and a wide brimmed hat seated in the waiting area. Sitting next to her was a young boy nibbling a candy bar.

"Mrs. Larson," Tom called, "you can come back now, we're finished in here."

The woman pushed her glasses up the bridge of her nose as she skirted around the table past Millie.

"What can I do for you dear?" Margie asked, gripping Millie's hands in a tender squeeze. "You're looking a bit tired, are you feeling alright?"

"Just fine, I was hoping to speak with Tom—actually, both of you if you can spare a moment."

Margie checked a book laying open on the counter. "All clear until later this afternoon. Can I get you something while you wait?"

"No thank you, I'll just have a seat and catch my breath. I've been a bee about the hive all morning."

Taking a seat across from the boy, Millie smiled at him, but he avoided looking in her direction. She took notice of his sneakers and blue cap; his style was unlike that of most boys in town.

"Jack, come take this while I settle the bill," the woman said, holding the dog's lead out to her side like it was a dirty sock.

She noticed the boy wince as he took a step forward, like he had a sharp pebble in his shoe, while tossing the candy wrapper on the table.

The woman set the money on the counter and walked briskly to the door.

"Wait!" Margie said, "before you go, I was hoping to get your house number, we like to send out mailings from time to time."

Millie listened closely, curious to know where the woman was staying.

"My husband doesn't like to share personal information; thank you for your service," she said tersely, quickly closing the door.

Tom looked perplexed, scratching the side of his neck.

"What a strange thing to say," Margie said, looking over at Tom, "did she say anything to you?"

"Not a word. I still haven't a clue how that hunk of metal ended up in that dog's leg—nearly cut it to the bone."

"Beautiful dog though," Millie said. "I've never seen a dog like that before, so fluffy and white."

"Not many folks can afford a dog like that," Tom said, "they're definitely not from these parts."

"Oh, and Tom, Millie has something to speak to us about," Margie said. "If it is a good time, that is."

Tom sat across from her, examining the candy wrapper. "Rockwood Confections, looks fancy, why I bet that bar cost a quarter at least… now, how can I help, Millie?"

"I'm hoping you could help me with a medicinal matter," she said, pulling her satchel to her feet and reaching for a notebook. "A patient of Frank's may have contracted diphtheria and the disease is progressing. Now, I've done some research suggesting a serum can be produced using large animals, like horses, if given the toxin by injection. Do you have any knowledge or experience in this practice?"

Tom loosened his collar, his eyes quickly filling with concern. "Millie, I think this is far beyond my scope. This is medical science on a grand scale, and the diphtheria antitoxin has had to go through much trial and error. I have read studies on bovine tuberculosis, which has similarities, but harvesting the antitoxin is difficult, and even if the process goes smoothly, tetanus infections are a grave concern. The sterilization process is rife with complications, not to mention the intermission between the first injection and the draw."

"And that leads to my next question," Millie continued, undeterred.

"I have read conflicting studies: One measured a viable serum within three to four days, and another produced in three months… I doubt we have that much time unfortunately."

"I'm sorry Millie, given my limited exposure, I can only make an educated guess. Considering the vasculature of, let's say, a horse, the processing of the toxin wouldn't be quick. I would say anywhere from twenty to thirty days, possibly more. How much time does your patient have?"

"I would say six days at the most without treatment. Frank is on his way back with a dose of the antitoxin, but I am unsure how much he was able to get."

Pacing the floor, Tom paused for a moment. "What about contacting the physician's board?"

"I sent a telegram this morning to the New York Department of Health. I discovered a farm lab conducting clinical trials, but time is not on our side. If you could find any information or consult any colleagues that currently have immunized animals, it would be greatly appreciated. I know this sounds strange, but I must investigate all options."

"I will do what I can, although I think the best course is through the farm labs. Even if we could provide a blood draw, the processing period is far too long without prior dosing."

"Thank you, Tom. I must be going—time is of the essence."

Millie rushed out the door, weighed down by all the papers and journals she was toting.

"Do you think this is possible?" Margie asked.

"Anything is possible. Whether it's probable is the true question—I'll be in my office."

She could see his wheels beginning to turn, delighting in the peculiar and miraculous, taking any opportunity to pour over unconventional therapies. Leaving him to his thoughts, she picked up the dusting wand; something about the change of seasons sparked her need for order and tidiness. Moving about the lobby, she picked up the candy wrapper, admiring the shiny label before tucking it into her pocket.

Millie hurried to the hospital entrance, pulling her scarf from her neck and wadding it up into a ball. Standing at the side entrance, a nurse she recognized was smoking a cigarette.

"Good afternoon, Hazel," Millie said.

Hazel wiped her forehead with a tissue. Her uniform was stained with blood and the hair underneath her bonnet was damp from perspiration.

"It looks as though you've had a hard morning."

"Not for me as much as the woman in our quarantine unit."

"Emily Paulie, the woman in hall two?"

"I'm afraid it is—she's having a time. We might need to do a tracheotomy. Dr. Clark is assessing; Frank is with him as well."

"Frank, as in my Frank?"

Hazel took a long drag and nodded. "They're in Dr. Clark's office now."

Fanning the smoke from the air, she ran to the entrance and rushed down the corridor.

"It's worth a try Frank," Clark said, taking the ampule out of a wooden container, holding the glass tube up to the light. "Two hundred and fifty units isn't much; wish we had five hundred at least."

Standing outside the frosted door pane, Millie looked through the opaque glass, listening to their voices. The doorknob turned and Clark greeted her. "Millie, nice to see you. Your husband may have arrived in the nick of time; please excuse me, I need to find Hazel."

"She was outside when I came in."

"Would you mind getting her for me?" he said, not taking his eyes off the ampule as he disappeared around the corner.

Leaning over, Frank kissed her on the cheek. "I was going to stop at home first but needed to deliver the antitoxin. I don't know if it will make much difference, but I have a lot to tell you."

"As do I. I have been researching all night and just left Tom Taylor's— after I fetch Hazel we must have a talk."

Millie called out to Hazel outside, who took one last drag before stubbing the butt into an ashtray. She straightened her apron and reclipped a pin on her cap before hastening down the hallway and through a pair of double doors.

Frank came out of the office; his eyes were bloodshot from lack of sleep and his hair was windblown.

"Dear, you look like a coffee would do you some good," Millie said.

"I could use more than coffee," he said, scrunching his nose. "A hot bath for one. But we have much to discuss—let's stop for a bite to eat first."

They found a corner table, which Millie quickly covered with stacks of journals she'd gathered. Between sips of coffee they read through studies, circling and scribbling notes. She pulled an article from the AVMA magazine and slid it over to him, pointing at the headline with the tip of her pencil: "Horses Helping to Heal."

"This is what I spoke with Tom about."

Frank readjusted his glasses to read the small print, giving her a perplexed look when he finished.

"I'm certain this has some merit, and just in case we can't get more in time, I think we should consider it." She continued to explain everything she knew about the clinical trials in upstate New York and the process involving injected horses.

Finishing the second cup, he listened to the excitement in her voice and thought about his words carefully. "Small town medicine has unique challenges, it's very different from all these advanced trials you're reading about in the big cities."

"Well, Mort was able to get it, obviously someone has supply."

"Mort has a larger practice that is hospital affiliated; Englewood is on a main rail route. He receives some allowance only on a case-by-case basis and it can still take weeks to get. The last delivery was months ago, and the antitoxin I gave to Clark was just about to expire—we're lucky we got it when we did. Likely, she has already passed seventy-two hours from onset; after day five, the prognosis is grim, and that's assuming the onset was at diagnosis. By the time we completed the culture, she could already be advancing into day four, possibly five. There simply isn't time, the toxin is likely already fixed to her tissues. If this does nothing to improve her breathing, a tracheotomy might be necessary, but even so, her organs are failing."

She tapped her pencil nervously against the pages of her notes while Frank settled the bill, then cleared the table and waited for him by the door. Looking outside, she remembered the strange encounter she'd had with the nurse at the foot of Emily's bed, recalling what she had said about the horses. As they drove home, she stared blankly out the window, her bag lying at her feet with papers spilling over the sides.

"Injecting a horse with toxin without the proper sanitization can be even more harmful: the threat of tetanus would corrupt any viable blood draw," Frank said. "I just don't see how this would be possible."

"I know dear, I'm just thinking about the children. They have been through so much."

Taking his foot off the gas pedal, he veered off the road, turning the car around, causing her sack of journals to tip over. "Where are we going?" Millie asked.

"Back to the hospital."

*　　*　　*

Margie leaned on the counter, catching her breath. After dusting, she rearranged the furniture and put out a stack of new magazines. Tom rushed out of his office to the door, plucking his coat from the pole and spinning as he tried to find the arm hole, the paper in his hand fluttering wildly. "I'll return later, please lock up if it's past four o'clock."

Dumbfounded from seeing him so worked up, she watched him scurry to the car, his bifocal head lamp still strapped to his head. In his office, she found his desk cluttered with papers and a half-eaten peanut butter sandwich. The top drawer of his filing cabinet was open with a mess of records piled on top. Envelopes were pulled out and her alphabetical tabs were all out of order. She picked up the file on top of the stack, which had a sticker labeled "Claremont Riding Academy" and a handwritten number beneath it. Opening the file, she skimmed over the papers and peeked at a record with a number matching the number on the front of the file, No. 111, with the words "Diphtheria Donor" in parentheses. The record was for a gelding, aged four and a half years. Color was noted as "bay," purchased August 25th for $215.00. The medical record had a "Final Disposition" column which was blank. Below the lines of handwritten entries was a column noting the number of bleeds measured in units, with horse's names and their assigned number. The last two columns were labeled "forwarded" and "destroyed." She saw nine horses listed on the record and followed the row for horse #111. The last entry was two years ago to the day and the column labeled "destroyed" was filled in with the word "sold" written in the box.

She picked up a small white receipt, which looked to be a bill of sale; only two names were printed on it. One side was signed by Theodore Cutler, represented by Claremont Riding Academy, and on the other side, typed in large font, was the name Charles D. Collins, "private owner for farm use" written under his name, with a purchase price of $75.00. "Oh, my word!" she said, restacking the papers and clipping the sale note to the medical record as she found it, noticing a telegram to Claremont Riding Academy on the corner table by the door.

* * *

Frank and Millie turned into the hospital entrance at the same time, distracted by Tom waving a piece of paper in the air.

"What's he got there?" Millie asked, "looks like he has something to show us."

Tom hopped out of his car, leaving it running, and leaned into their window, handing the paper to Millie.

Waves of surprise flashed over her face as her eyes scanned the document. "Could this be true?" she asked, continuing to examine it.

"It would appear so, but the question is: which horse. And I'm not sure if Charles would know or even still have the horse—not sure if they lost any during the storm."

Millie turned to Frank. "We need that ampule container."

Hurrying to Clark's office, Frank noticed the bright pink ball of packing sitting on top of a table. "This was in the container box."

"I'll check the wastebaskets," Millie said.

Frank and Tom looked through the double doors; at the end of the hallway was a pedestal sign that read "Quarantine Area."

"Wait here—I'll go down there," Frank said. Inside the quarantine area, Clark was standing over Emily's bed next to two nurses; he tapped on the glass to get his attention.

Clark stepped through the door. "Her breathing is slowly stabilizing," he said, pulling his mask down to his chin. "We may still need to use a tracheotomy, but for now, we'll watch and wait. It is encouraging, even with the small dose we gave her."

"That is good news. Actually, I was hoping to get a look at the serum container, if I may… we've had a rather remarkable discovery."

"It's in my office, follow me," Clark said. "I must say, I am surprised; two hundred and fifty units isn't much in this advanced stage." Entering his office, he rummaged around his desk and came around carrying a small box. "Here it is."

Frank looked up with an expression of shock and excitement, shaking the container over his head. "Claremont R.A. New York" was printed at the bottom of the wooden cylinder, and beneath that were the words "anti-diphtheria," and "No. 111," dated exactly two years ago to the day.

Tom held the paper next to the container; circled in the middle of the ledger was the number "111," assigned to the horse sold to Charles—an immunized horse purchased twenty-three months earlier.

"Incredible odds! We need to get to the farm!" Frank said.

*   *   *

As he rotated the pig on the roasting rod, Charles brushed on the last layer of oil and herbs. The aroma was causing his gut to growl, and he was glad this felt more like a celebration of Bernie's life than a wake. He could overhear Carl and Earl sharing stories on the porch, and even Paul was telling a few.

Patrick and Peter carried over large wooden trays to hold the meat; the buttery texture and dripping juices caused everyone's mouth to water.

Once the plates were full and the tea was topped off, Pastor John led a prayer and blessed the food.

While the ladies sat around the kitchen table nibbling and sharing their fall recipes, Claire's attention was elsewhere. She giggled watching Elliot swing his lanky leg over the porch rail, balancing his plate in his lap. Paul and Carl were on the steps next to Charles and the Kincaid brothers, laughing as they shared nostalgic moments. After enduring the tragedies of the past year, she felt closer than ever to everyone and brimmed with pride for each of them.

Bernice sniffled and dabbed the corners of her eyes at the end of the table.

"Bernice," Gretta said, "are you alright dear?"

"I'm fine, I truly am, but I will miss seeing him at the door tomorrow when the church bell rings."

"And Paul, I can't imagine how hard this is for him," Gretta said, gazing dreamily out the window, resting her chin on her hand.

Claire adjusted her seat to see what captivated her attention and saw Paul facing the window talking to Patrick. Claire looked at her with a side eye, deciding she was enjoying the view a little too much. "Gretta, dear, would you mind passing the blueberry pie, I would like to get a slice before the men come back for seconds."

Slowly turning from the window and pulling her eyes away from Paul, Gretta returned to reality to find Claire watching her with a peculiar expression, causing her to flush with embarrassment. "I'm sorry Claire, what did you say?"

"The pie dear, would you mind cutting me a slice," Claire repeated flatly, holding her plate in front of Gretta.

They continued their casual conversations, passing recipe cuttings from magazines and comforting themselves with berries and cream, while Claire subtly kept her attention on Gretta's wandering eyes.

Charles took his last bite of pecan pie just as Tom's car pulled into the driveway, with Frank and Millie arriving close behind. His eyebrows rose at the sight of the new arrivals, and he set his plate on the railing before heading over to greet them.

"Apologies Charles," Tom said, unable to contain his anxious excitement, "we didn't mean to pull you away from company, and we can come back later if you'd like."

Charles leaned back and patted his belly. "Food's already down, and there's plenty more if you're hungry." Tom, Frank, and Millie all exchanged glances before Tom shook his head.

"We have something important to show you," Tom said.

Stepping forward, Frank handed Charles a bill of sale. "Mrs. Paulie has been diagnosed with diphtheria. I was able to deliver a small dose of the antitoxin which appears to be helping for now—or at least it is buying time—but what is most remarkable is that the horse used to produce the serum may well be here."

Charles examined the document, pausing a couple times to wipe the sweat from his brow. "How is this possible?"

"Heaven only knows that answer," Frank said.

Handing the paper back to Frank, Charles stood with his hands on his hips in disbelief. "You know which horse this is?" Tom asked.

"I have an idea. Follow me, I'll show you."

He led them to the barn in the back, pulled the doors open, and stood in front of Juniper's stall. "Could he really be the one?" Charles asked, cupping his chin in his hand.

"Possibly," Tom said, "we can't know for sure, but he came from the lab facility in New York, Claremont Academy. We know for certain that #111 was the only horse sold before discard, and your signature is on this bill of sale."

Charles took a few steps back, still walloped by the coincidence. "How many draws you think they bled him for?"

Frank traced the column with his finger. "Says here… seven."

"What does that do to a horse?"

Millie walked up to the stall, taking hold of the bars and examining Juniper. "The toxin has little effect, usually causing a low-grade fever, but with repeated injections it can deplete their energy and the horse may eventually succumb to the toxin and die."

"Is this farm still in operation?" Charles asked.

"Unfortunately, it was destroyed in a massive fire: records, equipment, everything was lost, and they were slow to rebuild. My guess is rather than rehouse, they sold the animals. It takes three to six months to harvest the serum—it's a long process and the antitoxin expires after two years. They never did get the lab back up to full production and turned it into a riding academy once the insurance was settled."

"The last draw was exactly two years ago today, according to the medical record," Tom said. "And twenty-three months ago, he ended up here."

Charles took a deep breath, letting it out slowly. "I was using him for farmwork, never had the speed or agility for much else."

"Likely due to the repeated injections," Millie said.

"And here I thought he was just a lazy horse; he may well have saved many lives, who knows."

"He's a hero," Tom said.

"Is he still good for it? The serum?" Charles asked.

"Not likely. He most likely bled his limit or was released for quality. From what I researched, seven draws is quite high, and there is no telling if another would have killed him. My guess is if they sold him, he was unlikely to survive… or maybe the fire came first. We really don't know for sure."

"And Emily?" Charles asked, feeling his whole body tense up.

"The disease is quite advanced," Frank said. "She was declining rapidly before the antitoxin was administered."

"I don't understand, the serum is the cure?"

"If given the antitoxin at the onset, the likelihood of recovery is good, but she was likely diagnosed a few days after the initial symptoms started. If nothing else, it did give her a little more time. We need to alert Gladys, I think the children should see her soon."

Feeling a knot in his stomach, Charles sat down on a hay bale. "Gladys brought them to her house to allow Emily time to recover, and we were worried exposure could put them at risk as well."

"That was wise," Frank said, "children, especially the younger ones, are highly susceptible. You did the right thing. But now we must be going—no telling how much time is left."

*   *   *

Gladys and Margaret were carrying zucchini and squash to the kitchen counter after a pleasant afternoon in the garden. "I just love fall," Gladys said, "the vegetables are so hearty and colorful." With all her chopping and dicing, she didn't hear the tapping on the door.

"Someone is at the door Miss Gladys," Margaret said.

Setting the knife aside, she fixed her hair and dropped her apron on the table by the door. "Oh, it's Millie!" she announced, stepping outside and pulling the door closed behind her.

"We have good news: her breathing has improved," Millie said.

Lifting her face to the sky, Gladys clapped her hands. "Thank you Jesus! I have been wearing his ears out with all the prayin' I've been doing."

"We're hoping for a full recovery, but it's wise to bring the children now if it's a good time."

"Now?" Gladys asked, looking at Millie nodding slowly. She felt there was something she wasn't saying out loud, and an unsettling came over her. "We'll be in that buggy faster than I can polish off an apple turnover."

*   *   *

Angel Sarah

From the corner, Sarah stood watching the doctor skulk out of the room. She listened to the coarse breathing and smelled the sterile air as a nurse pushed a cart to the side of the bed, wiping tears from her eyes with her bloodstained apron.

Sarah gazed at the frail woman fighting for breath and lapsed into a memory of her own mother, who hadn't been much older than the woman before her. The sounds of her labored breathing was eerily similar, and Sarah remembered holding her mother's hand as she reached up, only to fall back against the pillow, lifeless. She recalled the years after her mother's death, feeling abandoned and struggling through life's hardships for years thereafter.

It was only her faith in God that kept her steadfast through countless disappointments and cruelties that plagued her when she was mortal, and having no children of her own, she ached at the reality that would soon come to pass.

*   *   *

On their way to the hospital, the children buzzed with excitement as they eagerly anticipated seeing their mother. Gladys was overjoyed by the positive report, imagining Emily's smiling face, healthy and happy, but something continued to bother her about the urgency in Millie's voice.

When they arrived, a nurse carrying a handful of linens crossed the hallway and waved Gladys over.

Ben reached for Margaret's hand, watching the women whisper. The nurse glanced over at them, then led Gladys to Dr. Clark's office and tapped on the window.

"Gladys is here to see Mrs. Paulie with the children."

Though exposing the children to their mother's illness was concerning, there was no way Clark could refuse. "We do need to take precautions to limit the risk of transmission. Miss Gladys, please step inside for a moment."

Once the door closed, she could see the concern in his expression.

"She is breathing better, but I'm afraid the disease has spread. Her heart is now failing, and her pulse is very weak. There isn't much time—it is good you brought them now."

She cupped her hand over her mouth, devastated by his words. "Medicine won't do?"

"We were able to buy a small amount of time due to the antitoxin we gave her, which is a miracle in itself."

"I wasn't prepared for this; I thought she would be coming home soon."

"I'm sorry. When you're ready, I will take you and the children to see her."

"Thank you, doctor," she whispered, dabbing the corners of her eyes with a handkerchief.

Gladys stood at the curtain as the children followed behind Dr. Clark to Emily's bedside. Opening the curtain, they saw their mother in a deep sleep, her breathing soft but steady. Margaret couldn't help but notice bloodstained towels in a laundry basket by the bed. In the far corner, pushed to the side of the room, was a tray holding what looked to be a large pair of metal clamps.

"There is a chance she will have difficulty speaking, and her vision is not clear," Clark said. "I'll be in my office if you need anything."

Clark leaned in close to Gladys before leaving. "They can stay as long as they want. I understand this time with her is precious."

"How much time is there doctor, really?"

He pulled up the sleeve of his overcoat and tapped his wristwatch.

"Her eyes are opening!" Ben said. "Hi Momma!"

Her lips quivered into a smile as she opened her eyes. Joy filled her as she looked at them, longing to wrap them up in her arms. She had so much to say—she wanted to apologize for being sick when they needed her most.

"How are you feeling, Momma?" Margaret asked, lightly touching the blanket covering her arm.

She watched their lips but heard no sound. She brought her arm up and cupped her hand by her ear. Her skin was pale blue, her veins barely visible beneath the surface, and the bones in her fingers stood out prominently.

"Momma, it's Jonathan, can you hear us?"

Gladys handed him a small notepad and a pencil from her bag, watching as they took turns writing her notes, holding them in front of her.

"Ben, what do you want to say, I'll write it for you," Margaret said, surprised when he took the pad and pencil and started to write. He brought the paper up, holding it out in front of her.

Emily smiled; running her finger over the seven crooked letters, it was the first time she had seen his handwriting. She placed the pad on her chest and looked at him curiously.

"She doesn't know what they mean," Jonathan said.

Ben pulled out a folded piece of paper from his pocket, turning the page around and holding up the last drawing he made for her.

A smile crossed her lips before she closed her eyes. She felt a warmth come over her and a vision of a white shimmering silhouette at the foot of her bed. A woman appeared, her long caramel colored hair was braided in the back and swooped along her shoulder over a silver-plated breastplate. The woman had a loving and comforting look on her face as she stepped closer to her bedside, touching her arm and reaching for her hand.

13

ONE MONTH LATER…

On a chilly fall morning, Claire came down the stairs in her robe to find Charles already standing by the window, sipping a mug of coffee.

"I didn't want to look outside this morning. I was afraid everything would be white," she said, giving his shoulders a squeeze. She glanced at the door, feeling a twinge of sadness when her eyes settled on a pair of boots in the mud catch, the crusty shoelaces frozen in place from dehydrated dirt and a boy's flannel hanging on the hook above them. It had been a long time since they'd seen any use.

As she listened for any rustling upstairs from their guest, a light tapping on the window startled her; Elliot's cheerful face appeared, giving her a wave, checking to see if anyone would be joining them as he did most mornings. She shrugged, shaking her head in disappointment.

Carl was busy saddling horses for warm-ups when Elliot walked up. "Not today either?"

"Not today," Elliot answered, grabbing two pails, letting them swing wildly as he walked along, whistling. Hearing footsteps behind him, he stopped suddenly and spun around.

"Is that really you?!" he said, staring at Paul as water swished and splashed over the sides.

"Yeah, it's me. Figured I would get some fresh air today—been locked away at the store for too long. I don't know how Bernie did it; he made it look easy."

"I didn't see your truck out front."

"That was intentional," he said, pointing across the field behind the paddock.

"*Golly*, would you look at her!" Elliot shouted.

"Bought it yesterday. The old man said it's better to pull than pick."

"Store's doin' good then?"

"Doin right well, and considering the lean times these days, I'd say that's a blessing."

Elliot crinkled his brows together, thinking it wasn't like him to be throwing out words like that.

"Yeah, I've been reading a little, too, about reaping what you sow; figured it time to start sowing."

Elliot smiled. "Let's go brother," he said, yanking on Paul's jacket sleeve to take a closer look.

Carl took the horses to the tie-off and heard nickering coming from the back barn. Picking up the pails Elliot left, he decided to make the feeding rounds. He felt a little disheartened on his way to the barn and did his best to avoid it altogether. Even though Elliot kept it clean, there seemed to be a sadness in the horse's eyes. As he dumped the feed into the bucket, the somber silence felt heavy in the air. The hand-painted letters on the wood plank, once fresh with new paint, looked dull in the dimly lit barn.

"Hey boy," he called, snaking a hose through the bars to fill the water bucket. Figuring he had at least an hour before the riders arrived, he opened the stall. The horse shifted, backing away from the wall, and drew in a deep breath, letting it out slowly. Carl stood to the side, observing his sunken posture as if holding his head up was a fight against gravity.

"You miss the boy," Carl said. "I get it, we all do."

The horse moved closer, and he thought about Tom's story and what he shared about horses used for antitoxin. It was quite remarkable, and it made sense. He calmly stood in his stall when most horses would be anxious and restless, and seemed more comfortable alone and secluded, but something changed recently. His appetite had tapered off and he wasn't as responsive. He had a hunch it was because of the boy's absence. Days had turned into weeks, and it was obvious that the horse was in mourning. He plucked the lead and bridle from a nest of webs and shook them out. "We're going for a walk boy, a brushing and some sunshine will do you good."

*　　*　　*

Claire held a tray over the sink, brushed off the crumbs from last night's supper, then set down a bowl of oatmeal and apples. She folded a napkin into a neat square and placed a spoon on top.

Charles, still standing by the window, glanced over as she passed by on her way to the bedroom.

Tapping lightly on the door, she left the tray on the floor and backed away, watching for a moment before retreating around the corner. Standing silently, she heard the door creak open, followed by the sound of clattering as the bowl and silver shifted, and then the door gently closed again.

*　　*　　*

Elliot climbed into the bucket seat of the tractor, caressing the smooth finish on the wheel. "What a beauty… can I start her up?"

"I was waiting for that question," Paul said, "come around the front here."

Elliot jumped down, rubbing his hands together in anticipation.

"First, you gotta turn the fuel on," Paul said, flipping a metal knob. "Then you pull this ring out to release the compression—go around the side and prime the oil pump and give that handle there about twenty cranks."

Elliot slid his shirtsleeve to his elbow and reached for the crank handle, counting rotations. "What do we do this for?"

"It moves the oil to the top of the engine," Paul said, reaching over to pick up the oil can. "Now, we take this can and lube the oil cups, like so. Then, we use this bar here to pump the fuel into the carburetor." Holding a flat metal bar against the pin, he gave it about fifteen cranks. "Now we're ready to turn her over. Let's just give this flywheel a spin."

Paul grabbed the top of the large wheel and pushed it down while Elliot pulled it from the bottom and covered his ears. The whole machine clanked and shook as the metal parts jumped to life, convulsing in a rigid rhythm of sputters and shakes.

"You'll get used to it," Paul yelled, reaching down to crank up the throttle. A loud burst of gas combustion echoed through the field, reaching all the way to the farmhouse. Claire jumped, peeking through the kitchen window.

*   *   *

Ben sat on his bed and pushed the tray aside, shuffling to the window to pull the curtain back. He rubbed his eyes, seeing Elliot waving his hat in the air sitting on the most magnificent machine he ever saw. Dropping the curtain, he grabbed the tray and pulled the door shut.

Distracted by the clattering silverware, Charles turned, catching the backside of plaid pajamas and a mass of dark hair scurry past into the kitchen. Claire froze, quietly watching him set the tray on the table and rush to the door, pulling his flannel over his pajama shirt and stuffing his feet into his boots, running out the door with untied laces flapping against his calves.

"I should have bought a tractor weeks ago," Charles said, looking around the corner.

Claire stared at him wide-eyed, following behind him to the door.

Elliot was enjoying the view and the rotation of the wheels, imagining the satisfaction of plowing all the surrounding fields, when he saw Ben running across the field. He decreased the throttle, looking at the pale, thin boy making his way over to him.

"She's a beauty, ain't she!" he hollered, tipping his hat and releasing the brake. The wheels lurched forward, flinging clumps of dirt.

Ben nodded, admiring the machine, watching him turn in a big loop around the field.

*   *   *

Carl pulled gently on the lead, trying to coax the horse forward to the edge of the tree line, clicking his tongue against his cheek. "Let's go boy, there's some nice sun out there."

Nearing the edge of the trees, he felt the tension loosen. The horse's sluggish narrow steps became quicker and longer, passing him at the shoulders. Suddenly, the horse stopped, looking out over the field and yanking up on the lead. Carl raised his hand to shield his face from the sun, feeling the horse's energy surge as it inhaled deeply and blew air through its nostrils. The horse tugged at the lead and began to whinny—low at first, with long pauses between, gradually becoming louder and more frequent.

He removed his hat and held it over his eyes, squinting at the small figure in the distance. "Well, I'll be daggum." Feeling a tug on his arm, the lead slipped from his grip and his foot sank into a divot.

Ben saw the horse trotting toward him in long steady strides; the tightness in his chest relaxed and the fear he had been carrying since his mother died faded. Suddenly, listening to Juniper's whinnying and low rumbling nickers, he didn't feel alone anymore. He stretched his arms out, laughing as Juniper tucked his head under his arm, sniffing at his hair and nuzzling into his chest.

Elliot rested his arms on the wheel as the engine rattled to a stop. "Had you not brought this over today, none of this would have happened."

"I'm sure the boy would have come out of his room eventually," Paul said, looking over at Carl leaning on the flywheel and rotating his ankle. "Say, you're walkin' a little funny."

"Stepped in a low spot, something this here machine might help fix."

"I reckon it will, but we need to go over some plans I got for planting first," Paul said.

"How you got time to be a farmer when you ain't even left that store for three weeks? Done missed three fishin' trips, had to take this one," he said, pointing to Elliot, "and you know he ain't good for fishin'. Talks too much—makes their ears hurt."

"I'll have some time after this month. Got a few more deliveries coming in for winter stock, then it will slow down. Bern always did more huntin' in the snow."

"You need an extra hand, that's what you need," Carl said, "train someone up so you can do more fishin' and trappin', or farming. How many hours you sleep son?"

"You can sleep when you're dead," they said in unison, reciting Bernie's mantra.

"How did you get that old mule out of the barn?" Paul asked.

"Darn near had to carry him on my back, but once I went into that damned hole and he saw the boy, he was gone."

"The boy sure does look thin. Must not have had much of an appetite," Elliot said.

"Same with the horse," Carl added.

Paul looked down at Bernie's watch. "I need some ground markers from the shed to stake out a plot before opening the store. I'll be by later to park the tractor by the paddock, and I'd think hard about slapping a steak on that ankle if I were you."

Carl shook out his leg. "If it falls off, I'll just grow another one."

Paul looked at Elliot with a smirk. "And you think I'm stubborn."

*   *   *

Ben wrapped the lead around his hand. Elliot could hear him giggling as the horse tickled his head with chuffs and rubs. "Mr. Elliot, will you teach me how to ride today, like we planned before…" his words trailed off, but Elliot knew what he was about to say.

Scuffing his hat against his trousers, Elliot scratched his head, unable to stomach disappointing him. "I suppose we could put you up there, but how's 'bout you put on some proper ridin' clothes. Folks 'round here might look at a man funny wearin' pajamas on horseback."

Ben handed him the lead and ran back to the house.

Patting the horse on the neck, Elliot laughed. "You best be careful with him boy, he ain't got a clue what he's doin' yet."

Ben kicked off his loose boots, leaving them lopsided in the mud catch as he rushed to his room.

Claire looked up at the ceiling, following his footsteps with her eyes as he hurried up the stairs, down the hall, and into his room. This time, the door didn't close. She stepped away from the sink, looking for Charles to share this happy moment, but only saw his coffee mug sitting on the corner table by the living room window. The quick footsteps clambered back down the stairs as she cut into a loaf of bread, holding a slice out to her side as he rushed by, like a relay racer handing off a baton.

He tucked it into his pocket, stepped into his boots, and fastened the top button of his flannel. "Thank you, Mrs. Collins!"

After tidying up the kitchen, she went upstairs to put on her day clothes. Surprised to see Ben's bedroom door was left open, she peeked around the corner. One side of the curtain was open, letting the sun pass through. The bed was made and the corners she'd tucked were undisturbed. The dresser drawers were closed, and the furniture was as she left it. Walking around the bed, she found the quilt his mother had made laying across the woven rug. His pajamas were under the bed, along with a box of crayons, a stack of papers, and his shoes. She kneeled, lifting the bed skirt, and pulled out his suitcase. When she opened it, she saw all his clothes, still folded neatly and unworn. At the bottom were his drawings and a brown paper bag. Inside it were clothespins, balled-up twine, three fishing bobbers, and a dollar bill. She closed the bag and carefully put it back the way she found it. A letter stuck out from the corner of the quilt. It was a letter from Margaret, telling him about her studies at nursing school. She told him she missed him and was planning to visit over the Christmas holiday. But it was the last paragraph that touched her deeply.

> *I know little brother, that you don't know the Collinses that well, but they seem like very nice people; Mother and Father liked them very much. Sometimes younger kids end up in orphanages or with people they don't know when these things happen. It will be fine, and I pray every night that you will love them, and they will love you.*

She sat back against the bed, wiping away tears, then tucked the letter back under the blanket and went to her bedroom. Sifting through her closet, still batting away tears, she slid a sweater off the hanger and noticed Charles's flannel hanger was empty. She looked to the corner, where his boots were, and they were missing as well. When she drew back the curtain, she could see him walking down the path away from the house.

*   *   *

"Good to see you," Paul said, tucking the stakes into his tool pouch.

Charles turned around, squinting at the silhouette in the barn. "Paul, is that you?"

"It's me," Paul confirmed, stepping out into view. "Been so long since you been out here, you forgot what I looked like."

"Nice to see you, friend; figured I would make my rounds, see what I could get to work on."

"You might be hard-pressed to find something—Carl and Elliot have most everything in top shape. I'm dropping a few stakes to mark for wheat and cover crops, then I'm off to the store, expecting a bulk feed delivery shortly."

Charles walked closer with his head lowered, like he was in deep thought. "I hear you been working your hind end off at the store, all hours of the day and night."

Paul tightened his belt, slightly annoyed. "I see Elliot has been keeping you updated. It will ease up before the winter months, at least enough to shave off a few hours a day." He could sense Charles going somewhere with the inquisition and waited for the question.

"How would you feel about taking the boy along, show him some basic tasks. He could give you an extra pair of hands," Charles said, doing his best to make it sound like a benefit rather than a hindrance.

"I don't need help, and I sure don't need to be looking after the kid right now. This is the end of the season, and I have a lot to get done. Maybe next month when things slow down."

Charles nodded. "Understood. I just thought it might lighten your load and give the boy some purpose. I won't hold you up—it's time I make use of myself around here and find something to get into."

Pulling gloves from his back pocket, Paul slapped them against his thigh, already regretting what he was about to say. "Alright… I'll show him some simple things, but he better not get in my way or make my day any longer."

Charles kept walking, looking up to the sky, whistling loudly, like he just set a bait trap and would collect in the morning.

"You walked right into that one," Paul mumbled to himself.

*　　*　　*

Elliot ducked inside the nook under the hay hatch, bobbing and weaving his way through a blanket of spiderwebs, baffled why Carl insisted on storing the spare saddles there. Nearly every day he batted down their sticky strings and every night they built them back again. He slapped his gloves together, shook out his hat, then took the raggedy saddle off its peg, brushing it off.

Ben rubbed Juniper's forehead while Elliot fastened the brow band and gave the nose bar a tug. He checked every part of the bridle and traced the leather that stretched under the jawbone and over his nose. His hand moved along the straps that hugged the ears and winced at the steel ring connecting all the pieces, putting his finger on the buckle of the bit. Juniper flicked his head upward and shook it from side to side. Ben didn't like the way the rod wracked against his teeth—the clanks and sounds of metal made him shiver.

"He'll get used to it. Might agitate him a little, and some don't mind it, but some will give you a fit over it."

Ben looked at Juniper's head, hidden behind a leather cage. It looked uncomfortable, and he kept shaking, pulling his head up, and occasionally knocking against him as if he were asking for it to be taken off.

Elliot gave the belly band a strong yank and pulled the buckle pin tight, flopping his arms over the saddle.

"Why does he need all these belts?"

"He's jumpy, you gotta be able to control him. These straps all have a purpose: they give you control, to make him turn when you tell him to turn. Think of a horse like a truck or a tractor. The wheel steers and the pedal stops and goes." He picked up the reins, gathering them up in his fist. "These here are the wheel." Then he grabbed the noseband. "This here is the brake," he said, giving the slender straps hanging along the horse's neck a tug.

"What about the one right there?" Ben asked, touching the metal rod that was anchored to the lower jaw.

"That's called the snaffle bit, makes it so you control lateral flexion, which is the direction you want him to turn. Puts pressure on the sides of his mouth, so he can't use his tongue."

Ben rolled his tongue along the roof of his mouth, imagining what it would feel like to have it stuck there.

"See how these are connected to the bridle?" Elliot said, running his hands up the reins. "When you pull one, it puts pressure on that side, makes it so you control which way you turn. That's important when you're learnin' to ride. Watch me." He stepped into the stirrup, throwing his leg around the saddle. Juniper sidestepped and snapped his head up, taking them in a jerky circle. Elliot pulled his arm straight back to his hip bone and leaned into the rein. As the bit drove in, it settled deeper against his gum. Juniper straightened and stopped sidestepping. Then he pulled the other arm down, sending another shock wave to the left side.

Ben watched Juniper's head jerk to the left. Elliot backed off and released his grip, bringing both reins forward again. "You see his head move? This is what you do to make him go this way or that, and he'll fight you for that control until he gets used to being told. He ain't too keen on havin' a rider either, never has been."

Jumping down, he patted Juniper's neck. "He'll be a good horse for you: he's slow, won't fight you for long. I'm more concerned he'll spook on you—he seems skittish with loud noises. I reckon somethin' spooked him during the storm, which is probably how he got banged up so bad, so watch for that."

Ben listened carefully, understanding most of what he was told. As he took hold of the reins, he noticed a drop of blood on top of his boot. Startled, he checked himself, glancing at his hands. Another droplet hit his boot, and he realized it was coming from the side of Juniper's mouth.

"Mr. Elliot! He's bleeding!"

"It don't work if it isn't in there snug. It won't hurt him, and we'll adjust it as we go, little by little until you get the hang of it."

Standing at Juniper's side, Ben looked at the bottom of the stirrup, then up at the saddle.

"I know, seems like a mountain, right? Grab hold of the pommel with your left hand."

Ben turned his shoulder to the right, looking confused.

"Nah, your left hand, here," Elliot said, walking up behind him and turning his body into the mount. "Reach here."

Stretching over the saddle, he reached for the pommel.

"That's good, now bring your foot up to this stirrup here," he said, tugging on his left pant leg. "Think left, left, swing right, right. Got it?"

Ben repeated after him, "Left, left, swing right, right."

"Now push off with your right leg and swing it around as hard as you can, bearing all the weight on the foot in the stirrup, and use the muscles in your bum. When your rear hits the seat, grab that pommel with your right hand." He pushed a hand under Ben's hip, giving him a shove into the air. Ben grunted and brought his leg around. The muscles in his weight-bearing leg twitched and his clammy hands slipped from the pommel.

"Open your eyes!"

His body shook with fear, and he clinched his eyes closed even tighter.

"You gotta open your eyes—it's even scarier with 'em shut."

"My leg feels funny."

"Ridin' takes strength, especially in the legs, and you don't have none yet. That's what farm labor is good for: builds muscle. That'll ease up the stronger you get, but you can't stay up there, shakin' with your eyes closed."

Juniper shifted his back legs, rocking gently and huffing big breaths of air.

Feeling his chest expand, Ben exhaled the air he'd been holding in his lungs.

Spitting out a corner of his thumbnail, Elliot watched nervously, waiting for him to open his eyes. At first, he didn't notice the gentle sway in the horse's movements, but he did see Ben's shoulders start to rock, making it easier for him to stay centered in the saddle.

"You're gonna make me chew off every fingernail I got—now open your eyes!"

When Ben let his breath out, the funny spots he saw dancing under his eyelids disappeared and the pressure in his head was gone. His forehead relaxed and he released the tension in his face. The gentle rocking loosened his hips and he began feeling more stable and balanced. The muscles in his legs stopped twitching and he felt a strange popping sensation somewhere along his hip bone as the pain he felt for weeks in his lower back disappeared. He opened one eye, then the other. It was a new world. He looked straight up, feeling like he could touch the clouds that rolled by.

"Whew, finally," Elliot said, "was afraid you were gonna fall asleep. Now, he's about thirteen hands, not too tall, but keep in mind you're about six feet off the ground, so it'll hurt right good if you fall off. Keep hold of the pommel and only work one rein at a time. Take him along the tree line until you get to the opening, using your right hand to keep him away from the woods."

Hesitating to pull back, he held the rein to his side, watching Elliot motion with his hand.

"Just like this, smooth and firm, not out that far—you got to pull it into your side, or else he ain't gonna go that way."

Afraid to engage the bit, he held the lead loose at his side.

"You got to pull it back, you ain't got control if…" He stopped yelling when he noticed the horse following Ben's hand with his head. "You're doin' good, keep hold of the rein now, keep him straight and bring your arm to your hip."

Juniper caught the scent of lavender along the edge of the trees and started to walk toward the thicket.

"Pull it!"

Holding the rein out to the side opposite from where Juniper was looking, he shook the strap and Juniper turned from the thicket. He shook the strap out to the side again and Juniper pulled further away from the thicket. When he pressed his thigh into Juniper's side and let go of any tension on the rein, Juniper straightened on the path, and they continued to the clearing.

"What's all the yelling for?" Charles said.

"Mornin' Mr. C, I'm trying to get him to use the bit, but he's afraid it hurts him."

"How you know it don't, you ever hear a horse answer that question?"

"He's gotta learn to control him," Elliot said.

"You're going to drive yourself bat crazy trying to control that," Charles said, pointing at the pair. "I reckon they'll figure it out."

Ben looked around, surprised at how far across the property he could see, even spotting Henry and Albert bobbing in their saddles in the pasture. He didn't understand why they moved that way and tried rising off the saddle like they did. It felt strange, and his legs shook when he put all his weight in the stirrups.

14

Paul stopped short of the turn, giving room to a large lumber hauler that veered onto the road. The bed was full of freshly cut timber, and in his mirror, he watched it roll over the hill before continuing to the store. In a rush to beat the feed delivery, he gathered up boxes, balancing them in one arm as he unlocked the door. Opening up the door, he dropped the boxes on the counter and took a deep breath. Little by little, the stale cigar smell had dwindled. He could sometimes still hear Bernie shaking the newspaper pages when he walked through the door, but even that memory was starting to wane.

He carried the boxes to the office and stretched out his back. The thought of spending the morning curled over the desk studying planting journals and plot measurements didn't appeal to him today—he wanted to move and use his body. Ever since he took over running the store, he'd been consumed with numbers, orders, and inventory, and he felt his body was starting to stiffen. He grabbed his gloves and headed to the stockroom when the high-pitched screech of squeaky brakes caught his attention, and the words "D&M Seed and Building" in green letters floated by the window.

"Good morning," Paul said, surprised to see Daniel, "wasn't expecting the man himself. You run deliveries now?"

"Not if I can help it, but I lost two men this week. The New Yorker with more money than sense offered twenty cents more an hour, can you believe that! Poached 'em right out from under me. The guy's been comin' 'round for weeks buying up all my lumber, can't get it in fast enough."

"Let me guess: Larson."

"That's him. Complete jackass if you want to know my opinion. I told the guys to be careful; those Yanks don't operate the way us small town folks do. Might seem like a hell of a deal now, but once the job's done, you're out on your keester lookin' for the next payday."

"Who did you lose? Peter, Thomas?"

Daniel shook his head, "Dale and Denny. Never dreamed they would cut and run, but money talks, I guess. Gonna be tough to replace 'em, been with me for years."

"Ten at least," Paul agreed.

"That's about right—long time. You start to know what each other's thinkin', sure makes runnin' a business easier with guys like that. You got it good being a one-man show here, at least you know who's sticking around."

"Yeah, if I get lonely, I just talk to myself. Let's get you unloaded."

They each took turns carrying feed bags, stacking them on pallets along the back side of the store. Daniel grabbed for the last bag when Paul stuck his arm out, "let me get that one," and slung the seventy-pounder over his shoulder like it was a knapsack. "I need the exercise; all this desk work is turning me into an old man."

"Better to use your brains than bones."

Paul grunted, wiping the sweat from his forehead. "Not for me. Look—I'm even losing my calluses. Sometimes I leave here at night and can hear my joints creak."

"Maybe it wouldn't be such a bad idea to get a second person; someone to mind the counter while you run around and flex your muscles."

"You're not the first person to suggest it, but I'm not exactly the boss type, and I don't need someone to watch over either. Sounds like more of a problem to me."

Daniel stepped back amused. "You're not a boss type, really?"

"What's so funny?"

"You're the most boss-type man I know. Always serious, level-headed, and you always know what needs to be done. And it would serve you good if you tried to have a little fun once in a while; it won't kill you."

"Sounds like you been talkin' to Elliot."

Daniel laughed. "You know he can't keep anything to himself."

"Let me get you a refill for the road," Paul said, looking at his empty thermos.

Walking to the door, they heard the crunch of stones under tires as a couple cars pulled into the driveway. "Looks like you got a rush here. I'll take a rain check on the coffee—got more deliveries to make before lunchtime, anyways. I'm finding out you have to run harder with less help, but I still find time for whiskey and women. Take care, Paul."

Paul waved goodbye and shook his gloves out, holding the door open for Peter Kincaid to enter.

"Mornin', Paul," Peter said and stepped inside. Gretta was standing at the counter fixing her hair. "Hello Mrs. Grover, nice to see you," Peter said.

Gretta turned around with a bright smile accentuated by the crimson red lipstick she was wearing. "Hello, Peter, nice to see you too," and quickly looked around him at Paul.

Paul felt his body tense, not wanting to invest the time in a twenty-minute conversation about her bird feeders. Gretta lifted her basket and put it on the counter. "It's time for a refill: my bluebirds are packing it in for the winter. They're not too worried about their waistline," she said, running her hands over the belt that hugged her hips to draw attention to her small midsection.

"I'll be right with you, Peter," Paul said, thinking that by filling Gretta's order first, he might usher her out the door faster. "What type of seed this week?"

She grabbed a strand of her hair and began to twist it with her finger. "I was thinking the same blend as last week—they seem to like that. Must be the right mix to satisfy," she said, with a hint of flirtatiousness. Peter blushed and took a walk down an aisle to distract himself.

Pretending not to notice the insinuation, and the lipstick, Paul reached under the counter for a bucket. "I'll be right back," he said flatly, passing Peter on his way to the seed bin, who gave him a mischievous wink and started to laugh. Paul felt uneasy; he could almost sense her watching him walk away and it made him walk faster.

Wandering up the aisle, Peter peeked through the shelving and caught her checking her reflection in a small compact mirror, which she promptly snapped shut when Paul returned to the counter. He poured the seed into her basket and waited for her to pay him.

"The color is so rich, it's such a good blend," she said, scooping up a handful and letting the seeds fall through her slender fingers.

"That'll be seven cents," Paul said.

Peter's elbow bumped into a rake, sending it rattling to the ground. "Be right with you Peter," Paul said, hoping that would put an end to her solicitation.

She reached into her skirt pocket and held the coins in her hand. Paul looked at her, unamused, preferring she just put them on the counter. With a sigh, he held out his hand. Her fingers tickled his hand as she dropped the coins, purposefully brushing her fingers against his palm. He pulled his hand back quickly and dropped them in the till, shutting it with a firm push. "Have a nice day Gretta—tell your husband I said hello."

Grabbing the basket, she looked over her shoulder at Peter, who was pretending to be looking at rolls of cord. "Hopefully they like it so much, I'll have to come back in a couple days for more," she said, and slid the basket to the crook of her elbow, leaning over the counter to admire the pocket watch Paul left sitting there. "What a handsome face it has... goodbye Peter," she called.

"Uh, umm, good day," Peter sputtered, dropping a spool of BX cable.

When the door closed behind her, Peter stepped out of the aisle. "Man, she's got some nerve—not to mention the hots for you buddy. Never heard a married woman talk like that. Chuck would have a fit; bet she doesn't wear that shade of lipstick around the house."

"I'm sure glad you were here. I don't have time for that trouble— listening to her stories is worse still."

Peter looked out the window, watching her get into her car. "Still, can't say she's bad to look at, could be worse I guess. You could have Earl's wife breathing down your shirt collar." Peter leaned against the counter, glancing around as a wave of nostalgia washed over him. "First time I been in here since we carried him out of here... feels strange. I can still see him sitting on that stool there spitting sunflower seeds. How you holdin' up?"

"I'm good. Some days better than others."

"I heard you're fixin' on farming, too, on top of this place. You'll be lucky to find time to sleep. Saw that new tractor sitting out front yesterday—that's some piece of equipment."

"If I figured right, it should pay for itself by this time next year."

"I'm sure it will. You're not exactly the guy who does anything before thinking it through—unlike myself, who put up cabinets and forgot the hinges. Got any?"

"For a standard twenty-four-inch door?"

"Sounds about right."

"I would think forty-five millimeter should work. How many doors?"

"We got six. Captain said we're getting new equipment, and he doesn't want it laying on the ground with the fire gear."

Paul returned with the hinges and sent Peter off with a thermos full of coffee. Gretta's perfume overpowered the nutty aroma, and he propped the door open to let some fresh air in when he saw Clint's car pull up. "Great," he murmured, and kicked the door stop away, letting the door close just before Clint could grab the handle.

Clint stepped inside, sniffing the air like a bloodhound. "Not sure a brothel smells better than a stogie, but she sure took a bath in it," he said, gripping the lapels of his sports jacket. Jack walked in after him, standing close to the door.

Paul held the empty coffee canister, wanting to break it over Clint's head—and if it wasn't for the boy, he might have.

"I could use a cup of that. Been putting up trusses since five o'clock this morning," Clint said with an obnoxious, haughty smirk.

"I'm fresh out, but there's a diner about thirty miles outside of town that serves it up hot."

Clint's smirk faded and his eyes narrowed, "I didn't come here for coffee anyway. You got any more saddles?"

He thought about lying and saying he didn't, but he could see four hanging just a few aisles down. "A few," he answered.

"Bits and bridles, too?"

"A few," Paul answered again, not offering anything further.

"Am I supposed to go on a scavenger hunt, or do you not know where they are or what they look like?"

Paul squeezed his fingers around the handle so tightly it began to shake and set it on the counter with a loud clank. "Third aisle, left side, twenty paces from the corner. If you get to the door, you passed them and you can open it and walk yourself out."

Clint chuffed a muffled laugh, his menacing stare breaking as the sound of Jack's zipper slid along the teeth of his jacket.

"Stay here—don't touch anything," he barked.

Paul gathered Clint was just as much of a jerk to his son as he was to everyone else and could see the faint outline of a bruise on the side of the boy's cheek, the bluish green pigment barely noticeable. He gave him a quick smile, pointing to a jar on the counter.

"Got some oatmeal cookies in there, help yourself, might be a little stale though."

Jack looked at the jar, then looked over to the aisle where his father was, seemingly scared to move. Paul kept an eye on Clint as he examined the stitching on the bridles, holding a strange lens up to his eye. He studied his stature: solidly built, a bit thin but with broad shoulders. His shoes didn't have a lick of dirt on them, which was curious, considering he'd been laying trusses all morning. *What kind of man changes his shoes before going to a hardware store?* he thought.

Clint pulled the bridles off the hook and grabbed the Waterford bit, walking up the aisle toward him. "I'll take those saddles too, and all the gag bits," he said, pushing past him.

Adding up the items, he fought the urge to ask about the equipment and lumber he's been buying.

He dropped two large bills on the counter. "You probably don't have change for that."

Opening the till, he lifted the coin carriage, feeling the bottom of the tray for bills, then reached for his money clip and set the change down with a smack of his hand, pointing to an empty box at the end of the counter. The boy picked it up, struggling to hold it as Clint dropped the heavy steel bits. The boy's grip started to slip. "Hold it still," he snapped.

Paul felt his blood run hot, seeing the boy's arms begin to shake under the weight.

Grabbing the saddles, Clint opened the door to let Jack pass. "Might want to leave this door open to air out the place—smells like a cheap whore."

Breathing through the flood of obscenities that sat on the tip of his tongue, he listened for the car to pull away. Feeling the tension in his shoulders, he shook his head and spread his hands out on the counter, immediately noticing something was missing. The pocket watch. He looked at the ground, thinking it may have fallen off, then checked the other side, but it wasn't there. *Clint couldn't have taken it*, he thought, he'd kept his eyes on him the whole time. The boy was the only one standing in that spot alone. He ran for the door, sliding out onto the gravel as they pulled away. The boy looked out the window at him, turning away quickly. He ran back inside to grab his jacket, shaking the pocket for the key, but stopped before his hand turned the knob, remembering the bruise on the boy's face. If he went after him and found his watch, he didn't want to imagine the punishment the boy would endure. He dropped his hand from the door, feeling another piece of Bernie slip away. For the first time, he was uneasy about leaving the counter unattended and briefly entertained the idea of having another person around, at least while he was occupied.

15

Gladys hummed loudly as she slid a spatula under a fresh tray of apple turnovers and put them in a picnic basket. Her midweek was no longer quiet and mundane. She eagerly looked forward to meeting the ladies for some afternoon porch-time, gossiping about the local happenings and swapping recipes. More than that, she enjoyed seeing Ben and checking in on him—Lord knows it helped ease her fretting. She walked to the pole barn, happy to see the empty spot where Morty's car used to be, recalling the memory of giving it to Jonathan for his graduation. It had always given her a fit to crank the engine; it was better suited for a young fella anyway.

Driving along, the mild breeze had her straightening the feather in her hat ribbon repeatedly, but she enjoyed it nonetheless. As she turned the corner onto the final stretch of road to the farm, she began to see the horses in the pasture. Squinting, she couldn't believe what she saw. She pushed her glasses further up the bridge of her nose, letting the car sputter to a slow roll. Gasps escaped her lips: "Oh my, oh my, thank you Jesus!" The car jolted forward, giving her head a jerk, but it wasn't enough to take her eyes off Ben in the saddle.

*　　*　　*

"Good day, Claire," Grace said, waving her hand above her head in a quick flapping motion that made her arm jiggle. Claire could see the large stack of recipe cards in her hand and figured she would need more sandwiches; they were likely in for a long afternoon.

Bernice held onto Earl's arm as they went up the steps, using him to steady herself.

"Good to see you both," Claire said, "we have a beautiful afternoon to enjoy together."

"Yes we do, dear! I went through all my recipe boxes, pulling out my favorites. Earl was curious if Charles was around to talk to while us old hens get to our gathering."

"He's somewhere around the farm, looking for something to get into," Claire said.

Earl tipped his hat, wished them a fine afternoon, and went to look for Charles, passing Gladys as she hurried up to the porch with the picnic basket swinging wildly, shielding her hat feather from the breeze.

"Miss Gladys," Earl said, stopping to remove his hat, bending at his waist.

She flippantly waved in his direction. "Hello Earl," she said, somewhat dismissive of his theatrical flair as she kept her eyes forward.

"Gladys, how good to…"

She rushed up the steps, set the basket in the middle of the table, and walked straight over to Claire, taking her by the shoulders with both hands. "What happened!? I saw him—he's riding!" She walked over to the corner of the porch, pointing to the field beside the house and cheered. "He's actually out there riding!"

"Yes, he is. It's been a glorious morning!"

"Do tell," she said, "I can't wait to hear how it happened."

"How what happened?" Bernice asked, unaware of the events since Ben came to live with them.

Gladys pulled out a chair, motioning for everyone to listen. "Sit down, ladies. I want to hear this."

Claire filled their glasses, talking through the last few weeks and how difficult it had been, especially for Ben. She explained how she agonized over his malaise, and how he never came out of his room except to use the bathroom, never communicating aside from a nod or a shake of his head.

"Then, this morning, we heard a loud pop outside—like an explosion!" Claire said. "I saw Elliot in the field with Paul and Carl, all gathered around the tractor. Next thing I knew, Ben ran plum past me, through the kitchen, and outside."

"And the horse?" Gladys asked, tapping her heel against the floor, "how did that happen?"

"Well, that is what is so incredible. Charles and I saw Ben run right up to Elliot, then the horse trotted over. Whatever Elliot said to him, sent Ben straight back to his room. He got dressed and back out he went. This all happened over the past few hours. He's been on the horse ever since."

"He looks at peace," Gladys said, turning to look out over the field. "He's where he belongs."

Claire took another sip, setting the glass down and spinning it by the rim. She looked up at Gladys with a fading smile.

"I was worried about how you felt about this," Claire said quietly. "I know it all happened so quickly and when he came home with us that day. I didn't know if—"

Gladys put her hand up, stopping her in mid-sentence. "Honey, I was there to help in a time of need. I never expected it to be long term. Once Jonathan and Margaret left, well… he wouldn't have been happy following me around the garden all day. Besides, he feels close to his father here. This is familiar to him, and I am certain his home is where that horse is. Of that, I am sure."

Reaching across the table, Claire held Gladys's hand. "I'm so relieved. I wanted to mention it last week, but it wasn't until this morning that I felt he wanted to be here at all."

"We were all terribly worried," Grace said. "After seeing you like that after last week's luncheon, I went home and prayed—been praying constantly!"

"Honey, it worked. I could see the grin on his face driving up here," Gladys said.

"Something smells divine coming from your basket," Bernice said.

"Would you like a peek?" Gladys asked, pushing her chair back and opening the lid. "Apple turnovers," she said, fanning the sweet scent with her hand.

Claire passed around the plates, the fruity aroma tickling her nose.

"This reminds me, I need to bake a batch of oatmeal cookies for Paul. He's been working such long hours at the store."

"Earl stops by every week," Bernice said. "He's very proud of him for keeping it open."

"I'm proud of all of us," Claire said. "We have been through some tough times over the past few months, and we stuck together." The women raised their glasses, which met with a crisp *clink*. Taking her seat, Claire watched a fancy red car pass by. A small round face looked over from the passenger seat, and she felt a shiver run down her back.

*   *   *

Charles stood at the corner of the paddock after clearing a spot for the tractor, watching Elliot run alongside Ben, feeling a bit nervous about him being in the open. He looked over his shoulder at the pasture where Henry and Albert were working and considered building a second enclosure. He had just enough space for a small one and was about to start staking it out when he saw Earl waving at him.

"How you been?" Earl asked.

"Wasn't too good for a spell, but things are beginning to look up. Getting ready for the Derby race—Henry seems to think we'll have a good run. Say, you think you could send Daniel our way? I want to build a second enclosure."

"Sure can, I'll be seeing him later today. He's dropping off a few supplies for my chicken coop, been runnin' the hauler himself. Lost his two best men to your new neighbor. That fella's been buying up all the timber, offering his guys more money… really got Daniel's goat."

Taking off his hat, Charles rubbed his temples hard. "Larson," he growled. "Who did he lose?"

"Dale and Denny."

Charles continued massaging his face to settle his nerves. Off in the distance, they heard lots of noise, and just beyond the hill they could see the very top of a roof being raised, and the sound of large wheels screeching echoed over the hill.

"Golly, that must be forty feet at the peak!"

"Every bit of it," Charles said through clenched teeth.

*　　*　　*

Paul placed the last box on a storage rack and brushed the cobwebs from his hair. Surveying the room, he felt good about the progress he'd made. Deciding to finish the day in the office, he dropped into the chair to calculate the day's sales and review outstanding orders. Pulling out a paper that had slipped under a folder, he noticed it was the order Elliot had given him, still folded just as it was when he'd put it in his pocket. After reconciling the orders for the farm, the revenue numbers didn't look as good as he'd thought. He figured if he fulfilled all the items, he would be lucky to break even. Moving his finger down the ledger across the past several weeks, he didn't see a payment from Charles in the books. To avoid carrying over another balance, he would need to have a tough conversation. Before walking out, he checked the calendar, reading the words "Empire Derby" scribbled across Saturday's square in Elliot's handwriting, remembering Elliot had told him not to place the order until the end of the month, after the race.

The door clattered and Denny peeked around the door. "Glad I caught you. The boss man wanted me to pick up about thirty feet of chain link. You got any out back?"

Paul tried to hide the disappointment on his face; the conversation with Daniel was still fresh in his mind.

"Boss man," Paul repeated, "I can think of another word for him."

Denny chuckled. It was an awkward sound, one that would normally amuse him, but now it was just aggravating. Paul put his gloves on. "Let's take a look," he said, noticing the wood shavings stuck to his Denny's sleeves. "Been doin' some woodworking?"

"Yeah," he said, brushing at the fragments that clung to the flannel, "just pulled up a barn."

"In town?"

"Nah, out at Larson's place. It's looking to be a big operation. Darn near the size of those big city buildings; never pulled a frame that high before."

"He's been buying up all my riding gear. Just had to replenish my saddles."

Denny nodded. "Man, this guy has plans for twenty stalls and a huge leather press: saddle molds, compressors, all the fancy equipment for crafting high-end saddlery. We're even talkin' boots, too! You might want to let Charles know about it—he could give him a run for his money. And I guarantee, it ain't as much as this Yankee's got."

"Heard you sold out to him for a little more change in your pocket."

Denny sighed. "Got a youngin on the way, due in June. Might not be a lot extra, but every bit helps these days."

Though he still wanted to pelt him, Paul felt his resentment subside a little. "This is what I got," he said, looking down the line of fencing material along the backside of the store. "Three rolls of chicken wire. This one looks to be about thirty feet, give or take. I'll charge you a dollar more, just in case it's over. Sounds like money is no concern for your new boss man."

"Any chance we can open an account?"

Paul narrowed his eyes, drawing a hand under his chin. "A revolving account?" he asked, knowing darn well what he meant the first time.

"I reckon."

"Larson set you up to ask?"

Denny's eyes darted around, avoiding eye contact. "He mentioned it."

"Mentioned it?"

"Alright, more like he told me to open it. I'm gettin' the idea that nobody tells him no."

"Well, allow me to be the first one. If he has a problem with it, he knows where to find me. And that'll be two dollars and fifty cents—no, make it two seventy-five for the extra aggravation."

Denny smirked, taking cash from his clip and handed him the bills, searching his pocket for change. "Ain't got the seventy-five, only got these dimes."

Paul reached over and plucked another dollar from Denny's hand. "I'll think about a twenty-five-cent credit, but don't hold your breath."

After Denny left, he flipped the window sign, grabbed the plot plan he'd been wanting to show Charles, picked up the oil can for the tractor, and left for the farm.

16

The Angels

Joshua turned the arrow in his hand, pressing his fingers around the arrowhead, admiring the sleek beauty and wood grain of the shaft.

"You ever gonna use that thing, or just stare at it?" Gabe asked.

Unamused, he turned the tip of the arrow around so that it was pointing at him and pulled his hand back. "Snap," he said with a wink.

"I was just curious. You sit there coddling and caressing it, I gotta wonder: Is it a weapon or a date?"

Sarah held her breath, trying to hold in her laugh.

"Why you always take his side?" Joshua said. "You know he's being a bully, but still, you go along with it, just stoking the fire, enabling bad behavior."

Sarah walked around the bar, her fingers gliding along the smooth marble edge as she watched specks of color dance around the room, reflected from the pendants hanging from the chandelier. "When do you think we'll find out who the last angel is, the tenth one?"

Gabe shrugged. "Look how long it took us to get this guy, the arrow smoocher."

"Time is not a part of our world. What is time anymore? Do you remember what it was like to know the day from the night?" Sarah asked.

Joshua and Gabe shook their heads, looking over at Jacob who was searching his own memory.

"There's so much about the human experience I don't remember—or miss. Time being one of them," Sarah said. "I get curious, wondering what we will be sent down to do once we're unified. We might end up fighting giants or a great battle for humanity. My mind gets so caught up sometimes. I imagine us all together, on the same mission, and I get…"

She saw their heads turn toward the door as the light grew brighter. They rose from their seats and fell into line. She felt warmth cover her in an embrace, and let her chin sink deeper into her chest. Her head felt light, and a hand gently pressed against her forehead, giving her a vision. She felt as if she were being carried on the wind, rising and falling like a feather—weightless. She brought her hands to her belly, a lighthearted giggle escaped her as the sensation radiated from her core—joyful, like a child on the high end of a teeter-totter descending back to the ground. The vision became clear, the sky and the ground moving together in a whimsical wave. Her skin cooled, and the brightness peeking through her eyelids dimmed. She opened her eyes and stepped forward.

"Enjoy the ride," Gabe said.

*　*　*

Angel Sarah

As she walked onto the lush soil, her boots brushed against the soft petals of dandelions blanketing the ground, sending the white fluff drifting into the air. Giggles and laughter could be heard in the distance. The sky was aqua blue, blending into the horizon in swirls of orange and turquoise. The air was sweet with the fragrance of lilacs and jasmine, while birds glided overhead, singing to one another. The distant rumbling of a herd of elephants trumpeting sent vibrations through her body. She walked along streams, listening to the water as it passed over rocks and bends, watching a brood of ducklings ride the current effortlessly, letting their weightless bodies rise and fall with the turns of the riverbank.

Nearing the edge, she gazed out over a field of clover at a mustang standing perfectly still. It was chestnut brown with a mane of silky black hair blowing wildly in the breeze. As she got closer, she slowed her steps, unable to look away from the majesty of the animal. Her boot sunk into a small branch underfoot. The sharp snap pierced the silence, and the horse sprang into motion, rearing up on its hind legs before galloping across the field. She watched its head stretch forward as it gained speed, the sound of its hooves fading as it ran faster and faster along the wide riverbed—its motion reminded her of the vision. Just before turning to the hillside, it jumped over the river. Its body stretched long, legs pulling high beneath its belly before landing in a graceful stride and quickly disappearing over the hill.

The ground gradually transitioned from spongy soil to hardened earth, the grass becoming sparse, giving way to sand and dirt. She stopped at the very edge, looking down into a swirl of cream and blue light that slowly curled around the opening. As she stepped into it, the colors seemed to envelop her, blanketing her body as she descended. The earth looked like a blue marble beneath her. Stars blinked around her as she moved faster, thick clouds passing underneath her. The opaque screen of bright white mist surrounding her suddenly dissipated, revealing the earth below in vibrant pools of green and blue. The ocean, unbridled and free-flowing, met the shores, patches of land silencing the waves, sending them back into the horizon.

The tunnel of colorful light carried her over plains and long stretches of trees that cut a path along squares of wheat and barley fields. She slowed, hovering over a large farm, seeing horses guided by men in a small enclosure. Nearing the ground, she saw a boy sitting on a horse and a small creek winding through some trees.

*　　*　　*

Scanning the farm, Paul was pleased to see productivity: Henry and Albert were working the horses, Carl guided a Thoroughbred into the trailer, and Ben was in the saddle riding Juniper. Grabbing a can of oil, Paul made his way over to the tractor where Elliot was keeping an eye on Ben.

"Figured you'd be by soon," Elliot said, "I wanted to stick around until you got here."

"Isn't this where I left you?" Paul said, glancing over his shoulder at Ben before turning back to Elliot with a displeased look. "Hope you got some work done and haven't been babysitting all day."

"Don't you worry that stubborn head of yours. All the chores are done—I even helped Mr. C and Earl measure for a second enclosure. And here," he said, handing Paul a piece of paper, "Mr. C asked me to give this to you."

"What's this?"

"Some material we need. He wants to get started on it right away. Daniel's crew is comin' in the mornin' to dig the posts and deliver the lumber. I'll stop by the store to pick up the rest."

Paul glanced over the list, his expression turning uneasy. He crunched up the paper and stuffed it into his pocket.

"Why did you do that?"

"Do what?"

"Crunch it up like that and cram it into your pocket."

"Don't worry about it," Paul said, not hiding his frustration. "I sure hope that prize horse he paid a season's wage for earns its keep this weekend."

"The account is behind again?"

"I said don't worry about it. Now help me crank this wheel. You remember how to grease it?"

Elliot took the can, feeling a bit disheartened about Paul's angst.

Paul turned the fuel on, primed the pump, and gripped the top of the flywheel, waiting for Elliot to finish filling the oil cups and grab hold of the lower part of the wheel.

"On three," Paul said. "One, two, three."

They gave it a hard pull, spinning the wheel and jolting the engine to life with a loud sputter. Elliot cupped his ears, turned his back to the clattering, and gazed out into the field. His heart sank when he saw Juniper's front legs batting the air, rearing up on his hind legs. Ben had his arms wrapped around the horse's neck, hugging him tightly. Elliot heard Ben shout and watched in terror as the horse sped off toward the woods. "Ben!" he shouted, sprinting as fast as he could, but the horse was not slowing down, bolting away even faster to get away from the noise.

Paul stood frozen with fear, unable to move his feet or look away as he watched helplessly. He saw Elliot sprint across the field, losing ground quickly as they got further away.

Ben's arms shook as he grabbed for the reins flapping wildly along Juniper's neck. Clinging to the horse with one arm, he grabbed the pommel with the other, desperate to anchor himself. But despite his efforts, he bounced violently in the saddle, his legs flailing against Juniper's sides. Closing his eyes, he silently pleaded for help. At that moment, a strange sensation washed over his body—like his hips were being drawn backwards. Suddenly, he felt the seat solid beneath him. The wind whipped against his face, and when he opened his eyes, the reins were firmly in his grasp. His thighs pressed against Juniper's sides, keeping him balanced. Juniper's long strides created a steady rhythm, each push off the ground flowing into the stretch toward the next. Ben's shoulders and arms moved in sync with the horse's motion, shifting forward and backward as he adjusted to the changes in his center of gravity, oscillating between the thrusts and pulls. His body relaxed, the reins resting loosely in his grip as he melted into Juniper's stride. It felt as though he was floating on the wind, the fear in his mind dissolving with each passing moment. The wind swept his hair away from his eyes, and he saw the tree line rapidly approaching. He pulled his arm to his side until Juniper pulled in that direction, barely avoiding the thicket. Ben and Juniper raced along the edge of the trees, skimming past the brush as they climbed the hill toward the creek that wrapped around the wooded area.

Paul took sharp, shallow breaths and dropped to his knees, punching the ground. As Charles and Carl ran out into the field, Charles pressed a hand to his chest, feeling his legs grow weak beneath him. Carl sprinted ahead, his eyes fixed on the horse's head, but caught sight of Ben's shifting posture. Their movement had smoothed out—the horse was no longer jerky or distressed. They were gliding. "Look," Carl yelled, pointing as he ran.

Slowing down to catch his breath, Elliot put his hands on his knees, his chest moving up and down rapidly. Fighting off his dizziness, he pushed himself into a sprint again, hearing Carl approach from the side.

"Help!" Elliot called to him as he continued to run.

Carl slowed down to a walk and then stopped altogether. The panic he'd felt a moment ago was replaced with a sense of peace and amazement. "He's got this," Carl said to himself, "hell, they got this!" He couldn't believe his eyes and turned back to Charles, who was still huffing and puffing across the field.

Just beyond the crest of the hill, Ben saw the creek and leaned back, pulling on the reins, but Juniper kept his stride. Elliot yelled into the wind, "Stop!" Pull back!" before collapsing to the ground, powerless to do anything more than pray.

Ben could see the wide end of the creek coming up quickly and felt pressure on his back, like a pair of hands straightening his spine and pushing his shoulders and hips down. Suddenly, they were weightless, taking flight over the water. A tickle rose in his belly and a giggle escaped his lips. He looked up briefly and glimpsed the blue sky before they swooped down to the ground on the other side. Juniper trotted up the hill, stopping when they reached the top. Ben straightened, pulling his shoulders back as the pressure holding him down lifted. He raised his head, glancing back at the creek, wide-eyed and exhilarated. Leaning forward, he patted Juniper's neck and clicked his tongue against his cheek, guiding the horse into a trot down the hill and back along the tree line toward the clearing.

Carl cupped his hands around his mouth and shouted, "Way to stay with him, boy," before bending over with a hearty belly laugh, wiping the sweat from his brow. Looking around, he saw Charles standing a ways behind him, utterly bewildered, still panting from the run.

Waving his hands in the air, Charles turned back to the hillside.

They all saw the jump. Elliot stood, his mouth hung open; Paul lifted his head, eyes bulging; and Charles stood on shaky legs, pinching off a cramp in his side.

Carl met Ben and Juniper at the clearing. "Boy, I think you just 'bout killed the old man, and Lord knows the shape the other two are in." In the distance, the tractor's engine shut off and everything went quiet. Carl rubbed Juniper's head. "You had him all along, didn't ya, boy."

The horse's nostrils flared, and he yanked against the pressure Carl put on the noseband.

"Mr. Carl?"

"Yeah boy?" he answered, still breathing heavily.

Ben pointed to the rod that clanked against Juniper's teeth. "I don't think he likes that."

Carl looked at the bit. "Well, if we take it out, how you reckon you're gonna control him?"

"Like this," and Ben tapped his boots against Juniper, leaning from side to side with Juniper following his lead effortlessly. He held out a hand with the lead hanging loosely and they weaved in and out of turns around the field. Ben sat firmly in the saddle and pulled on the rein, bringing it to his side like Elliot had showed him. Juniper's smooth turns got jerky, and his head yanked against the pressure against his tongue.

"See Mr. Carl? He doesn't like it when I pull back."

Elliot and Charles walked up—neither said a word.

"The boy wants to take the bit out," Carl said.

"Pull it," Charles said, "after what we just saw, let him ride the way he wants. I think they know what they're doing."

Ben's smile quickly faded when Paul walked over with an angry look on his face.

"Boy, you're lucky to be alive! You could have been killed!"

"It's alright," Elliot said, "he obviously knows what to—"

"He doesn't know anything!" Paul snapped, cutting Elliot off. "He could have just as easily been dragged across the field, and you all should be thanking your stars he wasn't. He got lucky—that's all! Get him down. I'll be by in the morning to pick him up—he's coming to the store with me. Clearly, someone has to keep an eye on him."

Carl started to go after him, but Charles grabbed his sleeve. "Let him cool off. I saw him from the paddock when the horse took off. Shook him up pretty bad."

They all watched him stomp across the field, but everyone kept their thoughts to themselves.

"I'm sorry, I didn't mean to make Mr. Paul mad," Ben said.

"You didn't do anything wrong son," Charles said, "he was afraid you were going to get hurt, and he deals with things differently than most folks."

Elliot nodded his head in agreement. "That's right, he gets madder than a puffed toad when he's scared. We better get up to the barn before he strikes that flywheel."

"Suppose I should give him a hand with it?" Carl said.

"I wouldn't. He's gonna have no problem giving it a hard pull."

*　　*　　*

Later that night, Claire set the table while Charles and Ben washed up. After the supper prayer, she glanced at Ben, then turned to Charles; both sat quietly, their eyes avoiding her. "That was quite a scene out there today, wasn't it?"

"Darn near sent me to the grave early, but I have to say, it was impressive the way he hung on there. And that jump... I've never seen anything like it."

Ben kept his head down while he scooped up potatoes, dropping them onto his plate.

"I bet that was scary," Claire said, "I'm so glad you didn't get hurt."

"I wasn't afraid at all; it felt like I was flying! I was a little scared at first, but then it felt like a pair of hands held me down, but I couldn't see them. After I got square in the saddle, I liked it!"

Charles slowly picked up his fork, not sure what to say after that. He just looked over at Claire with raised eyebrows and continued eating.

Equally perplexed, Claire smoothed the napkin in her lap. "And I hear you're going to the store with Paul tomorrow—that's exciting. He will teach you all sorts of things, and he does need a good helper. Are you happy about going to the store with him?"

Ben hesitated to answer. "Can I still stay here with you and Juniper some days?"

"I will talk to him," Charles said, "maybe we can work something out where you can help a little at the store and be here on the farm, too."

Ben happily agreed with a grin and another mouthful of potatoes.

"Good, that sounds good honey," Claire said.

*   *   *

That night, Claire and Charles lay in bed, the soft flicker of lamplight dancing around them as they spoke in hushed voices. "I never seen Paul so upset as I seen him in that field," Charles said, pulling the covers up to his chin. "He was pummeling the ground with his fists, wore himself clean out."

Claire nestled into her pillow, folding her hands under her cheek. "He is complicated; he's not like Elliot or even Carl… he's guarded and cautious and doesn't trust easily. To him, everything is a threat to his security. Even his own heart."

"You know, I never thought about it like that, but that's exactly right. I don't know how I never saw it before now."

"That's because you're close to him. It's easier to see from afar."

He kissed her on the top of her hand and snuffed out the oil lamp with a yawn. "Tell you what: I'm lucky to be married to such an insightful woman."

*   *   *

Lying in his bed, Ben couldn't sleep. He tossed and turned until he ended up on his side facing the window. The moonlight was bright, illuminating the windowpane. He pulled the bedsheet around his shoulders and walked to the window, pushing the curtain aside, just enough to see the corner of Juniper's barn. He listened for a moment, making sure Charles and Claire were asleep, then walked quietly to the door and tiptoed along the edge of the floorboards.

When he passed through the kitchen, he grabbed an oatmeal cookie from the basket and two biscuits left over from supper before quietly closing the door behind him. The wind gave him a chill, and he hugged the cover tighter around his body. The farm was still, almost unrecognizable from the hustle and bustle of the day, with only the sound of dirt crunching underfoot. The main barn looked majestic in the moonlight, and he could hear grunts and rustling as the horses bedded down for the night. On his way to the barn, he looked out into the pasture, noticing the spot along the fence where his father had pushed him through, urging him to run as fast as he could. He recalled the howling wind and the strong blasts of air at his back as he pushed through to get to the barn. But now, he wasn't afraid, and the courage he felt surprised him. The stars kept him company, lighting the path ahead. One star shone brighter than the rest, its twinkle framed by a delicate halo of blue and cream-colored clouds.

It was dark inside the barn, but slivers of moonlight streaming through the loft hatch lit just enough for him to make his way to Juniper's stall. He unlatched the door, and a soft rumble came from Juniper's throat as Ben crouched down on his knees, scooping straw that was piled up in the corner. He patted it down, spreading out the blanket. Juniper sniffed his hair and nudged him, making a wide circle before folding his legs and letting his weight fall to the side. Ben folded his hands behind his head and wriggled his feet into the straw. "I'll be at the store with Mr. Paul tomorrow. He wasn't very happy with us today, but Mr. Charles said I can stay here on the farm some days too," he said with a yawn. "It really was a good jump."

*　*　*

Jack knelt beside his bed, looking at the watch face, following the small twitch of the second hand. It looked just like the watch his grandpa had carried. Hearing his father's footsteps coming down the hall, he jumped into bed and slid the watch under his pillow, pretending to be asleep. Out of the corner of his eye, he could see his shadow cast under his door. He stayed quiet, his eyes landing on the candy wrapper he'd forgotten to hide sitting on the desk beside the door. His eyes darted from the desk to the door. A moment later, he heard his mother's voice, and the shadow went away. As soon as he heard their bedroom door close, he jumped out of bed, stuffed the wrapper into the bag he hid under the bed, and listened to the watch tick as he fell asleep.

17

CHARLES FELT AS THOUGH HE had only just closed his eyes when the sunlight spilled through the window. Pulling on his robe and sliding into his slippers, he shuffled quietly to the door. He tapped on Ben's door to wake him, knowing Paul would be coming shortly. When there was no response, he cracked the door open—the bed was empty. Finding no sign of him in the bathroom, he made his way to the kitchen, where he noticed Ben's boots were gone. Plucking his overcoat from the clothes tree, he stuck his bare feet in his boots and went out to look for him. Figuring there would be only one place Ben would be, he headed to the barn. Finding the latch raised, he slid the door to the side. "Ben, you in here?" He stepped inside, spotting snacks on the bench, then glanced into the stall. Juniper raised his head. Ben was curled around his neck, still asleep. Charles chuckled; it was the first time he saw Juniper laying down.

Ben stretched and rubbed his eyes.

"Mornin'," Charles said. "Sleep well? We better head on up to the house and get you cleaned up."

Back at the house, Claire held a coffee pot under the spicket, accidently overfilling it as she watched Charles and Ben walk by in their pajamas, Ben wrapped in his bedsheet like a cloak. Charles held up a hand to her with an arm around his shoulder. "I'll tell you later," he said with a grin.

A few minutes later, Charles and Elliot stood on the porch, watching Ben follow Paul to his truck. "We'll be lucky if they make it to lunchtime," Charles joked.

The ride to the store was quiet. Ben stared out the window while

Paul tried his best to think of something to talk about. He was still thinking when they pulled into the lot. He unlocked the door and tossed the keys on the counter. "First thing you do is flip that sign around," he said, pointing to the window. "Next, I'll show you how we get the coffee brewing. This is important: Folks don't like an empty pot before three o'clock." After they made the coffee, Paul walked him up and down the aisles, pointing out equipment and explaining how everything was organized.

"Do you know how to count?" Paul asked.

Ben nodded and started to count out loud, "One, two, three, four…"

"Good, have a seat," he said, pulling up the stool and opening the till. He pulled out a small stack of bills and dug into his pocket, dropping coins on the counter. "Can you count that?"

Ben looked at the coins. "Forty-five cents."

"That's good—how about the bills?"

Ben picked up the bills and counted them out, organizing them from smallest to largest. "Eighteen dollars."

"That's right. Good job, might give you counter duty." He grabbed the order book, "I'll show you this later, but when a customer buys something and pays for it, they like you to write it down and give them one of these. For now, I just want you to know where I keep it. Now let's go see the office."

Looking around at memorabilia on the wall, Ben leaned in closer to examine one of Bernie's pictures. "I know him, he's nice, he gave me Tootsie Rolls."

Paul walked over to the desk, leaning against it with his arms folded. "When did he give you Tootsie Rolls?"

"When I came in with my father. He gave me three pieces that day. One time, he gave us a fish to cook!"

"Let me guess: trout?" he asked, pointing to a picture on the desk behind him. "Did it look like this?"

Ben studied the picture for a moment. "That's you Mr. Paul; is Mr. Bernie coming to the store today?"

Taking a box from the desk drawer, Paul lifted the lid. It was filled to the brim with the rolled candies.

"Can I have one?!" Ben asked, his eyes wide as he stared at the container brimming with more candy than he'd ever seen.

"Help yourself; Bernie loved to prime kids with sugar. He would laugh when they left with their fathers, knowing they would be bouncing off the walls for the next six hours. But, sadly no, he won't be in today. He passed away."

Ben stopped chewing and looked at Paul. "He's not gone, Mr. Paul, he's in Heaven. And he will be waiting for you when you go to Heaven. So don't be sad."

For the first time, Paul realized they had something in common.

The bell clapped against the door. "We've got a customer," Paul said, handing the tin to Ben, "put this on the counter and make some friends."

*　　*　　*

Elliot rushed through feeding, keeping an eye on Carl and Daniel as they unloaded posts off the wagon. As he surveyed the fields, he spotted Charles standing along the fence line with his head down. Elliot set the feed buckets down and began walking in his direction. When he got closer, he saw the mail truck leaving the driveway and a letter in Charles's hand. He stayed behind the paddock, watching Charles, suddenly feeling that something was horribly wrong. Charles slumped his shoulders forward, pushed off the fence, and released the letter into the air over his head. The letter fluttered to the ground, tumbling along the breeze across the field. Elliot waited until Charles went inside, then went looking for the letter, which he found wedged between the ground post and the fence. Reaching down, he saw it was addressed to Collins Equestrian Farm, with large, stamped lettering across it that read "Foreclosure Notice." Words like "asset," "liquidation," and "market decline looming" stood out in bold, black letters as he scanned the page. He didn't understand most of the language, but knew it was bad news, not only for the Collinses, but for all of them. He looked back at the house before stuffing the letter in his pocket.

*　　*　　*

"Hello Mrs. Collins," Ben said from behind the counter.

"Well, don't you look purposeful."

Ben put his pencil down and pushed a notecard along the counter.

Positioning her glasses against the bridge of her nose, Claire leaned over to read the card. *Plez tak 1* was written in pencil.

"Spelling is a little off—we'll work on that," Paul said.

"I think it's a wonderful gesture! And I brought some freshly baked cookies," she said, tipping open the lid of the cookie jar. A smile crossed her lips as she peeked inside, but it quickly turned to a grimace. "Good heavens, these are well past their day."

"I can toss those for you," Paul said, "save you from carrying them."

"Good golly, no. This adds a little something special to my pie crust. Enjoy your day! I need to get back in time to see Charles off."

Ben saw a large man holding the door open for Claire. After the door swung shut, the man walked over to the counter with a boy about his age at his side.

"Good to see you, Paul," the man said in a loud husky voice, reaching for a handshake.

Ben listened to them talk as they walked to the back of the store. The boy stopped in front of the counter and looked at him. "You were in my class. Why don't you go to school anymore?"

"I don't like school. I'd rather be at the farm, or being here is good, too."

The boy stepped closer to the counter, looking at the cookie jar. "Are there cookies in there?"

Ben nodded.

"Can I have one?"

Ben lifted the lid. "Mrs. Collins just made them; she makes good cookies."

The boy took a bite. "Sure does," he said, crumbs tumbling out of his mouth as he tried to catch them with his hand. They laughed at the funny sounds he made as he coughed up crumbs between giggles.

"You like candy?" Ben asked, popping the lid on the tin box.

The boy's eyes boggled over the full tin and quickly crammed a large handful into his pocket, smiling at him with chunks of cookie stuck to his teeth.

"I'm Lucas; you stay at the old farmhouse, don't you?"

Ben shook his head. "I live with Mr. and Mrs. Collins now."

"Why don't you live with your parents? Most kids live with their parents."

"They died," Ben said, sitting back down on the stool.

"Both of them?!" the boy asked, flabbergasted.

Ben nodded.

Lucas didn't say anything, he just watched Ben's expression and pointed at the card in front of the tin. "That ain't spelled right."

"I don't know how to spell good yet."

"Hand me one of those," Lucas said, looking at a stack of cards next to the till, "and that pencil there. Watch, I'll show you."

Ben hovered over the counter on his elbows, watching Lucas write. When he finished, he placed the card over Ben's card. "Now, just tape it down."

Ben brought the roll of tape and a pair of scissors, cutting two long pieces, handing one piece to Lucas.

"Two bags of corn seed and a spool of sixteen-gauge copper wire," Paul said, tapping the spool on the counter.

"You got a helper now I see," the man said.

"Part-time, at least. Learning quick, too."

Ben made change from the sale, dropping the coins into the man's hand.

He shook the coins, looking at the change, then snapped his hand shut. "Looks right."

Ben tore off a note of sale and grabbed his pencil, looking at Lucas.

"He's good at math, but his spelling stinks."

At that moment, Elliot burst through the door, shaking off the raindrops and scuffing his boots along the door mat. "Hey, horse jumper," he said, seeing Ben at the counter.

"You jump horses?!" Lucas asked.

"I did yesterday," Ben said. "It was scary at first, but I really liked it."

"Father, did you hear that, he jumped a horse! Can I go to the farm sometime?"

"I suppose it would be fine, if Mr. Paul approves."

"Be right well with me. It'll be good for him to have someone his age to buddy around with."

Lucas jumped up and down in excitement, following his father to the door. "See ya Ben!"

Ben waved goodbye and plopped down on the stool, looking up at Paul with a grin.

"You gave him a tootsie roll, didn't you?"

"He took a lot more than one."

Paul laughed. "See, what'd I tell ya; like bears to honey."

Elliot poured a coffee, watching the boy and his father hide under their coats as they hurried to their car. When the boy lowered the jacket, his wavy blonde hair triggered a memory: that was the boy seated next to the mean kid, laughing and poking fun at Ben that afternoon they were in the yard throwing the ball.

"Do you like the coffee, Mr. Elliot? I made it myself."

Ben waited for a response, waiting for him to turn from the window. "Mr. Elliot?"

Elliot turned around, looking distracted and a bit fidgety. "Right, good," he said, taking a cookie from the jar and dipping it into his thermos.

Paul knew something was amiss; Elliot's nervousness was almost palpable, a sharp contrast from his relaxed, almost sloppy disposition.

"Can I see you around the corner?" Elliot said, stepping inside the office and closing it behind them.

Paul folded his arms, sitting on the corner of the desk, studying him with a curious look. "If you're acting goofy because of yesterday, you can just—"

Elliot shook his head and reached into his pocket, pacing around by the door. "This ain't about that."

"Well, come out with it already. Or do I have to watch you wear a groove in my floor?"

He pulled the soggy letter from his pocket and walked it over to the table. "I looked at somethin' I had no business lookin' at. It wasn't my place to, and I feel awful for doin' it."

"Why don't you just hand it to me," Paul said with his palm up.

"I'd rather thwart my conscience and pretend you found it on your own."

"As I'm standing in front of you watching you drop it on the table," Paul said flatly.

Elliot ignored his sarcasm. "Ain't my finest hour, Lord knows."

Leaning across the desk, Paul rolled his eyes and gave the letter a shake. Elliot watched for his reaction, but he simply read it, folded it up, and handed it back to him without a word.

"You ain't got nothin' to say after reading that? What do we do if everything just dries up? No work, no money, just gone like that!" Elliot said, snapping his fingers.

Paul lifted a large sketch from the bottom of some papers and smoothed it out. "Why do you think I'm doing this? I've seen this coming—I can tell what's going on. And not from some newspaper headline, but from what I see folks buying and storing. It's been real good for a long time… sooner or later, you get a reality check."

Elliot leaned over the large sketch. Plots were mapped out and measured with all sorts of calculations and a mix of crops. "What's this block here, at the east corner?"

"Fruit trees, mostly apple and pear. Should see production in two or three years."

"Two or three years! How you expect we get by till then!"

He pointed to three larger squares. "This is arugula and lettuce. Over here is your basic beans, carrots, beets, and spinach. Might throw turnips down, too; they can all grow close together. And this corner here is chard and radish. I got plans for pumpkins in the fall, and corn will go in over here, closer to the pumpkins and lettuce. I got scab-resistant seed, so I can lay down wheat with soybeans after, or interseed with the soybeans once the wheat is booted—this whole plot gets plenty of sun."

"I knew you were thinkin' 'bout this, but didn't realize the scale you were plannin' on. This is big, Paul—it will take time and money."

Paul took out a metal box and opened the lid.

"*Whoo-wee!*" Elliot's mouth hung open staring at the banded bills, "looks like you made a bank run!"

"The seed is being delivered today, so there goes half of it."

"This is a gamble of biblical proportions," he said nervously, still ogling at the bills. "What if it don't work? What happens to this place?"

"It's clear; there's no note on it or the property, so whatever happens from here, it's gonna come down to planning and preparation."

"I'd say you got both… but what about the farm?"

"The bigger question is whether this gamble will work," he said, tapping a finger over the calendar square marked up for Saturday's horse race.

18

CHARLES DESCENDED THE STAIRS WITH his bag slung over his shoulder, listening to Claire humming on the porch as she watered the potted herbs, content and blissful with her gardening. He didn't have the heart to cause her worry, so he walked to the study, dropping his bag at the door. Pacing along the bookshelves, his gaze lingered on the ribbons and awards pinned to the walls, stopping at a brass box that held the deed. He brushed his hand over the ornamental finish, took a seat at the desk, and removed a thin envelope. It only had forty-five dollars left. Taking the money out, he returned the empty envelope back inside the drawer and looked through the bookcases, thumbing over bindings for something to read on the train. Many of the books and journals were about finances, and just looking at them made his stomach tighten. He pondered whether to take journals on agriculture, but that didn't seem like suitable reading either. Walking farther down the row of shelves, he looked at a book tucked back in a corner and pulled it over to the edge. The binding was worn and dusty, but it felt right in his hand, and he dropped it into his bag.

Claire handed him a sack lunch when he stepped out onto the porch and kissed him. "I have a good feeling about tomorrow; it's going to be our new beginning."

He folded the bag and set it in his sack. "You are right about most things, darling, and I need you to be right this time."

She could tell he was fraught with nerves and rubbed the sides of his arms. "I just know that all the praying isn't falling on deaf ears," she said, looking down at his bag at the Bible sitting on top. "And I see you're sending up some of your own."

*　　*　　*

Closing the till, Ben waved goodbye to the last customer and unwrapped a Tootsie Roll.

"One, two, three, four… Looks like that makes seven rolls," Paul said, looking down at the wrappers in the trash bucket.

"For each customer I wrote a note for, I took one Tootsie Roll," Ben said, his words muffled by the chocolate-taffy chew.

"Only seven? I've been stocking pallets for nearly three hours," Paul said, brushing the splinters off his pants and shaking out his gloves. "That's a slow afternoon around here." He emptied the till, showing Ben how to record the sales in the ledger. Reviewing the balance, he noticed a sharp decline over the past few weeks. He couldn't quite put a finger on what was happening, but the writing was on the wall: something big was coming—or maybe it was already here.

On the drive back to the farm, Ben gazed out at the rolling fields, resting his head back against the seat. "Mr. Paul," he said sleepily, "will I still be able to ride Juniper on the days I don't come to the store with you?"

"Why do you like that horse so much? He isn't fast or particularly useful, and he ain't too nice to look at, either."

Ben folded his hands and looked back out the window. "I heard Mr. Charles and a man talking when my mother was buried. They said his blood might have kept her alive just long enough that we could see her before she died."

Paul glanced over at Ben, both of them vibrating as they jostled over the bumpy gravel road. Staring out the window with heavy eyelids, Ben's words lingered in Paul's mind, making him regret his harshness. "I can see he's a fine riding horse, and from what I saw yesterday, I'd say it would be a shame not to let you ride him. If we can agree you'll keep him on the ground, then we got a deal. Sound good?" Waiting for a reply, he looked over to find Ben fast asleep, his head rocking against the seat, tuckered out from the long day.

*   *   *

Charles scanned the crowd of passengers waiting to board the train, searching for Henry. Wading through bags and zigzagging through the crowd, Charles spotted him standing at the loading area with three other jockeys. He felt anxious about traveling to the derby by train, curious how his horse, Ranger, would fare on the journey. Looking around nervously, Charles tipped his hat to the gentleman chatting with Henry. "I'm not feeling good about this," Charles said.

Henry gave Ranger a rub, giving Charles a reassuring grin. "I'll wrap him up good. Got some blankets and the bumper—that'll help."

Charles looked around at the other horses. There were two large muscular draft horses, most likely Belgian and Shire, two Tennessee Walkers, and the prettiest Morgan he'd ever seen. The smooth, vibrant gold and brown coat of the Morgan stood stark in contrast to his midnight black Thoroughbred. The man holding the Morgan was standing next to Henry and held out his hand to Charles. "All the best at the derby race, Mr. Collins."

"Never took a racehorse by train before," he said, gripping the other man's hand in a nervous, sweaty shake, watching the first horse be led up the ramp. "He won't have a good run if he's stressed and unsteady."

"We'll load him next to Polly here," Henry said, "they took a liking to each other; that should help calm him down."

Walking over to the Morgan, Charles gave her a pat on the neck. "Where is she headed?"

"Taking her to auction. Most likely she'll be sold for driving, not sure how long she'll be good for, though. Her hindquarters are getting weak, but she was the best driver I ever had… age catches us all, I guess. I'll take whatever the auctioneer can get. I got a feeling these cars will be full of 'em—folks shedding the cost of feed to feed their own."

He felt his nerves buzz again. The man's words reminded him how important this race was to the farm. "How much you lookin' for?"

"Being that she's older than the socks I'm wearin', I figure she's worth forty. Be nice to get forty-five and make up the train fare."

Figuring Ranger would travel better with a companion, he took his last forty-five dollars from the money clip. "I'll take her off your hands— Ranger seems to like the companionship."

"That's a deal. I'm Reginald, by the way, but folks call me Reggie, Reggie Colburn. You have no idea how much this will help my family right now. I got four youngins at home, and you just saved me two days of travel. I'll be praying for you."

Henry looked through the travel bag. "We only have gear for one."

Reggie opened the burlap sack at his feet and took out some rugged looking gear. "It ain't as fancy as the one you got, but I made it myself. She does well with it."

Henry examined the homemade head bumper closely. The leather cap was sturdy enough and padded thick around the ear holes. Unlike most bumpers, it had a stiff hood that flared well over the eyes and hung low at the sides just above the jawbone. Charles rubbed his hand over the leather. "This is mighty fine craftsmanship—nice thick felt, too. You made this?"

"Yes sir, even has two extra buckles. I fixed 'em low so the halter crown is snug. I like it better than the high ones, prevents ear rub." He bent down, pulling a frayed buckled halter from the tattered bag. "I made this, too. Threaded the buckle on the outside and stitched an underlayer behind, so it sits flat against the jawbone. You won't find any gaps either," Reggie said, a hint of pride in his voice. "Runs to the seam of the crown. I made it for Polly. She'd get these big sores on her ears from chafing, so the hard ones never fit her quite right. Then again, she has a wider bridge than most Morgans—not all horses fit the same."

Charles and Henry were impressed as he fed the strap through the cap, demonstrating the design. "I would be interested in buying it from you, if you're open to parting with it?" Henry asked.

"Never thought it to be somethin' to sell, but sure, take it," he said, picking up the bag and handing it to Henry.

The first whistle blew for passengers to approach their cars.

"It was a pleasure," Reggie said, shaking their hands one last time before leaving.

Henry pulled Charles aside. "This here is better than anything I've seen. I know a lot of jockeys who would trade their gear for this design."

As Reggie walked away, Charles observed his shabby appearance. His trousers were ripped and worn thin, and he had a spoon in the sash around his floppy hat. He didn't appear, at least to Charles, to be skilled in the trades, but he respected Henry's opinion and expertise. As the harsh tone of the second whistle blew, Charles walked quickly to catch up to Reggie. Reaching into his pocket, Charles pulled a card from his pocket.

"What's this?" Reggie asked, turning the card over.

"I have a training facility—that's the name and address. Henry knows a good product when he sees it, so if you ever get a hankering to make more of this gear, I'd be happy to give you a fair price."

"I'll give it some thought," he said, staring at the card with curiosity as he turned to walk away.

Charles tucked his hands in his pockets, feeling only small change as they closed the gate behind Ranger. He walked slowly to the passenger car, handed his ticket to the conductor, and looked for an empty seat next to the window. As he settled onto the bench, he hoped for some privacy so that he could be alone with his thoughts.

A young couple with three small children were seated across from him. The smallest of the children, a sandy-haired boy who looked to be around five years old, had nodded off on his sister's shoulder. The man grabbed two large duffels and a canvas tarp from under the seat and slid them across the floor to the woman, who untied the rope around the tarp, spreading it out to cover their laps. The man stood up and stretched his back, crossing the aisle. "You mind if I sit here at the end, sir? The little ones could use the extra room to stretch out—we've been on this train for days."

Charles held out his hand, suggesting to the man he was welcome to sit. "Where are you and the brood headed?"

The man rested his head back and closed his eyes with a deep sigh. "I don't know yet, we'll stop where the work is I guess."

The sound of the whistle blew again and Charles reached into a bag for a handful of peanuts to help settle his nerves. The bag crackled as he rolled down the corners, catching the attention of the girl seated across the aisle. She glanced over frequently when he shook them into his hand. Unwrapping a stack of oatmeal cookies, Charles glanced at the man beside him, who was nodding off, and tapped him on the arm. "I have extra for the youngins if they like oatmeal and raisins. Lord knows I don't need them," he said, patting his stomach with a smile.

"I appreciate that, sir," the man said, taking the cookies in his large, calloused hands. "That is mighty kind of you."

Charles fell back into the seat, watching the girl take a cookie and pass the stack to her siblings. She ate it very slowly, savoring every bite, and looked over her shoulder at him with a grin.

"I have an extra bag of peanuts if you like roughage," Charles said to the man.

"I appreciate that, but I don't want to take more of your supply."

"It's alright. Please, I have plenty."

"Thank you, sir, that's very kind. Where you headed?"

"New York, for the Empire City Derby race."

"I've heard of it. Big race from what I hear."

"Largest in the Northeastern U.S. this late in the season."

"Nice payday for sure. You're a betting man I take it?"

"Not me," Charles said, "just bought a young horse, and hoping we have a good run with him."

"I sure hope you do mister. How fast is he, your horse?"

"On his best day, averages about thirty-four six, but this train ride might shake him a little. He's familiar with the trailer."

"Thirty-four six, that's faster than a minnow can swim a dipper! Why, the horse that won the Kentucky Derby back in the day wasn't that fast, what was his name…? Something… stone?"

"Stone Street," Charles said.

"That's right, Stone Street. He broke thirty-three, but there's been increases over the years—they keep getting faster and faster. You ever been to the Kentucky Derby?"

"Once. That's how I got my start in this crazy business. Had a couple real fine racers back in the day, and hoping for another go at it sometime. We'll see, never can tell what's around the bend."

"I wish you luck mister, I better get some shut-eye before the next stop. What's your horse's name, by the way, in case I cross a paper."

"It's Ranger. Ranger's Riot is his entry name."

The man nodded and pulled up his overcoat. "Good luck to you, and thanks again for the snacks," he said, and closed his eyes.

*   *   *

After dropping Ben at the farmhouse, Paul decided to head back to the barn for several more stakes, given that his planting plots kept expanding. Coming around the corner, he saw Elliot leaning over a stall with his head low between his arms.

"You alright back there?"

Elliot pushed off the door, snapping his head up. "All good, just thinkin' on some things."

"Thinking? Looks to me like you're praying."

"Ok, you got me. Doesn't hurt to pray buddy, it ain't like we got nothin' to ask for."

Paul pulled a few stakes from a bucket. "Here, help me plot this last acre, it'll take your mind off things for a while."

They headed out to the far east corner of the property. "Why we stakin' this corner?" Elliot asked.

"Wheat and beans need more sun, so does spinach and lettuce." He pointed over to the adjacent field. "See those plots over there? They can tolerate less sun and the ridge there is the dividing line. That plot will get more shade when the sun dips down like it is now."

"You really been diggin' into all this farmin' business," Elliot said, nudging him with his elbow. "You catch the play on words there?"

"Yeah," Paul chuckled, rolling his eyes, "I got it. Now take these stakes and pace out three hundred feet and we'll get these in the ground."

"You think the farm's in trouble?" Elliot asked bluntly. "You don't seem rattled one bit about that letter."

"Horse racin' is risky. Charles had a good long run, made a name for himself—put all of us to work and put food on our tables. He don't know any other way except this, so we're gonna let him handle it and back his play."

"And if the run is over?"

"Then we'll turn him into a farmer. Now let's get this plotted before the sun sets."

*   *   *

Ben worked on a drawing at the table while Claire cleaned their dishes. It reminded him of home, when he would listen to the sounds of his mother cooking and all the smells swirling around him as he sketched. He especially liked the special drawer, where Claire kept his drawing paper and crayons; she even added pencils and fancy-colored pens with feathers on the tip.

"How was the chicken tonight? I used a new recipe from Miss Gladys—the rosemary herbs sure made the kitchen smell nice."

"It was the best chicken I ever had! Thank you!"

"That's wonderful! I'll put a star next to that one."

After tidying the kitchen, she gathered her knitting tray and sat by the fire. Ben sprawled out on his stomach on the floor with his drawing utensils. When he finished his sketch, he rolled over on his side looking across the hallway. "What's in that room?" he asked, pointing to the French doors.

"Charles keeps special items in there—books and memorabilia and such. We call it the 'study.'"

"My father took me to the candy store every year for my birthday. They have books there, too."

"Yes, Miss Myrtle has been building her collection for years—she might need a second shelf soon. Did you read any of her books?"

"I can't read very well, but Mr. Elliot is teaching me to spell while we eat our lunches."

"Would you like to take a peek at some books?"

He looked over at the large doors. The room beyond was dark, except for the light of the oil lamp illuminating the corner by the door.

Claire set aside the knitting tray and picked up the lamp. "Let's take a look."

He followed her closely, nearly bumping into her when she pushed the doors open. She walked him along the bookcases, the lamp casting light across the room little by little, revealing shelves full of photos, awards, books, and framed newspaper clippings. A round stand holding a large globe on its axis caught his attention. He walked over, giving it a gentle push to make it spin. A picture hung above it, and she held the lamp up to the frame. "This is where it all started. His horse placed fifth in the Kentucky Derby that year."

He walked a little closer to get a better look. Mr. Charles was wearing a short, flat brimmed hat; his face was tan, and he was a lot thinner. He was dressed in fancy clothes standing beside a horse, and a small man was sitting in the saddle.

"That was Gale, he was one of the best jockeys around and a special friend to Charles."

"That's a very big horse!" Ben said.

"Yes, his name was Tad's Hopper. Charles named him that because he always hopped when they pulled the starting gate." Lowering the lantern, she led him along the other side, showing him more ribbons and artifacts, noticing he gave extra attention to the jockeys in all the pictures. "Charles has a collection of the *American Jockey* publications—here's a good one," she said, holding the cover to the light. "This is the fastest horse alive they say, his name is Man o' War. And that jockey in the saddle is Mr. Clarence Kummer. He's not much older than you are, maybe nineteen in this picture."

Ben accepted the magazine as if it were a precious stone. "Can I take this to my room?"

"Of course you can. I can teach you how to read it, too. It's more fun to learn when you read what interests you."

"Can I look at the pictures first?" he said, flipping through the pages.

"Certainly, you're welcome to look through as many as you like."

Raising his eyebrows, Ben looked at the box of magazines, in awe at the sheer number of options.

"How about we carry this whole box up to your room; you can look through as many as you like before bedtime."

Ben laid on top of his bed covers, waiting for the soft glow of the lamp light to go out in Claire's bedroom. Seeing the hallway finally go dark, he quietly gathered his sack and lifted the lid of the trunk, pulling out the spare blanket and stepping lightly down the hall.

Claire pulled the covers back and sat on the edge of the bed, listening to the creaks and light footsteps going down the stairs. A few moments later, she heard a faint rustling in the kitchen, followed by the side door closing gently. She thought it was a clever idea to put cookies on the counter, already wrapped. Walking over to the window, she watched him walk the path back to the barn with his blanket and a book.

Ben set the lantern down and nestled in next to Juniper, studying each image in the magazine. Before long, his eyelids grew heavy. Reaching for the lamp, he turned the wick down and blew on the flame, then pulled the blanket up close, falling asleep with the pages laying open on his chest.

19

Reggie splashed water on his face and washed his hands in the creek, looking around the camp at the clusters of people huddled over campfires. Children were huddled under tent blankets telling ghost stories while women were taking down clothes on the lines. Amidst the clamor of voices, Reggie's thoughts wandered back to his family's old house. A deep yearning stirred within him to have a place to call home again. For now, though, that remained a distant dream.

His wife, Cecelia, came walking over after having put the children to bed, rubbing her arms to shake the chill in the night air. "They went to sleep quickly tonight; had a big day playing with some new friends. A family just arrived from the Carolinas. The husband lost all his money on the stock exchange and his mining company closed its doors. Sounds awfully familiar, doesn't it?"

"Folks are hurtin' everywhere. Seems you got something to plan for one day, then you wake up to a different world and have to start all over again."

Feeling Reggie's sadness, Cecelia reached for his hand. "At least we're all together and everyone is healthy—can't ask for more than that."

Unmoved by her optimism, he shook his head. He knew that if he didn't make some type of move forward, they would live and die just as they were—homeless and living on borrowed land. "I need to travel north, and I must leave now to make it there in time."

The idea of splitting up the family filled Cecelia with anxiety, prompting her to barrage him with a flurry of questions. "Where are you going? Did you find work? How long will you be gone?"

"I will return the day after tomorrow. I met some nice folks at the train station. They're horsemen and took an interest in the gear I made. They have a horse runnin' in a big derby race in New York. I'm not sure if much will come of it, but I feel like I need to find out."

She hugged him and kissed him on the cheek. "We can make this work; you don't have to go chasin' after more."

Reggie wrapped his arms around her, holding her close. "I want more for our family; I want us to have a home again, somewhere with open spaces and good neighbors. It will just take time, and I will chase every opportunity to see that day."

*   *   *

Charles's sleep was interrupted by the shrill screech of the whistle, jolting his eyes open. Through the window, he saw the boarding platform approaching. Straightening in his seat, he lifted his head from the cradle he'd made with his overcoat and found a paper doll in his lap, sitting on top of his Bible. The doll was colored in with crayon and had brown wavy hair and a blue dress, just like the girl he had given the cookies to. Scanning the train car, he didn't see the family anywhere. When he opened the front cover to tuck the doll in the crease, his eyes caught large cursive handwriting on the back of the paper. "Betsy Price," was written in blue letters with a little pink heart at the end. Charles exited the train and pushed through a throng of reporters holding big, boxy cameras— none of whom paid him any attention—until he found Henry.

"Sleep well?" Henry asked.

"Better than I thought I would. Haven't been overnight on a train since our race in Tecumseh, three years ago."

"Look at these guys," Henry said, watching a gaggle of newsmen crossing into the infield, all clambering for their shot. "Well, I better get changed and saddled up. See you in the circle," he said with unwavering confidence.

The closer Charles got to the grandstand, the thicker the crowd became, and he searched for a seat along the railing looking over the paddock area. He lowered his glasses and scanned the showcard when a gray-haired man tapped him on the shoulder.

"Charles, is that really you? I thought you gave this up after that disappointing turnout last time."

"Somehow I managed to move on," Charles said flippantly, accepting Sid's handshake. "The track isn't in the best of shape; you got some rain here I see."

Sid chuckled. "Soggy soil won't make a difference to Rushmore; I don't think his feet will even touch the ground. I heard you bought into this one with a gelding from Sawyer's place."

Charles ignored the insinuation and swallowed the first reply that came to mind. "I just hope we have another contender on our hands. Henry's been reporting good times, so we'll see. He's still a young horse—one race at a time."

Sid nodded, likely disappointed his provocation wasn't entertained. "All the best to you Charles. Without Sawyer in your pocket, it could get tougher to compete. Prices are only getting higher, and as you know, talent is hard to come by."

Watching Sid take his seat in the box, puffing on cigars with his cohorts, made him want to watch the race from the moon. He tried to put the interaction out of his mind, but out of the corner of his eye, he could feel their ridicule.

*　　*　　*

Reggie grabbed his tattered sport coat with patches on the elbows and hurried to the betting booth where a small crowd of men stood in a line. In contrast to him, they were impeccably dressed. Thick, pungent smoke wafted from their fat cigars and swirled around their tall hats. He pulled the ill-fitting coat tight around his chest, fastening a button held by a thin string that broke free in his hand. He felt out of place and awkward among the wealthy gentlemen, keenly aware of the crude looks and whispers directed at him by men with money to burn just for a fleeting thrill. Stepping closer to the booth, feelings of doubt bubbled up when the man at the wagering window called him over. He placed the money on the counter, keeping his hand firmly on top of it.

"You placing a bet or holding it down so the wind don't blow it away?" the man asked.

Lifting his hand, Reggie let the man swipe it across the counter, holding the lapels of his jacket to dry the sweat from his hands.

"Forty dollars," the man said, handing him the bet card. "If you need to see the lineup, I have the charts on the wall behind me."

"No sir, I would like it all on Ranger's Riot."

The man looked at him curiously. "Ranger's Riot?" he repeated with little enthusiasm. "You sure about that? You're looking at seven-to-one odds standing."

Reggie felt like time stood still; the man stared at him as if doing him a favor by giving him time to reconsider.

Finally, the man in the booth raised his brows and processed his wager. "Good luck to you. You must know something nobody else does," he said and pulled the shutter closed.

*　　*　　*

The crowd cheered wildly as the horses approached the track, the jockeys poised in their saddles. Charles spotted Henry coming out of the paddock, sixth in line. Ranger moved in smooth, steady strides, seemingly unfazed by the people lining the infield. As the horses lined up, the crowd hushed and took their seats, waiting for the start. When the flag went up, Charles laced his fingers and rolled his thumbs, unable to watch.

Right out of the gate, Rushmore took the lead. Sid looked to where Charles was sitting just moments ago, humored to see him hunched over his knees and ringing his hands but found his seat empty. Looking around, Sid saw Charles exiting the ramp to the grandstand.

Charles walked past the paddock corridor, pacing along the backside of the stands where he could hear himself think. A storm of self-doubt churned in his mind, but after a few moments, the cheering hushed as a lead change happened. Charles suddenly felt a wave of nausea but fought his urge to flee as he hurried back to catch a view of the race. Rushmore's jockey pulled up, moving to the outside of the track. Ranger was fifth and struggling to break away from the middle pack. But by the quarter turn, Henry found an opening to move through, taking more ground on the backstretch, steadily gaining on Rushmore. Fourth, third, second… the crowd gasped in surprise as Ranger seemed to glide effortlessly through the pack until he was neck-and-neck with Rushmore. Coming into the final turn, Ranger seemed to gain a second wind, passing Rushmore on the inside. Charles's mind went blank; Ranger crossed the line two and a half lengths ahead of Rushmore.

Leaning forward with his hands at his knees, Charles finally took a filling breath. Listening to muffled groans and confused whispering, he chuckled, catching a bet ticket that had been discarded over the rail. He leaned against the wall, dropped the ticket to his side, and rested his head against the boards when a group of men passed by. One of the men gave him a pat on the shoulder. "Don't feel bad fella, none of us saw that coming either." He watched them walk away, shaking their heads in disbelief, and walked back down the corridor to meet Henry in the winner's circle.

After the newsmen snapped their pictures and the seats emptied, Charles stepped out onto the finish marker and stared up into the grandstand. He noticed one man sitting alone in a box. The man stood up and waved his hat in his direction. It was Sid. Charles returned the gesture and took one last look around.

A group of cameramen loitered around the hall outside the jockeys' quarters, talking amongst themselves about the unexpected upset, not recognizing Henry in his leisure clothes. Charles was sure that if it hadn't been for the green sash around the handle of Henry's duffle, he could have snuck right by.

One reporter, a taller fellow, pointed excitedly at Henry. "It's him, that's Henry Shoemacker!"

Henry was besieged by flashes of light as they encircled him, hungry for more content for their columns.

"I'll be at the stable, waiting on the all clear," Charles said, leaving him to the mob of story-hungry piranhas.

After the camera lenses closed and the crowds departed, they approached the station yard, decorated with banners and bright colored streamers. Small clusters of racegoers still clapped and waved. This was a feeling that Charles had long forgotten—even the handler holding Ranger's lead seemed to be enjoying the attention.

"Hey, isn't that the fella we bought the gear from?" Henry asked, pointing to a man sitting under a large tree across the field by the betting booth.

"I believe it is. What would he be doing here? Suppose he wants his horse back?"

Reggie stood, surprised to see them walking over. "Guess y'all are curious why I'm here."

"Charles seems to think you want the horse back," Henry said.

He chuckled, but his eyes looked red and glassy, wet streaks running down his cheeks. "No, that ain't the reason. Gee whiz, look at me... a grown man standin' here like this," he said, pinching his eyes to stop the tears.

"Something wrong?" Charles asked.

"You saved my family today," Reggie said, pulling out his bet card. "I'm not a gamblin' man, never dreamed of doin' such a thing as this, but I just had a feelin' about y'all."

"I believe your gear made a difference in the way he ran that race. Even had a few jockeys ask me where I got it," Henry said.

Charles reached out with a handshake. "Once you and your family get back on your feet, consider the offer."

*　　*　　*

Claire stirred a large pitcher of iced tea under the unseasonably warm late-afternoon sun. Using her elbow to prop open the door, she shimmied through with a tray of refreshments when a voice on the other side startled her.

"Here, let me hold that for you," a boy said, "I have a telegram for Mrs. Claire Collins."

Setting the tray down, she wiped the moisture from her hands, finding it a little unsettling to receive a telegram while Charles was traveling. But her nerves were calmed by the boy's friendly smile as he handed her the yellow envelope.

"I'm Mrs. Collins, and you are?"

"My name is Oscar. I'm a new mail carrier, this is my first delivery," he said proudly, touching the bill of his black felt cap, drawing her attention to the Western Union badge.

"I am honored indeed to be your first recipient. Thank you for the letter."

"You're welcome, Mrs. Collins," he said, hanging the messenger bag over the handlebars of his bike and peddling away with a wave.

The small white page was stamped with the Western Union Telegram emblem in the center in large bold print. Just below it, in small print, was the address: 445 West Street, New York, followed by a note that read: "Charles to return tomorrow. Race was a victory."

20

Two months later, Christmas time…

Ben warmed his toes by the fire, flipping a page of his new favorite book, *Dr. Doolittle*. It had been a snowy winter so far, with nothing much to do besides helping at the store and farm chores. Ben pulled his blanket over himself, rolling onto his back to continue reading when he heard footsteps on the porch and a knock at the door. He dropped the book and looked out the window, spotting Lucas holding a funny-looking stick with a round cup nailed to the end, waving at him. Ben grabbed his coat and toboggan, slid his socked feet into winter galoshes, and shut the door behind him.

"What's in your hand?" Ben asked, looking at the strange object.

"It's a snowball maker. Me and my father made it—let's try it out!"

Resting the newspaper on his lap, Charles watched them run off into the snow. "I miss having energy like that."

"I would argue that you still do," Claire said, "you added two new enclosures, we have three more horses, a new trainer… and let's not forget all the planting and ideas you and Paul have been busy with. Speaking of that, what were you two discussing earlier? Something about a farm market?"

"We calculated the spring and fall harvests, and if all goes well weather-wise, we're going to need a place to sell it all. We have space here at the farm, but a market near the store would be easier for Paul to manage."

Claire sat up with interest. "You know, I've been told I make a pretty good pie. I think having fresh baked goods would be something people might fancy."

Charles chuckled at Claire's infectious excitement. "I like it, they would sell like hotcakes, that's for sure!"

*   *   *

Scooping out the center of a snowdrift by the roadside, Ben and Lucas packed the round mold with snow. After a few minutes, they had an arsenal of snowballs ready, and Ben got an idea. He grabbed a lid from an old seed barrel and propped it against the trunk of a tree; then, they took turns launching snowballs at the target. Ben took a couple shots before he was distracted by Carl and Elliot moving horses around the pasture. "Want to go riding?"

"My father didn't say I could yet, but I'll ask him again. I heard him talking to my mother about it; she likes horses, so maybe he'll say I can." Pulling his arm back, he took aim at the target, hitting dead center.

"Alright!" he yelled, "look at that, bullseye!"

They ran up to the target, brushing off the snow and admiring the marksmanship. "That was a direct hit!"

In celebration, they jumped around, kicking at the snow and laughing.

*   *   *

Jack sat at the table, rolling marbles across the top, batting them back and forth while he waited for his mother to wake up. With the breakfast hour passing, he figured she wouldn't be down to make flapjacks, so instead, he took the last chocolate bar from a box he kept hidden under the staircase. Crouched in the pantry, he heard his father coming down the stairs and hurriedly pushed the box behind a sack of oats.

"Get in the car, we're going into town," Clint said.

On their way to town, Jack looked out the window and saw the two boys high-five each other, skipping around in circles. Anger bubbled up inside him, and he clenched his jaw so tight it made his teeth hurt.

Clint looked over at the farm as they drove by. "This guy thinks he's a big shot now. He wins one race and thinks he's back in the game.

Building up that rundown place—what a fool," he grumbled. "Hope the whole damn place burns down one day."

Jack didn't listen much to anything his father said, but he let his imagination run.

*   *   *

"What are you asking for this Christmas?" Lucas asked.

Ben thought about it but couldn't think of anything on the spot.

"I'm asking for a Gilbert chemistry set. Colt got one for his birthday; it even has hot plates and a blow torch and all kinds of powders you can mix up with skulls and crossbones on the bottles —isn't that cool?!"

Ben's eyes got wide. "That would be real fun if you get one."

"Darn tootin', we'll be able to invent all kinds of things! There's my father," Lucas said, practically jumping with excitement from imagining unwrapping presents under the Christmas tree. "I gotta go, but think of what you want to ask for. If you ask for a chemistry set, too, we can combine them and have twice the stuff to make!"

Later that night after supper, Ben picked up his book again, excited to return to the story. Sunday evenings were his favorite; they were more relaxed, and other than getting up early for church, the rest of the day was free for playing and reading. He rolled up a flannel blanket into a pillow and stuck it behind his head, listening to Charles and Claire talk about Christmas day supper. His attention toggled between the suspense of Dr. Doolittle's efforts to save a young rabbit with a broken foot and the conversation over honey-glazed ham.

"What would you like for Christmas this year?" Charles asked Ben from the kitchen.

Claire looked at Ben over her knitting needles. She gave him a nervous grin, sensitive to the fact that this would be a different kind of Christmas for him.

"Lucas asked me that earlier. I can't think of anything. He's asking for a chemistry set and thinks I should ask for one too so we can make twice the experiments."

"That's one way to get a bigger smoke plume," Charles chuckled. "You still have a couple days to think about it."

*   *   *

Bright and early the next morning, after Paul left with Ben on their way to the store, Claire got busy with cleaning. She started downstairs, then worked her way up to the second-floor bedrooms. While swiping the dusting cloth over Ben's desk, she uncovered a letter next to his drawing pad:

I canot thnk of a prsnt this yer. The Colins have givn me more then I need. Mabe soks and a xtra cemistree set and a bell for Juniper like the fanse horses. And I would like to see Jon and Margret.

She wasn't sure who it was meant for, but it delighted her, nonetheless.

*   *   *

"There's our seed delivery" Paul said, "grab your gloves. We're gonna have to work fast—it's cold out there."

Ben jumped off the stepladder and hurried around the corner.

"Mornin' Paul, mornin' Ben," Daniel said, giving Ben a nod. "What's it been now, 'bout two months? Surprised he ain't run you off yet."

"He's doing good—a quick learner and good with numbers," Paul said, handing Ben the delivery note. Two cars and a buggy pulled into the lot as Ben pushed through the door to put the note under the till.

"You better man the counter. I'll unload with Daniel and handle the outside work this morning," Paul said.

Ben worked the counter, filling orders and keeping up with the morning rush. Mondays were always the busiest day of the week, with folks coming in to redeem their government-issued seed vouchers. After the morning slowed, he grabbed the broom to clean up, sweeping his way to the back of the store. When he heard the bell clap against the window, he stopped sweeping to listen. Not hearing anyone, he figured it was Paul coming in to warm up. He rolled up a hose that came loose from its hook and hung it on the pegboard, when he saw a tall figure walk past the counter. A strange feeling crept up from the back of his neck and he shook off a wave of chills. Continuing to sweep, he suddenly felt like he was being watched. When he looked up, he saw a man standing at the end of the aisle scratching his chin with the blade of a small pocketknife. He leaned the broom between two garden hoses and turned around to help the man find what he was looking for, but the man was gone. He could hear footsteps on the other side of the aisle, stopping at the corner, just out of view.

"Hello, can I help you?" he asked quietly, feeling a tightness in his stomach when he saw the tips of white sneakers peeking out from around the shelf.

Jack Larson rounded the corner, glaring at the bug-eyed boy who was looking back at him. There was something about Ben that lit a spark of anger that grew hotter by the second. He couldn't quite put his finger on the reason; maybe it was because he had stolen his friend Lucas, or possibly the way he cowered, quiet and timid—but something about him stirred an awful temptation to knock his block off. Jack heard his father's voice in his head, and all the turmoil he had felt since the move came rushing to the surface. He took quick steps toward Ben, stopping just inches from his face, and wrapped his hand around the broom handle.

"Hey retard, remember me?" Jack said, curling his lip into a snarl, pushing him backwards and balling up his fist.

Losing his balance, Ben fell against the hard shelving, then felt an awful ache in his stomach from Jack's fist landing square in his midsection, doubling him over. Trying to catch his breath, he looked up as Jack drew back another punch, then saw a massive hand grip Jack's fist, holding it behind him and squeezing so hard Jack's hand turned white.

"Take your hands off him—let the boys handle it," Clint said, walking up the aisle toward Paul. "Seems to be some bad blood," he said coolly, snapping the pocketknife shut and dropping it in his shirt pocket.

Paul released his grip on Jack's hand, giving him a firm push forward,

"Get out!" he shouted through clenched teeth, "get out now while you still have two legs that work, both of ya!"

Jack stumbled forward, grimacing and rubbing his wrist, wincing from the pain.

Paul fixed his eyes on Clint and reached for a chain, plucking it off the hook without breaking eye contact. "I'm giving you three seconds to make it out that door before I take you out myself."

Clint held out his hands in submission. "We're leaving," he said, backing away.

Jack pushed the door open and ran out.

Paul stayed on Clint's heels with his hand cocked until Clint was outside, then stood in the middle of the lot, watching as they sped off, spitting gravel with their tires.

Elliot and Earl saw the ruckus from across the lot and knew something wasn't right.

Paul shouted as they pulled away. "You ever come back here again, I'll end your life Larson, you hear me—I'll end it!"

Rushing back inside, he found Ben sitting on the ground with his arms over his stomach and spit-up on his shirt. He strained to sit up straight, pulling his shirt sleeve across his lips.

Elliot and Earl yanked the door open, rattled by the scene. "What did he do, was that Larson?" Elliot said.

Paul looked up, seething with anger. "I'm going after that son of a bitch!"

Elliot flinched when he heard the door open and went to see who it was.

"Hey, Elliot," Denny said, closing the door behind him, "is Paul around, I wanted to grab a few more yards of wire."

Elliot walked toward him shaking his head and ushering him back out the door.

"What's the matter, why you want me to…"

Paul came around the corner, pointing at him. "You tell that piece of shit boss of yours, if he or his wretched son ever come around here again, he's a dead man, you hear me?! Go, get out, you tell that bastard I said that!"

"You better leave right quick," Elliot said, taking him by the shoulders and turning him around, walking him quickly out the door.

Denny looked over his shoulder as he jumped into the truck. The disappointment on Elliot's face stirred a wave of regret, and in that moment, he decided to end his dealings with Larson.

A few minutes later, Carl stepped inside, looking around frantically. "I just heard, ran into Denny at the corner."

"We'll talk about this later," Paul said, helping Ben to his feet.

Carl didn't say a word, just walked back out the door and got into his truck, reached for the revolver under the seat, calmly pulled out the ammo box, and loaded the chamber.

Carl's truck rumbled to a stop just short of Clint's driveway. Carl stepped out of the truck, fastened his holster, then dropped the revolver into the pocket. Crossing the yard, he noticed a large branch broken in half and heard glass breaking when he reached the door. "Larson, you might want to step out here, be better than me coming in there." Hearing rustling on the other side of the door, he heard a click and watched the knob turn slowly.

Clint opened the door just enough to look through and locked his eyes on Carl.

Cool-headed and unemotional, Carl lifted the bottom hem of his shirt, exposing the stock of the revolver and gave it a tap, drawing Clint's eyes to his hip. "You so much as look in the direction of that boy, the store, or the farm, and you'll meet your maker faster than I can tie down a calf, is that understood?"

Clint's gaze never left the revolver, even after Carl dropped his shirt. Without another word, Carl turned his back and walked off the porch.

*   *   *

Claire closed Ben's door and came downstairs, finding Charles standing at the edge of the steps, watching the sunset. She grabbed her shawl, shivering as the icy air lifted the bottom hem of her dress. "He's asleep now," she said, wrapping her arms around his shoulders. "Got him to eat two apple turnovers before nodding off." Tapping him on the shoulder, she pulled a letter from her pocket. "I wanted to show you this, it might cheer you up."

"What's this?"

"I have a hunch it might be his Christmas letter."

21

CHRISTMAS EVE MORNING...

The smell of butter and cinnamon enticed Charles out of bed. Wriggling his feet into slippers, he tied his robe belt and followed the wonderful smells downstairs. Ben already sat at the table pulling at the soft fluffy center of a cinnamon roll.

"How are you feeling this morning? You look good, got some color back in your cheeks."

"I feel better, a little sore right here," he said, rubbing the center of his stomach, "but it doesn't hurt that bad."

"Good, that's real good," Charles said, pulling out a chair across from him. Ever since Paul and Elliot shared the events of yesterday, he couldn't help but feel he'd somehow failed as a protector. "You know, Ben, you can talk to me about what happened. I don't know what the problem is between that Larson boy and you, but I do know it's not your fault."

Nodding, he reached for another roll. "He's a bully, and I hope I don't see him again."

"I talked to Paul last night," Charles said. "We think it's best you stay here at the farm for a while and not go to the store until we sort this out."

"I know, Mr. Paul already told me. I feel happy about it; Mr. Elliot said I could ride more too!"

"I reckon you can," Charles said, distracted by a scratching sound coming from the door. He turned his head, curious to know what was causing it. Lifting his finger to hush Claire and Ben, he got up to investigate. "Did you hear that?"

Claire shrugged, looking over at Ben with a smirk.

Charles leaned into the window to find a floppy-eared hound on the back steps with a ribbon dangling from its neck. "Honey, there's a gift-wrapped dog outside."

"The boys wanted him to have his present early. They thought he could use the company; he can keep an eye on him around here."

Charles raised a brow and looked over at Ben. "Looks like a mighty fine hound. What's his name?"

"That's just what we were trying to decide on, but we do like Buck," Claire said.

"*The Call of the Wild*," Charles said, backing off the topic when he noticed Claire holding a finger to her lips to shush him. When she set his plate down, piled high with food, he returned to the table, flattened a napkin in his lap, and ogled over the hotcakes, sausage, and biscuits. "Christmas Eve breakfast; almost as good as Christmas supper. Speaking of Christmas, you got any last-minute requests?" he said, glancing at Ben.

Ben was grinning ear-to-ear. "I just got a dog, Mr. Charles; I don't know what could be better than that!"

*   *   *

Daniel slung a concrete bag over his shoulder and dropped it at the corner of the pole barn. Wiping dust residue from his eyes, he spotted Denny pull in. "You can turn right around outta here," Daniel said. "You tell Larson his money don't control every damn body."

"I ain't here for material," Denny said, "I came here to ask for my job back; I ain't workin' for that guy no more."

"You too? Dale came by just yesterday for the same reason."

"I know he did. Neither of us knew Larson was as bad as he is. I don't want nothin' to do with him, especially after what happened at the store. And no matter if you take me back or not, I ain't liftin' a finger for that guy ever again. It was a stupid thing to do."

Daniel looked out over the snow-covered field, squinting from the glare, and reached into his pocket for an envelope. "Merry Christmas. Split that with Dale. See you Wednesday."

*　　*　　*

After breakfast, Claire carried a basket full of popcorn strings, marzipan cookies, and ornaments made of feathers and pinecones. Inhaling the Douglas fir, enjoying the woodsy scent, she heard a knock on the door. Oscar was standing on the porch with his messenger bag around his chest, covered up from head to toe in heavy clothes.

"Hello Oscar, chilly day to be out delivering letters," she said, nipped by a breeze of cool air that lurched through the doorway.

"Yes ma'am, but this is my last letter to deliver," he said, reaching into his bag.

"Before I take that, wait here for a moment," she said, stepping inside to pull a candy cane off the corner table. "Merry Christmas."

"Merry Christmas Mrs. Collins, and thank you!"

The letter was addressed to her and Charles from the Naval base where Jonathan was stationed. Opening it quickly, she read the letter, barely able to contain her excitement. Jonathan was to be released from base and would be visiting tomorrow along with Margaret. Pressing the letter to her chest, she decided to keep the news a surprise.

Ben came around the corner, beaming at the massive tree and running a finger over a feather-covered ball with his finger.

"That belonged to my mother," Claire said, "she made them out of carved corn husks and yarn. Those are real feathers, too."

Ben brushed his hand over a strand of tinsel. "It's so shiny!"

"I have an idea. How about after supper, you make an ornament for our tree."

"Really! I would like that," he said.

*　　*　　*

Jack hung his arm over the sink while his mother changed his bandage. After tucking the edges, she stroked the back of his head. "Ouch!" he gasped, pulling away from her hand.

"Jack, let me see the top of your head."

"It's fine, Mother. It only hurts a little. Just leave me alone," he said before shutting the door, leaving her standing alone in the bathroom.

The despair and hopelessness she had tried to squelch for years began to bubble up when she stepped in front of the mirror. She lightly touched the cut above her brow, staring at the blood that smeared on her fingertip. Normally, after Clint knocked her around, she would avoid mirrors for days. But this time she didn't look away. She memorized every bloody cut, burning scrape, and aching bruise. Minutes went by before she finally tipped the bottle of iodine over a cotton ball; it was the second bottle she had bought this month. Looking out the window at the light snowfall, she remembered past Christmases in the city. The grand storefronts and elaborate decorations and warm nights under a blanket with Jack on her lap, reading Christmas stories and eating chocolates by the handfuls. Overcome by a strange, wonderful determination, she swiped all the supplies she had prepared into a basket and dropped it into the bottom of the linen closet, then walked over to the mirror to take one last look.

Lying on his stomach, Jack hung his bandaged arm over the side of the bed, sliding his hand along the rug, when he heard a tap on the door. His mother entered quietly, and he felt the corner of his mattress sink as her hand began rubbing his back.

"I'm sorry this happened, and I want you to know it won't happen again. This will be the last Christmas we spend away from our family," she said quietly, almost in a whisper. He wanted to believe her, but it wasn't the first time she had promised things would change. He had lost hope and felt it was better not to have any in the first place.

She went downstairs, following the smell of cigar smoke. Clint reached for his bottle of scotch, the glass wobbling under the bottle's neck as he tried to steady his pour.

"Don't you think you should give your son a Christmas present? Something besides the backside of your hand?"

Clint turned his head quickly, looking at her with amusement. "You talk like you ain't got no sense woman, you might want to change your tone before—"

"Before what Clint? Before you blacken my other eye? Before you hurt your son again? You know there's a lot of talk about town… I would think twice about your actions from now on." Walking away, she could hear the clinking of his glass against the bottle, figuring it best to let him drink himself to sleep. She hoped that this time, he wouldn't wake up.

*   *   *

Before closing the store, Paul pulled a box from under the counter, unwrapped one of Bernie's cigars, and held it under his nose, letting his memories of past Christmases fill his mind. Holding the lighter in one hand, he cut the tip, just like he saw Bernie do a hundred times, and lit the end. He watched it catch fire, then blew on the tip to spread the heat. Holding it out in front of his face, he let the smoke swirl around him. He took a puff and blew out the smoke with a sputter and a cough.

*   *   *

Elliot relaxed in his chair with his Bible. Turning to the book of Job, he wanted to be reminded that when it seems like darkness is all around and the devil is breathing down your neck, the Lord can intervene and restore everything that was lost. Each time he read Bible stories, he always found a new way to interpret the words, like they spoke to a different part of his spirit each time he read them. Tonight, he felt like something new was about to happen—something he couldn't ever have dreamed of. He knew it would be good, and that everything was going to be alright.

*   *   *

Before turning in for the night, Charles and Claire gathered up the presents they'd hidden in the study, arranging them under the tree. "What's the tall one in the corner?" Charles asked, "it doesn't look familiar."

"That's a fire extinguisher. Seemed like a good idea. Myrtle said those

Gilbert chemistry sets pack quite a punch. Her nephew nearly blew up their chicken coop playing around with those chemicals."

"Good thinking dear."

*   *   *

Christmas Day...

By early afternoon, the house was full of food and family. Ben was sprawled out under the tree reading Jack London's *The Call of the Wild*, while the men played cards and smoked cigars in the study.

"You know I tried one of them yesterday; darn near coughed myself silly," Paul said.

"It's like an old army buddy," Charles chuckled, taking a puff and watching the smoke roll away. "You talk about the drama, then part ways when your body reminds you of the pain."

Gladys poked her head around the corner leading to the kitchen, the feathers on her hat coming into view before she did. "My lands, look at all this food!"

"Christmas is my one excuse to cook every cake, pie, and cookie I fancy most," Claire said, pulling out an apron with a hand-stitched Christmas tree on the front. "You ladies like this one? I just finished it last night. Been knitting it for months!"

"How wonderful," Bernice said, admiring the stitching. "You know, we should all get together and have a pattern-making party. We could do designs like this for all the holidays. Wouldn't that be a hoot!"

Claire took a seat at the table, leaning over to deliver a secret. "We have very special guests today," she whispered, checking around the corner for prying ears. "Jonathan and Margaret are visiting from the naval base! I haven't told Ben; I wanted it to be a surprise."

Gladys set down a pie plate and grabbed Claire's hands like they were two giddy schoolgirls. "That's wonderful!"

The low rattle of the egg timer went off, and Claire went to the counter to glaze the ham. She had just started when she heard a knock at the front door.

"That has to be them!" Gladys said, "nobody knocks at this house. It has to be!"

They all gathered at the corner of the kitchen, watching Ben set his book down and shuffle to the door, his mind still on the story. When he opened the door, the shimmer off a bronze-plated pin caught his eye. Jonathan stood there smiling in his uniform, with Margaret next to him, holding a letter. "We thought we would deliver this one personally."

Ben jumped up and down, then lunged forward with his arms spread wide, pulling them close.

"You have muscles now!" Jonathan said.

"And you got taller!" Margaret added.

"You're taller, too!" Ben said, reaching over to touch the brass lapel pin on Jonathan's uniform. "Wow, that's neat!"

Everyone had gathered around to enjoy the reunion. Gladys passed Claire a tissue to dry her eyes.

"Miss Gladys!" Jonathan called, seeing her through the doorway.

She wrapped him in a bear hug. "My, have you grown into a solid young man," she said, tapping the sides of his shoulders. "Look at you, all filled out and as broad as my waistline. How's that car running for you?"

"I love it, it runs like a top! I've missed you Miss Gladys," he said with a childlike smile. "And your cooking."

"Now that doesn't surprise me one bit; and Lord sakes look at you child," she said, turning to Margaret, touching the soft waves of hair that reached past her shoulders. "It's so long now—it's beautiful. And either I'm shrinking, or you grew three inches!"

"I want to show you my room!" Ben said, grabbing them by the hand, "and I want you to meet Juniper and Buck!"

"Who's Buck?" Jonathan asked.

"He's my Christmas dog! Mr. Elliot and Mr. Paul gave him to me as a present, even tied a ribbon around him. Come this way," he said, pulling on their arms.

"What a nice surprise," Gladys said, putting her arms around Claire as she watched them run off together like excited little kids. "That warmed my heart; they sure do sprout up fast once they leave the garden."

After supper, everyone gathered around the tree. Ben, Jonathan, and Margaret sat together on the sofa listening to Christmas songs on the radio. Gladys began to hum along to "Jingle Bells," and everyone began singing. Ben rested his head on Margaret's shoulder and laughed when Elliot danced in place with his arms flailing around.

Later that night, Claire gathered up blankets, overhearing Ben telling Jonathan and Margaret about the jockeys he's been reading about. "I'm going to be the best in the world someday!"

As the day came to an end, the guests said their goodbyes with full bellies, while the three siblings bunked together and talked long into the night. Claire tapped on the door, setting down extra blankets on a chair. "This should keep you warm. I hope you all had a good Christmas. Sleep well," she said, closing the door and listening to their happy voices as she turned in for the night.

22

Nearing Summertime...

The farm was getting busier each day, with more horses added to the stables for training and an uptick in student riders. Harold Williams was hired to assist Carl with training and brought extra hands with him to help manage the horses. Denny's crew stayed busy with construction work to expand the facilities, including a new training arena and a second enclosure, which took everyone except for Elliot by surprise.

One afternoon, Charles rested his hands over the fence, watching Ben in the saddle.

"I think he's ready, boss," Elliot said, waiting for Charles to give the signal to add another rail to the jump.

"His arc is perfect—impressive vertical lift. Go ahead and raise it."

Ben led Juniper along the perimeter of the course, trotting the vertical for the combination, clearing all three jumps with ease, then bringing Juniper around to a halt.

"I ain't no trainer," Elliot said, "but we've been at this for four straight weeks. They look better and better every time. He's itchin' to really run with it. I know how you feel 'bout this, and I ain't too keen on loosening the gloves either, but look at him. If you don't agree, then I'll keep my two cents to myself and keep makin' myself dizzy watching 'em circle the same tread."

"Sure does remind me of Gale," Charles said. "I reckon you can stretch 'em out a little more."

Elliot reached out and squeezed him on the shoulder to shake out some tension, then opened the gate and waved Ben over. "Great form.

He's shifting his weight to his back legs before that vertical; go ahead and take him out for a cool down."

Ben stayed along the perimeter of the property, close enough to the edge of the woods that he could listen to the water flowing through the creek. A light breeze brushed the treetops, rustling leaves on the ground, making them dance in circles. The movement of the woods fascinated him, and he kept snug to the tree line, watching the leaves spiral to the ground. Suddenly, he heard branches and twigs snapping and the sound of quiet laughter getting louder. Looking through the trees, he could see two figures holding out sticks, running through a path in the woods. A boy pushed through the thicket, holding branches away from his face, then Ben heard a voice calling after the boy, "Wait Lucas, wait!"

"Hey Ben!" Lucas said, pulling twigs from his hair as he walked out of the brush. Lucas looked back over his shoulder, cupping his hands to his mouth, and called out, "Jack, I'm over here."

Ben froze, keeping his eyes on the tree line, steadying Juniper as he started to dance and sidestep with a low groan.

"Hi boy," Lucas said, rubbing Juniper's forehead.

Jack stayed behind the thicket, pulling buds off a limb and throwing them on the ground, not looking in their direction.

"Come over, Jack, I'm tired of the woods," Lucas said, "let's do something else."

"I should get back," Ben said, "Mr. Elliot is waiting for me. I'm jumping today."

"Wait for me, I'm coming—I want to watch!" Lucas said, running to catch up.

Jack watched Lucas run alongside Ben and the horse; the excitement in Lucas's voice annoyed him as they laughed and talked. He plucked the last bud from a branch and threw it to the ground. Then he picked up the slingshots they had planned to use to launch pinecones into the creek and tucked them into his belt.

Once they reached the enclosure, Ben looked behind him and saw Jack throw a limb into the brush then disappear into the woods.

"I don't know why he don't like you, but he sure doesn't, does he,"

Lucas said. "We learned how to build a fire today in class using flint and steel. Gave me some ideas for our next experiment!"

Ben looked down at him curiously. "Maybe we can ask to have a campfire later and you can show me."

"You ever gonna come to school again?"

Ben shrugged. "Not if I don't have to. I know how to read and write now, and Mr. Paul says I'm good at math; not sure what's more to learn."

"My father says you need a good education to make it in the world; you think that's true?"

Ben wobbled in the saddle, giving it some thought. "I don't need to learn all that school stuff. I'm gonna be a jockey someday!"

"Yeah," Lucas agreed, "I can see that. It's all you ever talk about; I think you'll be a great jockey."

*   *   *

Elliot counted out the paces for the last cross rail and spotted Harold coming through the gate. "Thanks for letting us play in here, we won't be too long. Ben's hankerin' for a little more distance."

"Suits me, I figured he might be. Once he got the trot and canter, I knew it wouldn't be long," Harold said. "I might watch for a bit; can't say I know much about jumping."

"I been readin' up. That's how I learned how to measure this out," Elliot said, looking over the pattern of jumps. "This here is just the basic course to build confidence, but we'll move through slow."

"Sounds like you know what you're doing. Maybe I can learn a thing or two," Harold said, settling into a spot in the corner.

Lucas perched himself on the fence for a better view, clapping and whistling when Ben and Juniper trotted around the pasture.

Ben listened intently to Elliot explain the course and how to maneuver through and around the jumps.

"If you feel comfortable with your posts, go ahead and canter to the jump, and remember to always look straight ahead over the jump. If you look down, he's gonna feel it, so be confident."

Leaning forward in the saddle, Ben tightened his grip on the reins and cantered around each jump, even taking the double spread effortlessly. Ben and Juniper shared a language of their own. When Ben wanted to quicken their pace to jump, he squeezed his legs tighter and Juniper responded. When guiding turns, he leaned with his weight, moving in perfect harmony every step of the way.

Elliot made small corrections here and there, reminding Ben to count Juniper's strides so they didn't jump too early, to keep his hands wide when approaching the jump, and to pull his elbows in before takeoff. For the most part, however, he felt like they had it figured out and only needed to decide how high they wanted to go.

"That was cool!" Lucas said, "you make it look easy."

"It is! Hopefully we get to go higher tomorrow."

"How high you want to go?" Lucas asked, looking around for a point of reference. "As high as that?" he said, pointing to a hay bale hoisted off the ground about four feet by the trolley.

"He can jump twice that high, I seen it! Over that hilltop, he jumped the wide end of the creek!"

Lucas watched Ben climb down, unfastening his helmet. "You do this every day?"

"We practice jumping two days a week, sometimes three, but we walk everyday if the weather is nice."

"You don't ever get bored being around horses all the time?"

Ben shook his head. "No, I always want to be around them. What do you like to do?"

"Experiments! I like to watch my father in his shop. He takes all kinds of odd parts that end up working somehow. He's been working on a campfire iron; he calls it a pie maker, but I ain't sure why. You wouldn't cook a pie over a campfire! Got the idea from the snowball maker he made, the one we used to blast that target."

"I don't know about pies over a fire; but it makes me hungry. "Let's give him a wash and go ask about the campfire."

Elliot jogged over to Paul, who was coming in from the crop fields. "You see those jumps today? That was something, wasn't it?"

"I don't know if I'd call it jumping—looked more like a vertical take-off. That horse flies straight off the ground."

"Sure does. Harold had a guy come 'round the other day askin' if we was considerin' show jumpin' competitions!"

Paul leaned back and laughed. "That'll be the day. Charles ain't built all this to watch a horse with springs in his feet hop around all day. I'll be by tomorrow after closing the store—I'll need your help with the plow."

Elliot waited for Carl to close the barn then meandered over, noticing Paul was still amused by his suggestion. "You think Mr. C would ever consider…"

Carl shook his head. "I know what you're gonna say and you can forget it. Everything around here is about racin', and that horse is no racehorse."

"I know he ain't no racehorse, but he sure can jump. Never seen a horse that could jump like that. And you know, show jumpin' is becoming quite the draw—just ask the Brits."

"Let's call it a day," Carl said, "you been in the sun too long. It's startin' to affect your common sense."

They turned around, hearing quick steps behind them. Ben and Lucas ran by, giggling over a joke.

Elliot grinned. "It's good to see him happy, and with a buddy to boot. Ever since he got up on that horse, he's been a different kid."

23

Reggie held his hand out while his wife wrapped gauze around his thumb. "Now, how am I supposed to eat my ribs?"

"I'll have to pull the meat from the bone like I do for the children," she joked. "How long were you working that piece of hide?"

"Three hours just about. Without these new tools, it would have taken closer to five. Pulling and stretching is the tough job—the rest is easy with that mold. And with the time saved, I can make enough to sell."

"I think you need to let this heal first. Last time I checked you only have two of them."

After she rolled up the extra cloth, he reached for her hand. "I been kickin' around the idea of that business offer. Might be something worth thinkin' about."

"Didn't you say he's from the Midwest? That's not exactly across town. And what would we do? The children are settled, made friends, and started school."

He flexed his thumb to loosen the wrap and looked around at the hodgepodge of canvas shelters and pallet cabins. "I don't want to settle here; I don't want our children to feel settled here. This was only temporary until I found steady work."

"We will find a home again, but for now, this is home, and it's nothing to be ashamed of. I know it's not ideal, but something will turn around soon. I just know it."

*   *   *

Jack worked on a crossword puzzle at the table, enjoying the aroma of beans and paprika while his mother finished getting supper ready.

"Jack, go tell your father that supper is ready, please."

Laying his pencil down, he slid out of the chair in a huff and walked sluggishly over to the back door, pausing to glance out before opening it.

Observing his hesitation, she put her hands on her hips. "Go on, before it cools too much," she said, "you know how much he hates cold chili."

He stepped outside, hoping he wouldn't have to go looking far, and noticed a lot of the trucks and carriages that belonged to the men his father hired weren't around much anymore. The building on the property had been slowing down. Only a few guys had stuck around to pull up the pole barn, and two other buildings had been left only partially completed. He didn't see his father anywhere but heard voices coming from inside the barn. Crossing the yard into the driveway, he began to hear men shouting and ducked behind a large cart full of construction material.

"What do you mean you don't have my pay?!" the man shouted. "That's two weeks in a row, Larson! I don't work for free. And you might want to consider that before you lose any more help."

He crouched lower behind the cart, scooting along the side to get a better look. Before he could get around the corner, he fell back against the wheel, startled by a loud crack of smashing glass.

"That's it, Larson, you lush. You keep drinkin' every penny you got and not payin' guys, and you'll be done for! I ain't stickin' around either. I'm gone!"

He watched the man come around the corner of the barn, his father stumbling after him. His father yelled incoherently, shouting obscenities before sliding down against the doorframe, slumped over with a broken jug handle in his hand.

Jack began to return to the house, not wanting to look at his father any longer. His mother stood on the door stoop waiting for him to cross the yard. "Well, is he on his way?"

"He's asleep over there," he said, pointing to the barn.

She held the door open for him. "Start eating without me, I'll be inside shortly."

Knowing she would be busy with his father's drunkenness for the rest of the night, Jack poured a ladle of chili into a thermos and left out the front door for a nighttime walk through the woods. He didn't want to be around when his father came in to sleep it off. He crossed the road, heading down a long path lined with maples on both sides, never understanding why most kids feared the woods at night. He loved being guarded under the blanket of the moon and stars; it was the only place he didn't need to hide. He could walk around in the open, bare-skinned, letting the breeze tickle his arm hair and not worry about who might see the marks. Once he got to the thicket, he checked his pockets for the watch and unzipped the jacket, tying the sleeves around his waist. He shivered under the loose-fitting fabric of his tee shirt and swung his bare arms up over his head, stretching up into the cool night air. Looking out into the wide-open space where the moon fell over the fields in a blanket of soft light, he planted one foot on the crest of the bank. Turning his back to the breeze, he took a slim black box from his back pocket. He opened the lid, staring at the flashy wrapping around the cigar, then pulled the lighter from its pouch. With a flick of his thumb, the lighter cap popped up, and he held the tip of the cigar over the flame, just like he had watched his father do many times. Once he got a good burn going, he took a puff, holding it in his cheeks before blowing it out. The smoke cloud rolled past him, keeping its form before dissipating into the moonlight. After a few more practice puffs, he felt confident and walked into the woods. A few minutes later, he started to feel dizzy, and noticed he wasn't as agile through the ground cover as he normally was. A few moments later, his stomach started to feel a little sour.

He came to the narrow end of the creek, thinking some splashes of water on his face might help, when he spotted the glow of a fire and tiny shards of kindling being spit high into the air. He heard voices too, familiar ones, and pulled the branches apart to get a better look. His stomach felt even worse when he saw Ben and Lucas huddled around a campfire. They were eagerly reaching into a bag that sat between them to load their sticks with marshmallows. Their happy voices made his stomach churn as he listened to the volley of whispers followed by explosive laughter.

Despite his anger, he was curious to hear what they were talking about, so he moved as close as he could without being noticed, slowly swerving along the creek bed to keep his footing steady.

Lucus stuffed another marshmallow in his mouth just as another wave of laughter came over them. He spat out a sugary chunk onto his boot, causing them to laugh even harder.

"Where did you learn that joke?" Ben asked.

"Overheard my father tell it to a couple guys at the gas station. I don't think he knew I was listening in."

"You want another?" Ben asked, holding out a marshmallow.

Lucas shook his head, a little disgusted at the thought of more sweets, and rested back against the hay bale, putting his arms over his stomach and making a bloated face with his cheeks. "I can't eat anymore, or I'll throw up for sure."

"Me, too," Ben agreed, reaching for the bag to drop the marshmallow back inside. "We ate this whole bag!"

"No wonder we feel sick," Lucas said. Suddenly, Juniper blew out a loud blast of air from his nostrils, causing Lucas to sit up. "What's wrong with your horse?"

Ben noticed the rope he used to tie him to the fence post was lax, so he figured he was just shifting his footing. "He's probably going to lay down. We'll put him in the barn once the fire goes out."

"Or maybe it's a monster!" Lucas whispered, looking around nervously. "I can't see anything out there—it's pitch black beyond the fire."

Jack sprinted from the tree line to a small shed just beyond the fire's light, staying low to the ground, then crouched down at the back corner.

"Did you hear that?" Lucas asked. "It sounded like something on foot out there. Maybe we should head over to the barn."

"We can't leave the fire while it's this high. Mr. Charles said the ground is too dry and could cause a brush fire. We have to stay here for a little while longer. Why don't we tell a funny story—that will take your mind off being scared of the dark."

"I'm not scared of the dark!" Lucas insisted. "Why, I could run out there in the pitch black and not be scared."

Ben snickered, looking at him out of the corner of his eye, doubtful about his conviction.

"You wanna see? Watch, I'll run to that tree line and back." Standing up, he brushed the hay off his pants and leaned over his knee into a runner's stance. "Give me a countdown."

Ben sat up straight, intrigued by the challenge, and began counting out loud: "Three, two, one—go!"

Lucas sprinted straight ahead for the line of trees. It took seconds for the light of the fire to blend into darkness—even the moonlight was muffled by the tops of the trees. His senses heightened as he became aware of his breath and the sound of his boots hitting the ground. Everything else around him was completely silent.

Hearing footsteps fast approaching, Jack backed away from the corner, worried they could smell the cigar smoke. He looked around frantically for a place to hide it as the thumping grew closer and louder. In a panic, he threw the cigar down and ran in the opposite direction.

As Lucas sped past the shed, a strange scent hung in the air, convincing him something was out there. From the rancid smell, he was certain it was a big hairy monster. He turned back toward the campfire, a good forty yards from the tree line, and quickened his pace into a full out sprint. Fueled by adrenaline, he began waving his hands in the air. "It's out there, it's a monster!" Lucas yelled, getting closer to the campfire light.

Ben heard him hollering and squinted out into the dark, laughing when he saw him retreating so soon. He laughed so loudly that he didn't hear Lucas's shouts, and stood over the fire, knocking some logs to the base to hasten the burn. He propped his arm up on the stick, giggling under his breath as he watched Lucas sprinting toward him. Suddenly, a flash of light streaked across his peripheral vision and a loud explosion rippled through the field, followed by two more blasts. It was so loud that Lucas dropped to the ground on his stomach, covering his head.

Watching in terror as the shed went up in flames, Ben fell onto his backside against the hay bale. For a few seconds he couldn't move. He sat there panting as he watched the shed crackle and burst. Planks of wood were blown out by the force of the explosion, and flaming shrapnel fell all around, igniting the dry grass and setting a small bundle of damp hay ablaze.

Lucas bear-crawled over to Ben, staying as low to the ground as possible. "Let's go! The hay is on fire, the field is going up! Let's go!" he screamed, shaking Ben by the shoulders. Ben just sat there, paralyzed by the horror of what he was watching. Lucas yanked Ben's arm, pulling him to his feet. They stumbled along, weaving out of the rapidly spreading fires, flames already beginning to cut off clear paths of escape.

Hearing Juniper's high-pitched squeal, he broke away from Lucas's grip. Guarding his eyes with his hand, he batted away embers that landed on his neck. He could see Juniper's front legs smacking the air, trying to break loose from the lead.

"Ben, you can't get to him!" Lucas shouted, watching his friend step closer to the growing flames.

24

The Angel Joshua

SARAH KNELT BESIDE THE CURLING river, letting the current flow over the tips of her fingers. Looking out over the rolling hills, their emerald surfaces dotted with wildflowers, saturated her senses. A herd of wild mustangs nibbled on wheatgrass near a few bison. The landscape was beyond beautiful, it was poetic—animals and people living in harmony, with color and life abounding in vitality. She opened her hand and sprinkled water droplets onto her face, letting one roll into the corner of her mouth. Glancing over at the path, she saw Joshua walking toward the ledge, his quiver high on his back. She could make it to him before he reached the edge if she ran, but teleporting was much more fun.

"Where you headed?" she asked, appearing just behind his shoulder.

Joshua looked up from the ground in amusement. "Where you been? You missed the action."

"Saw you from the creek over yonder. What did I miss?"

"Gabe is sitting this one out because he can't hit the broad side of a barn with both hands."

"So you got an assignment! What did it look like?"

His face hardened with concern, and she didn't like the way he bunched up his brows. "Fire, lots of fire. And that horse Jacob saved…

let's just say if I miss this shot, that horse is toast. Wish me luck."

"Good luck," she said quietly, feeling the heaviness he carried on his shoulders. She considered walking alongside him, but sometimes the journey to the edge required solitude. It was a time for reflection, a moment to focus on the mission, and she could tell the outcome of this assignment was uncertain.

*   *   *

"Juniper! Junip—" Ben fell forward, drawing his hands up from the hot ground, coughing from the smoke that stung his eyes. Clenching his eyes closed, he crawled along on his knees, feeling for the fence. Even though the fire was encroaching on him from all sides, all he could focus on were the bursts of high-pitched whinnying and growling. Ben began to cry—the heat, the smoke, and the thought of Juniper in danger overwhelmed him. Feeling his way along the ground, he continued crawling closer to Juniper's screams.

Jack dashed into the trees, huffing and puffing. He didn't notice the brambles he rushed into were a cluster of thorn bushes. The sharp needles dug into his clothes and his hair. When he tried to shake himself loose, the thorns only sank deeper. He tugged so hard that he lost his balance and fell backwards, tearing himself free. Heart pounding, feeling the waves of heat from the burning shed, he ran as fast as he could for home.

*   *   *

Ben's throat felt like it was closing; he tried calling out to Juniper but could only manage a raspy cough. His hands stung like the worst sunburn imaginable, and his head was beginning to feel heavy. Pulling himself along the ground, he took one last deep breath, then collapsed, unable to keep going. For a moment, Ben felt as though he were dreaming. He felt his upper body being lifted from the ground, and through blurry eyes, he saw the tops of his boots as he was pulled through the tall grass.

"Dang, you're heavier than you look," Lucas said, grunting and panting as they reached cooler ground.

*   *   *

Joshua was too focused on his task to enjoy the trip down to earth. As the ground came into view, he spotted a small patch of flat land that was blistering in patches of yellow and red. A horse was rearing in the air, encircled by a rapidly tightening ring of fire. The fence line was concealed by wafts of thick smoke and the field was a violent storm of heat and flames. Long strips of fire snaked around hay bales, blocking most of the walkable ground. Gauging the distance to the horse, his eyes caught sight of a clearing up on a hillside. This was easily the farthest distance he ever took a shot from, but it looked to be the only option of getting a clear line of sight.

Joshua stood sideways to the target. Reaching an arm over his shoulder, he pulled an arrow from the quiver, nocking it in the middle of the bowstring. Looking down the shaft of the arrow, he saw the horse was beginning to tire and accept its fate. Joshua took a deep breath and took aim at the spot where the post anchored the lead. He followed the arch of the lead, aiming at the joint on the fence where it went slack as the horse reared desperately. Seconds felt like hours as he focused in on the target, but the horse kept rearing, and soon he realized there wasn't enough time to wait for the perfect shot; he would have to time it perfectly. The arrow would have to make contact at the exact time the horse landed, and before it reared again. He stretched the bowstring tighter, slowed his breathing, and released it when he saw the horse's nose lift and the withers drop.

*   *   *

"We need to save him!" Ben cried, weakly grasping at Lucas, trying to break his grip.

Lucas released his hold, pulling Ben to his feet. "We can't, Ben, the ground is hot and covered in smoke. Where is the well?"

"Back here!" Ben called, trying to shake the fog from his head. "It's this way, there's a bucket inside we can fill."

"Who's that?" Lucas asked, pointing out toward the barn.

Squinting through the smoke, Ben saw two men, each carrying pails, running toward the fence by the campfire.

*   *   *

"I'm going around this side," Charles hollered, disappearing behind a thick wall of white haze. The heat singed his forehead and floating embers stung his bare skin. He crossed a smoldering patch of grass, jumping across scorched strands of hay and running along a clear path of dirt to approach the fence from inside the pasture. The tightness in his chest gripped his airway and the smoke was getting too thick to pass through. He heard another bellowing squeal—and then nothing. The horse's screams fell silent. Charles doubled over in a coughing fit and set the pails of water down, turning around to retrace his steps.

*   *   *

Ben dropped to the ground, pulled his legs under his chin, and began to weep. "I don't hear him anymore, Lucas. I can't hear him," he sobbed.

Lucas sat on the ground beside him and put an arm around his shoulder, feeling his body tremble uncontrollably.

Joshua lowered the bow to his side and took a step back, hearing a crunch under his boot. Lifting his foot, he found a pocket watch with a shattered glass face. Holding it in his hand, he was surprised to see the hand still clicking forward. A moment later, a warm light descended around him, and he dropped the watch where he found it.

*   *   *

The reflection of headlights bounced around the farm's buildings as cars and trucks lined the road, making way for a fire engine that rolled in front of the main barn. The lights were so bright that they lit up the path all the way to the back barn.

"Ben, look!" Lucas said, shaking his shoulders and pointing to the hillside. "Look, over there! Do you see him? He's on the hill!" Lucas jumped to his feet, reaching down for Ben's arm, "Do you see him?!"

"That's him!" Ben said, looking toward the hillside.

They took off running, calling out to Juniper and keeping their eyes on the silhouette in the distance. The farther they ran, the colder the air became, and the ground cooled their feet. Ben called out again. "Juniper, here boy!"

Juniper stood perfectly still as they ran up. Steam seemed to rise from the bottom of his hooves, casting an eerie mist into the chilled air.

"You think he's burned?" Lucas asked, his voice shaky and soft.

They could smell burnt hair and were sure he had been injured. There was something like vapor rising off his body and his breathing was rough. The hair on his tail was singed, leaving it shorter and ending in a ball of matted hair.

Ben reached over for the short piece of lead that hung from the bridle and held it up. The end was cut cleanly in half.

"Is he ok?" Lucas asked, still standing at a distance.

"I can't tell. He doesn't want to move much."

Lucas flinched when he heard movement behind him. His father, along with Mr. Collins and a few other men, quickly approached out of the darkness.

"You boys alright?" Charles asked.

"We're fine, but the horse might be hurt," Lucas said.

"What happened? Did this start with the campfire?"

"No father," Lucas said. "We were telling stories and eating marshmallows, then I ran to the trees on a dare. But something didn't smell right, so I ran back. That's when we heard the booms and the shed exploded, catching the grass and hay on fire. We never even went near the shed!" Lucas pleaded, hoping the men believed him. "Ben tried to free the horse, but we couldn't see, and I dragged him out of the grass. We thought the horse was going to die; he was kicking his legs up because he couldn't get free. Then we found him back here, but he looks like he got burned!"

Charles walked around Juniper, knowing it would be a wait-and-see situation before they knew the extent of it.

"You think he's going to be alright?" Ben asked.

"I'll call Taylor in the morning. I am worried about his hooves. I'll put down some wet blankets for his stall."

"Wow, Ben, check that out!" Lucas said, looking at a huge spout of water shooting across the field. The boys ran out to the path, watching the firemen pull a large hose into the field beside the shed. "They're going to blast it with water—watch!"

They were relieved to see the fire put out. The ground was still smoking in some patches, but mostly it was steam billowing up from the water soaking the grass. They watched as men carried pails through the field, pouring them over the ground. A small section of fence was burned, and the shed was lost, but there was no other damage they could see.

"Probably won't be able to have another campfire for a while, but I bet it's in the morning paper!" Lucas said.

Ben looked over at his friend. "Thanks for saving me. Had you not dragged me out of it, I probably would have burned up!"

"Let's not tell them about that—we'll never get to have a campfire again."

*　　*　　*

After Lucas left with his father, Charles stared out into the field. "You say it just exploded with loud pops?"

"It did, we saw the whole thing! Lucas was running back because he was too scared to make it to the trees in the dark, and when he got close to the campfire, the shed caught fire and then it spread across the field. Once a hay bale went up, all the grass started to burn, real fast!"

"That hay was wet; caught fire like a matchstick. I know you want to stay with the horse, but we need to know what caused the fire, and I don't think you should be out here by yourself until we investigate. Go on to the house while I talk with the firemen."

Ben walked to the house, watching firemen roll up the hose after having doused the smoldering shed. Men were still pouring buckets of water over the grass, filling the hole they'd dug for the campfire—a soggy reminder of how the night's fun turned into a nightmare.

*   *   *

Charles waved down Elliot and Paul, who were watching the ground where the shed had stood to make sure nothing reignited.

"Suppose there's nothin' more to do till mornin' comes," Elliot said. "Can't see a daggum thing. Let's go see what Mr. C wants."

Paul kept glancing over his shoulder. "I just don't get it. Without a flame, there's nothing that would make those oil barrels burn. There had to be something to ignite it."

Elliot noticed a police car pulled in behind the fire truck. "That's Patrick right there. He'll be fixin' to investigate soon as daylight breaks tomorrow."

"You boys mind soaking some blankets? I think the horse could use them," Charles said. "I'll need to give some statements for the report."

On their walk back to the barn, Paul kept agonizing over the cause of the explosion. "I have a hard time believing the containers just popped on their own. The shed was well ventilated—hell, it was missing a plank in the corner. Mice and everything got through, and the gas cans and oil were sealed and anchored. It's not possible they went up without a heat source." He handed Elliot a large blanket from a storage box and threw another over his shoulder.

"Sure hope Juniper's gonna to be alright," Elliot said. "It'd be a real shame if somethin' happened to him."

Charles thanked everyone for their help and started down the path to the barn to help Paul and Elliot, gauging the distance from the campfire to the burned shed. The distance was too great for a spark from the fire to travel and ignite the shed, so he continued to ponder what could have happened. The scent of smoke wafted through the air until he passed the main barn, noticing a strange glow in the sky beyond the hillside. It reminded him of the northern lights, the way the sky flickered and twinkled.

25

JACK SPRINTED DOWN THE ROW of maple trees, hiding behind the large trunks every time the glow of headlights swept past. He untied his jacket from his waist and pulled it on, slipping his hands into the pockets to find comfort in the feel of the pocket watch. His breath quickened—it wasn't there. Anxiety turned to full-blown panic as he frantically checked his pants pockets. He shook them, turned them inside out. Still nothing. His heart raced as he looked out into the woods in despair, knowing it would be impossible to retrace his steps without a lantern.

He crossed the road and ran up to his house, slowing down when he noticed the back door was open. Looking from side to side, he quietly crept toward the kitchen to retrieve the lantern from under the sink when he heard a gurgled groan from the living room. Looking around the corner, he saw his father's arm hanging over the side of the sofa. An empty bottle of booze rested against his limp fingers. He hurried past into the kitchen, where his mother was sitting at the table holding a bloodstained rag against the side of her face. Jack felt sick to his stomach, the air full of cigar smoke, reminding him of the experimental drags leading up to the fire. The panic that had subsided on the way home roared back to life.

"You best be getting up to bed now," his mother said between sniffles.

"I need to get my lantern. I dropped something in the woods and need to find it," he said, not taking his eyes off the crimson rag. "That looks bad, Mother."

She pressed it tighter to her skin to hide the wound. "It will be fine. Don't worry about me, just get your lantern and come back quickly. It's getting very late."

As he walked to the sink to open the cabinet underneath, he saw more rags sitting at the bottom of the basin, all soaked with his mother's blood. She turned around in her chair, regretting leaving them out where he could see them. She looked away when he turned back toward her, unable to bear the sadness in his eyes. Thinking desperately of something to redirect his thoughts, she set her arm over the back of the chair. "Do you happen to know what all the ruckus was tonight? I saw a fire truck go by and lots of cars."

Jack turned away, crouching at the cabinet, and pulled out the lantern. "I don't know, must have been something in town. I'll be back soon," he said, rushing out the side door.

*   *   *

"You think he'll head on inside?" Elliot asked.

Paul lifted his cap, scratching his head with the brim. "Don't know, but I would think he's got instincts to do what he needs to do. Probably why he's standing out there in the open—to catch that stiff breeze."

"You boys got the blankets down?" Charles asked.

"All down boss, trying to coax him over," Elliot said.

"He'll go inside when he's ready. Horses want to be in their barns. That's why you draw the doors shut if a fire breaks out; they'll run back into it, even if it's on fire. If he does make it in, those blankets will help."

"You think he's gonna be alright? He looks pretty spooked." Elliot asked.

"I reckon if I were in the middle of a barbecue, I'd probably end up with some sauce on my britches, too. I don't know how much smoke he took in; his respiratory tract could be mighty rigid right now. Suppose that's why he's facing the breeze—that and to cool his heels."

*   *   *

Claire twisted a rag over the basin, handing it to Ben. "I'll get a band-aid for your elbow, then I want you to get into bed. I have a feeling it will be an early morning around here and you might have to tell the story of what happened to Mr. Kincaid so he can investigate. But don't be nervous about that—you didn't do anything wrong. I'm just thankful you two weren't hurt."

After sending Ben off to bed, she fixed a cup of peppermint tea, folded a shawl around her shoulders, and had a seat by the fire. Charles hung his coat on the post and slid into his slippers, taking a seat in the chair beside the window. "Don't feel much like looking at the fire tonight."

"I can't say I blame you. Ben told me what happened. Did Peter talk to you?"

"He did. He's coming by in the morning to take a look around."

Sensing he didn't feel much like talking, she relaxed into the chair and quietly sipped her tea.

"Something about this doesn't sit right with me," Charles said, as if to himself. We've stored the same equipment, the same way all these years and never had any issues. But now when the boys have themselves a campfire all hell breaks loose?"

She raised her cup, looking at him over the rim as he stared out into the night.

*   *   *

Ben rested his head against his pillow and shimmied under the covers. His mind swirled with worry as he wondered how Juniper was doing. He could hear Charles talking to Claire downstairs. Nothing about his voice seemed alarming, and everything was quiet. Ben turned to his side and stared out the window. An hour passed, and he was still awake. The full moon poured light through his window like a spotlight. Tossing and turning with his thoughts, he pushed the covers off, pulled his dirty clothes from the hamper, and crept down the hall. Keeping close to the wall, he stepped quietly down the stairs.

The air was chilly and the stench of burnt wood hung heavily in the air. He covered his mouth to muffle a cough, and as he approached the barn, heard Buck pawing from the inside. The crickets, normally alive with song, were quiet, likely busy finding ground cover in the woods. By the time he reached the main barn, the air was clear. Out of the corner of his eye, he saw a soft glow along the edge of the trees where Lucas had turned around to run back to the campfire. The light barely filtered through the cover of thickets, and he wondered if Paul or Elliot might be out there looking around.

As the light approached the clearing, a figure emerged, holding the light low to the ground and moving slowly from side to side.

Even in the dark, Ben could tell the figure didn't have a man-sized build—it was someone close to his stature, but a bit more filled out. The light lifted close enough to the silhouette to catch the dark waves of hair blowing sideways. A wave of chills rolled down his body when he realized it was Jack Larson. He thought about running back to the house, but his curiosity about what he was up to was heightened. Dropping to the ground, he crawled behind the wheel of the hay wagon, peeking through the wooden spokes with his hands tightly gripping the rim. He watched Jack hover over the ground, pacing back and forth, sifting through the planks and rubble. Hearing a shout, he saw the lantern fall lopsidedly to the ground. "Ouch, ouch!" Jack hollered, waving his hands at his sides, and using his boot to set the lantern upright.

Ben seized the moment to move closer to Jack, but as he did, a piece of burnt wood cracked under his foot.

Hearing movement behind him, Jack turned and stared straight at Ben.

Taking a couple steps forward, Ben stood in full view, unafraid. Without hesitation, he met the eyes of the boy who had struck him with stones, laughed in his face, and punched him at the store. He stepped forward again. He saw Jack clearly and waited.

Jack came closer, walking with a slight limp.

"Why are you here, Jack?"

He didn't answer, but kept walking in his direction, looking at the ground.

Ben's muscles tensed up and without thinking, he dropped one foot back and balled up his fist, just like Charles showed him in the car that day.

Jack took a few more steps, then stopped and looked just past Ben's shoulder off into the distance. Ben didn't turn away; he kept his eyes on him, noticing Jack's mouth beginning to move as he continued to stare.

Jack was awestruck by the horse's appearance. Surrounded by a ghostly mist, it stood perfectly still, like an apparition in the darkness. Suddenly and unexpectedly, he felt the gravity of what he had done, and all the shame and hurt he felt came out in a flood of tears as he dropped to his knees.

Ben felt his hand relax and took another cautious step, then another. Jack's shoulders shook with sobs as he wiped his face and sat down, pulling his knees up to his chin. Ben stood next to the lantern, not knowing what to think. He followed Jack's gaze, turning to look over his shoulder, seeing Juniper standing on the path at the edge of the grass.

"I didn't mean to do it! It was an accident," Jack said, wiping his eyes. "It was an accident!"

"You started the fire?"

Jack hung his head between his knees. "I took my father's cigar into the woods, then saw you and Lucas around the campfire. He was my friend first, you know! I had friends—back home in New York. Suppose you're going to snitch and tell everyone I did it, huh?"

Ben looked around the field, then looked at Jack. "How did it catch fire?"

"I heard you guys talking and ran behind the shed so I could hear, then I heard footsteps running up and figured you saw me. I panicked and threw the cigar down so you wouldn't know where I was, then ran off to that hill over there."

"Is that why you don't like me? You miss your friends?"

Jack shrugged. "I don't know, my father is always angry. Guess I'm turning out just like him. It wasn't always this way; we were happy in New York. I had a best friend. His name is Oliver. We were together every day until my father moved us out here, in the middle of nowhere."

Ben sat down cross-legged, snapping a blade of grass and twisting it around his finger. "My parents died. My father died right over there," he said, pointing to the paddock. "During the big storm, there was a tornado. Something broke loose and hit him. Then my mother died a short while ago from a bad flu. I don't know what it's like to have a mean father, but I know what it's like not to have one."

"I overheard my father say mean things about this place. That didn't help."

Ben looked down at his finger, unwinding the blade of grass.

Jack breathed a regretful sigh. "I'm sorry for punching you that day, I was trying to act tough in front of my old man, thinking he would ease up on the switch."

"What's a switch?"

Jack unzipped his jacket, lifting the bottom of his shirt. "He goes heavy on the bottle, then looks for something to hit on. Most of the time it's me, or my mother. One time it was our dog, Scooter. He's really going to let me have it when he finds out what happened here."

"What were you looking for?"

"A pocket watch, it must have fallen out somewhere when I ran."

"I'll help you look for it, then we'll figure out what to tell Mr. Charles so you won't get into trouble."

As they searched together, they shared more stories. Jack told him about his grandfather in New York and how different it was living in a big city, and Ben shared stories about the farm and jumping with Juniper.

"How are you out here in the middle of the night?" Jack asked. "Sneaking out of my house is like escaping from Newgate Prison."

"I couldn't fall asleep. I just walk really quietly, making sure not to step on the creaky boards going down the steps—and what's Newgate Prison?"

"A place where they send bad people in New York, looks creepy too."

After an hour or so, they gave up the search. Ben promised to look for it in the morning before anyone got up.

"You turned out different than I thought," Jack said, holding out his hand.

Ben smiled at him and shook his hand. "You did, too," he said, and watched Jack disappear into the night.

When he turned around, Juniper was at the edge of the path. He reached for the lead, unfastened the bridle, and coaxed Juniper to follow as he led him to the barn. He knelt at the edge of the blankets, sinking his palms into the moist fabric as he held his hands to Juniper's nostrils. Slowly walking backwards into the stall, he sat down against the wall, watching the corner. A few minutes later, Juniper came to the door sniffing at the ground, pushing the blanket against his face and making a soft chuffing sound. With each cautious step, Juniper's skin twitched and fluttered, until finally he folded his front legs and rolled onto his side in a loud huff. Ben sat against the wall, pulling straw over his legs for warmth, and thought about his night with Jack. Remembering the marks on Jack's side, he shivered and whispered a prayer that he wouldn't be hurt anymore.

26

Charles was awakened by voices downstairs, followed by a knock on the door which Buck responded to by barking. Quickly getting dressed, he came down the stairs to see Peter and Patrick on the porch.

"Good morning, hope we're not too early. We're going to start looking around if that's alright," Patrick said.

"Let me get my boots. I'll meet you out there."

Carl pulled in just as they started to spread out. Getting out of the car, he fastened his holster belt, tipping the barrel of his pistol into the socket as he headed out toward the woods. Buck followed close behind him, sniffing along the ground, shaking his head in sneezing fits. "Grounds still charred, you buffoon," Carl said, shaking his head at the clumsy pup.

*　　*　　*

Ben arched his back, shivering from the moisture that crept up his pant legs as he stretched his arms over his head, looking up at the backside of Juniper. He didn't see any obvious lacerations or burns anywhere on Juniper's legs, only two small patches of darkened skin on his cannon and shoulder. His tail had been singed, leaving a frayed wad of matted hair, but his breathing was steady, and he'd even drank most of the water in the trough. Ben pulled a feed bucket off the hook and opened the barn door. Across the field, he saw several men walking around, with Carl heading down the tree line.

Paul took to the perimeter opposite Carl and pushed his way through a cluster of thick branches. A sharp thorn scraped along the backside of his hand, and when he looked down, he noticed a small piece of fabric stuck on a thorny branch. He pulled it free and started heading across the field in Carl's direction. As he walked, he noticed broken branches and a pile of flattened leaves. He brushed his boots along the surface when something shimmered beneath the ground cover. Stooping down, fanning the leaves away, he uncovered Bernie's pocket watch; the thick glass face splintered with cracks.

*   *   *

Elliot dug around the shed with a shovel, tossing scoops of ash and debris over his shoulder. As he drove the blade in for another scoop, he noticed something in the mound of dirt—a cigar stub. He put it to his nose and inhaled. It hadn't been long since it was lit, he thought; the scent was still ripe on the tip. He dropped it into his pocket. In the distance, he heard Paul shouting from the tree line, waving his hand in the air.

*   *   *

Hearing the shouts, Ben dropped the bucket, watching the men hurry toward the tree line, and started to worry when he saw Paul standing over the spot where Jack said he ran to hide.

Paul kept yelling out the name "Larson," followed by every curse word imaginable. Ben started to breathe heavily, wondering if he should tell them what he knew, and that it was an accident.

When Elliot ran up to Paul, he could see the unhinged wild look in his eyes. His face was as red as a turkey's wattle. "It's Larson! That no good, shit-for-brains Larson!" he yelled, holding out his hand with the watch in his grip, waving it in front of everyone. "His son swiped it from the counter! One of them started the fire!"

"Cool down, Paul, you're going to give yourself a heart attack," Charles said. "We need to think this through. We ain't found anything close to where the fire started. That could have been laying out here for months.

Might mean he took it, but it doesn't connect him with burning the shed down. We need to keep our heads about us now."

Elliot reached into his shirt pocket and pulled out the cigar stub. "I found somethin', and it's fresh. Take a look at the label."

Paul snatched it from his hand. "Son of a bitch! Says right here on the label: New York City! Son of a bitch; it was Larson, I knew it!" Paul's face was red as he stomped off toward his truck. "I'm gonna get that smug prick!" he shouted.

Elliot's eyes darted around at the men, unsure what to do.

"We better go after him," Charles said, "this could turn sour real quick."

Carl's limp slowed him as he crossed the field, meeting Paul halfway to his truck. "What's all the noise about? Heard your hollerin' an acre away."

Paul held the watch in front of Carl's face, then showed him the cigar butt between his fingers before throwing it to the ground.

Carl watched the stub of the cigar roll across the dirt and unsnapped the buckle around his holster, following behind him.

"Does he have a gun?" Patrick asked.

"If that one don't, you can bet your ass the other one does," Charles answered.

By the time Ben reached the middle of the field, the men were already pulling out of the driveway. He ran as fast he could, yelling out into the wind, "Wait, stop!" He ran until his legs burned, the soles of his boots slapping the ground as he ran along the dirt, huffing and puffing and pumping his arms. "Wait, wait!"

He ran harder, losing sight of the back of Elliot's truck as it disappeared over the hill. He lowered his face to shield himself from the dust cloud rolling over the road. Suddenly, a surge of energy came over him, and he ran even faster.

"Paul, wait," Patrick called, catching up to him. "Let Peter and I go to the door first; we're the law and I don't want to book you for illegal entry."

Paul batted his hand off his arm. "That'll be the damned day, Patrick."

Carl held out his arm across Paul's chest to slow him down. "We can't go in there guns a blazin'. Let's be smart about this. One way or the other, his ass is grass."

Patrick and Peter took the lead and approached the porch, unsnapping their holsters. When Patrick pressed an ear to the door, he heard screams from inside. He motioned for Peter and drew his gun.

Paul looked at Charles, waving his hand for him to fall back behind him.

Peter drove his shoulder into the door, cracking the frame and forcing the door open.

"Police, police!" Patrick shouted, finding Jack huddled in the corner with his hands over his ears, red and purple marks all down his arms and legs. The sound of quick footsteps came barreling up the porch.

"Stop, he didn't mean it!" Ben shouted, pushing his way past the men, breaking the hold Paul had on the back of his shirt. "Let me go, he didn't mean it!" he yelled, running over to Jack, holding his head down with his arms around him.

Patrick and Peter stayed close to the wall, hearing shouting from the kitchen. "Police, come out where we can see you!" Peter shouted.

Carl barreled into the kitchen. Holding his revolver at his side, he pulled the hammer back when he saw Clint holding a woman by the back of the hair, face down in a basin full of water. Her feet were bloodied from a broken bottle on the floor.

"Step away and put your hands up!" Peter shouted. While Clint was distracted, Patrick circled behind him and broke Clint's hold with a firm shove, sending him across the floor against the table. Peter and Paul each grabbed an arm, holding them at his back while Patrick tightened handcuffs around his wrists and pulled him upright, pushing him to the door.

Carl held the revolver against Clint's nose with a smirk. "Told ya it wouldn't end well if I ever showed up again."

Elliot and Charles reached for Jack's mother, trying to catch her before she slid down to the floor, shaking and gasping for air. They covered her up with their jackets and gathered her wet hair from around her face, revealing deep purple marks around her neck.

Charles waved Paul over, "Go get Frank, hurry!"

Paul turned around and went back through the entryway. The boys were huddled together in the corner. "You two, come with me."

Jack stood up, limping as he tried to walk, leaning on Ben's shoulder.

"You hurt, son?" Paul asked.

"It hurts to walk," Jack said, looking down at his leg.

Paul bent down and scooped him up, his long legs dangling from his arms.

*   *   *

Millie was tidying up the waiting area when Paul, carrying a large boy, and Ben came through the door. Paul immediately called for Frank, pulling a rolling cot from the closet.

"His leg hurts and he's got some marks on his arms," Paul said.

Frank rounded the corner, cleaning his glasses, and was startled to see Paul and the boys.

"We need you at Larson's house. I'll drive," Paul said, reaching for the door.

Frank grabbed his bag and overcoat and closed the door behind them. "What happened?"

"Larson roughed up the kid and his wife. She ain't faring too good."

Frank threw his bag onto the rear seat and shut the door. "Where's this Larson fella?"

"Coming up the road here, in the back of Kincaid's car." Patrick slowed down, waving his arm out the window, and stopped next to Paul.

"I got Frank here with me, we're heading there now."

Patrick lifted his hand and drove off to the station with Clint handcuffed in the backseat.

"Son of a bitch!" Paul yelled through the window at Larson.

Frank felt like he was witnessing a true crime radio drama. "You boys had quite a morning so far," he said, not knowing quite what to make of the scene.

"You have no idea."

The men were standing around the porch when they arrived. Paul led Frank to the corner of the kitchen where Jack's mother was seated at the table. Leaving the doctor to tend to her, he stepped outside.

"Looks like he was fixin' to make some riding equipment," Charles said, looking out over the yard at one of the buildings. "There's a saddle cast sitting over there next to all those empty bottles."

"He ain't sticking around these parts, not if he has any sense. He'll be gone if he ever gets out of jail," Paul said, still shaking from anger. "Just being here gives me the heebie-jeebies."

"I got that same feelin' every time I drove by on my route home," Carl said. "That boy would be sittin' right here on these steps most days. Never dreamed it was like this though. To be honest, I had him figured to be the problem."

"Makes you wonder why he gave Ben such a hard time," Elliot said.

"I reckon it got so bad, he went looking for someone to take it out on," Charles said. "And what in the Sam Hill got into Ben… The way he ran in like he did, darn near ran me over!"

"There's more to this story," Paul said. "It'll all air out once the dust settles."

About thirty minutes later, Frank stepped out onto the porch. He tried to pull the door closed behind him, but it just toppled through the broken doorframe.

"That was like that when we found it," Carl said with a smirk.

Frank looked down the bridge of his nose at the men chuckling amongst themselves, then cleared his throat. "She's going to be fine. I bandaged some lacerations and fashioned a splint for her arm. I'll be reporting this to Judge Lambert personally, and recommend she speak to him herself to have this documented. Along with all the other times this happened."

Paul looked around, rubbing his shoulders with his hands. "Let's go. I don't want to be here."

*   *   *

Millie was relieved Jack's leg wasn't broken. "You have a sprained ankle. It should heal up nicely. Just keep this gauze wrapped tightly and use these crutches for a week or two, alright, sweetie?"

Jack nodded, looking at the brown wrap, and couldn't help but smile when he saw a roll of stickers behind her.

"You like those?"

"Yeah, I like frogs," Jack said. "My grandfather has a big pond at his house with lots and lots of frogs. They sit on top of lily pads and belch all night."

Millie and Ben laughed. "I'll make sure to send you home with some after we get these wounds cleaned up."

Paul had a seat in the lobby while Frank hung up his coat and disappeared around the corner.

"How's the patient?" Frank asked, peeking around the door.

"He's going to be just fine. We're rounding third base—a few more bandages to go then we're home free," she said, giving Jack a wink.

Frank gave Ben a tap on the back, then walked over to Jack's bedside. "Your mother is going to be alright, Jack. She's resting now."

Jack smiled, then turned his head to the side. "Thanks, Ben," he whispered.

Ben grinned, his red lips wrapped around a lollipop as he twirled it in his mouth. Reaching into his pocket, he pulled out another and held it up. "Grabbed a grape one for you," he said.

Jack looked up at the ceiling, a grin spreading across his face. Grapes were his favorite.

*   *   *

On the ride back, Ben and Jack told Paul everything. Jack confessed to accidentally starting the fire and trying to hide the evidence. And when he explained why he stole the watch from the counter, Paul couldn't help but forget the incident all together. Paul even offered him a job at the store if he ever wanted someplace to go after school. When they drove by the farm, Tom Taylor's truck was in the drive. "That's Mr. Taylor!" Ben said.

For some reason, Paul felt confident the horse would be fine. He only wished he were as certain about the fate of Jack and his mother.

Ben grabbed the crutches, tucking them under Jack's arms. "Maybe when you feel better, we can make a campfire. We'll get Lucas and some marshmallows and hot dogs and tell stories all night."

"That would be fun," Jack said, "thanks again Ben, and thanks Mr. Paul."

*　　*　　*

Charles fidgeted, wringing his hands as he glanced at Tom, anxiously watching his face for any hints about the horse's condition.

"I don't hear any signs of respiratory obstruction, and his hooves look good. He may have weakened the outer wall on the right one, but the line and bar are intact, and the angle is clean. No residue on the bulb, either. They look healthy to me, and I've seen my fair share. Other than that knotty looking tail and some singed hair near the cannon and shoulder, I'd say he once again defied all odds."

Charles gave a deep sigh of relief. "That's good news, Tom! Thanks for making the trip out here to look him over."

"My pleasure, just glad nobody got hurt last night. Man, what a story!"

"You aren't kidding—we sure do keep it lively around here."

27

One week later…

Patrick opened the cell, staring at the haggard figure sitting on the cot. "Time to face the music, Larson." Clint peered at Patrick with cold, hateful eyes, but kept his mouth shut as the handcuffs were slapped around his wrists. Patrick led him down two corridors into a humble courtroom, and sat him down behind a table, facing the judge's stand. Judge Bruce Lambert came through a door, looking across the room at Clint, slouched in the chair. He looked over some papers and pushed his glasses against the bridge of his nose, observing Clint's demeanor.

"Mr. Larson, you have a problem," Lambert said, his booming voice echoing through the room. "The way it works in these parts is simple: you got two choices. Either get real comfortable sitting behind bars, or make sure we never see your sorry face in this county again. So tell me… what's it gonna be?"

*   *   *

Ben was reaching through the vines to pick up the baseball that rolled through his legs when the school wagon passed.

Jack and Lucas waved at him. "Last day of school!" Jack hollered.

Ben waved back at them, then threw the ball to Elliot. "You think we can jump today?"

Elliot scratched his hairline with his cap. "I reckon we could give it a go. Taylor said Juniper would be the one to tell us if he can or can't."

"Yes!" Ben shouted, tossing his mitt in the air.

"You know," Elliot said, "there's lots of different types of ridin'."

"Like what?"

"Well, there's Western ridin', cross-country, racin'—all different styles."

"I like jumping. And I think we were getting pretty good!"

Elliot took his hat off and smacked it against his leg. "Guess we're jumpin' then!

*   *   *

Harold and Charles watched them run courses for most of the afternoon. As they watched the pair soar gracefully over the posts, they discussed the possibility of letting him compete. They both agreed that the boy showed real promise, but that wasn't enough. They needed to convince Carl.

"There he is," Charles said, spotting Carl working with some horses near the paddock. "Let's go talk to him, though I've got an inkling about the kind of response we'll get out of him," Charles said.

Carl watched them amble over from the corner of his eye. "Lord sakes, why do I feel a headache comin' on…" Leaning over the fence, he looked over at them, growing impatient waiting for one of them to say something. "You might as well come out with it. Go ahead—ask me if I'll drop real business to fart around with that jackrabbit over there."

Harold chuckled, but looking at Carl's stoic expression, his smile quickly faded. "That isn't quite how we were going to word it."

"You were going to dress it up, make it sound not so idiotic, I know."

Charles shot Harold a sly wink before sauntering up to Carl and draping an arm around his shoulder. "This might seem like a cat circus, but jumping holds the second biggest purse size across all riding disciplines, averaging close to five thousand but going up to fifteen. Not to mention all the prizes! Why, I heard of a third-place win on the East Coast of five hundred dollars in prime rib steaks. For third place! More importantly, the boy loves it, and the horse is pretty good at it, too. This might be something special, and you know how to groom riders. He needs that knowledge you got floating around in that head of yours."

"You say a fella got five hundred dollars in steak?"

"Sure did, got it delivered to his house every month for a year I think."

Carl pursed his lips and shook his finger at him. "Just one lesson, then we'll see what we're workin' with."

Charles pulled his arm back. "I knew you'd come around." Charles tipped his hat goodbye, walking away before Carl had a chance to change his mind.

"What just happened?" Harold asked, catching up with Charles.

"You just got to know how to talk to him. Throw food into the conversation and make it seem like his idea—works every time."

*　　*　　*

After filling the feed trough, Ben dusted his hands off, then raced off to follow Elliot down the driveway.

"Good practice today. He took those combinations like nothin' I'd ever seen before; figure I'll build out more fencing. Paul just took a delivery and has some extra pallets—let's go grab some."

When they got to the road, a long wagon with a high canopy rolled by.

"That's a long wagon!" Ben said.

"Yep, must be carting around some type of freight, probably headed for the train station."

*　　*　　*

After stacking seed for a couple hours, Paul sat down to take a break, drinking a soda while watching Daniel's crew lift plywood sheets to finish the roof.

"The market's comin' together. Look there—even got the sign painted!" Elliot said.

Ben hopped out of the truck, brushing his hand over the carved letters.

"Looks good, don't it?" Elliot said.

Paul tossed his soda can, pointing to the awning. "Even got Mrs. C's corner set up inside for her pies; everyone's waiting for the finishing touches."

"Guess you'll be trading in that old, tired cap for one of them straw ones like Carl likes to wear," Elliot said. "Should get yourself some overalls too."

Paul took his cap off, shook off some dust, and set it back on his head. "Give me thirty more years."

"There's Jack!" Ben said, pointing at a car with a flat-top canopy.

The driver got out and opened the rear door. Jack's mother stepped out, wearing a bright yellow dress, wide-brimmed hat, and sunglasses.

Ben ran up to Jack. "You don't have crutches anymore!"

"I can run now—doesn't hurt at all!" Jack said, shaking his foot.

Ben looked down at Jack's slick sneakers. "I always liked your shoes, don't see them kind around here."

Jack looked up at his mother. "You think I can send Ben a pair when we get there?"

"Sure, we can," she said, lifting her glasses from her face with a smile.

Ben looked over his shoulder at Paul and Elliot, then back to Jack. "What do you mean? Where are you going?"

"We're moving back to New York! We're gonna stay with my grandfather. I get to see my friends and go back to school in the fall, my old school! I'll write to you once a week. We can be pen pals; you can tell me all about the farm and jumping and I'll tell you stories from the city!"

Ben tried his best to force a smile. "I'm happy you get to see your grandfather and friends again. And I'll write you back, I promise."

Jack's mother placed a small box, wrapped in brown paper and tied with a shiny gold ribbon, into Jack's hand.

"This is for you, Mr. Paul," Jack said and handed him the box.

He turned the decorated cube around in his hand and gave it a shake, his curiosity sparked. "What's this?"

"Open it!"

Untying the ribbon, he pulled a small brown leather case from the wrapping.

"Looks fancy!" Elliot added, leaning over his shoulder for a peek.

He opened the box, taking out a blue velvet pouch. Out dropped a gold Waltham pocket watch, with an engraved frame and a double sunk dial. He cradled it in his palm, looking over at Jack.

"I know it can't replace the one I stole," Jack said, guilt etched across his face.

Paul shifted his feet, his heart swelling with gratitude. He reached into his pocket, pulled out Bernie's watch, and handed it to Jack. "It belonged to the owner of this place; his name was Bernie. He raised me when my father passed. The face is busted, but it can be fixed; I found it in the woods."

"Gee, thanks Mr. Paul!" Jack said with a wide smile.

His mother reached for Paul's hand. "Thank you for everything. I'm Elizabeth Larson, and in three weeks, I'll be Elizabeth Rockwood again."

Paul felt his face flush and his shirt collar felt tighter. Her eyes were emerald green and her skin was pale with a few freckles around her nose and cheeks. He was distracted by a few loose waves of silky auburn hair peeking out behind her hat, falling in soft curls down her shoulders.

Paul stood stiff like a statue. Feeling the tension, Elliot coughed into his elbow, gave Paul a discreet nudge, and excused himself.

"It's very nice to meet you. I, I… don't remember ever seeing your, your… face," Paul stuttered.

Elliot rolled his eyes, trying not to laugh and walked over to the boys, giving Paul space to embarrass himself some more. "You guys want to head inside? There's a full cookie jar," he said, following behind them into the store, fighting the urge to peek out the window.

Elizabeth brushed a stray strand of hair from her face. "During our short time here, I managed to keep a low profile. You can imagine why," she said with a cool demeanor.

Paul was charmed by the way she spoke. It was rare to meet a lady with such poise, sophistication, and extraordinary beauty. "So, you're leaving now, for New York?"

"We are. Our luggage was just taken to the train station, and we'll be on our way shortly."

Paul nodded while he thought of something to say to stall their departure, looking down at the watch. "This was so generous and thoughtful. Thank you."

"He really felt awful about the situation and wanted to make it right. It was all his idea, I can assure you."

"I sure do appreciate it; I'll carry it with me always."

Pulling her glasses down and adjusting her hat, she noticed the driver checking the time. "I suppose we best be going; it was a pleasure to meet you Paul," she said, holding out her hand.

He looked at her slender fingers wrapped around his hand, not wanting to let go. "This might seem a little forward, and I feel ridiculous asking, having just met you… but would you consider giving me your address? I would like to write you. To check on you and Jack, make sure you're doing fine."

She giggled, trying not to notice his nervousness while feeling butterflies of her own, rather taken by his handsome, rugged face. She felt entranced by the intensity of his kind eyes as he waited for her reply. She felt the pockets in her skirt. "I don't seem to have anything to write on with me. But here, take this," she said, handing him a chocolate bar.

He stared at the shiny blue wrapping, turning it over in his hand. "I remember seeing this same wrapper, I found it in the bucket by the door one day. There doesn't seem to be any place to write an address though— I'll step inside for some paper."

She laughed again, this time out loud. Her full, happy laugh rang out, and Paul thought it was the best sound he had ever heard. She reached out, flipping it over in his hand, pointing to the small print on the back. "There, in the corner. You can write to that address."

He looked closer at the small print, holding it up to his face. "Rockwood Confections," he read aloud, looking back at her with surprise. "Elizabeth Rockwood," he said with a smile.

"Henry Rockwood is my father—Jack's grandfather. He's made an empire off his sweet tooth."

The door swung open, and Jack and Ben came running out. "I have a pocket full of cookies, Mother!"

"Well, that's a relief. I just gave our last chocolate bar away."

*   *   *

"You fixin' to eat that?" Elliot said, eyeing the bar in Paul's hand. "I skipped lunch today and got a rumble in my stomach."

"Not if it's the last thing in the cupboard after the apocalypse."

"What are you smirking about?" Elliot asked, "'Cause, I know you didn't impress her that much with all the stuttering you were doing."

Paul looked at the address again, then tucked the bar in his pocket, pulling out his gloves with a grin, unable to stop the smile from spreading across his lips as he walked across the lot.

"Paul," Elliot called, "Paul, what did I miss, Paul!"

*   *   *

Peter held Clint's wrists by the handcuffs and walked him to the front door of the house before removing them. "You got thirty minutes Larson, not a minute more."

Clint stood at the door, rubbing his wrists before stepping inside. The living room was bare, the floors were clean, and the air smelled of fresh lemon and flowers. The kitchen was cleared, and the cabinets empty. He noticed one pantry door was half open, and inside were his last few bottles of gin. Looking around, Clint suddenly felt lost and alone. Maybe it was sobriety—it'd been a week since he drank—but his own home felt unfamiliar. He turned back toward the door, reaching for a saucer on a small corner table. Turning it upside down, he took the key to his car and stepped out onto the porch.

"That was fast," Peter said, checking his watch.

Clint gave a terse nod, making his way to the side of the house where the car was parked.

Driving behind him toward the county line, Peter wondered what could make a man destroy his own life, then figured some things were simply beyond understanding. The sun started to settle as they neared the border. After a long drive, Peter finally pulled to the side of the road, watching Clint drive away. Looking in the rearview mirror, Clint saw the dust rise over the road as Peter turned around. Clint stared forward as he crossed the county line headed south.

28

Reggie lit the oil lamp after the children had gone off to bed, sat on a three-legged stool, hunched over a piece of paper, and began to write a letter. Struggling with the first sentence, he set the pen down and pushed the paper aside, looking off into the corner of the one-bedroom cabin. His eyes ran over the head bumpers he'd made, placed along a shelf so the mice couldn't get to them. He looked at his hands, covered in calluses and blisters from pulling leather and stitching, figuring that for as much as it was nagging at him, he might as well see what could come of it. He picked up the pen.

*   *   *

Ben sat up in bed, flipped down the blanket, and hung his legs over the side, wiggling his toes. His shoulders felt stiff and his chest was sore. Walking to the dresser mirror, he paused to look at his reflection. Turning his shoulder to the mirror, flexing his biceps, he was surprised to see his muscles starting to show. Taking a few steps back, he could see more definition in his shoulders and back. He trailed his fingers along his stomach and over the ridges of his abdomen when the aroma of bacon found its way to his nose.

Charles and Carl were sitting at the kitchen table having a cup of coffee when Ben came around the corner. Carl tapped his fingers against his mug, hoping Charles would have forgotten this whole training idea, but doubted that was possible after the coffee invitation.

"Good morning," Charles said, "smelled that bacon sizzling I bet.

Have a seat—we have something to chew over with you."

Ben rubbed his eyes and sat down gingerly.

"You feel alright? You're moving a little slow," Charles said.

"I'm fine, just a little sore from training and pallet loading."

Carl chuckled to himself, then shook his head and looked over at Charles. "You best reconsider this cockamamie idea, especially if throwing a few pallets has him all stiffened up."

Charles dismissed Carl's cranky attitude and folded his arms on the table. "We—"

"We?" Carl interrupted.

Charles grimaced at Carl, then continued, turning to face Ben. "We have been talking about your talent and passion for jumping and have noticed the time and effort you've been putting into it. Harold and Elliot have both suggested we take this a little more seriously, if you fancy that idea." Waiting for Ben's reaction, he looked over at Carl again. "*We* would like to help get you ready for that if it's something you really want to do."

Ben sat up, wide-eyed. "Would I ever! That would be great! Will you be training me Mr. Carl?"

Carl hesitated to answer, taking a slow swig of coffee, then lowered the mug to the table. "That seems to be what we're here to discuss."

"Yes! This is the best thing ever; I can't wait to learn from you, Mr. Carl!" Claire couldn't help but giggle over Ben's animated excitement. The odd pairing seemed like a recipe for disaster to her, but she finished plating the eggs, enjoying the rhetoric.

"Lord sakes!" Carl said, watching Claire set a large tray in front of them. It was filled with eggs, bacon, biscuits and gravy, and fresh baked rolls. "You eat like this every mornin'?"

"We put gas in the tank early around here," Charles said, heaping a large spoonful of eggs on his plate, handing the spoon over to Ben.

"Now I am impressed," Carl said. "Not sure how that horse can get up in the air like that at all."

*　*　*

Over the next couple months, Carl worked with Ben nearly every day. On their rest days, they worked on perfecting techniques like hand placement and weight distribution on high and broad jumps. The higher Elliot set the rails, the more they scratched their heads, wondering if there was anything they couldn't clear. Carl went home each night after training, combing through articles on the discipline of show jumping, learning all he could. He read stories on competitions in England, Canada, Australia, and New York, surprised to even find commentary on the Olympic games in Paris. He quickly became consumed, studying course diagrams and mechanics.

One morning, while drinking a cup of coffee, Charles had a visit from Oscar. He peddled his bike up the driveway with his messenger bag hanging from the handlebars.

"You got something in that bag for me?" Charles asked.

"Yes sir, Mr. Collins, all the way from Kansas!"

"Kansas… not sure I know anyone from Kansas. Why, that's a few hundred miles from here."

"Four hundred and fifty, sir," Oscar added, pushing his glasses against his nose. "Have a good day, Mr. Collins!"

"Have a good day Oscar, and thanks for the letter."

Claire heard voices on the porch and stepped out. "Who are you talking to dear?"

"That bookworm, Oscar. He delivered this letter. Smart kid, and a hard-working one to boot."

"Who is it from?"

"No idea, someone from Kansas—says R. Colburn on the address. Colburn, Colburn…" he muttered to himself. "Seems like I heard that name somewhere."

She turned, hearing Ben's clunky steps coming down the stairs. "Poor boy is plumb wore out. Maybe it wouldn't be a terrible idea to have him take a break?"

"Believe me, I have tried; that boy is dialed in on this competition like cutworms on cornstalks. Carl too. Why, Harold said he can't get him to time trainers anymore. All he talks about are these jumping courses, spouting technical jargon nobody understands. Rambles on about lines, paces, and faults… nobody knows what they're saying. It's like a secret language."

"I'll let you get to that letter and get back to my cookies; I told Paul he would have a few batches for the store."

He took another sip from this mug, shaking the letter from the envelope and reading:

To Mr. Charles Collins and Henry Shoemacker,

I have given the idea of starting a business some thought and as I sit here, writing by candlelight while the youngins are sleeping, I can't help but dream of a better life for us. I have just finished my gear from the last piece of hide I bought from the winnings and will be sending a package with the headpieces by rail in the morning.

If you think this is worth an investment and potentially moving my family, please send a return letter. Much appreciated.

Reggie Colburn, Route 66, Elgin, Kansas

*   *   *

Carl turned into the farm's drive and gathered up some papers from the passenger seat, noticing Charles waving him over from the porch.

"Y'all are starting earlier and earlier," Charles said, "that boy can barely shuffle to the kitchen."

"The *boy* can't. Heck, it takes me an hour just to get out of bed nowadays; I'm getting too old for this lifestyle."

"What you got there?" Charles asked, seeing the disorderly pages flapping in his hand.

Carl held the papers above his head, shaking them around as he spoke. "Turns out this competition we been training for has an oxer, a liverpool, and brush jumps. It'll be a daggum miracle if I don't drop dead just readin' up on it!"

Charles pretended to understand but didn't have a clue what he was carrying on about, and before he could say anything, Carl was already halfway down to the pasture.

*   *   *

Elliot was busy making fencing according to Carl's measurements and configuring the course, counting out his steps for the spacing of the broad jumps. He lifted the top rail onto the vertical jump, feeling a bit apprehensive about the height. "Every bit of five feet," he thought to himself.

"We got to rethink this whole course," Carl said, pointing to the pages in his hand.

"What do you mean? This here jump is higher than anything they ever jumped before!"

Carl looked at the jump dismissively, waving his hand across it as if shooing off a fly. "That ain't nothin'. This show is wall-to-wall obstacles. Not too concerned with these ones," he said, pointing to the single jump on the diagram. Elliot noticed sweat beginning to bead on Carl's forehead as he tapped his finger over a shape that Elliot didn't recognize. "This here's what they call a box oxer, and this funny looking picture right here is a brush jump. Now that worries me, because it's set wide. Juniper's gonna need to really stretch his chest and legs to clear it. And he don't ride loose like that, he's got a short middle; he ain't long and lanky like these young horses."

"How's 'bout we just go out there and find some covering, get him used to it. He can learn to skim it instead of thinkin' he has to clear it."

Carl shook a finger at him. "Not a bad idea. Gather up some brush, I'll put up some combinations."

*   *   *

When Ben walked into the arena later that morning, he noticed twice as many jumps as before. Every obstacle was marked with hand-painted numbers on wooden paddles attached to the fence posts, one having a small trench under the center.

Carl approached Ben, not wasting time on small talk. "Warm him up good," Carl said, pointing to Juniper. "Take him through the woods for a nice long walk then practice posting the trot. Come back the same way. When you get to the hilltop, walk him back by the lead. We want him warm and loose for this today."

Ben took the same path he remembered from when he was younger, when he would cut through the woods to get to the farm. They went deeper into the trees to a clearing in the center of the woods, walking along the narrow path that ended near the edge of town. Ben felt calm, listening to the sounds of Juniper trotting and the leaves rattling. His eyes wandered, drawn to the Virginia creeper winding itself around tree trunks. Spotting a cluster of poison sumac, he instinctively scratched his leg, recalling the time he had run through it as a child and his mother spent weeks dabbing pink liquid on his shins. The path narrowed, and they continued through a tangle of low-hanging branches to a dirt drive where his father used to push the wheelbarrow as he collected firewood.

The backyard looked the same as when he'd last seen it, only the grass was taller, and the crack in the shed's window stretched a bit longer. The backdoor stoop had been overtaken by switchgrass, and all the overgrowth made the house look much smaller. He closed his eyes for a moment and could hear his father's voice, remembering the conversations with him as they stacked wood. Even the sound of creaks and clacks from the back door resonated in his memory. When he opened his eyes, he had a vision of his mother standing at the door, blowing a kiss to him with a dish towel folded around her shoulder, just as she had every morning.

29

Paul pulled up to the store just as the mail delivery arrived, jumping out of his truck with a rush of adrenaline.

"Morning Paul," Clark greeted. "You got one today, flew in all the way from New York City!"

He felt a catch in his stomach and reached for the letter, quickly looking for the address: "Miss Elizabeth Rockwood" was written in slanted cursive. It was artwork to him.

"Thanks Clark!" he said, in a rush to get inside. Dropping his keys on the counter, he pulled the stool under him and set the letter in his lap, rubbing the sides of his jeans to wipe the sweat from his hands. He carefully separated the seam and pulled out the letter:

My Dearest Paul,

Thank you for the nice letter, it is delightful to hear that your business is expanding. I am excited to hear how the market's preparations are coming along, I am certain it will be a success. Maybe one day Jack and I will make it back there to stock up for winter canning.

As you may have surmised, I have officially regained my family's last name and Jack and I have settled once again. He is so happy now. He is back at school and taken up with his old friends. My father is pleased we have returned, but it is not without heaviness of heart. There are many nights we talk about small-town life and how different it is from the city and just as I write this letter to you, Jack is sealing his letter to Ben. It is sweet how they became friends through all the obstacles and hardship that unfolded during our time there, and I am so grateful that experience is behind them.

I do look forward to your next letter, it is the highlight of my day when I receive them, and I hope to hear about your endeavors soon.

Many thoughts to you,
Elizabeth Rockwood

He exhaled his breath slowly, not realizing he'd forgotten to breathe as he focused intently on every word. He could only remember one other time in his entire life when he'd felt such certainty and contentment. Looking over at the picture hanging on the wall, Bernie's voice came to his mind: *"Go find that woman, she'll melt that hunk of ice in your chest."*

Claire came through the door, her curiosity piqued as she noticed Paul just sitting there, smiling at the wall, seemingly lost in a daydream. She called his name twice before he even realized she was there. "You look like you're in another world," she said, smiling. "I brought some fresh cookies and a few baskets for the market."

"That's right good, Mrs. C," he said, pushing the stool away and walking around the counter like he was on air.

"Something's different about you today, Paul. You seem… happy."

"Just another workday around here, nothin' special. Now let's get you unloaded. You're going to like the space—the boys did a fine job."

* * *

Harold and Elliot leaned against the fence, their arms draped over the top as they watched Ben guide Juniper through the course. Even though they were focused on the riding, they couldn't help but notice Carl's limp seemed to be getting worse.

"He's not moving around too good, is he," Harold said.

"Nah. He took a spill a while back, stepped into a divot. But you know Carl—he's bullheaded as ever, and he's determined to see this through. Walks around with those diagrams all day long."

"He is bullheaded, that's for sure. But this show jumping venture is only going to get more rigorous. Most riders compete in ten shows a year, sometimes more depending on rank, and the international competitions can add even more travel."

Elliot looked at him like he had his hat on too tight. "International?" he repeated, "I don't think he's anywheres close to that level."

Harold pushed off the fence and pointed to the high jump. "I ain't never seen, nor heard of anyone having been training for this short of time, that can ride like that. If that ain't world-stage talent, I don't know what is."

Elliot turned around, watching them weave through the jumps, easily clearing every rail. Gliding over an oxer-to-vertical combination in perfect rhythm and ending with a row of five cavaletti, Elliot looked over at Harold again.

"What you just saw… that ain't normal," Harold said.

The next couple of days were much the same. Training started early in the morning and finished with lighter exercises in the afternoon. The day before the show, Carl skipped the morning routine, deciding to start early in the afternoon instead, thinking Juniper's muscles would be quicker to loosen on the day of the show.

Ben took Juniper on another long walk, eventually settling under a sprawling oak tree in the clearing. There, he lounged in the shade, reading the last few chapters of *The Call of the Wild*. It was peaceful and calm. When he finally returned to the farm, Elliot and Carl were bundles of nerves, and everyone seemed eager to give him attention. Even Henry and Albert struck up conversations, advising him to not let a case of the nerves deter his focus. The irony was, he wasn't nervous at all.

Just before Ben came in for supper, Claire wrapped a package and placed it on his bed along with another letter that arrived from Jack. About to leave, she noticed the box that he usually kept tucked away under his bed was sitting on a shelf, and all the letters he had received were sandwiched between bookends.

Suppertime was quiet, which usually meant the food was too delicious for conversation. When she mentioned the letter from New York, Ben quickly finished his plate and asked to be excused from the table, running upstairs to his room after Charles gave him a nod.

Claire smiled as she watched him hurry away, then turned to Charles. "You're awfully quiet tonight. Anything on your mind?"

"One or two thoughts are turning over in there," Charles said, dabbing his mouth with a napkin. "Don't know why, but I feel like I'm the one competing! I haven't been this worked up since Ranger's race, and it was a darn miracle I didn't keel over in that grandstand. Talk about a nail-biter!"

Hearing loud footsteps coming down the stairs, she gave Charles a reassuring pat on the arm, waiting for Ben to come around the corner.

"Thank you so much!" he said. He beamed in his brand-new riding boots and helmet, proudly holding up a pair of beige breeches and a navy tweed jacket. "I've never had clothes this nice before!"

"They should fit like a glove! Why don't you try them on in case I need to make any alterations."

"You bet I will!"

"Thanks Papa," she whispered, massaging his shoulders. "You've spent the last two months telling me how much you enjoy watching him ride. Don't let what could happen take away the joy of what is happening."

Charles let his shoulders relax, closing his eyes when she kissed his forehead. "I've been working on a touch of flare, wait here."

She returned with a blue velvet blanket with two gold tassels hanging from the ends. "It's very popular in dressage. Do you think he'll like it?"

Charles cocked his head to the side and pinched his chin. "Honey, I think that's suitable for the medalists, but with this being his first show, maybe it might be a little—"

She shushed him before he could finish, but he didn't mind. He delighted in her happiness as she combed her fingers through the silky gold threads, her face glowing with pride and a tender expression of love.

Later that night, with his helmet hanging from the corner post and the boots beside his bed, Ben rested against the pillow and began reading the letter from Jack:

Dear Ben,

I hope this letter gets to you before the show. I want to wish you luck. It's been fun hearing about your training. Sure is a high jump, but I know you can do it. I got seated next to that girl I told you about in writing class, Madeline. She's not a very quiet girl, but she lets me look off her paper during tests, so I like that. My mother has been talking a lot about being in the country. I think she misses it. I miss being around you and Lucas. We never had that campfire we talked about, maybe someday we will.

My letter is short this week, I have a math page to finish before bed.

Hope you win the show, write to me as soon as you can and tell me how it went. I want to hear all about it. I bet there will be lots of horses there.

Your friend,
Jack

Ben rolled over to face the window, watching the breeze carry the edges of the curtains, thinking about the show. He folded his hands and said his prayers, thanking God for every good thing in his life as he quickly fell asleep.

Claire sat by the fire, carefully sewing the hem of Ben's breeches, while Charles sat in the study, engrossed in a project that had occupied him all evening. Securing the final stitch, she tucked her needle into the spool and shook out the fabric.

"Are you turning in soon?" Claire asked, speaking loud enough so that Charles could hear her.

"Almost finished. I'll be out shortly to put the fire out." After a few minor edits, he read his letter one last time. Deciding he was satisfied, he tucked it into an envelope and stood up to leave.

Examining the stitch, Claire gave the breeches a tug, making sure the hem would hold, and folded them over her arm. On her way to the kitchen for a cup of water, Charles came out of the study holding an envelope. "Would you mind sending this off tomorrow?"

She looked at the envelope with curiosity. "Who is Reginald Colburn of Kansas?"

"I'll tell you later. Right now, I need to get some shut-eye before the big debut tomorrow."

On their way to bed, Claire hung the pants over the back of Ben's chair and pulled the bed cover over him, noticing the blue sash at his feet.

"He liked the sash," she whispered, joining Charles in the hall.

"I know, dear. He'll be the best dressed horse if nothing else."

*　　*　　*

The crowing of the rooster agitated Carl from sleep, his quilt lumped in a ball at his feet and a half-eaten sandwich wedged under his arm. He rolled over the diagrams he had fallen asleep studying and limped out of bed. After dressing, he grabbed a thermos of oatmeal he had made the night before, grabbed his bag, and headed out the door. On his way to the farm, he passed the Larson house. The house surely wasn't much to look at, but those unfinished pole barns and all that space and equipment were just wasting away. *Such a shame*, he thought. *Somebody in the trades should make use of it.*

*　　*　　*

Ben awoke to a clamor outside, the sound of voices echoing throughout the house. He hurried to the bathroom to brush his teeth and comb his hair, then packed his new clothes into a duffle and went downstairs. Pulling the kitchen curtain aside, he saw Juniper being led into a long trailer. Elliot and Paul stood off to the side talking to Carl and Charles.

"You ready for some breakfast?" Claire asked.

Ben shook his head and put his hand over his stomach. "I'm not hungry, I think I'll skip breakfast this morning."

"Butterflies starting to flutter, are they?"

"I think so."

An hour later, they were pulling out of the driveway. Ben sat in the backseat, his eyes darting back to the trailer behind them every few minutes, wondering if Juniper knew what was happening. "Mr. Carl?" he asked, "suppose he doesn't fancy riding in that trailer?"

"What would you suggest? We can't carry him. Horses prefer being trailered—most don't like trains and certainly prefer it over a boat—and no horse that I ever heard of has been in an airplane. So I would say he's making out just fine back there. I'd be more worried about Elliot eating himself into a corn dog coma."

Charles laughed, remembering the last time they visited the state fair. Elliot had been sick for hours. Rolling over the hill, he noticed the vacant property with the discarded horse sign leaning against the barn, surrounded by broken pieces of wood and overturned crates.

"Say," Carl said, "that headpiece you put on Juniper for the trip is good quality. Never seen a cap like that before. Where'd it come from?"

"Bought it off of a gentleman on our way to the derby race. Real nice fella with an eye for craftsmanship; we need someone with that kind of skill around here."

"Well, heck, tell him there's a place already chock full of leather-making tools. Even got a saddle cast in there."

Charles looked out at the property, resting his arm out the window. "I actually did just that."

*　　*　　*

Ben watched as endless rolling hills of corn and soybean fields passed by. He saw roaming horses, small towns with ice cream parlors, and women carrying large umbrellas wearing fancy dresses. As they got closer to the state fairgrounds, cars started to fill the roads and the towns got closer together. Folks were busy visiting window shops, outdoor markets, and buying fresh vegetables from farm stands.

"Elliot's nose has to be tickling by now," Carl said. "Those dogs are spinning on the stakes sure enough."

Signs with large arrows lined the roadside with "Iowa State Fair" painted in bright green letters, and a line of cars led to a large grandstand in the distance. Rows of flags boxed in open fields, with men directing people into parking areas. There were other buildings surrounding the grandstand, and some of them looked to Ben to be a mile long. Banners hung from every entrance and advertisements and posters were everywhere, with booths stretching as far as he could see, with crowds of people gathered around them.

Charles pointed to a sign with the words "Horse Show," with an arrow pointing to the right. "Looks like we head that way, to the grandstand area."

A man dressed in a white suit wearing a black cap waved them over. "You here for the horse show?"

"The jumping competition," Carl said, showing him their entry ticket.

The man backed up, looking at the trailer. "You'll want to follow this path along the back of the grandstand. There'll be a couple men over there that will show you to the lot, closer to the arena. Good luck to you—there's a lot of good jumpers today!"

Carl continued driving, mumbling to no one in particular. "Private lot. Sounds fancy."

Two men guided them to a roped-off area lined with horse trailers. When they pulled up, one of the men took down a large rope and ushered them through. Ben watched horses being unloaded by men in crisp white shirts and riding boots. Some even wore long jackets with tails on the back and tall hats. The horses had head gear guarding their eyes, some had braided tails, and others had ribbons braided into their manes.

"Let's stretch our legs," Carl said, shutting down the engine. "I'll find out where we're heading before we unload him." Before he put his hand on the door, a man was standing at the window.

"Good day, sir. Might I show you to the resting quarters?"

Carl looked over at the man, not expecting such formality, then glanced over at Charles, who had the same surprised look on his face.

They followed the man to a white booth where he stopped and let them walk ahead. "The show staff will direct you to your quarters and issue your line placement. Good luck to you today gentlemen." The man tipped his hat in a half-bow, making Carl feel that much more out of place. The booth was decorated with ribbons of every color and ticket rolls sat along the counter. A well-groomed man greeted them at the window. "Ranking card please."

"We don't have a ranking card, just our entry ticket," Carl said, pulling the ticket from his pocket and handing it to the man.

The man looked unimpressed as he stamped the entry ticket and handed it back to him along with a scoring card and course layout. "Each rider has an opportunity to walk the course prior to the first competitor called to the gate. The Novice group begins their round at one o'clock sharp, with an opening ceremony call ten minutes prior. All riders and their horses are to be on the green for the participation announcement. Once the first placement takes their spot at the gate, all riders and horses must stay at their quarters until escorted to the arena by the paddock master. Do you have any questions for me at this time?"

Carl slid the papers over at Charles, thinking he could better comprehend all the instructions.

"Not at this time, no sir," Charles said.

"I got one. What placement did we get?" Carl asked.

The man pointed to the stamp on the entry ticket in Carl's hand. "Placement twelve. All other riders have ranking cards with previous competition stats."

"Well, we all got to start somewhere, don't we. I'll bet they all started with just an entry ticket, too."

Charles nudged Carl with his elbow, thanked the man in the booth, and pushed him along. "I'll be a son of a gun," Carl said, pointing to passersby holding thick white sticks topped with cotton candy. "Where you suppose that booth is? Bet they ain't as cantankerous as that last fella was."

Charles chuckled to himself. "You call *him* cantankerous?"

They unloaded Juniper while Ben changed into his riding clothes in the backseat, then made their way to the long stable marked with a banner that said "Resting Quarters." Carl noticed horses walking along the back of the building, while others warmed up in a field beside the stables. "Why don't you walk him; we got an hour. Use the long rein to stretch his topline long and low, then ride across this backstretch here in a trot or canter for ten minutes. Just like you did in the woods."

"I'll find our spot in the stable and meet you there," Charles said.

Walking into the stable, Charles saw a long row of numbered doors according to the rider's placement. The first several doors had ribbons decorating the front, and some even had signs with the horses' names and home state. The first door was decorated with a row of first-place ribbons and pennants across the front. A sketch of the horse with the name "Brazin'" was written in block letters. As he walked down each pen, the ribbons seemed to diminish, which made sense. The novice riders likely won fewer competitions, although the tenth placement had even more ribbons than the third, so possibly there were experienced riders with multiple horses in different classes.

He stopped at a door with a round plaque clipped to the bar and the number twelve carved on it. The straw was fresh, and the pen was deep, giving the horses lots of room. Riders and handlers along with their horses began to filter through the entrance, adjusting gear and making sure their wardrobe was tidy. It wasn't the same crowd as racing. Their voices were hushed and they whispered, meticulously looking over details and manicuring their horses. Some even dressed to match the colorful ribbons woven through their horse's mane. Most riders didn't even acknowledge each other, keeping to themselves.

As the pens started to fill up, he checked his watch and began to look for Carl. The horses looked to be a mix; he saw Dutch and Belgian Warmbloods, Westphalians, Trakehner, and a Holsteiner. Seeing Carl and Ben at the entrance, he waved them over. Juniper looked relaxed and unbothered by the commotion, and Ben seemed just as relaxed, although he was a bit distracted and awestruck by the other riders and their colorful displays.

"This is us!" Charles said.

Carl looked at the bare door, then looked down the rows at the others, frowning. "Guess we should have brought something shiny," he said.

"I have something," Ben said, digging through his bag for the blue sash. "We can put this over the door!"

A few minutes later, a tall slender mature man wearing riding clothes with a long-tailed overcoat began to speak at the far end of the stable. Charles noticed Carl looked a bit winded, so he walked down by himself to listen in. The man directed the first three riders to follow him in sequential order. The first rider was to be in the saddle while the riders in succession were to walk their horses to the paddock area. After the first three rounds concluded, those riders would return to the stable and he would escort the next three. Walking back down the corridor, he noticed one rider who looked to be about twenty years old, close to Ben's age. The others looked well into their twenties and thirties, and the man in ninth placement appeared nearly as old as he was.

"I think this is going to move fast. He's moving them out in groups of three," Charles said, watching Carl swipe his forehead with his sleeve. "You alright, Carl? Looking a little out of sorts."

"Twelve obstacles," Carl murmured. "The upright, liverpool, double and triple combinations; an ascending and… a descending oxer, which we didn't train for. Not to mention the course runs diagonally, and there's a tight transition going into the double—and I mean tight!"

Charles leaned close to Carl and set his hands down on his shoulders. "Answer me this: did you do your darndest to train him for something like this? You been walking around for weeks with your head in those course manuals, chattering about things none of us could translate."

"I believe I did," Carl sighed, "as good as an old jockey from the flat track could. But this is an entirely new game."

"So, sit back and watch him ride. Maybe he's more prepared than you're giving him credit for, although I will say, some of these riders look well-seasoned."

The man in the announcement box came over the speaker, calling the names of the first three riders. The roaring cheers from the stands echoed through the stable. "Jackrabbits can sure bring a crowd," Charles joked, slapping Carl on the back. "I must say, I didn't expect this. Not sure what I expected, but it sure wasn't this."

The first rider entered the arena on a Trakehner, a horse known for its jumping ability. Carl noticed the horse's arch was a few degrees off from

Juniper's, even though he was a much broader horse. The pair drew a penalty when its hind leg tapped the rail on the third combination.

The second rider, atop the Holsteiner, had two faults right out of the gate and struggled in the turns, popping its head, and the rider had too much bounce. Watching the riders intently, he observed their speed, angle of transitions, and other mechanics, and was quite surprised to feel a certain degree of confidence building.

The third horse was a Westphalian, which made him nervous. In his opinion, there was no better breed for agility, lightness, and power in the hindquarters. The rider had a decent run and their rhythm was tight and focused. The horse's neck came out high from the withers, and the shoulders had good angles. But again, he accumulated two faults, one of which was a transition to a small vertical at four and three quarters, just like the first two riders. Reviewing his notes, as the next three riders approached the gate, Carl calculated that Ben had a good chance for a clean run and might even score better than the three most high-ranking placements.

The next round of riders performed much like the first group. And even though one rider completed the course with zero faults, they were a bit sloppy over the liverpool, incurring point reductions for a short landing. For a Belgian Warmblood at seventeen hands, that was surprising. The crowd, he noticed, was much more reserved and composed than your average horse-racing enthusiast. They clapped quietly, and when the riders were on the course, you could hear a pin drop, which was astounding given the packed grandstand. Scanning the crowd, he easily spotted Elliot along the rail on the second tier; he stuck out like a corn cob in a row of lettuce.

Finally, it was time for the last group. The paddock master escorted the riders to the announcement deck. Carl could hear Elliot from the grandstand, whooping and hollering and whistling loudly, so loudly that Carl couldn't hold in the laughter, which helped to relieve the rising tension. Two Thoroughbreds towered over Juniper at the withers; he was the only Quarter Horse in the show. The first rider had a strong run, even clearing the tricky jump at the turn, but rubbed the rail on the descending oxer enough to cost them a perfect score.

The next rider was the boy closest to Ben's age, and to Carl's surprise, the announcer introduced the boy as being from Iowa as well. In fact, all the other riders were from different states, as far as southwest Texas and even Idaho. The first half of the course was smooth, but the horse faltered on the vertical. The boy's upper body was too far forward—he got ahead of the horse, impeding its balance. The next trouble spot was the liverpool. The horse hesitated at takeoff, which happens if the rider isn't confident with timing and jumping from the edge. It was a problem Carl noticed with the other riders as well. For some reason, he didn't fear that jump for Ben. Ever since he'd cleared the creek that day, he was certain they wouldn't have any lag.

It was finally time for Ben's ride. Carl looked around for Charles, spotting him pacing the ground along the grandstand, nervous as ever. They approached the gate and settled into forward motion. Ben's legs were positioned just behind the girth and his calves made even contact with Juniper's body. His elbows were tucked, and his head was lifted. They moved through the first turn effortlessly, well-balanced and with quick time. Ben paced the jump over the liverpool with ease and confidence and came into the next transition with more quickness and agility than all previous riders. Carl's knuckles were gripped into tight fists, holding his breath at the vertical and the third combination, but they ran a clear course toward the oxers. It was a flawless run so far. In fact, they made it look easy. The height and broadness of Juniper's jumping ability hushed the crowd, and when they landed the final combination, the quiet-mannered patrons erupted in loud cheers; even the spectators in the fields and walkways clapped and whistled.

Carl rolled up his papers, tapping the end against his hand, turning around as folks celebrated the only perfect run of the show, and by an unknown contender on a Quarter Horse, no less.

The announcer soon called all riders to the ring while men cleared the obstacles and set up a small podium in the corner of the arena. Once the riders and their horses spread out along the perimeter, a man stepped out into the arena, directing the top three competitors to the center. Ben stood off to the side as the Trakehner's rider was called forward, followed by the Westphalian. The man held out three ribbons with medals over his arm; announcing the Trakehner rider as the third-place winner and placed the bronze medal around his neck, clipping a white ribbon to the horse's bridle.

The second-place ribbon went to the Westphalian's rider, taking the silver medal and receiving the red ribbon.

Elliot tapped Carl on the shoulder, giving him a nod, and bumped his elbow against Charles's arm with a wink, rubbing his hands together in anticipation. The announcer turned to Ben and held up the blue ribbon, congratulating him for a zero-fault performance. The crowd erupted in a wave of cheers when the medal was presented. Camera flashes flickered, as reporters angled for a shot when the navy-blue ribbon was clipped to Juniper's bridle. The paddock master handed Ben the blue velvet blanket for their victory lap around the arena. He unfolded the blanket and draped it over Juniper's shoulders, stunned to see so many people waving and clapping for them. He smiled and waved, which made them cheer even louder, halting at the center of the arena with the golden tassels caressing his legs.

*   *   *

It took a couple hours for the crowd to disperse, and they received many congratulatory handshakes and accolades from people wanting to make their acquaintance. Ben made fast friends with a group of boys that came up to him wanting to know how he started jumping and where he learned to ride. Packing up their gear, Charles even had people ask about training and came away feeling quite overwhelmed by all the attention and publicity. On their way to the lot, they passed by the man in the white booth.

"I reckon next year, we'll have that ranking card for you, fella," Carl said, giving the man a sly wink.

"You just couldn't resist, could you," Charles said.

*   *   *

By the time they got back to the farm, Ben was fast asleep in the backseat.

"I think the sugar rush finally wore off," Charles said, looking over the back of his seat when they turned off the lights.

"Cotton candy and Baby Ruth bars will turn you off after dark. Once that sun goes down, so do you," Carl said. "Let's get these two put away for the night."

Charles headed up to the house with Ben, while Carl took Juniper to the barn, hanging the blue ribbon on the door.

30

The next morning, the town was buzzing with the news of their win at the state fair. The front page of the *Iowa Press* featured an article highlighting their performance in the show jumping competition, their picture plastered across the page. By noon, everyone in town had the story in store windows or spread across kitchen tables over coffee. Friends and neighbors came in droves to offer congratulations, along with curious motorists who drove by, hoping for a peek at the blue-ribbon horse.

Over the next few months, they traveled farther, entering horse shows across the country. They amassed a collection of blue ribbons and medals, prize money and trophies; and Carl finally got his steaks. Ben's ranking shot up, becoming the youngest rider to clear the high jump at six feet, four inches. By the end of that summer, he was among the top performers in the show jumping circuit, receiving invitations to compete from around the country, and even drawing attention from the national press. As economic times became more volatile and folks sank deeper into the era people began to call the Great Depression, the country was hungry for underdog stories, and Juniper quickly became a favorite among show fans, outperforming horses bred specifically for jumping athleticism.

*   *   *

Late one Sunday morning, Charles picked up a large envelope sitting on his desk. Imprinted on the seal was the logo of the National Horse Show Administration. It was an invitation for Ben to participate in the National Horse Show's Show Jumping Competition in August at

Madison Square Garden in New York City. Fourteen competitors would compete for the Show Jumping National Championship. Charles knew that most national champions catapulted into serious competitions, eventually leading to the coveted Grand Prix and even potentially the Olympic arena.

It wasn't like Charles to bother Carl on a Sunday, but he couldn't wait another day to talk to him. He hurried to his car and started for Carl's house. Slowing down as he crested the hill, he stuck his head out the window, waving at Reggie's children who were playing kickball in the front yard, still in their church clothes. Reggie was applying the last coat of lacquer to the sign for the pole barn that read: "R.C. Saddlery and Tack."

"Looking good, Reggie!" he hollered as he drove by.

*   *   *

Charles drummed his fingers impatiently, waiting for Carl to finish reading the invitation.

"I reckon since he's underage, you'll need to sign off on the entry," Carl said, looking up from the letter. "If you're waitin' for my answer, I would say let him compete. No doubt about it."

Charles sat back into the chair, looking at Carl's swollen leg soaking in a basin. "You do this every day?"

"Every day. Hurts like a fly in your whiskey. I think this next stage in his training will be better suited for a younger lad, someone more experienced than I am. These big-time trainers in this business know a lot more than an old broken-down jockey like me. I think it's time to find someone who can take him as far as he wants to go."

Charles was uncomfortable with the suggestion but pragmatic nonetheless; neither one of them were equipped for this level of riding.

"This discipline only gets more technical the farther you go," Carl said. "It ain't like racin'. With a racehorse, it's simple: If you go faster than the other horses and don't fall off, you're home—simple as that. But at the level of competition he's gettin' to, he's looking at timed courses and more difficult jumps against world-class competitors. Some of these riders jump different horses, competing several times a week. I read of one fella who trains on four different horses each week, runs in six to eight competitions a day—hell, I can barely make it through one!"

"I understand that, I do, but you got him this far. I don't know how well he'll take to someone new. What if we don't find the right one?"

"You don't give yourself enough credit. You hired Harold, and he's doin' right well. When the right one turns up, you'll know it—and Ben will know it, too."

Charles nodded in agreement, and Carl got to his feet, stretching his lower back as he walked him to the door.

"It won't be an easy thing to tell him… maybe we should do it together?" Charles said.

"It'll work itself out. No need to make a big deal over it—just trading in an old model for a newer one."

*   *   *

When Charles returned home, he found Ben reading a book on the couch and handed him the envelope. "You let me know if this is something you want to do."

Ben put the book down and took the envelope, a smile widening across his face when he read the insignia. He pulled the invitation out, scanning it quickly. "They're inviting me to compete! In New York City!" he said, sitting up and gripping the papers, reading them again.

"It's the largest horse show that I know of. Doesn't get any bigger than this, at least not in your ranking."

"Alright!" he yelled, waving the papers in the air. "I'm going to write Jack and tell him I'm going to New York! Thanks Mr. Charles. Mr. Carl is going to be really surprised tomorrow!"

Ben grabbed his pen and started to write his letter to Jack, excited to tell him about the trip to New York and plan a meeting between them so that Jack could show him around the city.

31

OVER THE NEXT FEW WEEKS leading up to the show, Charles spoke with several training prospects, settling on one fella with a British accent that had a solid portfolio and experience training on the national level. The only issue was he lived in New York, so they agreed that the show would be the best place to meet, figuring that if he performed well there with his current skills, the next level of training would be appropriate.

*   *   *

Paul hurried through his bookkeeping for the day, relieved to see some profits. Finishing up, he locked up the store and farmstand, excited to get home and read his letter. When he arrived at his house, he immediately sat himself down and began to read.

My Dearest Paul,

It is incredible to hear about the news of the Horse Show, it's all Jack can talk about. He's so excited to see his friend again and just as excited to watch the show. I must admit, I am excited as well. I do love horses and have never been to a show like this before. I look forward to each letter you write. You are very skilled at running the business and I am so happy the harvest was successful. I wish I could taste all the fresh vegetables you will be selling. I am also happy to hear you have help working the farmstand. Everything you have told me about Mrs. Collins and Miss Gladys makes me feel like I know them already—such wonderful women indeed.

I think your idea of having Elliot work the store with you is a great idea. You can certainly use the extra pair of hands, and with all the years together, you've built a friendship you can depend on.

I do hope you can accompany the others on the trip to New York. I would love the opportunity to show you around and enjoy a walk through the city. There's so much to see, and the theatre is quite entertaining.

Please consider this an invitation for a visit, it would be so very pleasing to see you again.

In my thoughts,
Elizabeth

*   *   *

One month later...

Paul stood in front of the mirror, turning his head from side to side, evaluating the shave. He combed through his hair with his fingers, which was easier now with a couple inches taken off, and it felt better under his hat, too. The collared shirt felt tight and restrictive around his neck and tugging on it didn't help loosen the fabric. He walked to the closet, looking through his boots for a lightly worn pair. He selected black dress shoes instead and pulled pressed trousers off the hanger, folding them neatly into his bag.

On the way to the train station, he pulled into the store to give Elliot the delivery schedule and check in on Claire and Gladys, who were already sorting vegetables into baskets.

"Claire," Gladys called, "you might want to come out here and take a look at this; someone got a hold of Paul and trimmed the bear off him."

Paul felt his face flush. "Good looking vegetables."

"Vegetables? Who's looking at vegetables with your handsome mug standing in front of them?" Gladys said, leaning over and giving him a tender pat on the side of his face. "So that's what you look like."

Claire stood at the door holding a tray of caramel apples. "Paul," she said sweetly, "you look so handsome. Not that you didn't before, but I can finally see your face without all that scruff hiding it."

"And look at the shoes!" Gladys said, "how do those feel? Bet you wanna kick 'em off."

Paul smiled, "I do, actually. They're a little tight."

"Fashion comes before comfort, at least in the big city, or so I hear. That's why I keep my wide behind in the garden: the corn stalks hide it."

Elliot whistled, coming out of the store. "You look like you're fixin' to see a special someone! Either that or you shaved with a bush trimmer!"

Paul took the jokes in stride, knowing he looked about as different as he felt. "Yeah, yeah, just thought I would try to class it up a little."

"I'd say you better double back to the class, because you overshot it by a few miles. You look like one of them advertisements for Stetson."

Paul handed over the orders. "Here, make sure we get this all tagged before I get back. Most folks save up till their vouchers come at the end of the week, then it's high gear on Monday."

"Sure thing, boss," he said, "now go get that lady you been writin'."

He could hear Claire and Gladys whispering as he returned to his truck, which made him walk even faster.

Gladys turned to Elliot with her eyebrows raised. "What lady has he been writing to?"

"Lady?" Claire said, "what's this about a lady now? Has he met someone, finally?!"

Elliot sputtered, trying to grab his words out of the air and stuff them back inside his mouth as he slowly backed away from the inquisitive and persistent women.

"No, you don't!" Gladys said, "you're telling us what you know, or guess who won't be getting a lemon meringue to take home tonight."

Paul pulled away, laughing when he saw Elliot trying to escape, knowing he didn't stand a chance.

The train station was decorated with banners, colored streamers, and balloons tied around light poles. Crowds of townsfolk gathered at the boarding ramp to send them off. Daniel and the crew held up a plywood sign with "New York City Bound" painted on it, and Tom and Margie honked their horn as they pulled into the parking area.

As soon as he stepped out of the truck, he noticed Gretta pull away from Chuck and saunter over, prompting Paul to duck behind a group of boys tapping on drums hanging from their waists. He weaved through the crowd, taking hold of Charles's hand to pull him onto the platform.

"Isn't this something!" Charles said, shouting over the cheers and drum snares. "I feel like Louis Armstrong playing the Sunset Café!"

Reggie lifted his youngest onto his shoulders for a better view as the train whistle blew. Friends and neighbors cheered and waved as the train pulled away from the station.

Paul sat down next to Carl, who was busy studying course diagrams and peeling an orange. Carl briefly stole a glance over at Paul when a scent of cologne wafted under his nose, then looked back to the page, then looked back at Paul again, tilting his head to the side. "Something's different with you, besides those goofy shoes you're wearin'. I can't quite put my finger on it."

Paul shook his head and put his head back, closing his eyes with a smile on his lips.

Ben pressed his face to the rear window, waving back at everyone as they got farther and farther away and the train rounded the bend. He could barely sit still—excited for the show, but even more excited to see Jack again.

32

THIRTY HOURS LATER...

Ben's head bumped roughly against the seat as the uneven tracks jolted him awake. When his eyes fluttered open, he saw the tallest building he'd ever seen and sat straight up, pulling the window down to stick his head out. He was awestruck by the immensity of the structures, his jaw dropping at the sight of a row of men sitting on a beam seemingly a mile high in the air. The greenery faded into brick and stone and rivers of people flowed every which way. Trolley cars, bridges, and streets could be seen through rows of tightly packed buildings that were so tall they seemed to scrape the sky. Crowds of people waited in lines outside of shops, and they even passed a section that was bustling with street vendors and delivery carts.

Paul's eyes widened, waking up to a sea of metal and glass, tapping Carl on the arm and pointing out the window.

"Sure looks much bigger in person than in pictures, doesn't it," Carl said. "Never seen anything like this."

The train's whistle blew as they pulled into the packed station. People stood in massive crowds with luggage, waiting at terminals with attendants in long coats punching tickets. The station looked like a castle, complete with ornamental designs, steeple tops, and stone pillars. Exiting the train, the sound of people's voices filled their ears. Horns blared and the streets rumbled with activity. People walked in every direction as they splintered off, disappearing into the alleys and trolley cars.

"Which way do we go now?" Carl asked.

Charles unfolded a map while they waited for the horse car to unload.

"Says here we take Eighth Avenue to our west. It's somewhere between Forty-ninth and Fiftieth Streets. Must be impossible to miss—they even have boarding facilities.

Once Juniper was led out of the car, they made their way through the street, following a few other horses escorted by handlers; they figured everyone with a horse was headed to the same place. The sounds didn't startle Juniper; they kept the face gear Reggie made on his head, which helped muffle the noise and kept his legs wrapped for protection.

"Maybe I can ask Reggie to make me head gear like that. I don't know how folks adjust to this much commotion," Carl said.

Paul's senses were on overload as he watched the chaos of the street, cars and people bustling around every block. The only thing that relaxed him was the thought of seeing Elizabeth again, and even that wasn't very relaxing.

Upon reaching Madison Square Garden, they were greeted by a truly grandiose building, with cars lining a curved walkway that wrapped around it. With its four high towers at each corner and rows of arched windows on all sides, it looked like a coliseum. The entrance along Eighth Avenue had a balcony above the entryway with flags waving over the railing. Posters advertising the grand horse show lined the corners, and a black pointed gate encircled the entire structure. Each tower had a decorative display of lights at the very top with ornamental stonework along the columns.

Their necks began to ache as they walked around, staring above their heads at the skyline. Paul remembered Elizabeth telling him how there was so much to see. *Boy, she wasn't kidding*, he thought.

A small group of school-aged boys loitered on the corner trading baseball cards and women walked along carrying large shopping bags. The scenery was constantly changing around them; everywhere they looked there was something going on, and cars of every different shape and size raced by. Charles tucked the map into his pocket and pointed to a side entrance off the main street. The two horses they had been following were standing outside a large wooden door. "There, let's head that way."

The noise subsided as they turned the corner onto a sidewalk nestled between two buildings. It was eerie how dark it got in the narrow alley, the sun unable to penetrate, even in the middle of the day. Two men opened the wooden door and stepped aside, allowing the horses to pass through, directing them down a wide corridor to the staging area. The walls echoed with the clacking of horses' hooves and the vibrations of wheeled carts being pushed along ramps. Everyone working was dressed in black pants and shirts. They followed the two men to a large door on rollers with ropes at each side. Together, they pulled the door along the rail. Inside was the largest arena they had ever seen. Manicured dirt stretched for what seemed like miles, with dark green grass along the perimeter. The seating was nearly as high as the building, wrapping around them like a giant baseball stadium, with an upper level enclosed behind glass windows and overhanging suites. They walked a short distance off the main grounds and passed through a tunnel that separated the arena from the staging area. The stables were stocked with food and water for the horses, and a large outdoor pen lined with trees and haystacks along a wooden fence surrounded the area. Two young men with waste scoops and hoses were stationed at the corners.

Ben walked Juniper over to their stall, pointing excitedly when he saw what was on it. "It has a sign with his name on it!"

"Kinda makes the state fair seem like a pony ride," Carl said.

"The hotel is across the street and down a couple blocks; we should drop off our bags and get settled in," Charles suggested.

Once Juniper was comfortable and fed, Carl sat down in a chair at the corner of the stall and stretched his legs, folding his arms over his chest and closing his eyes.

"Aren't you coming?" Charles asked.

"I don't fancy the idea of leaving him here alone; figure I'll stay close by."

"Suit yourself. We'll be back once we check in and get our bearings."

Several horses waited at the wooden doors as they walked out into the street. A small group of reporters stood around three men wearing tall black hats walking out of a door marked "private." One of the men took notice of Ben, then looked at Charles with a curious expression, but turned away when a reporter pushed through the gathering crowd, asking for his thoughts on the competitors. The man noticed the *New York Times* press badge pinned to the reporter's lapel and decided to entertain his solicitation. When the man began to speak, his thick British accent caught Charles's attention.

"It wouldn't be my place to wager a bet or offer speculations until I have reviewed the rankings, and even then, there's always room for surprises."

Charles waited until the reporters parted, and finding a small opening in the crowd, he approached the man. "You wouldn't be Arthur Davies by chance, would you?"

Overhearing his question, the reporters laughed, covering their mouths and whispering amongst themselves. Some even stood on their toes looking over the heads of people to get a glimpse of the person who asked such a ridiculous question.

"I am indeed. And who might be asking?" Arthur said, somehow already guessing at the reply, just by the Midwestern drawl.

"I'm Charles, Charles Collins."

"Nice to meet you, Charles!" Arthur said, shaking his hand firmly with an approving smile. "And hello to you, young man. What is your name?"

"Hello sir, my name is Benjamin Paulie. I sure like your hat!"

Arthur laughed and tipped his hat to Ben, giving Charles a wink as the reporters began to crowd them out.

Charles put his arm around Ben's shoulders, walking him across the street. He overheard the conversation between two men as they passed by. "Can you believe that guy? Who doesn't know Arthur Davies, he's only one of the best horse trainers in the country!"

Charles turned around just before crossing the road, watching Arthur maneuver through eager men holding notepads and pencils before slipping into the backseat of a car. Just before the driver pulled out onto the road, Arthur waved, touching the brim of his hat.

"He seems nice. I like the way he talks; it's different."

At that moment, Charles knew he had found the right trainer.

*   *   *

Paul loitered around the hotel lobby, waiting for Charles and Ben to check their bags. The aroma of smoked sausage stoked his appetite, drawing him outside to a cart vendor wearing a white apron. His mouth began to water as the scent of oregano and basil sifted through the air, and he saw a quaint restaurant across the street with people seated at little round tables under an awning. He began pacing back to the hotel doors when he heard a familiar voice.

"Mother, come on! He told me in the letter where they were staying—it's just around the corner. Maybe I can see him before the show!" Jack pulled her by the arm, tugging her toward the door when she stopped, pulling her hand over her mouth. Jack spun around in the direction she was looking. "Mr. Paul, is that you?!"

Paul looked around, touching the sleeves of his shirt and rubbing his head. "Sure looks and feels like it. Good to see you, Jack. I bet you're looking for Ben."

"Sure am! I wanted to see him before the show. He said you would be here before noontime, and it's almost noon right now!"

Paul heard a commotion from the hotel entrance and, turning around, saw Ben jogging down the steps with Charles trailing behind him. "Looks like you found him," Charles said.

As soon as the boys saw each other, they were talking a mile a minute, pausing only to take in more air before sharing a new story or thought.

Elizabeth's face lit up with a bright smile that made her cheeks swell and pinken. "What a pleasant surprise! I wasn't expecting to see you standing on the corner next to Freddie's sausage cart."

"And I almost went over for one, but there are so many options; I wanted to make the right choice."

Charles hung back for a moment, discreetly observing the interaction between them, and suddenly it all made sense: the trimming, the shirt, and shoes. He looked playful yet awkward, but his eyes lit up when he looked at her as they talked and laughed.

"Can we go to Uncle Tony's, Mother? Please!" Jack asked. "Ben has never been to a pizzeria before!"

"What kind of host would I be if I didn't introduce you to the staple food of every New Yorker," Elizabeth said. "Wasn't that Charles over there by the door? Maybe he would like to join us."

Paul looked around but didn't see him. "Maybe he forgot something. I'll be right back." When he stepped back inside the lobby, he saw Charles waiting by a hostess podium in a small room next to a cigar shop. Paul approached him and tapped him on the arm. "We're about to be introduced to the local cuisine. Come join us—they call it a pizzeria."

Charles leaned in and put his hand on Paul's shoulder. "I want you to experience something better than a pizzeria, and by the looks of it, you already are. Now, get out of here, take that lady out for a meal. I'll see you at the show."

As they strolled down the street, Jack explained the history of the New York-style pizza to Ben, and how it migrated to the city from Naples; he'd heard his uncle tell the story hundreds of times to tourists who stopped in for a bite to eat.

Elizabeth pointed out the theatre district across the block, which had the best cheesecake bakery in the city, in her opinion. "It is so wonderful to be here showing you the city. I do hope you find it enjoyable as well. Just around this next corner is my brother's restaurant; he opened it last year and it's been very popular."

Paul noticed a woman sitting beside a flower cart with a basket of red roses. He excused himself and selected a rose from the bouquet. He returned to Elizabeth with a rose and a smile.

She accepted it graciously, twirling it under her nose as they walked, swinging her arm at her side. Paul felt a flutter when their hands touched briefly, and he wondered if she had felt it, too.

Jack and Ben giggled under their breath. "We might get that campfire night sooner than we think."

33

The Angels

"How long you think it will take before he realizes lifting that log over his head won't make him any smarter?"

Jacob walked over to the window to see the spectacle Joshua was snickering at and shook his head, watching Gabe grunting and moaning, his biceps quivering under the weight. "Lord only knows—literally—but if he had any sense, he would realize it ain't about lifting heavy, but how many reps you can press."

"I had a dream last night," Joshua said, noticing Sarah's stoic gaze turn in their direction.

"You, too? Mine was so vivid and, quite frankly, alarming. I haven't been able to relax since waking up. Tell us what you dreamt."

Joshua turned away from the hulk-fest outside the window and spun his chair around to face them. He lowered his elbows to his knees and leaned forward, like he was about to speak a secret. "I saw people gathered in a large city, almost like a town square, looking up at a building with large windows. They were all gathered in the center, and even more were outside, spilling into the streets. There was a grand balcony wrapping around the entire room of this place with small enclosures on the ground floor. Men hung their hats on hooks and were busy pushing small pieces of paper through numbered slots. Large numbered signs were posted around the floor, and the noise… It was deafening. Everyone was shouting and waving these small pieces of paper in the air. Some were running from slot to slot. Some were talking over each other, others were in full sprints running around, holding their hats on their heads they were moving so fast."

Sarah and Jacob were so focused on his story that they didn't hear Gabe come in, even though he was still grunting and breathing heavily. Gabe grabbed a cloth and ran it under the bar sink, wiping the sweat from his face, and heard Joshua begin to whisper.

As Joshua's voice lowered, Sarah felt a rash of goose bumps shudder down her spine.

"Then, I saw people running out of this building, stepping over all these pieces of paper and shouting at the top of their lungs, pushing the doors open. They cupped their hands over their mouths to call to everyone gathered outside and yelled, 'It crashed! America has crashed! Everything is gone!' One guy walked down the street, right in front of a moving trolley car, and didn't get back up. People were scared. Grown men hung their heads and wept, some were angry, throwing these white pieces of paper on the ground, stomping their feet, looking for someone's neck to ring. Other people just slunk down where they stood, silent and depressed… but that wasn't the worst of it," he whispered. "The worst was what happened after. I saw people standing in lines as long as five blocks, some maybe even a mile long. They were destitute, their clothes were mangy and tattered. They were dirty, some just skin and bones—even children! Some had no shoes on their feet, and others had just given up. The ones lucky enough to get to the front of the line walked away with nothing but a loaf of bread and a bag of wheat flour. But the scariest thing of all was the look in their eyes. They looked hollow, almost soulless—like they had no hope at all. Just an empty, dark, painful reality. To them, it seemed like death was preferable to another hour of existing."

No one said a word after he finished. Even Gabe was drawn in by the premonition, although only half-listening and somewhat skeptical.

Sarah looked like she was in shock, her breath labored as she nodded in agreement.

"I had the same type of dream!" she said. Her eyes darted around, shifting from the ground to Joshua and then to Jacob. "I saw towns boarded up, small shops and markets with signs on the doors and windows: 'closed,' 'broke,' 'out of work,' 'out of money'… these signs were everywhere. It was happening everywhere: cities and countryside, east and west. People were so sad. Families were barely holding on, the small children clinging to their parents in fear. It was so real, they were so burdened."

Jacob looked over at her, surprised and a bit terrified at the visions, and feeling that something big was coming. "You guys think we could be on the cusp of what we've been waiting for?"

Joshua raised his brows and leaned back against the chair. "I don't know, none of us do. So far, we have been assigned to help people. None of us have seen anything great and world-changing yet, but I have a strange feeling you might be on to something. I think we're being prepared; our gifts are being tested, and we're being refined and trained. It might seem like small potatoes now, but we're here for a reason. You can't tell me the nine of us, brought together over the span of nine hundred years, have been brought here just to heal animals and see visions. And, I mean, we still don't know what this guy is good for," Joshua joked, pointing over at Gabe. "We're waiting on the tenth one to do something big, I just know it. Something that will require all of us to accomplish."

Gabe rolled his eyes and dropped his sweat rag on Joshua's head.

"Get that nasty thing off me!" Joshua said, lifting it off with just his fingertips and tossing it at Gabe's feet. "Except for this numbskull. He'll be lucky to make it out the door without tripping over his laces. There ain't much we can count on him for."

"You all are getting carried away; just because we got a seat on the bench don't mean we are taking part in some monumental shift of prophecy. Maybe we're just supposed to keep order, ya know. Keep things moving in the direction He wants them to go," Gabe said, admiring and flexing his bicep.

"Seriously, guys," Sarah interjected. "You all know in the past, when we had similar dreams, it was something to pay attention to. I think Joshua and I are being shown something. Something awful is coming, and we need to be ready."

"The only thing I see coming is a nice warm shower," Gabe said, "and later, a fillet, and a big ole tater, with butter and…"

Gabe's words faded into the background as they watched him walk to his quarters, still talking to himself and rubbing his stomach, completely oblivious to their serious conversation.

"What a buffoon," Jacob said, "I sure hope when the doo-doo does hit the proverbial fan, that big dummy isn't anywhere near me."

Sarah looked over her shoulder, waiting for Gabe to shut his door, then rested her chin on the backrest and hugged her arms around the spindles. "There's one more thing," she said in a hushed whisper, almost too quiet to hear.

"I overheard the other angels talking last night before I fell asleep."

"Which ones? All of them?" Joshua asked.

"Not all of them, just the ones that don't talk too much."

Joshua looked over at Jacob with a confused look on his face. "That's all of them, Sarah. Can you be more specific?"

Sarah sighed. "There were three of them huddled around the campfire. There was the one with the goofy mustache that looks like a French baker, the shorter fella that likes to mumble to himself, and the super quiet one that wears the same shirt day after day that ties in the front. He's the one Gabe makes fun of and says he looks like a pirate."

"Ah, yeah… that guy. What a weirdo," Jacob said.

"Quiet, let her talk," Joshua said.

"Anyway," Sarah said, "I heard them talking about the other ones. Angels like us, only… different."

"What do you mean, 'different?'" Joshua asked, biting the tip of his thumbnail.

"By what I could make out, the pirate said they were like us in that they have powers, strengths, and abilities. The difference is that we come from light, and they come from darkness. The mumbler said he had a vision. He said that these other angels were being held, locked away, but one day they would be set free. And when that happens, our tribe will meet their tribe and the final battle between good and evil will happen. These other angels rule the dark places, even places down on earth. Then the mumbler told them that some of the less powerful ones are roaming the earth now, and when we get sent on assignments, they are watching… and waiting."

The three of them stayed quiet for what seemed like minutes, not wanting to break the silence and unsure what to say, unsure of whether to believe the speculation of the other angels. Joshua glanced up at Jacob, giving him a quick head tilt in Sarah's direction, who was sitting there looking quite troubled.

Jacob lightly tapped her with his elbow. "Eh, who listens to those guys anyway. Maybe they knew you were listening and spun that tall tale just to get us riled up. And I wouldn't be surprised if Gabe were in on it; he was prowling around last night—probably helped them conjure it up. He'll do anything for his own amusement."

"Yeah, I can see that," Joshua agreed, "they're probably just yanking our chain."

Sarah gave them both a doubtful look but accepted their efforts to make light of the situation.

"Let's gather some wood for a fire tonight, Gabe talking about fillets made my stomach growl," Joshua said, smacking his hands on his knees to break the dreary mood. "I'll scrub down the rack. Jacob, season the steaks."

34

CHARLES AND CARL LOITERED AROUND the grand entrance to the Gardens, taking in the sights and sounds. As they rounded the corner, they noticed a private entrance. Charles stopped them, pointing to a man wearing a black split-tail coat and tall hat. "That's Arthur Davies," he said to Carl, "that's the trainer I was telling you about before you nodded off last night. By the way, are you aware how loud you snore?"

"That's the second time you pointed him out to me," Carl grumbled.

"Let's try and follow him," Charles said. "I'll introduce you."

Charles swallowed the lump in his throat and followed Carl, moving out of the way as a flurry of excited spectators pushed past them. "Folks in New York seem to be in a hurry for everything. No wonder there's so much concrete around this place; they don't stay still long enough for grass to grow."

Carl opened the door marked "private" which led to the stables, and they stepped inside. The crowd could be heard cheering from a full city block away. "Ben must be getting ready to saddle up—there's the paddock master heading over to that stage over there."

"Do they call them "paddock masters" at a place like this?"

"Probably not."

Paul waited by the main entrance, tugging at his shirt collar and regretting his choice of attire, longing for the soft flexibility of a flannel. He checked his watch for the eighth time in ten minutes. He stretched his neck, peering over the crowd of bobbing heads, hoping to spot Elizabeth and Jack. After a couple minutes, he gave up, only seeing strangers in the sea of faces. As he was about to step into the stream of people herding themselves inside the gate, he felt a tap on his back and heard a giggle. When he turned around, he was greeted by Jack's dimpled grin and Elizabeth's bright smile.

"Hi, Mr. Paul, sorry we're late. I had to use the bathroom real bad—we stopped at Freddie's sausage stand outside your hotel on our way here."

Paul laughed, meeting eyes with Elizabeth who was shaking her head at his earnest excuse. "It's a miracle we ran into each other," Paul said. "I ain't seen this many people in all my life."

"I saw Ben! I seen him right before he left. He ate some sausages, too, so I hope they don't bother him like they did me."

"I must have just missed you then. I couldn't sleep, so I got up and walked around the block about twelve times. Figured if I went any further, I'd get lost for sure."

"You do look a little frazzled," Elizabeth said, eyeing the pizza sauce on his chest pocket with a grin.

"I only got one of 'em," Paul said, rubbing the stain with his knuckles. "Next time I'll bring an extra," he said, his face red with embarrassment.

"There's no better testament for a New York pizzeria than that," she joked.

Jack tugged at her arm, growing antsy. "Let's head inside—I hope we have good seats!"

Elizabeth complied, and to Paul's surprise, she reached back for his hand. The way her cheeks plumped under her eyes and the curls of her hair framed her face made Paul's legs feel like spaghetti noodles. He reached to take hold of her hand, taking a moment to look at their clasped fingers as the mass of people funneled through the gate.

The high-pitched voices bounced off the arched walls, and the bustling of bodies bumped off his broad shoulders. Even though he missed the slow pace of home, he would trade just about anything to be holding her hand, even if it meant slaying dragons or being swept down a corridor with thousands of strangers.

Men with long coats, white shirts adorned with gold buttons, and sashes for belts stood along the ramps, waving patrons to the seating areas. Large signs with numbers counted the rows for each section. Jack skipped along, jumping up to get a peek inside the arena. "Let's go down this one," he said, pulling them along like a happy train. "I think this is in the middle, Mother."

"Alright, alright, settle down. We had displeasing seats at the football game and were able to see everything. Truly, there is no bad seat in this entire place."

"You're football fans?" Paul asked with a surprised look on his face.

"Don't let these fancy dresses fool you—I grew up with two older brothers."

Paul smiled. There was so much to learn about her, so many surprises and unexpected layers. He couldn't wait to find out more about this amazing woman who was holding his hand.

Jack took the large steps two by two, making it all the way to the top of the section in five quick strides. He stood with his hands on the rail, looking back, waiting for them to catch up. "I see him, I see Ben! He's coming out now, quick, come see!"

Elizabeth wrapped her arm around his shoulder admiring the grand arena. When she turned back to Paul, his mouth fell open, and his brilliant blue eyes widened as he looked from one end of the arena to the other. His eyes followed the endless rows of seats and balconies on the other side before he turned to Elizabeth in amazement. She pointed behind them and Paul turned, his head tilting upward, ogling at the high pitch of the ceiling that met the upper rows above them.

"Quite impressive, isn't it."

Paul was speechless and could only nod. People filled the balconies, standing in long, wide aisles as they found their seats. Women shrugged off fur coats and took off colorful hats, while men shook each other's hands and lit fat cigars, sizing up the riders and their mounts. Paul noticed what looked to be private bets being wagered in the upper balconies and even saw butlers carrying small trays of hors d'oeuvres and cocktail glasses.

"This sure does put the state fairs in perspective. We ain't seen nothing like this."

"Ben must be highly talented to have received this invitation. You must be very proud of him," Elizabeth said, releasing her grip on his hand and giving his arm a comforting squeeze.

"He sure has worked hard for it; him and Carl both. Carl must be outside his socks over this. Can't imagine what the old man is thinkin'."

"Look!" Jack pointed to the line of riders facing the crowd for the opening ceremony. Three men carrying trumpets walked out to the middle of the grounds followed by at least a dozen more carrying flags representing the United States, Canada, and numerous European countries. Five stagecoaches were rolled out, each with dignitaries and influential sportsmen in the carriages, waving at the crowd.

"There's the senator, Mr. James Wolcott Wadsworth," Elizabeth said. "My father had dinner with him just a few months back. Such a wonderful man."

Paul was once again surprised by this elegant creature of very fortunate beginnings. Sometimes he felt inadequate to even breathe the same air or be standing so close to her, and yet, it was so comfortable and easy. It was a paradox, and he was grateful for the mystery of it all.

*   *   *

"Mr. Charles Collins, good to see you my friend," Arthur said, reaching for a handshake.

"Arthur, it's a pleasure. This is quite the show—it sure makes Iowa look like one giant cornfield in a desert," Charles said. "This is Ben's trainer, Carl Ebbers."

"Nice to meet you Carl," Arthur said, shaking his hand and giving him a sincere smile.

"Apologies for the soggy handshake," Carl said, "I'm a little out of my bucket here."

"No apology necessary. I still get worked up myself over shows like this. The stakes keep getting more astounding the further a rider gets. It's a business, and just as with any business, the higher you soar, the bigger the stage. I best be taking my seat now; I'll be in the suite above you."

"Thanks Arthur," Charles said with a wave, "hopefully we'll find you afterwards."

"Not to worry. If Ben does well, I'll find you."

Charles turned to Carl with a big grin and slapped him on the shoulder. "Did you hear that? He'll find us!" When he brought his hand away, he could feel the perspiration through Carl's shirt. "Boy, you are really nervous."

"I could use a lip full of chewin' tabacca 'bout now," Carl said.

"Oh yes, among the grandeur and privilege, your spittoon will fit right in."

The audience was guided to their seats by the soft sound of trumpets, which gradually grew louder. The carriages made their way off the grounds as the men holding flags stood in formation. The crowd clapped and cheered as the riders guided their horses to their markers to await the ceremony introduction.

"Lord sakes," Charles said, "these are the finest thoroughbreds I ever seen, except for that one oddball Quarter Horse."

Carl grumbled. "I'll take that oddball any day of the week. These other horses are all bred for this. Years of breeding and manipulating so-called genetic traits. Juniper is special—no test tube or high-dollar, fancy-pants bloodline. Just one organ that makes the whole machine run: his heart."

Charles turned his head, quite amazed at the unusually eloquent and touching words coming from Carl's mouth. "Look, over there," Charles said, pointing to the areas along the arena roped off for reporters and cameramen. There was even a large booth filled with equipment and men speaking into mounted microphones. "I bet this is on the radio!"

The announcer stepped onto the stage and instructed the riders to remain on their posts until all competitors were introduced in their riding order. A few of the horses sidestepped, some making full turns around their marker to shake off energy, but Juniper and Ben stayed on their spot, seemingly enjoying the scenery.

"He looks relaxed," Charles said. "You think he's as calm on the inside as he looks on the outside?"

"I ain't never seen him bristled before. Don't know why all this hubbub would make much difference."

One by one, the riders and their mounts were introduced. Ben was one of eight riders representing the United States competitors. Europe had five riders, and Canada had three. Once the riders exited the arena to their staging quarters, the crowd erupted in cheers and whistles for an all-brass band that marched out to the center. There were trumpets, tubas, and saxophones playing a catchy jazz number that had people swaying and dancing in the aisles. Folks waved flags in the stands and leaned over railings in front of cameramen that walked the perimeter.

Charles and Carl watched until the last horse disappeared behind two large wooden gates before even hearing the music. "Suppose we can get back there?" Charles asked.

"Already tried—twice. You can't get near them horses. They're guarded like Fort Knox."

"But we're family, and you're his trainer."

"You think I walked up to one of them guards acting like a hot dog vendor? Believe me, I tried all angles."

*　　*　　*

Elizabeth chuckled, observing Paul's foot tapping the floor. It was obvious he had no rhythm, but she enjoyed seeing him loosen up. He even patted his thigh through the chorus when the snare drum chimed in. "You look like you're having fun."

Paul felt his collar grow tighter and start to strangle him as he looked at her rosy cheeks. The loss of control over himself was unsettling and delightful at the same time. "I am. I haven't been this uncomfortable, yet content in a very long time, if ever."

Once the band concluded their skit, one trumpeter walked up a set of stairs to a platform that reached over the first row. Blowing his instrument, he sprayed a colorful tapestry of colored confetti into the stands. Elizabeth laughed and clapped, watching hands raise up to catch the tiny flecks of paper. Paul didn't see any of it; his eyes were on

Elizabeth—her smile caused her eyes to twinkle and her head to fall back just a bit. Jack jumped in place and giggled. At that moment, Paul knew his life would never be the same.

The announcer's voice echoed through the building from a platform high above the grounds, elevated over the center of the arena. Several judges were positioned evenly at each side of the platform. The people took their seats as the announcer waited for the course groomers to complete their final checks. The paddock master escorted the first rider to the staging area just outside the gate.

"Sixteen jumps: four diagonal lines to clear five hogs back, topping out at four poles. Six-and-a-half-foot spreads, with a five-footer going vertical. Three of the five oxers are just off the turn, and the second scoot is trouble. Seven combinations and that water tray is three and a half meters. Not to mention three combinations have absolutely no flex in counting strides."

Charles pulled his glasses down to the end of his nose and peered over the frame at Carl. "I know this isn't our first rodeo, but I still haven't the foggiest idea of what you say sometimes."

"I said… this is gonna be a doozy."

A Canadian rider was first out of the gate, red and white ribbons woven through the horse's mane, braided in four sleek strands. The rider had remarkable balance and cut the diagonals perfectly. Every stride was precise, and the lead-up to the jumps was confident and explosive. Carl sighed audibly and pulled out his tattered notebook, the spiral binding barely attached to the crinkled pages.

"You still carrying that thing around?" Charles said, looking at it pitifully.

Carl ignored him and began taking notes.

"That horse is running darn near perfect," Charles said, "looks like we got some stiff competition."

Carl pointed the tip of his pencil to the course as the rider approached the high jump. "This is where we'll see what we're up against. If he ain't gassed after this pass, we have a tough couple days ahead of us."

Charles squinted as he watched the horse position for the jump. The head lifted and the hind legs pulled under the body. He could see the large frame compress like a coiled spring. The weight distribution shifted to its hindquarters, cutting the last stride shorter than the others, and it thrust forward in an effortless leap, clearing the jump by several inches. With eyes widened, Charles turned slowly to look at Carl, who tapped his pencil on the page and tucked the notebook back into his pocket.

"Why aren't you scribbling?"

"I don't figure it'll help much; we're matched—either we will, or we won't."

The last two turns led into a rollback: two oxers and three double and triple bar combinations. The Canadian horse faulted on a short turn, with just a slight hesitation costing them a mere fraction of a point. When their run concluded, the stands came to life as red and white pennants waved through the crowd. The announcer gave the score, and the crowd fell silent as the next rider entered the staging pen. The European rider hailed from the Netherlands and started the course on an upset at the first spread but quickly gained momentum, beating the Canadian rider's time, although stacking up two faults.

"That's two down, and not a flawless run yet," Charles said, hoping to hear Carl take a breath.

"Even so, these lads are just shaking off nerves. Once the travel stiffness wears off, they'll be finding their stride."

Two Americans followed, running neck to neck until the second turn into the vertical water tray jump. The first rider cleared by an inch, but the second rider took a fault when the landing fell short.

Carl channeled his stress into being a diligent narrator, grading every movement of the riders. "That second turn has a bite to it… if he doesn't jump on his backside, he'll never straighten up in time to clear that five-footer… he's sloppy on the pivot, pulls his front legs too high."

Charles began to sweat, filled with anxious energy. Even though he didn't understand everything Carl was saying, he could pick up the inflection in his tone, and it wasn't helping his jitters.

"I think I see Ben!" Jack said, standing up and looking over toward the pen by the gate. "There he is! He's next after this one!"

Elizabeth felt the vibration in her seat as Paul's foot tapped an agitated rhythm against the seat frame.

The next rider represented France, donning a shoulder cape embroidered in blue, white, and red, while the horse sported matching ribbons woven into its mane. The rider untied his cape and handed it to the paddock master. The horse reared its head on cue as they stopped at the gate. The rider was taller than most but had the slim build of a jockey. Carl had noticed him when the horses were on their marks before the competition started; he was the only horse other than Juniper who didn't fuss at the line.

The clock began once the horse engaged in forward motion, and that was the last time Carl saw its feet on the ground. The speed was dynamic—he had never seen such controlled speed in a jumping course. Not only was he fast, but the control was remarkable. The power was all in the back end, like he was powered by jet fuel. Once he took to flight, he hung there like a balloon and hit the ground running. He turned his long body on a duck's bill and shot off like a rocket.

"That's the best jumper I ever seen," Carl said in a breathy exhale. "If we come close to that, it's the best we can hope for. We ain't catching 'em."

The crowd's silence quickly transformed into a roar of shouts and whistles as the rider exited with a zero-fault score.

"Here he comes, he's at the gate!" Jack said, shifting in his seat for a clear view.

Paul drummed his fingers on the arm rest and crossed his feet at the ankles to stop his foot from tapping. He felt the gentle brush of soft, slender fingers over the top of his hand and was instantly soothed by her touch.

"Don't worry, Mr. Paul," Jack said, "he's going to fly, just wait and see!"

Charles felt like the air suddenly got thin, forcing him to take deep breaths. He turned around and looked up at the suite behind them, catching Arthur looking back at him. Arthur gave him a nod and lifted his hand before turning his attention to the arena. "Here we go. You ready for this?"

Carl was as still as a statue. "No more than I am for my own funeral."

The gate was drawn open. Ben slid three fingers under the leather strap and felt his grip slip. For the first time since he'd started jumping, he was buzzing with nervousness. The endless rows of faces closed in around him like a snuffer on a flame. He took a deep breath and looked forward, picturing in his mind the handmade hurdles and Elliot's ragtag leafy camouflage tied to palleted wall jumps. Before Juniper engaged, Ben heard a peculiar sound. He tilted his ear to his shoulder and listened again. Once the crowd was hushed, the sound came again. It was a high-pitched whistle—three short bursts, just like his father made when the horses were walking by the gate. He looked down at the paddock master who was waiting for his start, but when he didn't move forward, the man looked up at him and wrinkled his brow. Ben looked up into the rafters and cupped his hand to his ear. Juniper heard it, too. His ears twitched and turned and he let out a loud snort. The whistle sounded again, like it was being sent from above. It was unmistakable—he'd heard that sound every morning along the cart path. He closed his eyes and gripped the smooth leather straps in his hands, remembering a time when jumping—gliding over rails and fences—was only a daydream. Juniper let out another snort and pawed the ground.

"You alright young man?"

Ben opened his eyes, the sound still ringing in his ears. "We're ready, sir."

Juniper launched forward, keeping his head low, which gave Ben a clean line of sight on the first series of jumps. First a single, then two doubles leading to the first turn.

"What's he looking at!" Carl grumbled, "he's mopping the dirt with his snout!"

Ben approached the first fence, feeling a snap against the reins when Juniper blew out a loud puff of air. Just before taking off, Juniper lowered his head more than he ever had before, like he was only focusing on the ground and nothing else. Ben pulled his hips back at the bounce to shift his weight, hoping to encourage Juniper to raise his head, but he barreled down, springing off his hindquarters in a long stretch over the rails.

"Get his head up!" Carl yelled, "he ain't gonna see that triple out there. His snout is so low he can smell the worms."

Charles wiped his hands along his pant leg, wishing Carl would keep the narrative to himself.

The ascending oxer was next leading into the turn. Juniper fell out of the vertical, causing his back legs to kick out too far on the landing, but Ben maintained the two-point position through the gateway.

"Here it comes, boy," Ben said softly, anchoring over the saddle and giving Juniper a loose hold. Lining up and counting their strides, Ben felt Juniper snap his head for a brief moment, then lower it down again before launching off the ground like a spring.

"Turn him, turn him!"

The first turn had already begun before they even landed. Juniper's body flexed as his muscles stretched, swiping the pass and slingshotting straight to the water tray.

"There he goes again. I ain't fussin', but Lord almighty, what's that horse looking through, the top of his head?" Carl rubbed his temples as he watched.

"We got this one boy, it's just a creek," Ben whispered.

They cut the path lining up the water jump and gauged the takeoff. Ben felt no hesitation and watched Juniper's belly lift away a stride short, adding a foot to the width. The wind brushed his face, and he felt a laugh escape his lips.

"I can't look," Carl said, shaking his head, "they're runnin' this like two rogue wildcats!"

Light claps and gasps rumbled from the upper deck when they cleared the extra distance with ground to spare.

"Calm down Carl, you're going to give yourself a heart attack."

By now, Ben was picturing every jump and turn like it was just another day on the farm. He could even picture Elliot stomping and waving as they approached the high jump. "A little more, boy," he said, giving the rein a shake and pulling his thighs and elbows tight. Juniper popped his head just before their takeoff, lengthening his body over the top rail. Ben tipped a little too far forward, putting more weight on Juniper's neck as his body descended.

Charles saw Carl drop his head in his hands.

Juniper pushed against the extra weight as Ben tried to pull behind the saddle, but his elbows were too far forward. He leaned into Juniper's pull, cutting the descent and coming within fault zone. Ben felt a flutter of vibrations ripple down Juniper's neck as the horse strained against gravity to keep his arch high and his hind legs tucked. Juniper stuck the landing with a grunt and sped for the triple off the second turn.

Carl raised his head when he heard the excited humming of restrained voices, and one not-so-quiet woman at the end of the aisle making an inelegant whooping sound and pushing her fist into the air.

"Look at him go, Mr. Paul; they made the high jump!" Jack said, bouncing in his seat.

Paul smiled at Jack. Seeing how proud he was of his friend made his heart feel like an overinflated tire.

Ben gave Juniper a soft pat on the neck as they wore a new groove around the last turn to take the stretch of combinations. He knew he was putting too much pressure on his neck, so he released the tension, dropped his weight back, and stayed low as they approached the double. Juniper responded in kind by giving them a whole new gear. Juniper lowered his head, pulling all his power from his underbelly and drove hard against the ground, using all his hind strength. Their momentum was palpable—they were closing in on the day's time record, leading by three full seconds.

"Take off with him Ben!" Jack yelled, cupping his hands to his mouth and standing up, "run with him!"

Elizabeth giggled and glanced over at Paul, then turned back and started to clap, pulling her hands under her chin in tense anticipation of the finish.

Paul stood up and held his breath as he sunk his hands into his back pockets.

Ben didn't have time to fully recover out of the turn and regain center balance before they were on the next approach. He lined up with Juniper as best he could, leaning a bit too far into his right leg on takeoff, causing Juniper to kick out early and brush the top rail—not enough to knock it off the post, but costing them a fault for contact. They maintained their speed on the vertical and hit the triple on the nose. Their paces were balanced as they floated effortlessly in a graceful stretch, clearing the triple and setting a new show record.

"Yes!" Jack yelled, reaching for his mother's arm, pulling her hand from her chin. "He did good mother, he really did!"

Elizabeth got to her feet and rubbed Jack's shoulders while they watched Ben exit the gate, then turned to Paul. He was standing still, hands in his pockets. He wasn't shouting or outwardly excited, but when she looked into his eyes, there was a noticeable sparkle. He watched Ben until he was out of sight, then looked at her and smiled.

"You still breathing, old man?" Charles said with a chuckle, shaking Carl by the shoulder. "You see that?! Wildcats! You were right, ran that like their tail was on fire!"

"Poor choice of words there, don't ya think?"

Charles nodded in shameful agreement, but then the smile crossed his lips again. "You done good, Carl. Done real good."

Carl shook his head. "Ain't nothin' this old fool done, but one thing is for certain; they need control. Any more of that and I'll be under this here seat."

Charles laughed a hearty belly laugh as he looked out over the rows of spectators. The stadium buzzed with clapping and cheering, even as the next rider was being ushered to the staging pen. He glanced up at the suite behind them and saw Arthur standing at the balcony, lowering his binoculars and clapping.

By the time the next two riders had completed the course, Carl had pulled out his notebook and resumed his notetaking, focusing on the turns. He drew geometrical shapes and triangles with degrees and numbers scribbled on the page; looking at it made Charles's head hurt.

The announcer introduced the final rider, concluding by asking spectators to remain seated for the announcements of the finalists for the following day.

The last rider was another American from Salt Lake City. Charles pointed to the stable name listed in the show program and held it up for Carl to see. "Look here, that mount came from Sawyer's Acres. What are the odds?"

Carl continued with his diagrams, not paying Charles any mind. The first and second turn hurt the American on time, which was unrecoverable; after two faults, including one knockdown, they were all but out of the finals.

"Shucks," Charles said, "I'd like to talk to that fella, ask if he knows of Sawyer's whereabouts."

Carl kept his head down, adding up numbers and drawing more columns.

"What are you so engrossed in over there?"

Carl tucked his pencil into the spiral binding and slapped his finger over a diagram. "I think we got a shot at the finals."

A group of groundskeepers hurried out to the arena and made space for the podium by clearing a couple fences. Two men strung banners while others unrolled colorful streamers, attaching them around the base of a stage they rolled out to the center.

"These folks have this operation wound tight. They leave no room for the ordinary, do they," Charles said, watching the men run back and forth, tidying up the stage and assembling the décor and microphones.

Within minutes, the riders were gathered at the entrance to the arena, and the announcer and judges were seated on the stage holding large prongs with oversized numbers attached. The announcer took his appointed platform in the middle of the judges and lifted the microphone.

"Ladies and gentlemen, I ask that you turn your attention to the center of the arena while we receive the judges' scores for the top five finalists. These riders will advance to the final round tomorrow at ten o'clock, which will conclude with the closing ceremony and award presentation. May I present our fifth finalist, who accrued two and a half fault points on Course A: Ralph Messier from Spokane, Washington, in the United States. Our fourth finalist accrued two and a quarter fault points on Course A: Bjorn Achterberg from the Netherlands. Our third-place finalist accrued two faults on Course A: Benjamin Paulie from Greenfield, Iowa, in the United States. Our second-place finalist accrued one-and three-quarter fault points on Course A: Ethan Bergeron from Edmonton, Canada. Our first-place finalist accrued one fault point on Course A: Pierre Auclair from Strasbourg, France."

The crowd cheered and confetti showered down from overhead. The band played in a roped-off section behind the stage as the riders exited the arena.

Charles and Carl stretched their legs, looking for an opening as people made their way into the aisles.

"What a show. Suppose we should head to the stable?"

"I reckon. If we start now, we should be there by suppertime," Carl said, his eyes boggling at the congested exits.

"I can't wait to see Ben!" Jack said, "I bet he's excited about tomorrow. Would it be alright if he comes over tonight, Mother? We can play baseball with Oliver and Tommy in the park!"

"Let's be respectful of their time, dear. We don't know the preparations they need to make for the second day. Let's wait until we hear their plans for this evening."

Jack pushed out into the aisle and waited for Paul and his mother to follow, then hurried around the corner and down the ramp.

"That was such fun," Elizabeth said. "Thank you so much for the invitation. It was a spectacular show, and I am utterly beside myself that he made the finals. You must be so proud."

"I didn't know what to expect, but it sure wasn't anything on this scale. Ever since I stepped off that train, it's been one shockwave after another. But yes, I am proud, very much so. I've been thinking... since we have an extra day, I thought it would be nice to take you and Jack out for supper. Something that isn't too saucy—I'm running out of shirts."

"I would be delighted, and I'm sure Jack will be, too. And just in case you're missing some comfort food, I know of a quaint little café on 81st that serves fillet and potatoes."

Paul laughed and smacked his lips together. "How did you figure me for a steak man?"

"Just a hunch," she said slyly.

*   *   *

Charles slowed at the end of the ramp, waiting for Carl, who had been absorbed by the masses coming down the corridor, when he felt a tap on his arm. Turning around, he was met with Arthur's beaming face.

"I told you I would find you if I liked what I saw."

"I'm happy to see you, my friend, but how did you get down here so fast?"

"The suites have a private entrance and exit—it bypasses the congestion," he said with a grin and a wink. "Are you meeting up with Benjamin at the Garden Stables?"

"Yes, sir—or at least we're hoping to make our way there. Seems like quite the journey—this place is a mile wide!"

"Please, allow me."

Charles motioned at Carl to step out of the herd and watched as Arthur waved over two men wearing long overcoats standing by a small black cart with a bench seat. The men peddled the cart under an archway to a roped-off corridor, and Arthur slipped a large bill into the hand of one of the men.

"Right this way, gentlemen," Arthur said, motioning to the long black bench seat under the canopy.

Carl and Charles enjoyed the light breeze as they rolled down the quiet underlay of the massive structure. They veered into a two-lane tunnel, passing other lucky passengers in their carts.

"Thank you, Arthur, this is quite the treat," Charles said.

"Only reasonable way to get around this place. I'll have passes for you to watch from the suite tomorrow. The view is spectacular and will serve Carl well in his analysis of form."

Charles bumped Carl with his elbow. "You hear that? You'll have a bird's-eye view."

Carl checked his pocket to make sure his notebook was secure and closed his eyes, enjoying the soft rattle of the cart's wheels.

35

BEN HUNG THE SADDLE, PULLED an apple from his bag, and held it out, stroking Juniper's head. He watched the other riders shake hands, listening to them speak in foreign tongues; some even had cameramen take their photos. He took a few steps further into the corner of the stall, speaking softly to Juniper and rubbing his muzzle.

"Benjamin Paulie? Young man, are you in there?"

Recognizing the man's voice, Ben let go of the apple, allowing Juniper to finish it as he walked to the door and found the paddock master smiling at him.

"Might you be available for a photograph? I have the chaps gathering out front, and the photo wouldn't be complete without you."

"Yes, sir," Ben said, latching the door behind him and following the man to the front of the stable area. When he joined the other finalists, he was bombarded by camera flashes and rapid-fire questions from journalists hankering for commentary. The men behind the lenses shouted at Ben and the other riders, gesticulating wildly, each wanting a specific angle. Ben began to sweat, turning his head from side to side in the direction of the loudest voice. The bursts of bright flashes blurred his vision, and all the noise and movement made his head throb. The reporters crowded around each other, their fingers clutching small pencils over handheld notebooks, their questions blending together into unintelligible noise. He rubbed his eyes, stepping behind the other riders and turning away from the mob of hungry news hoarders, leaving the other riders to the relentless attention.

"Ben, Ben! Over here!" Jack yelled, jumping up and down just beyond a gated entrance.

Ben's eyes strained toward the direction of his call, until three silhouettes slowly came into focus. "Jack!" he said, running the length of the stable, swerving around stable helpers and past two relaxed guards that gave him a polite nod as he approached the gate.

"You done real good, Ben! That was wild! I can't believe you done this good!" Jack said, patting him on the shoulder. "I mean, I knew you wouldn't fall off or nothin', but you made it to the next day!"

Ben smiled and laughed. "Come this way—you won't believe this!"

Jack and Ben walked shoulder to shoulder, looking around the inside of the fancy stable. Ben pulled on Jack's sleeve, guiding him away from the newsmen still swarming about as the riders tended to their horses and gear.

"Where we going?" Jack asked.

"You'll see. Follow me, it's over here."

Ben led him to a large white box in the corner, glancing around to ensure no one was watching. "Look at this!" He opened the lid, revealing loads and loads of ice cream bars and popsicles of every kind of flavor, heaped all the way to the top.

"I had four, but I can eat another!" Ben said, ogling over the assortment.

"Holy cow, I seen ice cream bars before, but not this many!" Jack pulled out a grape popsicle and unwrapped it quickly, stuffing the wrapper in his pocket and taking a large lick off the side.

"I knew you were going to pick the grape ones—that's why I didn't take one."

Hearing quiet giggling from behind, they turned to see Paul and Elizabeth smiling at them.

Paul stepped forward, placing a hand on Ben's shoulder. "You looked good out there."

"Thanks, Mr. Paul!"

"You looked very elegant," Elizabeth said, "it was truly a privilege to watch you ride."

Ben smiled, feeling his cheeks flush. "Thanks Miss Elizabeth. I just imagined the farm and Mr. Elliot in my head—that seemed to help."

Paul snickered, knowing just how much that sentiment would mean to Elliot, and made a mental note to tell him just that.

"Have you seen Mr. Carl?" Ben asked.

"Not since they left the hotel, but I reckon they'll be slow-moving. Carl ain't too quick in a herd, and there's a lot of ground to cover around here."

"Look! There they are!" Ben said, pointing to a riding cart with two men peddling.

"Looks like they got a ride," Paul said, curious to know who they were seated with.

Charles joked with the dapper-dressed man as they exited the cart. The man extended his arm, giving Carl a steady post to cling to as he dismounted. Paul examined the man's appearance; he was tan with dark brown hair cut high over his ears and a side part that looked too slick for a random spectator. His overcoat was accented with gold buttons, making his crisp blue shirt pop against the metallic black coat and slacks. The buckle around his waist highlighted his trim physique; he was obviously in superb shape and stood a full four inches taller, which surprised him more than anything. At six-three, he wasn't accustomed to looking up to anyone. As they approached, he picked up on the man's accent, making him that much more curious.

Charles and Carl walked toward them while the man slowed his pace, letting them greet Ben and celebrate in a private space. Paul kept his eyes on the man, watching him linger at the last stall, keeping his head down and checking his watch.

"Boy, you sure do know how to knock us out of our boots!" Carl said, reaching over and giving his shoulder a shake, "how you feel, you feel good?"

"I feel great, Mr. Carl! Sorry for the turn there. I know I dropped my shoulders too soon… really made Juniper fight for that one."

"Boy, you done us all proud. You ain't got nothin' to be sorry for— that kinda thing is gonna happen from time to time. Juniper can handle it. He don't expect you to ride perfect, ain't no such thing."

Charles looked back at Arthur and noticed his annoyed facial expression as he shifted his body to face the wall, then turned to Ben.

"I'm proud of you, son. That was great fun to watch you out there! Wonderful!

Ben and Jack slurped the last of their frozen pops, exchanged wide-eyed glances, and turned back to the box.

"You picking another cherry one?" Jack asked.

Ben shook his head, scanning the assortment. "This time I'm picking the root beer one!"

Suddenly, a growing clamor of voices rose from the stable entrance and the swarm of cameramen and reporters filled the path between them and Arthur. Shouts calling after Arthur echoed through the corridor as the large group of men crowded around him, leveraging for a spot in front, shouting questions at him.

"Arthur Davies, Arthur Davies!" His name was called repeatedly, accompanied by flashes of bulbs and men talking over each other.

Charles looked over at the commotion and then turned back to Ben. "I guess that is a good segue into the introduction."

Paul and Elizabeth looked confused as they looked at Arthur and then back to Charles.

"That's Arthur Davies—he's here to meet Benjamin," Charles said.

"We'll catch you up later," Carl said, giving Paul a wink.

"That's the man we saw before the show!" Ben said, "the one that talks different!"

"Yes, it is," Charles chuckled, "he's originally from Great Britain, but now he lives upstate."

"He's here to meet me?" Ben asked, looking over at the tall man, heads above the cameramen. "He sure is tall."

"He likes the way you ride," Charles said.

Ben pursed his lips and nodded, still watching the spectacle.

Arthur appeased the excited frenzy, giving a short commentary on the show before politely excusing himself.

Paul watched Arthur as he walked over, remarkably calm amidst the horde of cameramen continuing to take shots as he moved further away. He approached with a warm smile, his confidence unmistakable—so much so it was slightly aggravating to Paul.

"Pleasure is all mine, Benjamin, sir," Arthur said, reaching out for a handshake, "my name is Arthur Davies."

"Hello, Mr. Davies," Ben said, losing his hand inside Arthur's firm grip.

Arthur looked at Elizabeth, and Paul could almost see a blush of red cross his cheeks. "Hello, miss, pleasure to make your acquaintance."

Elizabeth shook his hand. "My, you look familiar, but I cannot place it."

"As do you; have you visited Westminster Abbey in the last four days?"

Elizabeth giggled. "Not lately, no."

"Westchester perhaps?"

"Yes! My father purchased two colts over the years from an exceptional breeder. They are remarkable creatures, and with such good temperaments. Wait… are you of the Davies family from Westchester Stables?!"

Arthur lifted his hat with a slight bow. "I am, although my father deserves the credit for the breeding. Most of the brood resides in England, except for my mother and father. Who is your father, if I might ask?"

"Henry Rockwood, have you heard of him?"

"The famous New York chocolatier? Who hasn't heard of him! Surely every person who fancies fine confections. What a remarkable chance meeting. So remarkable," Arthur said, giving her a gracious nod.

"This here's Paul Rogers," Carl said, observing Paul's awkwardness at Arthur's exchange with Elizabeth.

"Paul!" Arthur said with enthusiasm, "it's a pleasure, sir, nice to meet you."

"Likewise," Paul said in a cool tone, returning the stiff handshake with a tight squeeze.

Arthur could sense Paul's territorial nature—it wasn't the first time he was met with distrust. He never got tired of male skepticism, and in fact welcomed it. It only proved that he wasn't lacking in charisma or good looks—or, heaven forbid, getting any shorter.

"I haven't met you yet, young man," Arthur said to Jack, whose lips were covered in a deep purple hue.

"I'm Jack, sir! Ben is my buddy—we met back in Iowa and stayed friends even after me and my mother moved back here when my father left. This is the first time we've seen each other since!"

Elizabeth felt awkwardly shy and slightly embarrassed as she listened to Jack divulge their sensitive story, but grinned and shrugged hopelessly at his overshare nonetheless.

Arthur was humored and entertained by his innocent honesty, then reached for his sticky hand with a smile. "I am happy you two have reunited."

"I suppose we should find a place for a bite to eat; I'm sure everyone is hankering for a meal. I know I'm starting to grumble," Charles said, placing his hand on his belly.

"Ben and I wanted to go to Alberto's for ziti! Can we, Mother, please!"

"Alberto's is hard to beat, but I would love to bring you all to my home for a catered meal," Arthur said, "complete with the pasta of your choosing and strawberry shortcake."

Ben and Jack smacked their chops and tossed their popsicle wrappers.

Carl wriggled his hands in his pockets, shaking loose change. "I suppose we could catch one of them yellow taxi cars," Carl said, "how far is the drive?"

"Not necessary," Arthur said. "Allow me to arrange your ride. They will pick you up in an hour outside your hotel and drop you off after we conclude the evening. I'll send for two cars, so you have ample leg room."

"Much obliged, Arthur," Charles said. "That sounds dandy."

Arthur checked his watch. "I'll plan for your arrival around four o'clock, and I will request an early banquet to get you back before dark. We all have another early morning ahead of us."

Carl raised his hand, like he was in a third-grade classroom, "I ain't too swift on leavin' the horse unattended. Seems like this racket doesn't die down—ever."

"Rest assured, Carl, I'll put one of my apprentice trainers in the car to watch over Juniper until you return," Arthur said, giving them a wave as he walked to the two cyclists waiting by the cart.

Carl looked at Charles, hoisting his suspenders and raising his eyebrows. "I can get used to this—that man's got some clout!"

"Wow, Ben, we're going to his place! I bet it's really nice!" Jack whispered.

"I think we should mosey back to the hotel and put on fresh britches," Carl said.

Paul looked over at Elizabeth, feeling a bit deflated as his plans for a special evening were muscled-out by a big shot looking to make an impression, but he was happy for Ben's budding opportunity.

"I don't want to intrude on your evening," Elizabeth said. "Jack and I can meet up with you all in the morning—I can clear my calendar another day."

"The invitation was for all of us, little lady, you ain't off the hook that easily," Carl said, giving her a grin before he headed to the gate.

"We're all in this together," Charles said, following behind Carl.

"I personally wouldn't have it any other way," Paul said. "It isn't quite what I had in mind, but I do hope you and Jack are coming along."

Elizabeth smiled and nodded her head.

"Yippee!" Jack hollered, smacking Ben on the arm as they hurried over to pet Juniper.

Paul looked down as Elizabeth turned to him. He stared at his funny-looking shoes and scratchy pleated trousers, still feeling like he didn't quite measure up to someone like Arthur with his fancy suits and droves of admirers.

"I know of a great little spot, and if we hurry, we can make it back in plenty of time to meet the drivers," she said. "Boys, you want to catch a carriage ride?"

"Let's go, Ben, you're going to love this!" Jack said

They climbed into a carriage pulled by two large horses, Ben and Paul admiring the shiny buckles and elegant embellishments along their reins. The man seated atop the carriage tipped his hat at Elizabeth as if he recognized her and took her instructions to the destination. Ben and Jack climbed over the first seat into the rear bench where they had an elevated view, and Ben listened and watched as Jack pointed out everything along their path.

The driver pulled up to a small boutique on the corner, and they all exited just in time to see men carrying boxes through the door. A younger fella tugged at a mannequin to get it through the front door, knocking the arm off, causing everyone to smile.

"It's coming together quite nicely, Miss Rockwood. Wish I could say the same about the mannequin," the driver said.

Elizabeth laughed into her hand, not wanting to draw more attention to the young man's bumble, and waved goodbye to the driver.

Paul's attention was fixated on the chaos of the street, lined with outdoor vendors and bustling shoppers dressed in fine suits and dresses, some carrying bags as big as suitcases.

"Never seen so many people concerned with what they wear," Paul said, watching a lady pull out three pairs of shoes and show them to the lady walking beside her.

"Fashion is everything here in the city," Elizabeth said, admiring the woman's silver slingback heels.

"It's right over there!" Jack said, pulling Ben by the sleeve.

Ben and Jack hurried across the street. Ben stopped at the center of the sidewalk, gawking at the tall building and the two-story train track that wrapped around the exterior.

"Watch, Ben! It's coming—do you hear it?"

Ben turned his head to listen. "What are we listening for?"

"That! Look up!"

Ben heard a whistle blow and looked up to see a train coming from the second story, running along a small track with its own platform extending out from the windows. It tooted its whistle again before clacking along the track and disappearing into a small tunnel that ran back inside the building.

Glancing at Ben, Jack laughed—his friend looked like he had just seen a magic trick, standing there speechless with his mouth hanging open.

"Let's go, they got more inside!"

Paul admired the architecture and design of the signage that ran the length of the storefront. The lettering was carved out of vibrant gold material and affixed to a red awning. The shape of each letter was beveled at the corners, creating a three-dimensional effect. He stepped out of the path of a group of small children as they hurried inside.

"FAO Schwarz," Paul said, "I take it they are popular with the youngins?"

"The most popular," Elizabeth said. "It's the landmark every kid in New York cherishes—two floors packed floor to ceiling with every kind of toy, train, doll, and instrument you can imagine. How about you join them and enjoy Ben's reaction? I'll find you inside—I have a quick errand across the street."

Paul approached the doors, eyeing a man dressed as a toy soldier. He flinched as the man moved unexpectedly, opening the large, brass-trimmed door with white-gloved hands for him to pass through. Glancing behind him as the man closed the door, he turned to face a grand display of humming motorized miniature cars and trains rolling around an extravagant display of tiny houses in a countryside setting. He leaned over the tiny farm with tiny plastic farm animals and felt the pang of longing for the familiarity of home.

"Mr. Paul, look!" Ben hollered, "we're up here!"

Paul gasped as his eyes trailed upward, seeing Ben and Jack holding the largest stuffed bear he had ever seen. It was twice their size, requiring both of them to support its floppy head. The second floor was alive with whimsical music, and every square inch seemed to be occupied by some type of mechanized gadget. As he slowly made his way up the stairs, a miniature airplane whizzed past him overhead, carried by a metal arm that swung in a wide circle.

"Can you believe this place Mr. Paul?" Ben said, following Jack as he bounced from aisle to aisle, touching and marveling over shelves of tiny figurines, moving their arms and legs.

Jack picked up a small army man holding a rifle. "This is the new military set. Look, the heads even turn! I'm asking for this one for Christmas!"

Paul followed the boys through the store, getting a kick out of their banter as they held up the newest gizmo that caught their attention; he even checked out a few himself after he got acclimated to the assault on his nervous system. After a lap around the store, they headed for the stairs.

"There's my mother!" Jack said, pointing to a waving hand at the door.

She smiled, watching them get closer, their eyes still beaming with excitement and overstimulation.

"Well… what did you think?" she asked.

"That was the best store ever!" Ben said, "I can't believe what I saw! There's things in there I've never seen before, and Lucas would flip over those chemistry sets!"

"And what about you?" she asked, giggling at Paul's ruffled appearance. "You came out with all your faculties, so it must have been mildly entertaining."

Paul glanced back a few more times and ran his hand through his hair. "What a place… there's something around every corner."

"Strange and wonderful," Elizabeth sighed, taking in a deep breath of air, and lifting her chin up.

Paul looked at her, watching her hair dip below the middle of her back as she turned in a half circle, swinging a bag in her hand.

"Strange and wonderful indeed," he muttered.

"Here, this is for you," she said, handing him a brown bag with thin tissue covering the opening.

"What's this?"

"Not much. Just a little comfort maybe—something that brings home a little closer."

Paul grinned, his cheeks flushing bright pink, momentarily accentuating his blue eyes as he peeked inside and pulled out a blue and red plaid flannel. The fabric was brushed cotton and felt as soft as silk in his hands, with two-tone buttons and pockets at the waist and chest. He slipped it over his collared shirt, running his hands along the sleeves.

"It's a perfect fit—just a touch below your back pockets, and it falls squarely at your hips."

"I have to say, this is the best gift I have ever received. If we don't count that candy bar and the pocket watch, that is."

Elizabeth dropped her head and pulled her shoulder up to her ear with a shy grin.

"What's behind your back?" Paul asked.

She handed him another bag, noticing his awkward expression.

"You didn't get me another gift I hope!" Paul said, feeling a bit self-aware as the boys stood over his shoulder looking at the bag.

"I promise, this is the last one. It's such a good complement to the shirt, I couldn't resist."

Paul hesitated, but accepted the bag, pulling out a box.

He lifted the lid with a laugh, turning the boot over in his hand. The leather was just as smooth as the shirt and the embroidery of the branding on the ankle pads were an obvious clue that these boots were out of any price range he could muster.

"I don't know what to say… I can't accept all this Elizabeth. As fine as these are, they are way too expensive. I can't let you pay for boots like these."

Jack giggled and covered his mouth. "Mr. Paul, my mother has more money than she knows what to do with."

"Jack, my darling, that is not the way we discuss our matters."

"Sorry, Mother," he said, still snickering with Ben.

Paul examined the boots and lifted the tongue. "Size twelve… how did you know?"

Jack slapped his hand across his thigh, laughing even harder.

"What's so funny?" Paul asked, watching a grin cross Elizabeth's lips.

"It's my job to know these things—I'm a fashion designer. That store we stopped in front of is mine. If I don't know a shoe size when I see it, I'm in the wrong industry."

Paul looked at her in surprise, glancing toward the boutique across the street where men continued to carry ladders and boxes through the door.

"Show him, Mother, show him the store!" Jack said. "It don't look good yet—there's stuff everywhere—but it looks better than when she bought it."

"I don't want to take too much of your time," Elizabeth said. "Perhaps you and Ben would like some time to relax in your rooms before the trip to Westchester."

"I can get changed faster than a hiccup," Paul said excitedly. "I would love to see it."

"Me, too!" Ben said. "I think it's neat—you both have stores of your own!"

"Now it makes sense," Paul said as they waited for cars to pass before crossing.

"What is that exactly?" Elizabeth asked.

"It's everything—your style, your grace." He held up his boots. "Your impeccable taste. You're an artist. You make everything… well… beautiful."

Jack snickered and leaned in close to Ben's ear. "Did you hear that? He said, 'beautiful.'"

When they got to the side of the store, Elizabeth was greeted by a man carrying a ladder. "Nice to see you today, Miss Rockwood. We're almost finished with the light fixtures, and your desk and measuring tables will be here shortly."

"Thank you, Eldon, I do appreciate that. Would you mind if we had a quick walk-through? We will be out of your way quickly."

"Not at all! Just watch your step—we have tools lying about, and Scotty's in there. You know how he is—he isn't too aware of his surroundings."

Elizabeth smiled knowingly at his warning. As they stepped through the door, a large plank of wood floated by, carried by a pair of legs pivoting beneath it.

"Duck!" Jack shouted, tugging Ben out of the way.

Scotty turned to see who had entered, unintentionally swinging the opposite end of the board toward them, only to drop it at his feet at the last moment.

"Hey, Jack! Hello, Miss Rockwood," Scotty said.

"Hello, Scotty, nice to see you," Elizabeth said. "Looks like you are very busy today."

"Yes ma'am! And I got the big dolls put together for you."

Elizabeth's eyes scanned the interior, and a small chuckle escaped her when she noticed a mannequin with its arm on backwards.

"I see, and you did a very fine job, I must say."

Paul was impressed with the woodworking and enjoyed the smell of cedar tickling his nose. The comforting aroma soothed his nerves, and he inhaled deeply as they stepped over mounds of sawdust gathered on the floor beneath sawhorses. One corner of the room was wallpapered in a creamy tapestry of pale yellow and cream that lit up the room as the sun hit the wall. Sparkling glass and crystal shimmered from a grand chandelier, casting light onto a platform surrounded by mirrors below. The windows in the front reached from the floor to the ceiling, giving an ample view of the buzzing street outside.

"It's not quite ready for show, but I should have it completed within a few weeks. Do you like it?"

"Like it? I think it's wonderful," Paul said, turning his head in all directions and running his hand along a carved beam of wood. "I can see you have some skilled tradesmen on the job—this is impressive."

"I am fortunate that my brother Tony is building another restaurant on the west end of the city and his workers go back and forth between here and there. Most of the materials came from what he couldn't use or ordered too much of. Of course, he didn't order dressing mirrors and pastel wall wrapping," she laughed.

"And probably not those," Paul said, pointing to the two boys poking each other playfully with the mannequin arms.

"Definitely not," Elizabeth said, shaking her head in amusement.

"How'd you think that looked right, Scotty?" Jack said, holding his hand out to his side and turning it as far backwards as he could reach. "Your arms don't look like this! If they did, you wouldn't be able to swing a baseball bat."

Ben helped Scotty attach the arms in the right direction while Jack ran in circles holding the torso of another. The boys looked at the headless models and laughed at the bare, curvy form, giggling and pointing at the bosoms.

"Boys will be boys," Elizabeth said. "The jokes around here never cease."

Paul agreed, trying his best not to entertain their fun, and looked at her. "I am happy for you, Elizabeth. This is something else, something to be very proud of—you have a great future ahead of you."

He was surprised by her reaction. She shrugged her shoulders and gave it one last brief glance. "It's one of many ideas taking up space in my head. We should probably head back now boys."

"See ya, Scotty!" Jack said as they hurried to the door.

"See ya guys, bye Ben!" Scotty said, picking up the board and turning, nearly toppling over a tool bucket as he got back to work.

Walking to the carriage, Jack noticed a group of men at the corner, their cameras all pointing in their direction.

"Look, Ben, they're talking about you. I bet they recognize your clothes from the show! Maybe they will take our picture and put it in the paper!" Jack said.

As the men started to walk in their direction, the carriage driver held the door open and ushered them to their seats.

36

Everyone waited in the hotel lobby while Ben and Paul went to change. Jack's attention was drawn to a fountain in the corner, and Carl was busy reviewing his notes. For the first time, Elizabeth and Charles were alone, giving them time to get to know each other.

"I'm glad you decided to join us," Charles said awkwardly, keeping his chin lowered.

"Why, thank you Mr. Collins, we appreciate the invitation. The show was incredible. It is quite a shame that I have lived here all my life and have never been to this marvelous event; I guess if you're not in the know about horses, it will pass you by."

"I can't say I'm surprised. Seems to be things pass you by faster than your head can turn in these parts."

"It's true—it can be a lot to take in. I do hope Paul is enjoying it. I know it has been overwhelming for him."

"Darlin', I can tell you for certain, wherever you are, you can best be sure that that boy is enjoying it."

Elizabeth smiled, her pink lips parting, and the brightness of her face relaxed Charles. She was pleased to hear his remark and charmed at the fatherly way he spoke of Paul. His care and concern for Paul's well-being was touching, and she could feel that this group of strong, hard-working men were becoming a comfort to her soul.

"I am pleased to hear that, Mr. Collins, and do know that I adore his company greatly. He is a very good man indeed."

Charles nodded, finally meeting her eyes. She could almost see the water welling, and he turned quickly and walked toward Carl, looking back at her after rubbing his eyes. "Please, Miss Elizabeth, call me Charles."

Elizabeth grinned.

The ding of the elevator chimed, and Paul and Ben stepped out. Ben spotted Jack at the fountain and hurried over. Carl pursed his lips and whistled at Paul. "That is one fine shirt, boy!"

Paul stood in front of the door as it closed, smoothing his hands down the front, looking down at his feet and lifting his toes.

"Doggone, now those are some trodders," Carl said, walking over for a better look.

Charles looked over at Elizabeth and gave her a wink.

Paul walked over to her, feeling a bit bashful as he waited for her opinion.

"You look more like you. Very handsome—and comfortable," she said.

"Thank you again. You have no idea how good it felt to drop those slick-soled cages in the waste can."

Her infectious laugh echoed throughout the lobby. "If you ever need a good pair of dress shoes, ones that don't feel like cages, please write me, and I will send you a pair you'll fancy."

"I believe that's them," Charles said, looking past the bellman at two yellow cars pulling up in front of the building. The first car stopped, and a young thin man stepped out, buttoned his jacket, and greeted the bellman. When he noticed the group exiting the lobby, he introduced himself as Arthur's assistant in training.

"I'm Andrew Madison, nice to meet you."

"Likewise," Charles said, giving an introduction as they all gathered by the cars.

"And you must be Benjamin," Andrew said, extending his hand to Jack.

"I ain't—I can't ride a horse at all!" Jack said, stepping to the side. "This is Ben, he's my best buddy."

Elizabeth put a hand to her lips, touched by the sentiment, and fluttered a look over to Paul who was obviously moved by it as well.

"Hello Ben," Andrew said, shaking his hand. "Do you have any special instructions for me? I want you to feel comfortable with your horse in my care while you pay a visit to the stables."

"He's probably had too many apples today; he'll eat a bushel if you let him. He likes the left side of the grazing area near the fence—one of the attendants gave him a handful of raisins so he keeps to that side."

"He ain't too quick to welcome strangers neither, so you might need a little help with that," Carl said, reaching into his pocket. "Here, take this. Just watch your fingers, he won't bat an eye to take one of 'em."

"Peppermint," Andrew said, holding the sprigs up to his nose, "always a favorite."

"Should make him follow you out to stretch his legs, at least he won't take a nip at your britches" Carl said.

"Thank you for the pointers," Andrew said, stepping to the side as the drivers walked around the cars and opened the doors. "Enjoy your visit to the stables."

Elizabeth gazed out the window as they drove through the city, while Ben and Jack speculated about whether the bronze fish in the fountain had once been a real fish. She always enjoyed the view of city life, so many things rushing by. Her eyes fell upon a young family; two small children were nestled between their parents huddled around a baby stroller. It gave her a warm feeling, but it was fleeting. She often found herself turning away from happy couples laughing together over coffees in outdoor cafes or taking a midday stroll through the park holding hands. Her own picture-perfect family ideal had been fractured.

During the drive, she caught herself looking at Paul in the front seat. She memorized the structure of his jawbone and the angle of the stubble as it wrapped around his lower cheekbones. His features were rugged, as if chiseled from fine stone. The dark hair of his short beard somehow made his eyebrows lighter in comparison and she was surprised by the length of his lashes. She also noticed a dimple that would appear when he clenched his jaw, adding even more mystery to what thoughts went on inside his head. Her stomach muscles tightened when he quietly turned his head to look over his shoulder, catching her look away rather quickly.

A sly grin crossed the corner of his mouth, and he gazed back out the window.

Distracting herself with vistas of the calm picturesque countryside, she recognized the hills and valleys as they caravaned along windy roads cutting through vast grasslands. It was a familiar trek, as she often traveled upstate with her family during the autumn for a large picnic at their cabin.

"Mother, look—that's the way to grandfather's cottage!"

The driver glanced in the mirror. "Abbey Springs is quite the eye opener. Your family has a place there?"

"Yes, we do. It's our retreat for whenever we all need to touch grass again," Elizabeth sighed, momentarily missing the natural wonders outside the city limits.

Paul noticed the driver's eyes get wide, as if he were impressed by her answer, and Paul's eyes followed the private path as it curved upward to a wooden bridge. He began imagining what Elizabeth's family was like, and before he knew it, he was daydreaming about being surrounded by a large family, with Ben and Jack playing and people enjoying each other's company. He caught himself, startled and a bit scared by his own desires, and decided to distract himself by thinking about what Elliot might be doing right now.

The rest of the drive was quiet—aside from the boys. Jack and Ben covered everything from insects to planets and still had gas in their tanks when they arrived at a large archway that had the name "Westchester Stables" displayed in iron letters across the gated entrance. Two statues of horses stood in the middle of landscaped flower beds, one on each side.

"Whoa," Jack said, pressing his face to the window, "this place is neat!"

Ben looked left to right across wide-open fields, lined with straight white fences that stretched over acres of rich green grass, rolling like waves over the ocean. He saw large, covered trailers rolling past buildings, and several open training areas that were just as big as the horse show arena. One enclosure had jumps set up and even its own liverpool. He saw wall jumps covered with vines and shrubbery wrapped around the posts, and in the corner, a man stood on a high platform holding binoculars and watching a rider. Horses were everywhere, being walked or ridden, no matter which direction he turned. They were in the fields, arenas, grazing pastures—he even saw a small group of young kids riding in a line following a man who looked to be an instructor.

As they curved along the driveway, they passed long stables—Ben counted at least eight. All the buildings were uniform in color, with rich brown walls, windows trimmed in bright white, and red roofs. Perfectly groomed paths weaved around and through the stables as riders and handlers walked horses in all directions. Two men waved at them while they sat on a bench outside a watering house scuffing horseshoes.

The drive narrowed as they ascended a hill, the view of the stables gradually obscured by low-hanging weeping willows, vibrant wisteria trees, and clusters of white dogwoods. Elizabeth gasped when she saw the most beautiful blossoming cherry trees she had ever laid eyes on.

"This is absolutely stunning!" she said, rolling down the window in hopes of smelling their fragrance.

Carl was flabbergasted. He hadn't uttered a word since they entered the gates.

Paul marveled at the architecture of the house coming up on their right. The porch wrapped around the entire home, supported by grand columns on each side. The black shutters were a stark contrast to the white exterior and large glass windows. The roof had several pitches providing shelter over third floor balconies, and there was a large pond off the west corner.

"Nice place," Paul commented to the driver.

"That is the stable worker's quarters. Some are seasonal and only stay during the busy training season, and others only stay for specific shows. But our manager, Jerry Doogle, is year-round; he stays in that cabin set back near the pond."

Paul saw a small rowboat pulled up to a bank, and a row of casters hung along a rack attached to the side of the cabin. "That would be the one I would pick too."

"The main house is just up ahead," the driver said.

"Did you hear that?" Ben whispered to Jack. "This ain't even the main house."

They rolled up one more hill and over a wooden bridge that crossed a creek. Ben and Jack stuck their heads out of the window, ogling at the lampposts and apple trees that lined the drive. Four massive white columns held up the roof covering the grand entrance.

"This looks like Buckingham Palace!" Jack said.

Tall, slender trees and short bushes curved around cobblestone walkways and sitting areas around the property. Elizabeth admired a fountain nestled in the center of a pergola, a canopy of wildflowers and greenery woven through the beams above.

"Reminds me of Italy," she said, leaning forward between Paul and the driver and repeating the words in French. Her breath sweetened the air, and the waft of her light perfume hung softly around her. Paul listened to her voice speaking foreign words and took a deep inhale, feeling his blood run hot; everything about her kept him in a constant state of intrigue and delight.

The cars stopped under the stone arch of the main entrance. An elderly couple stood up from their rocking chairs in the corner of the stately porch. A man wearing a butler's uniform opened the door with a white towel over his arm.

"I don't know about you, but I feel a little underdressed," Carl said, snapping the shoulder of his exposed suspender.

Jack and Ben poured out of the seat, staring up at the painted glass windows that curved around the stoney structure.

"Reminds me of a castle!" Ben whispered, shifting his eyes to the man holding the door open and the couple shuffling to the top of the stairs.

Through the entrance, Ben saw someone coming down a wide, curved staircase just inside the doorway. As the man came into view and checked his watch, Ben recognized him instantly.

"Right on time," Arthur said, walking down the stairs and greeting them with a welcoming smile.

The first driver nodded and closed the door after the last passenger exited.

"Simon is the most punctual man I know. He also moonlights as one of our course timers," Arthur said. "Please, come inside, the terrace is a wonderful setting for the meal and has a view of the orchards."

Arthur led them up the stairs, walking over to the couple who were standing off to the side. "These are my parents, Arthur Sr. and Patricia Davies."

As they greeted each other, Patricia held Elizabeth's hand for an extended moment, complimenting her on her dress. The couple made them feel welcome, and it softened Paul's initial judgment of Arthur as a puffed-up, egocentric bachelor. After all, he housed his aging parents. *How bad can the guy be?* he thought.

Arthur introduced Gerald, their butler, giving him a pat on the shoulder. There was no haughty pretense, just a warm family feeling about all of them. They walked through the large entryway and were led through double glass doors to the outside terrace. The space was simple yet elegantly designed and gave them a superb view of the surrounding vineyards, woods, and rolling fields with clusters of fruit trees.

"I thought this would be a nice setting for our dinner. The weather is perfect, and it offers the best view of the grounds—we might even see a few deer pass through," Arthur said, inviting them to gather around the table. "After we have dined, I can take you for a tour before your departure."

"This is such a treat," Charles said. "We very much appreciate the invitation and the opportunity to visit."

"Sure beats the backwoods of Greenfield. I ain't never seen a spread like this before," Carl added. "Makes me think we should have turned to this jumpin' business a long time ago."

Arthur laughed. "We didn't get here solely from the horse business, although, I must confess, it's been an extraordinary journey."

"You ain't been in racin'. I know that much," Carl said.

Gerald brought a pitcher of iced tea and a tray of tall glasses, doing his best to keep from cracking a smile, like he knew a secret. He placed the glasses down slowly, hoping he would catch some of the conversation—

he enjoyed the reaction most people had when they heard Arthur's story for the first time.

"I don't know a thing about horse racing, never saw the allure," Arthur said, uncorking a bottle of merlot and carrying it to the ledge, looking out into the vineyard. "The idea of watching horses run fiercely in a large circle always felt like a disservice to their power and elegance. When you watch a horse jump, for example, you see them in their natural state. The way they maneuver, their agility, grace, and momentum. There is something majestic and harmonious in their movement, like a melody that flows through their spirit, and we are the lucky violinists they sing to."

Arthur waved the glass under his nose to inhale the fruity elixir and looked back at the table. Everyone was staring at him with the same expression of wonder and euphoria, like he had spoken something so profound it stunned them into silence.

"Please, don't interpret that as criticism toward the sport. I simply prefer to see their grandeur and performance in a more primal and natural way," Arthur clarified, not meaning to offend their area of expertise.

"I certainly didn't take it that way," Charles said. "I'm still caught up in the way you described it. I never thought of it that way, but it sure makes sense."

"Arthur Sr. brought his love for fine wine here from England, and before that, my great grandfather owned wineries across Italy. Growing up, I was fortunate enough to work alongside them, learning the family business. And with so much ground to cover, I was allowed to own a horse. It wasn't long before I was spending more time riding than picking and grinding. One thing led to another, and I convinced my father to let me take formal riding lessons in turn for weekends at the vineyards."

"You're a young, strapping lad. Why don't you ride now?" Carl asked.

Charles winced, feeling like that was getting too personal for a casual meal and a view.

"After four national championships in Dublin, Paris, and London, along with an invitation to the Olympics, I had my run and just wished to be home. When my grandfather passed, his legacy was largely dependent on my commitment to managing the family business. My father is getting up in age, and it was my turn to step in.

"So, you run two businesses. How do you manage that?" Charles asked. "This isn't exactly what I call a small operation. I can barely keep eight horses on the track."

"It sounds more exhausting than it is, I assure you. Over the past few years, I have managed the wineries, implementing processes that have proven to be highly successful. As such, my day-to-day involvement isn't as necessary as years past, and I guess you could say that the old pleasures began calling. That's how I ended up building what you see here, training the world's best riders. Most come in seasonally, and a few stay and train only around competition season. But as the business expanded, and more riders sought us out, our seasonal schedule has filled up nearly every calendar month. It is always riding season somewhere, after all."

"You won all those shows in all those places?!" Ben asked, his eyes open wide.

Arthur pulled out the chair opposite him and sat, folding his hands on the table. "Yes I did, Benjamin, and I can tell you, you have the ability to do the same if that is your intention. Riding for fun is one thing, but competing on the national circuit requires an entirely different level of professionalism. It takes monumental commitment and talent—and we already checked off one of those requirements today."

Jack bumped Ben with his elbow. "He's the best, Mr. Davies! We didn't get along too good when we first met, and I thought it was strange the way he only wanted to be around horses. But he's not weird at all; he's just really good at that one thing!"

"Jack," Elizabeth interjected, quietly embarrassed.

Arthur chuckled. "You have a good friend with you, Benjamin. He's honest and he supports you—don't let him slip away," he said, giving Elizabeth a wink.

Paul felt a twinge of jealousy when he saw her reaction to his polite gesture of understanding. Even though he was certain he didn't mean anything elusive by it, Paul was still unnerved by his quick wit and cool demeanor.

"I would really like to compete, sir! I would train all the time to do something like that! Mr. Carl worked out a deal with the jockeys, where I get to train in the morning around the big enclosure some days, then Mr. Elliot and I train in the smaller one on other days. Mr. Elliot has lots more wood to make more jumps, doesn't he Mr. Carl!"

Carl and Charles looked at each other awkwardly, both shifting their posture and taking a long drink of iced tea.

Paul knew where this conversation was headed and decided it best to leave the four of them to discuss it in private, inviting Elizabeth and Jack to take a quick walk around the grounds.

"I would like to stretch my legs for a bit and I think I just saw a deer," Paul said, turning to Elizabeth and Jack. "Would you both like to go for a quick stroll down to the garden?"

"I would," Elizabeth said, "that sounds lovely!"

Gerald led them down a stairway to the ground floor, through a narrow hallway with wooden beams overhead. Hanging from above was a light fixture made of buck antlers; it was the most fantastic piece Paul had ever seen.

"The garden path takes you along the edge of the vineyard," Gerald said. "If you keep to the left, you'll come out just before you reach the fountain at the pergola."

"Thank you, Gerald," Elizabeth said, "it certainly looks incredible."

*　　*　　*

Carl folded his hands, rolled his thumbs in slow circles, and exhaled. "Elliot would be happy to build more jumps Ben, but we need to have a more serious conversation."

Ben brushed the hair from his eyes, then tucked his hands under his legs and looked over at him. He noticed Charles glancing down, his expression distant and thoughtful, knowing that Carl was about to say something heavy.

"Ben, you got the ability and gumption, but this old fart is simply... too old. My joints creak, my back aches, and I ain't got the skills you'll need to jump against riders on this level. I done took ya as far as I could, and even that was a miracle from our maker. I read what I could and dumped all my ridin' knowledge into ya, but this kind of ridin', this level of competin' is over this old man's noggin," Carl said, tapping his forehead with a crooked grin. "Mr. Davies here is willing to take you under his wing—you're ready for that now."

Charles knew how hard this was for the old man to admit, and that if Carl were able, he would give it all he had. He looked at Ben, gauging his reaction, but Ben just looked at Carl blankly for a moment.

"You aren't fixin' to train me anymore?"

Carl shook his head. "It's time for me to do what old jockeys do—sit and watch."

Ben slunk down in his chair. "Will I have to leave the farm? Because I don't want to leave. I like it there."

Charles felt a boulder form in his throat and was preparing to speak when Arthur nodded and lifted his hand.

"You don't have to leave the farm, Benjamin. I have riders visit from all over the world who stay here to train and compete. Some are here for longer, but they all have homes they return to once their competition or season has concluded."

Ben stayed quiet, his thoughts a confusing tangle he couldn't quite unravel. He wanted to do well, and jumping was the only thing he'd ever wanted to do, but thinking about leaving the farm and all his friends made him sad.

"Take time with this, Benjamin," Arthur said, "this is a decision all competitors eventually need to face, and it's a very personal one. This is a commitment to yourself, and with that, you need to be ready to make sacrifices. For some riders, that means lengthy absences from their families. It won't serve you well if your heart isn't in it—take time to make the right decision for you."

Ben loosened his posture and sat a bit straighter in the chair. Arthur's words made him feel more comfortable thinking about his future.

"That's exactly right," Charles said. "This is your decision, and we will support you no matter what you decide."

Ben grinned, looking at each one of them before his gaze stopped on Arthur.

Carl relaxed, sliding his elbow over the table closer to Charles. Charles sensed it, too—Arthur and Ben shared a connection, and they trusted that the rest would take care of itself in time.

*　　*　　*

Paul smiled as he watched Elizabeth and Jack lean in to sniff the fragrance of a lilac bloom. Jack gripped her hand, leading them off the path so he could investigate a ceramic frog perched on a log beside a sitting bench.

"Grandfather has one just like this!" Jack said, rubbing his hand across its head.

"Yes, he does enjoy his bullfrogs," Elizabeth said, "only his make a lot of noise."

Elizabeth strolled over to Paul on the path. "We have a large pond, and the bullfrogs sit atop the lily pads and croak all night long. It can be quite disruptive if you're not accustomed to it."

"I find them peaceful," Paul said, "Then again I can sleep through just about anything if the day was productive."

"So, what do you like to do for fun when you're not working yourself to exhaustion?"

Paul thought about it, then realized he hadn't taken the time to find out. "I fish from time to time with Elliot and Carl, but that isn't exactly pleasurable—Elliot can't keep his lips from moving most times."

Elizabeth giggled. "Well, we will have to explore that; it would be good for you to tap into your joy. You might surprise yourself and find there's something you enjoy about the world that doesn't require strenuous effort on your part."

Paul liked hearing her say the word "we"—it gave him hope that she wasn't planning on saying farewell after their New York trip was over.

"This doesn't require any effort—being here with you and Jack."

Her cheeks reddened and her eyes softened. She found herself lost in his gaze, momentarily losing all perception of the world around them.

"Do you like frogs, Mr. Paul?" Jack asked as he jogged back onto the path.

Paul broke eye contact, fighting against the butterflies buzzing around his stomach. "I do like frogs. They taste good, too."

Jack gasped. "You don't eat them, do you?!"

"Only once. The last time I took a lake trip, Elliot tried cookin' the legs. Let's just say they weren't anything I would choose a steak over."

Jack shook his head in disgust, sticking out his tongue and shivering.

"I see a light coming from the door," Elizabeth said. "We should join the others for dinner now."

As they approached the door, Gerald asked how they liked the garden walk, leading them back to the terrace where the others were listening to Arthur tell a story of his trek through England's countryside.

Gerald escorted Arthur's parents to their seats while several suited waiters carried trays of silver platters to the table.

"I didn't know what each of you would fancy, so I took the liberty of ordering a variety."

The waiters lifted the lids presenting an assortment of duck, fillets, steamed whitefish, and lobster tails.

Carl's mouth watered as he tucked his linen napkin into the collar of his shirt. "Glad I wore my suspenders."

During dinner, Ben quietly thought about what Arthur said. He listened to their conversations and stories, joked with Jack, and thought about how nice it would be to be able to spend time with him if he visited more. The more he thought on it, the more he liked the idea. Ben got a kick out of listening to Arthur's parents tell stories of how he would disappear into the vineyards on his horse and sleep in the stables. The stories resonated with him, stirring memories of his own experiences and how he sought comfort lying with Juniper.

At the end of the meal, they went on a tour of the whole property, even the stables. Arthur introduced them to the men who worked there and three of his trainers. They met the new student riders who were working on trotting and cantering. They met a Gold Cup championship winner and a rider from Ireland, who proudly showed them a real four-leaf clover that he kept in his pocket, pressed between wax paper, when he competed. Arthur made a point to bring Ben into the conversations and introductions as "the next rider-in-training." It gave him a sense of comfort knowing he wouldn't be a stranger if he chose to train there.

Arthur checked his watch as the sun began to dip. "I think we should conclude the evening to ensure you are well rested for tomorrow," he said, placing his hand on Ben's shoulder. "It will be an even bigger production in the finals. It always is."

When they reached the courtyard, they thanked Arthur for his generous hospitality and the meal. Arthur accepted their gratitude with humility, inviting them to visit any time they wished.

During the farewell handshakes, Ben stepped off the driveway, plucking an apple from one of the trees and tucking it into his pocket, knowing Juniper would appreciate the treat.

Arthur watched as they dispersed into the vehicles, lightly touching Elizabeth's arm. "Simon will take you and Jack to your residence from the hotel before he journeys back; I want to make sure you get home without incident."

"Thank you again, Mr. Davies, we appreciate that very much," she said.

Paul took a small offense to the protective insinuation; he was more than capable of getting them home safe and was planning to do so anyway. Paul gritted his teeth but politely shook Arthur's hand and resisted the urge to squeeze until he heard bones crack.

As they passed the horse statues, Ben turned around in his seat to look back. He took out the apple, rubbed it against his shirt, and smiled.

37

The Angels

GABE'S SENSES WERE AROUSED BY the rich smells wafting through his room. When he crossed the room to his door, a flicker of movement outside his window caught his eye. Creeping toward the window, he peered out into the darkness, seeing fire embers shooting up into the sky. He moved closer and cupped his hands around his temples to block the glare of candlelight. Just as he turned to head back toward the door, he saw a dark figure whiz past the edge of the trees, a black cloak flailing behind, brushing the ground in long tattered shreds. Gabe pulled his knife from its sheath and ran outside, the door slamming shut behind him and rattling the stained glass window.

"What's gotten into you?" Jacob said. "You that hungry?"

At first, Jacob didn't see the knife, but when Gabe pulled his hand from his side, Jacob dropped the steak tongs and focused on the direction Gabe was looking.

Joshua hopped off the picnic table bench and closed in behind them, grabbling a metal prong used to stoke the fire.

Sarah picked up a glass bottle, breaking it at the neck over a large rock, causing them to turn their heads in her direction.

"That was impressive," Joshua said coolly.

Jacob turned his attention between Gabe and the tree line. "What are we looking for?"

Gabe stopped at the spot where he had glimpsed the figure. Dropping to one knee, he brushed the ground with his fingers. "No footprint," he said quietly, stabbing his knife into the dirt.

They gathered around, exchanging worried glances and looking out into the brush.

"What did you see?" Sarah asked, "or thought you saw?"

"I saw it, and it wasn't the first time."

"What? What is it?!" Joshua said, growing impatient from the lagging explanation.

"The shadows," Gabe said eerily. "Saw one a few nights ago. The time before that was the day you left to play with your arrows when the fire broke out. Every time I see them, it signals some impending disaster, and one of us gets called for duty."

"What do they look like? Where have you seen them?" Sarah asked.

"I just said they are shadows, you know—persons without bodies," he said with a snarky tone. "They are black, but not solid black... you can see through 'em. This one was wearing a cloak, shredded at the bottom."

Gabe pulled his knife from the ground and stood up. "It went by my window, then disappeared into the woods there. They aren't allowed to stick around; they have to pass through quickly on their way to the outer limits, or to earth."

Jacob looked around nervously. "How do you know that? You haven't been conversing with the oddballs again, have you?"

Gabe walked to the table, dropping his knife onto his plate. "I know what you're gonna say before you say it, so let me save you the breath. Abram's no dummy. Yes, he mumbles to himself, and yes, it's weird, but he's battled them before. He calls them dark angels. He earned his spot with us from overcoming their poison and spells, and he's taught me a thing or two about them. He mumbles the Lord's prayer whenever he feels their presence."

"Oh, that's just lovely," Jacob said. "Sarah overheard them just last night telling ghost stories by the campfire."

"Jacob!" Sarah said. "That was a secret!"

Gabe faced them with a stern expression. "This is no time for secrets, Sarah. What do you know?"

"I don't know much. I overheard the other three talking last night. They mentioned something about other angels roaming about, angels from the darkness. But he said they only roamed the earth… and…"

Gabe set his foot on the bench and leaned on his elbow. "And?"

"And that one day we will do battle in a war between good and evil."

"So why in the name of our holy one are we seeing floating apparitions?" Joshua asked.

They watched as Gabe stabbed his knife into one of the steaks on the table and walked off, tearing off bites with his teeth like a Viking with a drumstick.

"Should we follow him?" Sarah asked, looking over her shoulder into the woods. "I don't feel like hanging around out here."

Jacob watched Gabe cross the field that separated their barracks from the others. "We better stay here. Let him go do what he's gonna do— he'll do it anyways."

Sitting down to eat, they chewed quietly, listening to the wind sail between the tops of the trees.

Joshua was the first to break the silence. "This don't add up—they shouldn't be able to touch this world. Didn't you say these dark angels were being held someplace? How can they mingle down on earth then, or float by our windows?"

Sarah nodded. "That's what I overheard. Maybe there are different varieties—some that are more powerful and are being restrained and some that can be among the humans, or whiz by our backyard whenever they feel like it."

Joshua blew out a sigh. "This is just great—like I'm going to be able to fall asleep now!"

"Hush," Sarah said, looking around at the darkness before leaning over to Joshua. "I bet this has something to do with our dreams. Gabe said he sees them just before something bad happens."

Jacob shivered. "I don't like this, guys. I don't like it at all."

"Relax you two," Joshua said. "You really think Jesus would let us walk into a fight we didn't know was coming? He's always given us the battle plan. We are His soldiers, and He is our general; we'll know all we need to know when the time comes—rest assured of that."

"You're right," Sarah agreed, "this is our territory, and we're protected. If they want to dance, we'll give them a tango they'll never forget."

*   *   *

Abram drew his blade down the end of a smooth branch until the tip was a fine point, stopping when he heard heavy footsteps coming up behind him. He spun around holding the point at eye level like a javelin.

"Calm down, Curtal Friar, I'm armed with a T-bone," Gabe said, tossing his steak bone into the fire pit. "We need to have a chat."

Abram lowered the stick and leaned it up against a tree. "I know what you're here for. You seen them, too."

"Sure did, right outside my bedroom window, ruined my appetite," Gabe said. "Sarah told me she heard y'all chirping about the other angels last night, and now I have three sniveling pansies to console. I thought we agreed to keep this between you and me—and away from the other big-mouthed yappers."

Abram shrugged. "I thought we were being quiet; we didn't mean for anyone to hear us."

"Next time you want to tell campfire stories, do it on your side and away from the communal pit. Delicate ears are listening."

"Apologies, Gabe."

"Too late for that now. Just tell me what you know. What are you sensing?"

Abram watched Zelach walking out of the woods and pointed in his direction. "Zelach was already hunting it. I sense their shackles are wearing thin. Those bound in the earth will soon be set free, but not yet. The ones we are seeing have no power. They are going to and fro, only passing between realms. They cannot see us, they have no authority— they are only vapors. Their spirits were lost, and their souls given to the dark triad. They never had an earthly body as a host. They were hatched from the spirit realm out of dark rituals and symbolism."

"Layman's terms please, Abram."

Abram waited for Zelach to join, then continued. "They are not the ones to worry about—they can't touch, see, or interact. They aren't even really here. They are illusions that pass between here and earth, eternally lost."

"Still ain't clearing it up for me, big guy. How do we stop them from zooming past the windows and freaking us out?"

"That will come later. We will battle the others, the ones bound in the hidden places. And when we wipe the floor with them, the spirits, shadows, and vapors will perish into the Lake of Fire forever."

Gabe nodded but rolled his eyes. "Yeah, yeah, we all know that story. I guess we have to put up with their poor sense of direction until then, is that it?"

"Pay attention, my friend, for they signal a force coming upon the earth. I believe the more of them we see, the greater the calamity that is building on earth will be. Shine up your armor, Hercules. The day will come when all that heavy lifting will serve you in a far greater way than filling out those shirt sleeves."

"If you say so, Ezekiel, but it sounds like horse doody to me. And before you make fun of my sleeves, talk to your boy here in the pirate pajamas."

Zelach brushed at his white shirt with puffy sleeves and pulled the neck string. "What's wrong with my shirt?"

Gabe chuckled, shaking his head. "See you two chumps later, I have three thumb-suckers to bottle feed."

*   *   *

"Let's clean up and go inside, I don't like being out here anymore," Joshua said.

Jacob began stacking their cups when Sarah touched his arm. "Wait, put them down. Here comes Gabe. We don't want him to think we're scared and running inside over this."

"But we are," Joshua said.

Sarah sighed with annoyance. "Just wait a minute, act normal."

Gabe walked toward the door and waved them over. "You can quit acting tough now. And tell Jacob he can pick up the sippy cups."

38

THE DRIVE BACK TO THE city was peaceful. Elizabeth relished the stories going back and forth between Paul and Simon. They spoke of fishing, farming, and what they loved about the country. It was quite surprising how much they had in common, and she learned a lot about Paul. As the sun began to set, the sky dimmed, casting a soft light against Paul's face, revealing the smoothness of his skin. Elizabeth found herself staring at him, curious to know what made him laugh over a lost catch wriggling off the line or why he furrowed his brow in deep thought. He had many quirks and facial expressions that seemed more purposeful than a reactive reflex.

As the cityscape drew near, Paul was quieted by a heartache. He had just a few more hours to be around Elizabeth and Jack, and he was perturbed that he had to sleep through eight of them. The drivers stopped the cars in front of the hotel. Andrew Madison and the bellman were there to greet them. Paul opened his door and crossed the back of the car, stopping at her window and placing his hand on the roof, bending down as she lowered the window.

"Have a safe ride home, Elizabeth. Rest well."

The cool night air wafted his scent over her, and she felt intoxicated. "We will meet again in the morning, same time, same place?"

Paul nodded and looked at Jack. "Don't let the frogs keep you awake."

"Good night, Mr. Paul, see you tomorrow!" Jack waved, not stopping until the car turned down 87th Avenue.

Andrew gave them a good report on Juniper. "He had plenty to eat, a good walk, and the peppermint worked like a charm."

"Glad to hear it, I thought it might," Carl said.

Andrew shook Ben's hand. "If I don't see you tomorrow, good luck at the show, and have a fun ride."

Ben watched Andrew climb into the car, then followed behind the men into the lobby.

Carl shuffled across the floor while rubbing his belly, which was stuffed full of shellfish. "I'm gonna sleep good tonight. Ain't ate that much since Christmas supper."

Charles agreed. "What a nice evening," he said, turning to Paul, who was gazing outside as the elevator dinged and the door opened. "Might want to stop those love bugs from buzzing around your head and get on inside before you lose your ride."

Paul chuckled, stepping over the threshold, giving the operator a nod.

"What's a love bug, Mr. Charles? Is it like a firefly?" Ben asked.

Paul gave Charles a look.

"Yes, that's what I meant, fireflies," Charles said, giving Paul a wink.

"I didn't see any of those, but I sure wish I did," Ben said with a yawn.

"You're fixin' to be asleep before your head hits the pillow," Charles said, yawning himself as the elevator lifted. "You ever wonder why a yawn is contagious?"

Later that night, lying in bed, Paul lingered in the memory of his evening with Elizabeth. He thought on everything they did, from the carriage ride to the walk at Arthur's, and the sweet sound of her speaking French played over and over in his mind until he faded off to sleep.

*   *   *

Charles listened to the ticking of his pocket watch, unable to fall asleep amidst Carl's loud snores and sputtering breaths. The sounds of the city never quieted. He finally began to drift off to sleep, only to be jolted awake by the screeching of brakes and the grinding noises of large sliding doors being opened and closed as street merchants and bakeries received their early morning deliveries. He finally gave up hope and decided that coffee was the only antidote for his sleepless night. He quietly dressed and combed his hair, leaving a note on Carl's bedside table telling him to meet downstairs in the lobby when he woke up.

When the elevator doors opened, he was bombarded with rolling carts carrying small silver dishes pushed by waiters scurrying in all directions. The relentless, inescapable noise was a gut punch to his grogginess, and he missed his quiet country mornings sipping coffee on the porch, watching the sun poke up from the tree line. He rubbed his eyes and walked wearily to the hostess podium.

"Good morning, sir, might you join us for breakfast this morning?"

"I'm still full of last night's supper, but I'd fancy a mug of black coffee."

"Right this way, sir, we have plenty of fresh coffee. I made it myself about twenty minutes ago."

"Does this city ever slow down?"

She laughed, then realized the question was sincere. "It does not. That's our slogan sir—the city that never sleeps."

Charles followed her to a high-top table in the corner with a view of the street. "Might I trouble you for a table that isn't so exposed? I would like to have my eyes fixated on something that isn't moving until the coffee does its job."

"Of course, sir, I have a booth in the corner, follow me."

*　　*　　*

Jack turned over on his pillow, listening to his mother sing and hum while rolling her hair in the bathroom. He had forgotten how beautiful her voice was; it had been years since he last heard her sing. She sounded so happy that it made him smile, and he moved the pillow away from his ear so he could hear her more clearly. He suddenly remembered the big show was today, and pushed off the covers, excited to see Ben and Mr. Paul. As he got dressed, he wondered if there was a reason for his mother's high spirits. *Yes*, he thought to himself, remembering the many interactions that him and Ben would giggle over as they watched them walk about, not to mention the flower Mr. Paul gave her. It made him feel happy, and he knelt beside his bed and said a quick prayer, asking that his mother fancy Mr. Paul.

39

Charles thumbed through the newspaper, flabbergasted by the sheer number of pages filled with articles. There were even separate sections for sports and finances. He nearly spat out his coffee when he discovered a crossword puzzle. While searching his pockets for a pencil, he looked up to see Paul loitering near the hostess podium and waved to catch his attention.

"I like this spot," Paul said, sliding along the bench across from him.

"I asked for the most secluded spot available. If I could have found one thirty miles north, I would have sat there."

The waitress delivered an extra mug of coffee and topped them off. Paul hugged it to his face like it was liquid gold.

"You must have had a night like I had. Be thankful you didn't share a room with Carl—snores like a grizzly bear."

Charles folded the newspaper in half and set it on the table. "You look good. There's a twinkle in your eye."

Paul looked down at his mug with a dismissive grunt.

"What's wrong with having a twinkle? You ain't so macho that you can hide it you know. Let yourself feel it, be bold—you're in love."

Paul shook his head, but the grin he fought so hard to suppress crept out anyway.

Charles laughed and shook out the paper, pulling out his glasses and flipping to the crossword. "Help me out with this one: What has four letters and starts with an 'L' and ends with an 'E'?"

"You got a lot of humor for a man who got no sleep."

Carl and Ben soon joined them, and after a bite to eat, they packed their bags and loaded them onto a cart. The bellman hung a tag around the handle and rolled it into a large closet. "Good luck at the show today! Your bags will be ready when you return."

Ben stopped at the mirror, adjusted his riding coat, and fastened his boot strap.

"Don't forget this," Carl said, handing him a helmet.

Ben glanced at it twice and then looked up at Carl. "This isn't my helmet. This is much nicer than mine. Look, it has a velvet liner and a neat bill. And it's shiny. It must have got mixed up with my gear somehow."

"Only if by 'mixed up' you mean me throwin' out the old one and replacin' it with this one."

"Gee, thanks, Mr. Carl! This is so nice!" Ben rushed to the mirror and strapped it onto his head, running his hands over the smooth surface.

"Where'd you sneak off to get that?" Charles asked.

"I made some friends," Carl said smugly.

Paul held the door open while Luis stowed their luggage. "We best be on our way; we got a show to win."

Ben hurried for the door, tucking the helmet under his arm.

Charles smirked at Paul as he passed through the door. "Someone is in a mighty big hurry this morning, and I doubt it's due to the coffee."

*   *   *

The walk to Madison Square Garden was much the same as the day before. People gathered at the same spot, trying to push their way through the entrance like cattle loaded into the feedlot. Paul stayed behind, wishing Ben good luck as Charles and Carl escorted him to the staging area. Rather than stepping into the current of the crowd, Paul raised up on his toes, looking over the heads of the people waiting at the ramp to get to their seats. Whenever he saw a shade of auburn red hair, his heart thumped. As the seats began to fill and the snack vendors suited up, he started to wonder where they were and checked the signage to make sure he was in the correct aisle. When the crowd thinned out, it was easier to see the corridor, but as far as he could see, there was no sign of them.

The band began to play softly in the corner of the arena and people cleared the walkways to hurry to their seats. He was just about to turn away when a silver Bugatti Royale pulled to the curb followed by a bronze Rolls Royce convertible. The passersby stopped to admire the fine automobiles and the lady seated in the front seat of the Rolls. She untied the scarf around her head and long curls of silky auburn red strands fell below the low back of her black dress. A pair of thin legs touched the ground and stood up in tall slingback heels. The tapered hem hugged the woman's slim figure, flaring out with subtle ruffles just below her knees. She turned her head to the wind, pushing up large dark sunglasses to the crown of her head.

Paul felt his knees buckle and his cheeks hurt from the smile that broadened his face. A man with equally fine taste in attire, who Paul assumed to be her father, came around the front of the car with Jack following close behind him. The man was robust in the middle with white hair and a mustache that curved upward, making it appear as if he had a permanent jolly expression. He was quite tall, every bit of six feet, wearing a scarf around his neck that matched the car. He bent down and hugged Jack, lifting him off the ground. Paul took a few steps closer, maneuvering around a beam for a better look.

He watched intently as her father walked to greet another man exiting the stunning silver Bugatti. Paul's wide smile quickly dissipated when he recognized the other man he was shaking hands with. It was Arthur Davies. The two men shared a familiarity as Arthur opened the door to the car for the white-haired man to inspect. After a quick conversation, they shook hands again and Arthur led Elizabeth and Jack through a private entrance, disappearing out of sight.

Paul walked over to the ramp and leaned against the cool brick, feeling his temperature rise. He rested his head back and stuffed his hands into his pockets.

"Sir, can I show you to your seat? You don't want to miss the opening ceremony."

When Paul opened his eyes, a man stood grinning at him with a lapel covered in flag pins and a colorful pocket square poking out from his blazer. "Sure, lead the way."

The man chattered as they walked but Paul didn't hear a word. He thanked him for the escort, then sat down, glanced over at the two empty seats, and folded his hands across his stomach. The arena looked the same, only now there were large flags representing the countries of the finalists hanging in a line above the judges' platform. He did his best to block out his thoughts and focus on the show. The riders were announced and entered the arena one by one, following the same order as they scored the previous day.

*   *   *

"Where's your notebook?" Charles asked, looking at Carl.

Carl frantically patted down his pockets. "I ain't got it—must have left it in my trousers."

"Guess you just get to sit and watch, but for the life of me, I don't understand why we have to sit down here when we could have watched from Arthur's suite. Why did you turn that down?"

"I like the view just fine from here. Besides, I'm afraid of heights."

Charles chuckled. "A jockey who's afraid of heights, never heard of such a thing."

"I think the boy will take the help from Arthur—that conversation went better than I thought it would."

Charles nodded. "Sure didn't start out that way, but he came around right quick. I think once Arthur took a turn at talking to him, it made an impact. Look how confident he looks. And that helmet sure does look nice."

"It might give him a boost, and it sure beats that turtle shell he was wearing. Say, you notice anything different about Paul? He seems a bit… smiley."

Charles let out a belly laugh. "He's in love with the fine Miss Elizabeth. But don't let on that I told you that, he'll have my hide."

"Shoot, I knew that—knew it before we got on that train. First time I saw him in a shirt with a collar, he smelled different, too—I think he finally uncorked a bottle of cologne. And trimmed the grizzle off his face.

If you didn't catch onto that, you're as blind as a possum on a sunny day."

"Look! There he goes," Charles said, pointing at Ben. "Next time we see him it's show time."

*　　*　　*

The Angels

Jacob, Joshua, and Sarah sat along a beam hovering over the center of the arena.

"You think that big dummy will notice we skipped out on him?" Jacob asked.

"Are you kidding me?" Joshua said, looking over at him with an amused expression. "He's too busy admiring his reflection in the mirror to notice."

"Forget about what Gabe's doing; look at the horse you guys!" Sarah said, pointing to Juniper. "He wouldn't be alive if it weren't for you two. And look at how far they've come! Have you seen such a place? Look at all the people in the stands, so excited and happy. And look, there's even a band!"

"Yeah, Juniper sure looks different than when I first saw him, but that boy got him here—they're like peas and carrots those two. I got a hunch they will do great things—that is, if they don't screw this up."

"Isn't that what *we're* here for?" Sarah asked.

Joshua shook out a handful of roasted almonds, popping them up in the air one by one and catching them on his tongue. "I thought we were here for the food."

"Good grief," Sarah said, "sometimes you're as intolerable as Gabe."

"Let's not be overdramatic," Jacob said. "Nobody is that bad."

*　　*　　*

Paul watched Ben until he couldn't see him anymore and then sank into the seat. The crowd was so lively around him he didn't hear Jack calling to him from the railing. He leaned forward, staring at his boots, when the tips of pointy heels came into view. He looked up to see Elizabeth and Jack, scanning the crowd for the charming Mr. Davies but not finding him.

"So sorry we are late, I hope we didn't miss much," Elizabeth said, shrugging off a woven shoulder covering.

"Hi, Mr. Paul!" Jack said. "I heard those bullfrogs all night long! I even slept with my window open!"

Paul nodded, forcing a smile.

"Did you see Ben? Did he come out yet?" Jack asked.

Paul pointed to the end of the run leading to the staging area. "He just dipped behind the curtain—you just missed him."

"Oh man!" Jack groaned.

"Sorry dear," Elizabeth said, then turned to Paul. "My father gave us a ride; he is leaving for Connecticut for a few days to attend a culinary conference. He loves his morning scone, so we stopped at a café and ran into Mr. Davies. As soon as they met, they were lost in horse talk, chatting about the horses my father purchased from his stables. Such an incredibly small world sometimes."

Paul snapped out of his stupor after hearing her explanation. "I thought I saw you on the sidewalk, but I was moving so fast with the herd I wasn't sure if it was you," he said, knowing darn well that he'd just told a bold-faced lie.

"Yes, it was! Oh, I wish you would have noticed. I would have loved for you to meet my father; he's such a wonderful man. He and Mr. Davies share an interest in automobiles, so that delayed us a bit, but we were lucky enough to be escorted by Mr. Davies through an entrance that bypassed the crowd, only I got lost and took the wrong corridor."

"I told you, Mother, Mr. Davies said to go right, not left."

Elizabeth shrugged, admitting fault. "I am not too keen on directions."

"That's for sure. Remember the time we went to Stanley's baseball game? You drove around the west side for what seemed like hours!" Jack said.

Paul laughed, feeling foolish and a bit immature, but that insecure feeling only solidified the strong emotions that churned inside of him, like a boiling pot tipping the lid.

*   *   *

Charles turned in his seat, looking up at the suite overhead. Arthur was holding his binoculars, scanning the arena. When he lowered them, he gave Charles a wave. The stands were full, not an open seat in the house. Some stood in the aisles, and a wide gate that opened to a side street was lined with spectators five rows deep. Smaller children clung to the metal bars with their feet on the top rung. People in the crowd held up signs and waved small flags to cheer on the competitors from their home country. The Canadian fans were the most visible, seated together in a section near the main stage, dressed in their country's colors. The announcer took his spot in the center stand among the judges as the first rider approached the arena with the paddock master.

"The jumps are arranged differently, ain't they? I hope I'm not losing that much of my mind," Charles said.

"We still got a good number out there, but that tight turn at the second crossover isn't any less forgiving today. The water tray and wall are still planted, but notice the height of the oxers, and the count between the combinations is two paces shorter, give or take a foot."

Charles wrinkled his brow, leaning forward. Even knowing they were looking at the same thing, he couldn't wrap his head around Carl's perspective. "You're going to miss this, old man. All that figuring and geometrical analysis you been doing... what are you going to scribble down now?"

"I'm still breathin', ain't I?" Carl said, patting his hands on his chest and pretending to check his pulse. "I ain't fixin' to hang up my notebook yet."

Charles nodded his head. "That's good, Carl. Arthur might need a statistician on payroll."

The fifth-placed rider took the reins from the paddock master and readied himself.

"That's the fella from Spokane. He had a good run yesterday, right?" Charles asked, probing for commentary.

"Eh, somethin' 'bout that liverpool wasn't his brand of mustard. He was faulted for hesitation, but it could have been the rider. They really have to count those paces leadin' to a jump like that; if they don't, they'll come down short nine times out of ten."

Out of the gate, they looked a hair slow, and it wasn't until the second turn that they found their rhythm. They cleared the liverpool without hesitation but clipped the top rail of the ascending oxer, accumulating two faults after the rollback turn. Taking the first jump at speed, they knocked themselves off course on the jump-off. At the end of their ride, it was obvious Ralph Messier was disappointed, pulling on the bill of his helmet and smacking his thigh as they trotted to the gate.

"That's one down. Hate to see a ride go sideways like that, especially at this level," Carl said.

The fourth-place rider had a delay at the gate when his boot strap buckle broke and he had to wait for the paddock master to retrieve a replacement.

"This ain't lookin' too good neither," Carl said.

"Why's that? A little break might do 'em good to settle their nerves."

"Not that one. Last time, he came out of the gate like a tumbler out of a hot barrel. Kicked off with more energy than a jack-in-the-box. The more time he spends saddled-up, the more that bullet is goin' in every direction. Got too much pent-up energy."

It happened just like Carl said it would. When the rider engaged in forward motion, the horse snapped its head up, taking one full pass to smooth out and correct a fishtail after the first jump.

"He needs to hold him real tight. You see the placement of his hands, high up on the reins like that? It didn't hurt him too much yesterday, but it ain't doin' him any favors. With a horse like that, he'd be better off runnin' loose and just lettin' him go," Carl said. "Although, he could end up at the bottom of that water tray."

*   *   *

"There's Ben! He's over there coming down now!"

Elizabeth twisted her shawl in her hands. "I can't remember the last time I felt so much nervous energy," she said, looking over at Paul. "What's your secret? You look so calm and steady."

"Don't let my composure fool you, inside I'm a live wire."

Something about the way he said that was deeply honest, and she knew that if he would only let his emotions show… what a light display that would be.

Ben trotted to the gate after another rider exited with a fault count. This time, instead of imagining Mr. Elliot out there waving his hat in the air, he looked around and saw the course for what it was, without imaginary images. He wanted to face this challenge head-on and give it his best, showing Carl all that he taught him. He wanted a perfect ride this time—a perfect run to honor the man who got him here.

Out of the gate, they moved in unison. Ben switched his seat, riding high on the canter and falling back at the swing, using his outside leg to pull Juniper's motor around. After the oxers, they were leading in time, only getting faster as they came into the first turn. Their rollback was flawless, setting them up for the jump-off, clearing the combinations and cutting the turn into the vertical with perfect execution. Ben loosened his grip on the reins, dropping his shoulders and centering over the saddle, keeping his elbows in and squaring his hips. He tightened his core and focused on his thigh muscles, making the second turn in course-record time. Approaching the wall, they had a forty-five-degree vertical, and their arch and landing took the best distance by a full twelve inches. Rounding the last turn, he tucked his elbows and counted paces, just like Carl had taught him, keeping his rear back on the approach and hovering at center and forward at touchdown. The crowd stayed quiet, although clapping could be heard after they cleared the liverpool.

The couple seated behind Charles and Carl *ooh'd* and *ahh'd* over the performance. The man clapped and whistled. "Whoever trained that chap sure knows a thing or two."

When Charles glanced over at Carl, he saw a tear rolling down his cheek. Charles quickly turned away, pretending not to notice, wanting him to enjoy this moment without inhibition.

The last stretch of the course required a hairpin turn and flawless timing to cut into a double, followed by two short verticals and the high jump. Ben lowered the reins as they turned into the straight. Juniper's breath was steady, and Ben flexed and balanced as they approached the takeoff.

Charles and Carl had a front-facing view of the straight, each holding their breath as Juniper sprang off the ground like he had coils for hooves.

The crowd sprang to their feet before Ben and Juniper reached the gate. As they exited the arena, Ben finally understood what Arthur had said. Jumping a horse was like a wild melody, and the rider was the violin. For the very first time, he could hear the music.

Charles looked up to the balcony where Arthur was standing, watching as he pumped his arm in the air, tilting his head back in extraordinary laughter. He looked at Charles, and they both exchanged smiles filled with pride.

Elizabeth clapped and Jack jumped out of his seat, bouncing on his heels. "Way to go Ben! Way to go!" he shouted. "Mother, Mr. Paul—he was the best one yet!"

Paul's breath caught in his throat as he waited for the judges to submit their scores. The announcer raised the speaker. "The first zero-fault score and a new course record for time."

Elizabeth gasped, putting her hand on Paul's shoulder and resting her head on her fingers. Jack skipped in place, turning in a circle while pumping his arms up and down. Elizabeth hugged Jack as he dropped back into his seat. "That was amazing," she said, "truly amazing."

Arthur raised his binoculars just in time to witness something he had never seen before; the second-place finalist, Ethan Bergeron from Canada, congratulated Ben before walking his mount to the gate.

"What's your feeling on this rider?" Charles asked, settling into his seat.

"Don't count 'em out. If he runs loose, the horse is less likely to hesitate like last time. But once that blood starts pumpin', he might tense up.

Following Ben's run, it can't be easy to settle down."

The crowd grew quiet again and the paddock master allowed extra time before ushering them forward.

After a minor infraction on the diagonal, they took the course by storm, trailing a touch behind in time. Their turns were tight, and coming into the first approach on the combinations, the rider choked up on the reins, pulling a smidge too tight on the right. The horse slowed, costing them time, and their jump wasn't vertical on takeoff, taking a fault for the delay.

"You were right again," Charles said.

"Hate to see it, but he was just wound a bit too tight."

Their hesitations plagued them coming out of the second turn, but the remainder of the course was flawless, and they nearly matched Ben's high jump, which was impressive. The minor deduction in points put them in second place, which could be upset very easily if the French rider stayed the course he ran yesterday.

"This fella is good," Carl mumbled. "Cool-headed, just like his horse; you can tell they been workin' together for a stretch. Some of these lads turn horses like I do sweat rags, riding multiple horses a week at this level, but these two... they run like stink on a sow."

The Frenchman had good form; his posture was upright with no bend in his shoulders. He pivoted at the waist and kept the crown of his head centered over his middle.

"If Ben had form like this, they would be unstoppable. Look at this!" Carl said, lifting his pointer finger. "Watch how he moves, his body is perfectly symmetrical. Look at his lines—that's balance!" Carl watched closely as they paralleled Ben and Juniper's performance, arguably turning smoother corners. "He rides like he's liquid, no catches, no jerks—flowin' like water."

*　　*　　*

Jack leaned over and whispered, "Mother, that guy is a good rider; Ben's still too short to look like him."

"He is very graceful—oh, here comes the high jump," she said, pulling her shawl through her fingers.

"Wow, that was high!" Jack said, "Ben might need some more practice to beat him!"

*   *   *

Carl scratched his chin, watching them approach the stretch. He remembered Arthur fancy-talking about seeing horses as athletic marvels of power and motion, but never did it materialize as it did now. The crowd was so still, so quiet as they watched; everyone was just as captivated as he was. And just like that, their run was over. The rider with ice for blood exited the run as coolly as he entered, not paying any mind to the eruption of applause.

"I don't know quite what to say," Charles said.

"Me either."

After revealing the score of the first-place finalist, the announcer consulted with the judges and stepped to the center podium after a brief pause, giving the riders time to line up by rank. "Our finalists have completed Course B today, and their scores reconciled with their Course A performance. May I present you, ladies and gentlemen, the National Horse Show competition finalists. In fifth place, Bjorn Achterberg from the Netherlands. In fourth place, Ralph Messier from Spokane, Washington, United States. In third place, Ethan Bergeron from Edmonton, Canada. In second place, Benjamin Paulie from Greenfield, Iowa. In first place, Pierre Auclair from Strasbourg, France. Ladies and Gentlemen, please stand for the presentation of medals."

The infield was quickly overtaken by newsmen and journalists, vying for their column photo or front-page accolades. Ben enjoyed being with the riders more than the medals and attention. After the photos were taken, the riders congratulated each other, sharing their thoughts, faults, and misgivings they felt before their runs. Ethan and Ben exchanged friendly banter as they unsaddled their horses in the stable, admitting their mistakes and recognizing they could have just as easily had a jump-off, given how close their scores were. Ralph wandered over, snapping the cap off a Coca-Cola, and perched himself on a large wooden storage tote, unbuckling his helmet.

"You ride good. Who's your trainer?"

"Mr. Carl Ebbers, but he's old now and can't get along the way he used to, so I think I might train with Mr. Arthur Davies."

"*Gee whiz*, going straight to the top! Never heard of Carl Ebbers, but everyone's heard of Arthur Davies—he's a legend! Been stacking up that gold for years. Not much silver, right, Ethan?"

"I only know of golds, but he probably took second at some point in his career. You must have one hell of a rabbit's foot to get that break—he don't look at just anyone."

Ben waved at Pierre as he passed by their huddle, but he walked on by without so much as a glance.

Ralph finished his soda pop and wiped his lips. "We have tried that more times than we can count. You're wasting your time, kid—you could be set on fire and he wouldn't even spit in your direction."

Ethan chuckled. "Hell, he wouldn't even spit on you."

Pierre was tall for a jockey—slender but strong. Ben watched him throw his bag over his shoulder, not giving any of the other riders so much as a glance before he disappeared around a corner.

Ralph belched and hopped down, giving Ben a handshake. "Maybe I'll see you again, Ben. Keep riding the way you do."

Ethan and Ralph walked around each other, putting their fists up to guard their faces, pretending to throw fake jabs and shadow box each other.

"See you next year, pops," Ralph said, sidestepping with a shuffle.

"Pops? Who you calling Pops? You're older than me!"

"I might not catch you in the ring, but twenty bucks says I can take you to that feed trough and back."

"Deal," Ethan said, spitting into his palm as Ralph did the same. "Count us down, Ben."

Ben grimaced as they mashed their hands together in a firm shake, then took their spots in the center of the long stable. Ben looked around, then counted: "one, two, three—go!"

As they took off running, Ben heard a man speaking loudly in a foreign language he had never heard before. When he looked around the corner, he saw Pierre drop his bag, reaching out to shake Arthur's hand, gripping him at the elbow. Pierre was obviously excited to see Arthur, pulling him close in a manly, bent-elbow hug around the neck. As they conversed back and forth, their voices sounded happy, and the language was pleasant to listen to.

The patter of footsteps got louder as Ethan and Ralph returned to their starting spots, doubled over, and breathing heavily. "Pay up," Ethan said, wiggling his fingers with a palm out.

Quieting their breath, they heard the lofty chatter and turned around, walking behind Ben, staring at the interaction. "He does talk!" Ralph whispered.

"Sure he does, if you're Arthur Davies," Ethan said.

Ralph flicked Ethan in the arm. "No, knucklehead, he only speaks French. Obviously."

Arthur turned, waving Ben over. "Come, I want you to meet a good friend of mine."

"See you around, Ben, good luck to you," Ralph said.

Ethan rolled his eyes. "You don't need luck, you got Davies. See ya, Ben!"

Ben waved goodbye to his new acquaintances, then hurried over. As he approached, he felt small in comparison, looking up at Pierre with a nervous grin. He was just as intimidating up close as he was from a distance. His features were sharp, and his dark eyes and bushy brows made him look permanently serious. Arthur spoke to him and put his hand around Ben's shoulder. Pierre's face softened; he folded one arm around his torso, pulled his shoulders back, and bent at the waist to shake his hand.

He said something Ben didn't understand but heard his name—which sounded neat in a French accent.

Familiar voices carried through the breezeway, and Ben spun around. As soon as he saw Jack, the two ran to each other. Jack picked up the shiny medal from around Ben's neck, turning it over. "This is really something! Is it heavy?"

Ben slipped it over his head and put it around Jack's neck. "A little."

Carl and Charles walked over to the stall to pack the equipment while Jack and Ben checked the ice box for popsicles.

Elizabeth grinned at the boys as they pulled back wrappers and climbed up on a storage bin to snack. Overhearing Pierre and Arthur's conversation, Elizabeth would giggle under her breath every now and then. She heard Pierre complain about the blister on his hand from the reins, cursing his trainer like a sailor for not packing his old ones. She opened a small handbag and pulled out a small packet of ointment and a band-aid, then walked over.

Paul listened as the three of them laughed and spoke to each other. Paul felt intoxicated as the exquisite words rolled off her tongue. Even though he didn't have a clue what she was saying, he could listen to her for hours. After a few minutes, she returned.

"If we ever have more than a day or two, you'll have to teach me a few words," Paul said. "At least the bad ones, so I can holler at Elliot without him knowing what I'm calling him."

"I would like that. I do hope we can continue our letters; it is most enjoyable to write to you and hear about your life. You must be anxious to get back to the quiet country after this trip."

Paul felt a stone drop to the pit of his stomach. His muscles tensed as the reality of leaving began to weigh heavily on him. She noticed his jaw clench and his cheekbones flare, just as they had on the drive upstate when he'd looked contemplative or restless.

He avoided looking at her, knowing it would break him to tell her how he truly felt about leaving.

"I have been dreading this departure for the last forty-three hours and twenty-five minutes."

Once the gear was packed, the paddock master arranged for a cart. Two gentlemen cycled over and asked if anyone was interested in a ride to the main gate.

One by one, their hands shot up—except for Paul and Elizabeth, and Jack and Ben, who were still licking their frozen pops, fueled by sugar.

"I can take two at a time comfortably," one cyclist said, "three if you squeeze and hold your breath, but it's a short jaunt."

Arthur held up his hand. "Give us a quick moment please."

"Rather than say our goodbyes here, let's meet at the bridge in the park. I have to travel that way, and it is close to the train station. Juniper can have a stretch before loading time."

"Carl and I will go first and wait at the hotel lobby, and once we're all together, we will walk with the horse," Charles said.

"Can Ben and I ride together mother? We know our way!"

Elizabeth agreed. "Go straight to the hotel and be polite about their time—no stopping at Uncle Tony's for a slice of pizza."

"We know, Mother," Jack called as they rushed to the doors to wait for the next cart.

"Guess who's riding together?" Jack whispered.

Ben smirked and nodded. "Did you plan that?"

"Sure did!" Jack answered.

Soon, Paul and Elizabeth were the only ones left. The stables were quiet, with only the rustling of one or two horses waiting to be escorted by Garden handlers to the side entrance.

Paul's sigh was audible, and he felt like if he spoke, he would get this all wrong. They stood shoulder to shoulder, Elizabeth holding her hands together in front of her as they stared blankly forward, neither knowing what to say but both feeling quite down. After what felt like an eternity, their heads slowly turned inward until their eyes met.

"I'm sorry," Paul whispered in a low strained voice, "I can't not do this."

He gently reached behind her, placing his hand over the dip in the small of her back as he turned to face her. He took his other hand and pulled her closer at her waist, turning her so she was facing him directly. He tilted her chin upward and caressed her cheek with the back of his hand, trailing down the contour of her face to her neck. He leaned down, breathing in her sweet scent, stopping just before their lips parted. He watched her eyes flutter shut and pulled her in tighter, lifting her up. She let her weight fall into his embrace, her toes barely touching the ground as she felt his lips press into hers.

"Look, Ben, look!" Jack said, turning around on the bench.

They pushed their faces between the two seat cushions and looked behind them, giggling as they watched them share their special moment.

"That's gross! I'm never kissing a girl!" Jack said.

They turned back around in the seat, sticking out their tongues in disgust and shivering at the thought, but Jack was happy on the inside.

"You know what this means," Ben said.

They raised their arms into the air. "Campfire!" they shouted.

"I can taste those marshmallows already!" Jack said.

*   *   *

Paul released his hold and held her face as she found her footing. The squeaky cart wheels shattered the silence as they stared at each other, not breaking eye contact until the cart came to a stop. Paul helped her inside, then maneuvered in next to her. She was trying to steady her breathing as he lowered his hand over hers, turning her palm and sliding his fingers through hers. Her pulse quickened as their fingers intertwined and he squeezed. She couldn't remember the last time her hand was held; it felt wonderful, and she didn't want him to let it go.

Jack and Ben crossed the street, weaving around slow walkers. They passed hot dog vendors, but it was the roasted peanuts that made their stomachs growl.

"Boy am I hungry!" Jack said, seeing his Uncle Tony flipping pizza dough through the restaurant's kitchen window.

"There's my Uncle Tony," Jack said, waving as they walked by. Jack saw his uncle put his finger in the air. "Wait, he wants to see us. Let's go over real quick."

"But your mother said—"

Jack's uncle walked outside carrying two pepperoni slices wrapped in wax paper. "Here. Just don't tell your ma, and make sure to eat all your dinner tonight, or else she'll find out."

"Thanks, Uncle Tony!" Jack said, handing a slice to Ben. "Quick, woof it down! She'll never find out."

They devoured the slices, tossing the wrapping in the last trash container before the hotel's block. Wiping their faces with their sleeves, they waited for a trolly to round the corner before continuing their walk.

"If I train with Mr. Davies, I will get to come back more often. Maybe we could see each other more."

"Tell him you want to! He's a real big shot and will take you far, Ben. You'd be an idiot not to take him up on it. Maybe you can stay with us on the days you're not riding and play baseball in the park with me and my buddies—you'd really like them."

Ben nodded, convinced it was the right thing to do. "I'm going to tell him. I will miss Mr. Carl, and I worry about hurting his feelings. He trained me up real good."

"I get that, but Mr. Carl seems to like him, and it might keep him from hobbling around like he does. Just tell him before you leave, that way we can make a plan for when you come back. You can come to our house and meet my grandfather. We can even go to his chocolate factory—makes popsicles look like spinach. He has every kind of chocolate treat you can imagine! Sprinkles, coconut, caramel, fudge—all put inside the bars so when you break them apart, it all oozes out!"

Ben's eyes widened as he imagined the chocolate fantasyland, as they skipped across the street and saw everyone gathered out front of the hotel. "There's your mother and Mr. Paul, looks like they're all waiting for us."

Elizabeth looked at Jack's face, swiping her thumb over the sauce on his chin. "I see you saw your uncle."

Jack grimaced, dragging his sleeve along his chin, and leaned over to Ben. "Where were ya on that one?"

*　　*　　*

Carl stepped outside the Garden's side entrance with Juniper, waiting for the others to cross the street, then they all began their walk to the park. Ben and Jack walked alongside Juniper, talking about their next adventure and where they wanted to go together. Charles walked alongside Carl, giving Paul and Elizabeth some space as they followed.

Elizabeth deliberately held her arm further from her side, craving the touch of his hand in hers, feeling her heart race when their hands brushed as they walked. Paul's thoughts splintered as busily as the people rushing by, and he longed for just a few more minutes of her time.

"There's the bridge, just down this street and across that path next to the station," Charles said.

Feeling those minutes slipping away, he blurted out the first thing that came to his mind: "I wish I could build a bridge that stretched all the way to Greenfield."

"I know you have a lot of responsibility, and your days are long and difficult, but promise me you will write. It doesn't have to be every week, or even every two weeks, but just knowing that on any given day, I might come across one of your letters makes me so happy."

Paul listened to the delicate click of her heels along the cobblestone and wondered how such an elegant, beautiful, successful woman from the big city would ever desire to hear anything he could ever write. He didn't speak different languages, didn't own expensive cars or wear fancy clothes, and he certainly hadn't made a name for himself—but her words cast a spell on him, and he trembled at the thought of losing her.

"I promise."

Arthur had just arrived at the bridge when they came down the path. Charles and Carl thanked him for such an enjoyable evening and for making the time to watch Ben compete.

"I sure hope to see you again soon, Arthur," Charles said. "I appreciate you being here to share this experience with us."

"Tell him, tell him now!" Jack whispered to Ben out of the corner of his mouth.

Ben walked up beside Carl and stood facing Arthur. "I would like to train with you, Mr. Davies. I would like that just fine."

Arthur straightened his posture and held a stiff hand out to Ben. "Once we shake on it, consider it a pact—trainer and pupil."

Ben shook his hand with a smile. "Thank you, Mr. Davies."

The train whistle blew in the distance, the approaching engine sending smoke plumes curling into the air as it rounded the bend.

"Damn," Paul mumbled.

"We're on our way home," Charles said, picking up his bag. "Should we write to you, Arthur, once we get there to work out the details?"

Arthur walked with them, carrying Carl's bag so that he could load Juniper. "Send me your current training schedule so that we can make a plan. We still have a few months of riding weather—even longer if we make the trip south to my facility just outside Savannah. It's fairly popular during the winter months for those who train in the off-season."

The train whistle blew once more as the cars clacked into the station. As Paul watched it pass by, he felt a poke at his back.

"It was good to see you, Mr. Paul. Maybe next time you can see our frogs—just promise me you won't eat their legs," Jack said.

Paul shook his head and laughed. "It was really good to see you too, Jack." Paul held out his hand, taken by surprise when Jack went right in for a hug, wrapping his arms around Paul's waist.

Elizabeth put her hand over her chest, deeply touched at the trust and security Jack drew from Paul's company.

Paul wrapped his arms around Jack with a squeeze. "I promise, Jack, your frogs are safe around me. Can't say the same for Mr. Elliot." Slinging his bag over his shoulder, he walked over to Elizabeth. "Thank you," he said, looking around at the city's landscape. "Thanks for showing us around, and for the shirt and the boots, and for your company—I will write to you, you can count on it."

"Best of luck with the grand opening. I know it will be a huge success, but be sure to tell me how it went."

Paul nodded. "If it's still standing, that is. You know who I left in charge."

"I hate to leave before you all board, but I need to open the store for an afternoon delivery."

"My car is here Elizabeth," Arthur said, "I can take you and get you back to the estate after."

"That would be delightful, thank you, Arthur."

Jack and Ben ran up ahead to watch the train rolling into the station house.

Paul pushed away the thought of Arthur escorting Elizabeth and Jack, catching Charles giving him a smirk as he walked by behind Carl.

The train rested in the terminal as passengers crowded around the vestibule. Carl and Charles walked Juniper to the loading ramp and fastened his head bumper.

"You see Paul's face when Arthur offered to take Elizabeth across town? Darn near had to put this bumper on his head."

"I saw. He's sweet on that young lady—can't say I blame him," Carl said.

"Sweet on her? That man's in love. Isn't anything sweet about that—that there's torment."

Elizabeth and Jack watched Paul and Ben board; Ben grabbed a window seat and opened the window, sitting on his knees and sticking his head out of the window. "I'll write and tell you when I'll be back," he said to Jack.

"Write when you get home! And bring your baseball mitt when you come back—I'll tell Oliver that we got another player."

Paul took a seat opposite the window, not wanting to see Arthur leave with them; he didn't trust himself not to hurl himself off the car.

Charles reached over the seat and squeezed his shoulder. "Kind of feels like your insides are in a meat grinder, don't it?" he said with a chuckle before taking a seat on the bench behind him.

The whistle blew as the train slowly gained momentum, pulling out of the station. Paul fought the urge but glanced over just before the train reached the park—and instantly regretted it. Watching them walk away with Arthur was the image that lingered in his mind for the next thirty-some hours.

As the skyline of the city faded behind them, Carl stretched out his legs and folded his arms on his chest. Charles and Ben were still gazing out their windows, soaking up the scenery.

Ben pulled out his medal, rubbing his hands over the lettering engraved in the thick metal.

"I'm so proud of you Benjamin," Charles said.

"Thank you, Mr. Charles. I can't wait to show Mrs. Claire and Mr.

Elliot and Lucas! Maybe when I come back to train, Lucas can come with me, and we can see Jack together."

"How do you feel about coming back and training with Mr. Davies?"

"I wasn't sure at first, I was sad mostly. It wasn't anything to do with Mr. Davies, he has a neat place and all, but I will miss Mr. Carl."

Carl kept his eyes closed so it appeared he was nodding off, even though he was one row separated and turned his head to listen.

"Mr. Carl taught me to ride, and I liked the way he would draw for me and show me how to do things with pictures. I know it took all his time and he don't particularly like this jumping stuff—he calls jumpers "rabbit jockeys."

Charles laughed. "He isn't closing that notebook anytime soon—I have a feeling you're going to have to put up with him a little while longer."

Ben looked out the window and dropped the medal in his lap. "I hope so. I would give this medal back to make him young again so his knees don't hurt."

Carl suddenly felt an ache in his heart. It was a pain like no other— the sting and warmth of a tear pooled beneath his lid before rolling down his face.

Ben looked at the medal and cupped it in his hand, sliding his fingers along the silky neck strap. "I never thought I would get one of these. I just wanted to ride for Mr. Carl and do everything right, just like he taught me… I wanted to ride perfect, for him," he said, then slid along the bench to the aisle closer to Charles and handed him the medal. "Will you give this to him? I want him to have it, and I know he won't take it from me," he whispered.

Charles was at a loss for words over Ben's expression of gratitude and couldn't deny the request. "I'm not too sure he'll take it from me either, but I will give it to him."

Ben grinned and slid back to the window.

Paul leaned his head back, hating each rotation of the track assembly turning the car wheels and every chuff that carried him farther away from her. "Estate," he mumbled to himself, recalling the last words Arthur said. He shook his head, thinking on his one-bedroom house with a cedar shake roof and a fish-carving table out back next to a drying line.

40
The Angels

"WHAT TOOK YOU SO LONG?" Gabe said as they came through the door. "I already played two games of solitaire, sharpened all my knives, and got stuck with cleanup. Where did you guys run off to?"

"We had something to…" Sarah paused, searching for the best word that wouldn't give too much away.

"Oversee," Jacob interjected with a confident nod, looking at them for agreement.

"Yeah, that's right, we had to oversee something," Joshua said.

Gabe watched them closely, his gaze sharp as their eyes darted around. "Whatever."

Jacob scratched the back of his neck, thankful he dropped his interest. "Haven't seen any more floaters, have you? You talk to the others?"

Gabe slid his blade into the sheath on the card table. "Don't worry about it—yet," he said, then shuffled the card deck and began another round of solitaire.

"You can't just drop it like that; tell us something! We need to know if there are spooks in our midst!" Joshua said.

"And what are you gonna do about it? Pull out one of your feathered sticks? Good luck with that—you got nothing for it to sink into."

"So, you *do* know more than you're letting onto," Sarah said, "and the other angels know about it." Standing with her hands on her hips, she fixed Jacob and Joshua with an accusatory glare. "That proves what I overheard last night wasn't a hoax like you two said it was."

Joshua raised his eyebrows at her and Jacob started scratching his neck again, sensing the impending interrogation.

Gabe smacked the deck on the table and slid it aside. "What are you rodeo clowns insinuating?"

Sarah tapped her foot, waiting for their responses.

"We aren't insinuating anything," Joshua said. "Last night, when she heard them talking at the campfire about other angels—dark ones—and something about a battle between good and evil. We just figured it was another one of your pranks, you know, to get our goats—like that time you filled my quiver with flowers or the time you hung that decoy from the roof outside Jacob's window and started screaming about flying reindeer."

Gabe laughed under his breath at the pleasant memories.

"Or the time when you took lanterns and put them under the door and imitated Jesus! Telling us to put our right hand out, then our left hand out, then shake them all about. Remember that one?"

Gabe laughed even harder. "That was a good one. You guys didn't catch on until it was time to turn yourselves around."

"And that's what it's all about!" Jacob sang.

"You three would be the driest lumps of flat sawn if it weren't for me. But this isn't a joke—not that you would recognize it if it were. Abram and Zelach have seen them, too, but say they're illusions. Apparently, they have a broken compass and are lost in our dimension. So a lot like you guys if you think about it."

Jacob looked around the room nervously. "So what do we do about it?"

"Point and laugh," Gabe said. "They can't see us and they have no bodies, so it's not like they can lick their finger and touch your ear."

Joshua shuddered, remembering Gabe's wet willie phase.

"I heard them talk about 'dark ones,'" Sarah said. "The mumbler said they were bound, but one day they would be set free—and that's why we're here: to fight them."

Gabe grunted. "His name is Abram. There's only three of them—learn their names already. They've been living beside us for six hundred years."

"You're the one who calls the puffy shirt guy 'the pirate,'" Sarah said sarcastically.

"Well, that's what he looks like, am I right?"

Joshua and Jacob nodded quietly in agreement and took a seat at the table for a card deal.

"Have a seat, horse whisperers," Gabe said. "Tell me how the kid did today."

"How did you know about that?" Joshua asked. "We were only gone for a few hours!"

Gabe just chuckled and started to deal.

41

Gladys held her hat on her head, looking up at the swaying treetops. "I hope this breeze eases up, or we'll never get these streamers wrapped in time."

Claire hurried to catch up, picking up the end of an uncurled ribbon dragging across the ground behind Gladys. "Denny is bringing a ladder to hang the sign. If he can attach one end to the base of the lamps, we can wrap it around the poles and anchor it down with the clothespins. I still can't believe it! When that telegram came, I nearly reached out and picked little Oscar off the ground. He will probably think twice about coming to our door with a letter now."

"Poppycock, the whole town is buzzing. He's probably delivered more newspapers today than he has all year. Why, this is the biggest thing that has ever happened around here, and I have the corns to prove it! Been walking myself all over town—folks ain't talking about nothing else."

*　　*　　*

Daniel's truck pulled into the station, a long line of cars trailing behind him. Townsfolk honked their horns, waving to each other. Elliot pulled in from a side road with the signs and a box of tools, with Buck seated next to him, hanging his head out of the window.

"Here they come, Gladys, it won't be long now!" Claire said. "It feels like they have been away longer than just a few days… I can't wait to give Ben a big hug!"

"Me, too, dear. And after I do that, I'm getting the juice on this lady friend that has Paul licking his chops like an old coon hound. Getting the goods from Elliot has been tougher than I thought."

Gladys held one end of the spool and handed the ribbon end to Claire. "Don't be silly, Paul isn't going to tell us anything," Claire said.

"That's what Elliot is for. And I baked two extra lemon meringue pies for bartering. We might want to hush ourselves, here he comes now."

"Mornin', Miss Gladys, Mrs. C. Y'all need a hand with that?"

"That would be delightful," Claire said. "I see Denny with the ladder."

Reggie and Cecelia held handfuls of balloons and began tying the ribbons to armchairs, benches, and station signage, while Bernice and Earl passed out plastic kazoos and noise makers as folks gathered. Tom and Margie held the leash of a cocker spaniel with a decorated collar that Buck found out wasn't very playful.

Lucas came running down the sloped hill toward the vestibule with his father and mother trailing behind.

"Lucas!" Elliot called, waving him over. "Give me a hand with the sign—between the two of us, we should be able to carry it over."

"How much time till they get here?" Lucas asked.

"'Bout an hour, I figure, maybe less. Just listen for that three o'clock whistle—we'll hear 'em comin' from the county over."

"I can't wait to see Ben! You know he saw our buddy Jack, don't ya?"

"I sure do; it's all y'all been talkin' 'bout for days."

*　　*　　*

Paul opened his eyes, instantly recognizing the view out the window and feeling discontented by it. He heard Carl snoring, and laced his boots, rubbing the sleep from his eyes.

Ben was standing at the front of the train car when the whistle blew, then turned around in excitement. "We're almost there, Mr. Charles!"

Charles was in the aisle, stretching out his back and gathering his bag. "I sure am ready to get off this car—got a crick in my neck," he said, leaning over and tapping Carl on the arm.

Carl sputtered awake, disoriented and hungry.

"Next stop is ours," Charles said.

Ben started to jump in place, pointing up ahead and pulling the window down. "Look up ahead, look at all the cars—everyone is here!"

Carl wiggled his toes and rubbed his stomach, lifting his hat off his face. "What's all the ruckus for?"

With one last whistle, the train entered the station. Everyone blew their noisemakers and cheered.

"There's Mr. Elliot and Lucas… and Buck!" Ben said, waving to them from the window. Ben marveled at the reception; there were signs with his name on them, and everywhere he looked was decorated with balloons and colored streamers. As soon as the train stopped, he was already at the door, anxious for it to open.

Seeing Elliot waving from the loading platform, Paul buttoned his shirt and slung his bag over his shoulder. It felt good to see so many happy faces on everyone he knew, and for a moment, he forgot to feel miserable.

As soon as they stepped off the car, they were met with hugs and handshakes; even the men who worked in the barber shop were there to greet them. Charles leaned into Claire while Paul was swallowed up by Gladys, pulling him down by his shoulders for an embrace. Margie gave him a squeeze on his cheeks. "How did you like the big city!"

Claire and Gladys moved in closer with their ears tuned in.

"It was a city, not much to speak of—big, loud, and busy. Ben was a champion, though; that boy did good," Paul said, excusing himself when he noticed Elliot waving from the back of the crowd.

"Not to worry, we'll get him talking," Gladys whispered to Claire, opening her arms when she saw Ben moving closer. "Boy, you look like you grew an inch! What are they feeding folks over there in the city?"

"We had duck and mussels and all kinds of food at Mr. Davies's house. It was nice!"

Gladys looked at the gals and raised her eyebrows. "Fancy!"

Claire reached out, placed her hands around his face, then scooped him into a hug. "I'm so proud of you! I want to hear all about it!"

Paul got through the mob and dropped his bag in front of Elliot.

"Didn't recognize ya at first with that froufrou shirt… and *whew-wee*, look at them boots! Where'd ya get those? Didn't figure city folk as havin' workin' togs."

Paul grinned, admiring them as he crossed them right over left, propping one toe on the ground.

Elliot bent over to get a peek at the tread. "Figures—ain't got no grip. Them soles are slicker than spit; must just be for show," he said with a wink.

Paul snickered at the teasing and grabbed his bag, looking up at the sky as dark clouds rolled in from the west. "Get any rain while we was gone?"

"Not a drip, but we're fixin' for some after dusk—wind is startin' to pick up. If we hurry, we can make a stop at the store. It's shapin' up, got most everything ready for the opening."

"Let's scoot then."

Ben and Lucas chased after a streamer that was rustled apart by the wind, then another and another.

Charles, Carl, and Reggie made their way to the ramp to unload Juniper. "Best be getting him put up, looks like rains a comin' and comin' quick," Carl said.

"How'd he manage the ride? That was quite a stretch… 'bout how long it take?"

"Thirty-four long hours coming back," Charles said. "Didn't seem as long getting there, but he did right well. Sure handled the noise better than we did, right Carl?"

Carl shook his head, bringing Juniper down the ramp. "Sure did; maybe you can craft one of these for my noggin' if I'm ever need'n to go back, Reggie."

Reggie examined the fit, placing his fingers under the crown strap. "Didn't shift or bunch an inch," he said, unbuckling the fastener. "Got several orders for custom caps just after you left town, someone by the name Pemberton. In the letter he mentioned you and Henry. You heard of this fella?"

Charles pushed out a sigh and looked at Carl, who seemed amused by the question. "Good ole Sid. He's like a bad penny—keeps turning up."

"I ain't said I'd do the work, and if you ain't fond of the fella, that's all I need to turn him away," Reggie said.

"Take his work, Reggie, it will get your name out there. Sid has clout in the racin' business; ain't got much humility, but he can get you exposure if you can get past the entitlement."

Paul climbed into his truck, mildly pleased to be back in the driver's seat after spending the last few days as a passenger. He watched the station clear out, cranking the engine when Elliot rolled up. He pulled out behind him, following him to the side road.

When they pulled into the store's lot, Elliot jumped out of his truck and jogged over to the market's storefront with his arms out wide. "You like it?" he said, turning his head up to the sign and pointing. "Took us dang near two hours to get that bugger centered—had to fashion a support post to the back."

Paul pushed the door closed, staring up at the sign.

"Look through the windows here: Claire and Gladys put all those racks together for their baked goods, even got ribbons on all the carrying baskets for shoppers, and Denny built these vegetable bins from scrap. And the fence here, I painted it!"

Paul looked around, walking the rows of bins under the awning, touching the fabric overhang.

"That was Daniel's handiwork, he made a pulley track. Watch this!" Elliot grabbed the rope that fed around the wheel and pulled it down. The fabric retracted and hung neatly under the lip of the roof. "How's that for curb appeal! We noticed when the sun comes up in the east, the vegetables would be gettin' baked, but this keeps the shade over 'em!"

Paul tugged at a hook overhead, noticing a few more in a line. "What's these for?"

Elliot put his hands on his hips and shook his head at the ground. "Wasn't my idea, and I tried my darndest to talk 'em out of it, but Mrs. C and Miss Gladys got it in their bonnets that they wanted hangin' flowers. I told 'em it might bring more bees and other flying critters, but they wanted 'color,' whatever that means."

Paul chuckled.

"We got buckets and barrels for fruit—seems like enough color to me—but sometimes it's best to just oblige and go forth 'cause when they team up on ya, you're sunk. And you should know, they pressed me hard 'bout you and all your googly eyes with Miss Elizabeth."

"You better not have—"

Elliot smacked his thigh and snickered. "Calm down Romeo, I ain't let onto nothin'. But you'd better fix your stutterin', 'cause you ain't foolin' nobody for long."

Paul reached out for a handshake. "You done good. This was hard work—real hard."

Elliot batted his hand away and wrapped an arm around his neck, giving him a firm squeeze before backing away and playfully flicking him with the back of his hand, feeling the softness of the shirt. "Boy, that's slicker than those boot bottoms—you sure do clean up good. Ball's over come tomorrow, though, so you'd better leave these fancy clothes on the hanger—we'll need to get up on that roof and drive a few more nails into a corner beam."

"Is it just a gap or pulling up?"

"Seems to be pulling. Daniel had a few lengths we had to scrap and put down new; must have been split on an angle, some were warped pretty good."

Elliot followed him around the building to the back corner, gripping the sides of his floppy hat and pulling it tight to his head against a gust of wind. "See it there?" he said, holding his hat with one hand and pointing with the other. "Looks to have pulled up higher today."

Paul nodded. "That won't take much; I can slap that down with a mallet."

"Not in those you can't," Elliot said, pointing to Paul's boots. "Ain't got no grab to 'em. Besides, we're fixin' to get rained on, so let's meet back here at sunup."

Elliot turned around and started walking, expecting Paul to be beside him. When he looked back, Paul was staring up at the roof. "You fixin' to get struck by lightnin'? Let's be on our way."

"You go on ahead. I need to stop in the store first."

Elliot hesitated, trying to gauge where Paul was on the knucklehead meter. "Promise me you ain't climbin' up there and you'll wait till mornin', 'cause if ya don't, then I ain't leavin'."

"Alright, alright. I promise," Paul said, then turned and waved him off as he crossed the lot.

Elliot watched a line of dark clouds rolling in fast and jumped in his truck, feeling confident that Paul meant it. Paul hated working in the rain as much as he did.

Paul yanked the door open and stepped inside. The face frame of the counter had been painted a deep mocha brown, accented with white trim board. He walked over and brushed his hand over the surface. It was sanded down—all the chips and divots, even the burn marks from cigar ash had been smoothed out, sealed, and finished. The windows were spotless, the casings freshly painted, and a valance hung from a wooden curtain rod. The coffee counter had a new coal grate and a cubby stocked with cups, and a small basket held wooden stir sticks. A large panel of perforated hardboard was mounted behind the till with hooks and pegs that held an assortment of tools, keys, wire, scissors, and twine. The cabinets underneath had been given a fresh coat of paint and hardware. He leaned over the counter and saw trays and bins organized in neat rows underneath and a clean pad of writing paper and a newspaper with the front-page article on the horse show.

On his way to the office to grab the mallet, he pushed the storage room door open. Looking around, his jaw fell open. The cobwebs were gone, the grain in the floorboards was now visible, and all the boxes and random items had been organized. The biggest surprise was that the cracked yellowed window had been replaced, and even though the sky was darkening, a good amount of light poured in. It smelled different, too—it wasn't as stale and musty.

On his way out the door with the mallet, he took a look down the aisles. Everything was in order: bins and tooling were straightened, and the seed bins were full. Paul shook his head in disbelief—it was like the whole place had been spit shined.

42

The Angels

SARAH FOLDED HER HAND ON the table. "I'm out, again. And I'm bored. That's four hands in a row now.

"Hey, sweetheart, since you can't play cards worth a toot, how about whipping up a snack for us that can?" Gabe said.

Joshua could see the irritation on Sarah's face and was a little concerned Gabe would end up wearing the lager in her mug. Just as Sarah bent her arm, tilting the mug in Gabe's direction, Joshua watched Gabe's amusement fade, his attention focused on something in the distance.

"What, you see another one?" Joshua said, still jumpy from their prior discussion.

Sarah relaxed her grip and turned around to see what had grabbed his attention, noticing the light under the door get brighter.

"Two pair!" Jacob yelled, laying down his hand. "Put that in your quiver, chump."

Sarah thumped him on the back of his head. "Not now, dummy. Turn around."

Standing in line with his head lowered, Gabe felt a warm glow and a touch on his shoulder. His eyes then fell upon Jesus's scarred feet. He was amazed how gentle and loving Jesus was after having been tortured and slain. Gabe felt Jesus's palm rest on his chest, and he suddenly felt vulnerable and scared, insecure and unworthy. These sensitive emotions caught him off guard, and before he could fidget from the awkward feelings, he was given a vision of a brooding man that was battling heart pain. The man was terrified of something; there was an inescapable force threatening to penetrate the fortress around his heart. The man was trapped, his fear of love throwing him into turmoil. This man didn't want to need anyone, he desired solitude and a simple life. He was running— running from memories of love lost and of people taken away from him, leaving behind a void he filled with work and responsibilities. To him, love meant loss and pain, and he wanted nothing to do with it. Gabe felt a startling kinship with this man; he knew about building walls to keep from being hurt. It was his calling card, and he played it very well.

Jesus stepped back and turned to the door. When the light faded, they looked to each other, curious which one was selected for an assignment. They knew right away it was Gabe by the way he looked like he had just bitten into a lemon.

"Well?" Sarah said, "what did you see?"

"Me," Gabe said.

"You saw an egotistical, stubborn, musclehead prankster?"

"Let's be real," Gabe said, "next to me, nobody has muscle."

Sarah sighed. "I'm sure you will lift something heavy and throw your weight around gallantly. Just stay clear of any thinking, feeling humans and you'll be just fine."

Gabe shook his head, amused at the irony of the assignment he'd been given. "Better watch your six guys, I'm not the only jokester around here."

*   *   *

Paul grabbed a ladder, tucked the mallet into his belt, and looked at the clouds rolling in, quickening his pace. The wind picked up as he hoisted himself onto the roof, straddling the pitch for stability. He looked out across the landscape, awed by the beauty of the sea of corn swaying in the fields. His spirit was quieted by the silence and isolation. He felt at peace—untouchable.

Gabe lowered onto the roof on the opposite side, shaking his head. He could feel the tug-of-war inside Paul and closed his eyes, meditating on Paul's heartbeat. He resurrected all the angst Paul was feeling, bringing it to the surface for him to confront. He stirred up his past and the pain from losing his parents and Bernie. "This is gonna sting," he said quietly.

Paul reminisced over the past two days, his emotions stirring like the clouds overhead. He thought about Elizabeth and how her life in New York was just getting settled; she had a new beginning and a corner boutique with her name above the door. She had style and class—she was smart and driven. She didn't show the pain and hurt she had endured; it was like it had evaporated off her like morning dew. She had family close by and was privileged, she had no cares or worries and probably many well-to-do admirers. His heart ached, and he couldn't stop himself from going back and forth between their differences and similarities. They laughed together a lot, and he remembered the way he'd caught her looking at him in the car; it was obvious she liked what she saw, but he couldn't fathom why. He was a simple country boy, no wealth to speak of, no prominent family legacy. Everything he had required calluses and heavy lifting, things that would eventually become a tether for a free-spirited city woman. Then, an even darker thought came to the surface, one that he was afraid to even acknowledge: What if she left, what if she died? His mind took him on a journey through losing his mother, then his father—the only security he had known. He remembered holding Bernie in his arms and lowering his casket into the ground. He wouldn't be able to go on if something happened to Elizabeth, or Jack. He couldn't handle it if they were taken away. It would be the end of him.

Gabe drew his breath in deep, then exhaled, letting it go to be carried off by the wind. He could feel Paul's struggle, and even though he was impressed by his rigidity, he was equally frustrated by his brittleness. He wanted to give him a good shaking and hopefully knock some sense into him.

Paul pulled out a small black box from his pocket and opened it. The tiny inset diamond was barely visible in the gold pronged cradle. He lifted it from the velvet holder and held it up, then placed it on the tip of his pinky finger. He imagined what he would say and how he would ask her, but he could only imagine himself bumbling and stuttering, just like Elliot said. He'd seen the rings the women in the city had been wearing and they were a lot bigger than this. *What an embarrassment*, he thought, *how could he ask her to marry him when he couldn't even afford a proper ring.* A raindrop landed on his hand, then another. When he looked up, the cloud was directly above him, unleashing a relentless downpour. He reached for the ring box but his hand slipped, causing it to slide just out of reach. When he stretched to grab it, he lost his balance, and the ring toppled off his fingertip and rolled down the roof and over the edge.

Gabe rolled his eyes and hung his head, feeling pity for this bumbling, clumsy, lovesick fool. Gabe caught the jewelry box as it skidded past, then slowly stood up, stretching his back, and doing a side twist to loosen a cramp.

In a hurry to retrieve the ring, Paul quickly got to his feet and pulled the mallet from his belt. Crossing the pitch, he lost traction and slid down a few feet until he regained his balance. The rain stung as it pelted his neck, making him flinch and scurry faster down the pitch. He walked on a diagonal until he was close enough to the corner to see the raised beam. As he took another step, his boots slipped, and before he realized it, he was free-falling over the edge.

Gabe stretched out his arm, grabbing Paul by the front of his shirt and yanking him forward. Paul hit the roof with a thud, landing flat on his stomach. As Paul started to right himself, the loudest sound he'd ever heard exploded around him. Panicking, he clapped his hands over his ears and gazed around, convinced lightning had struck a tree. He jerked his head toward the corner of the roof, but instead of seeing a falling tree, he saw a massive white figure standing near the edge. He wiped the rain from his eyes and looked again. The misty silhouette moved slowly along the edge, stopping at the ladder, then shot up into the sky like a bullet and vanished.

Paul rolled onto his back and sat up, touching his shirt and his head, wondering if he was suffering from a head injury that caused a hallucination. Looking up, he saw nothing but blue sky as the storm clouds separated and rolled eastward. He pushed up onto his feet, but his shaky legs gave out, so he decided to scoot on his backside until he reached the ladder. Carefully putting one leg over the top rung, he saw the ring box sitting upright in the center of the top step. Leaning over, he picked it up and opened the box—inside was the ring.

43

The Angels

Gabe pushed the door open, squeezing the dampness from his shirt hem, leaving a puddle on the floor.

"That was fast," Sarah said, "didn't even have time to whip up that snack you wanted."

Jacob held his cards close to his chest as Gabe approached, sensing him peering over his shoulder. "Not this time," he said, pulling his shoulder around and staring at Joshua. "And don't you be trying to cheat with him—you two can't be trusted."

"What was the assignment?" Sarah asked. "Did you throw any punches, save a town from flooding by pushing over trees to build a dam? Or perhaps lifting a car off a little old lady?"

"None of the above. I got to listen to a man whine and fall off a roof. It would have been hilarious if it weren't so pathetic."

"What happened? How did you save him?" Sarah asked, knocking her stirring spoon against the pot, and setting it aside to listen.

Gabe pulled his shirt over his head and tossed it on the back of a chair. "Had to snatch him up—he was going over for sure. A good smack on the head might have done him some good. Poor sap was driving me crazy, but he'd have a broken neck had I not grabbed him."

"You think he saw you?" Joshua asked.

Gabe flexed at his reflection in the window. "Oh, he saw me. I wasn't completely visible, but he definitely got an eyeful. Lucky lad."

Joshua shook his head and sorted his cards.

"Deal me in," Gabe said, pulling out a chair.

"Not until you put a shirt on," Jacob said. "Unlike the roof guy, I can see perfectly."

44

Paul sat on the roof, staring at the ring before raising his eyes to the sky in bewilderment. The storm had passed and the warmth of the setting sun warmed his back. He touched his chest, expecting it to be tender from the impact of being hurled onto his stomach, but there were no scratches, no pain—in fact, he felt better than he had in years. He sat with his legs dangling over the edge, swinging them back and forth like a child sitting atop monkey bars, thinking about what happened. He felt lighter than ever, like a weight had been lifted and his heart no longer ached with insecurity and fear. He didn't understand why, but he vaguely recognized this feeling—like how he used to feel before the pain. He tried thinking on what had troubled him before the fall—all the unpleasant thoughts and defeating speculations—but couldn't resurrect that fear anymore.

Hoisting one leg over the top rung of the ladder, he turned around and saw the mallet on the pitch of the roof, remembering he hadn't even fixed the beam. Carefully, he bear-crawled up the roof, grabbed the mallet, and scooted down to the corner slowly, making sure he relied more on his hands and legs for grip than the boots. When he got to the edge, the roof line was flat—there was no heave. Turning over on his stomach, he ran his hand along the corner edge, but it was flush with the ridge. He inspected the wood shakes closely and found an impression directly over the spot where the warped beam was raised. He moved his hand over the surface, feeling an indention in the wood. It was large and had a peculiar shape, like an imprint of a fist with wide knuckles. Paul made a fist and placed his hand over the area.

Surprisingly, the shape matched the outline of his own.

Keeping his eyes on the imprint, he slowly slid the mallet into his belt and crossed the roof to the ladder, climbing down. Walking away with the ladder, he looked back at the corner of the roof, knowing that whatever he just experienced, he would keep it to himself.

*　　*　　*

Claire fluttered around the kitchen, adding the finishing touches to the meal. Charles emerged from the study, following the scent of freshly baked oatmeal cookies, counting eight ribbon-laced baskets on his way to the counter.

"I see you have been a busy bee; if you keep baking like this, we'll need to sleep outside with the horses," he said, giving her a peck on the cheek.

"If you think this is busy, you should see Gladys's kitchen. She has been glazing and basting for three days straight—the opening of the market has really turned up her timer."

"Where'd Ben run off to?" Charles said, rubbing his belly.

"He was excited to read the letters that came from Margaret and Jonathan; such a shame they didn't make it in time before the trip."

Charles followed the sound of footsteps coming down the hall from upstairs and broke off a corner of a cookie.

"Put that down!" Claire giggled, "you don't want to squander that appetite. Bernice gave me some of her garden herbs, and I used them on the roast, the gravy, and over the potatoes. It's positively scrumptious!"

Ben came around the corner as he finished reading the letter from Jonathan and slipped it under his utensils.

"How are they doing?" Claire asked. "The letters came just after you all left."

"Jonathan is in the Pacific Ocean! He said they are working on drills, and he might be able to visit for Thanksgiving! Margaret said she has been studying a lot and will be going to a real hospital to watch other nurses soon!"

"That is wonderful!" Claire said. "Oh, I do hope they can visit over the holidays—that was so much fun last year."

Over supper, she listened to Ben recount every step of the trip. Resting her chin on her hand, she couldn't help but be amused by his animated expressions as he described the toy store and how much fun he had with Jack.

Charles delighted in recounting the memories, noticing Claire pay particular interest when Ben spoke of all the things they saw with Mr. Paul and Miss Elizabeth.

"Jack's mother sounds extraordinary!" Claire said. "I am so impressed; it must be exciting to be a fashion designer in a big city like that."

Ben rested against the chair, satisfied after cleaning his plate and already eyeing the cookies on the counter. "I think she's really nice, and Mr. Paul thinks so, too. Me and Jack saw him give her a flower and then we saw him kiss her! But he doesn't know we saw that part—Jack and I peeked through the cushions on the cart ride."

Claire dropped her hand, turning to look at Charles who spat out a mouthful of lemonade.

Ben continued his narrative, giving her every detail of the show and all the cameramen, the riders he met, and how much he liked Mr. Davies. He talked and talked until he started to yawn. "Thank you for supper Mrs. Claire, can I take a cookie to my room? I think I'll write my letter to Jack, then go straight to bed."

"You sure can—in fact, take two. I am certain Miss Gladys has dozens more at her place."

Claire waited until she heard him upstairs, then leaned over the table. "Did you know about this budding romance? Why, I nearly fell out of this chair sideways! Is he... does he..."

Charles exhaled with a grin, then shook his head and shrugged. "I don't believe in airing another man's affairs, but I can say with certain confidence... yes, that man has some feelings for Miss Elizabeth, and I believe it is a mutual admiration."

Claire wriggled in her seat and clapped her hands together. "This just tickles me silly. Gladys and I have had a sneaking suspicion he had—"

Charles put his hand up. "I think we best keep this to ourselves. If he finds it something to make a fuss over, he will make it known in his own time."

"You are right dear. I will pretend I never heard a word about it. Gladys, on the other hand… she's already on the scent. It isn't hard to discern he's been quite distracted lately, and Elliot nearly spilled the beans once or twice. Gladys has been up to her eyeballs in lemon meringue to get him talking."

*   *   *

Paul balled up another piece of paper and dropped it beside his chair, positioning his pen to start over. He knew what he wanted to say but writing it down was a problem. Taking a moment to think, he rested his feet on the table, moving the toe of his boot to look at the ring box sitting next to an empty can of soup, then stared blankly at the sheet of paper again before giving it another attempt.

Dear Elizabeth,

I hope this finds you well. By now, you are likely close to opening your store. I was wondering if you would like to consider moving back to Greenfield instead; you and Jack can begin your life here with me. And by the way, would you marry me?

Shaking his head in frustration, he crumpled it up and tossed it into the heaping pile of laughable, preposterous mush. Realizing it was futile to put his feelings into words, he dropped the notepaper on the table and walked to the bedroom, defeated but still consumed by the need to let her know what was on his mind.

*   *   *

Elliot slept soundly and woke up with a sudden jolt of energy. The sun's rays were in the middle of the window curtain, which meant he'd slept well past six o'clock. "The roof," he said out loud to himself, hurrying out of bed, gathering his clothes in one arm and his boots in the other. He knew Paul wasn't going to wait and would be up on that roof as soon as he got there. He splashed some water on his face after dressing and swiped his thermos off the counter, not even stopping to give it a rinse, and jogged through the wet grass in his bare feet.

When he pulled in, Paul's truck was pulled back into the cornfield and he was perched on the tailgate, just sitting there. He tied up his boots and went to the store to fill his thermos, figuring Paul had already got it percolating, but when he turned the knob, the door was still locked, and the sign wasn't flipped. Checking his watch again at half-past six, he unlocked the door and took care of the opening, thinking that once Paul noticed his truck, he would be coming around shortly. But after starting the morning brew, balancing the ledger, counting the till, and catching a mouse, he got curious why Paul hadn't been in, so he opened the door and poked his head around the corner. Paul was still in the same spot, just sitting there, looking out into the fields with his elbows on his thighs and his hands folded. He checked his watch again: seven o'clock. The seed delivery would arrive soon and Daniel was expected to drop off some building material. Elliot scratched his chin, arguing with himself about whether to walk over or let him sort out whatever he was dealing with. After a few paces, Elliot filled his thermos and started across the lot into the field.

As he got closer, he could see Paul clearly. He looked relaxed and had his eyes closed with his head turned up to the sun, letting it warm his bare chest and shoulders. His shirt was laying over his knee, fluttering in the cool breeze as he looked over at Elliot approaching from the side.

"You feelin' alright?" Elliot asked, holding up his wrist. "Ain't like you to be sunning yourself before havin' the store and market spinnin' like plates on sticks."

Paul pulled his arms behind him to lean on and reclined his head back. "I'm feeling just fine, Elliot, just wanted to breathe in the morning air and take some time to admire the work we done."

Elliot looked at him curiously, walking slowly over to the corner of the truck, setting his thermos on the bed rail. "You ain't never took time to breathe or admire anything. You groomed twenty acres, plowed and harvested, raised a roof, and stocked five hundred pounds of fertilizer without breathing, and that was all before openin' time. What's goin' on with ya? Did you catch that city bug? Suppose you'll be wantin' cream in your coffee now and a dust shield on the tractor."

Paul smirked, slowly and methodically putting on his shirt, enjoying his last few moments of soaking in the sun. "Store looks good—you worked your tail off."

"I can't hog all the glory; we had a lot of hands. Mrs. C, Miss Gladys… they done all the frills. Me and Daniel and Denny did most everything else, and Earl hung the counter peg."

Paul jumped down, stretching his arms over his head, and tapped Elliot on the shoulder. "Looks good, and you got a good head for business. You kept good order."

Elliot glanced over at him, unsure of what was going on with him, but accepted the sincere compliment, as unexpected as it was. Elliot kept his eyes mostly on the ground as they walked, still feeling somewhat awkward about the touching words, but every now and then he would peek at Paul as they walked. *He has something goin' on*, he thought; his face wasn't so tense, and his brows weren't drawn together in a constant furrow—he could actually see two eyebrows instead of one. His lips were parted and somewhat lifted, not pulled downward into a scowl, and his steps were a bit lighter, almost boyish, with a little spring in the ball of his feet. Rather than keep hounding him for the reason, Elliot simply welcomed it and hoped it would last.

Just as they reached the door, Daniel pulled in with a load of material. "You want me to run it out back?" he asked, waving his hand out the door.

Paul nodded. "We'll meet you back there."

Daniel gave a thumbs-up and turned the wheel, straightening it out and rolling past to the back of the store.

Paul reached for his gloves on the ledge behind the coffee station, but his hands just felt a smooth surface. He looked at Elliot who was pointing to a wooden slot anchored to the wall beside the door, half hidden by the valance. Paul dipped his hand inside and pulled out his gloves.

"That was Miss Gladys's idea; she was fixin' to throw a label on it, but I had to draw the line somewhere."

Paul tossed a pair to Elliot and pulled the door open. "Flip the sign on your way out."

"We can pound that beam in place after we stack this load," Elliot said, wiggling his hand into a glove.

"Beam's fixed."

"You didn't crawl up there when you done promised…" Elliot shook his head and blew out an audible exhale. "Why did I think otherwise," he murmured under his breath, catching up to Paul. "Sometimes you ain't as wise as you think you are. You could have landed dead on your back in those vegetable bins," he said, pointing to the market's awning.

Paul chuckled, remembering the strange encounter as he looked up at the roof, feeling a chill roll over him. "I might have, but I didn't—did I."

Daniel dropped the tailgate and jumped up in the bed, unhooking the straps holding the lumber down. "I told Denny to keep this wrapped, and now look at it; it's gonna take at least a day or two to dry out from all the rain we got."

"We got room in the back for it to bake," Elliot said, sliding a plank from the pile.

"We got more fresh-cut timber this morning; got more than I can sell, and still got another order comin' in from what that Larson fella called for. I couldn't cancel it, now I'm stuck with four cords of wood."

Paul got an idea, turning to look at Bernie's house sitting across the field nestled among the pine and birchwood trees. "I'll take it off your hands."

They both turned and looked at him, then looked at each other with curiosity. "What you plannin' to do with all that timber?" Elliot asked.

"Don't worry about it," Paul said, turning back around and pointing to Bernie's place. "Roll it back there and drop it around the back beside the shed."

Daniel raised his eyebrows. "You got it, boss. I'll bring another load by this afternoon. Do I need to tell the boys we got some work ahead of us?"

Paul adjusted his cap, wiping the sweat with the brim, then setting it back on his head. "Not yet. I'll see how far I can get."

Elliot glanced over at Daniel, then steadied the plank on his shoulder and carried it off. As they unloaded and stacked, every time he passed Paul, he discreetly observed him and could sense he was deep in thought. But whatever he was cooking up in his head seemed to make him happy, and sooner or later he would find out what it was.

45

Elizabeth walked the long driveway, quickening her steps the closer she got to the mailbox post. She could feel her stomach flutter and her skin felt warm and tingly. She lifted the cast iron cover and slowly peeked inside, looking for the blue-and-white checkered pattern of an envelope. As the light entered the box, she flipped through the letters, feeling saddened. On her walk back to the house, she wrestled with her angst, knowing it had only been a few days. Even if he had written her as soon as he returned home, it would be days—if not longer—to receive a letter.

Jack closed the door behind him and looped a strap around his books. His white short sleeved-shirt was neatly pressed, his tie slightly off center, and his knickers didn't quite reach the tops of his knee socks.

Elizabeth giggled as she looked over his appearance. "We might need to release that hem; it appears you have hit a growth spurt."

Jack looked down at his knees. "Ben said boys grow taller and bigger in farm states. I hope I don't stop growing now."

"Is that right? I never really considered that before, but I can see the possibility."

"It's true, look at Mr. Paul, he's real tall!"

She smiled watching him sluggishly walk down the steps. "Are you excited to begin your new lessons?"

"A little… I hope I don't have to sit next to Madeline again—she never stops talking."

They walked to the end of the driveway and waited for the school trolley. Elizabeth shuffled through the letters, turning over one from the city zoning office and opened it. She scanned the letter and saw the seal at the bottom with a stamp marked "approved." "It's official," she said, turning the letter around, "your mother is the owner of Rockwood Fashion Boutique."

Jack touched the embossed stamp, rubbing a finger over the texture. "Whose signature is that?"

"The mayor of New York City."

Jack looked at her proudly. "You're going to be great, Mother; you have always looked better than other mothers—most don't wear shoes like yours."

"I have seen other mothers wear heeled shoes. Oliver's mother does."

"Only when they meet us for church. Other times she wears flat-soled man shoes."

Elizabeth giggled again, pulling a finger through an uncombed strand of his hair. "You sure know how to make me laugh."

The trolley bell sounded and could be seen coming up the road. "Can you pick up some more paper today?" Jack asked. "I need to write Ben when I get home."

"Yes, my dear."

Jack stepped onto the trolley and turned around. "Get some for you, too, so you can write to Mr. Paul. I used the last of it for my homework," he said with a wave.

Elizabeth stood at the end of the drive until the trolley disappeared behind a row of tulip trees, examining the letter again. She didn't understand why she felt so indifferent; this was all she had worked toward over the months and weeks leading up to this moment. She had collected fine fabric for years, designing and cutting—it was her escape from the trials of the life she had endured. Then, suddenly it became obvious: it was a distraction, something she had turned to when she felt hopeless and sad. It brought comfort and something to focus on instead of the unrest and hurt. But now she felt exhilarated and hopeful, no longer desperate to lose herself in her work. It wasn't just about her own identity and freedom anymore; she felt her heart begin to open up to something much more meaningful.

46

Arthur checked the schedule as usual, making sure his staff was properly assigned to their posts. He held his morning meeting to cover the training agenda and announced the upcoming competitions the riders were preparing for, noticing an entry for his youngest rider at the St. Louis Charity Horse Show a week from today. "Simon, this is the first I am seeing this on the calendar. I wasn't aware this was clipping at our heels."

"That was my oversight; I apologize—I didn't cross-reference this month with our annual charity events and missed that one. Will you be able to attend on such short notice?"

Arthur rubbed his forehead, erasing some names from the calendar boxes and writing in new ones. After making some adjustments and counting the ratio of students and trainers once more, he tapped the pencil against the paper. "I think I can make time for it. We will need to fill my seat at the Manchester Auction Fundraiser and allocate a proxy for our contribution—and I do want that painting of the Fighting Temeraire."

"Yes, sir," Simon said, "I will coordinate that for you, it was my mistake."

"Thank you, Simon. Now excuse me, I have a letter to prepare for mailing immediately."

Arthur entered his writing room overlooking the courtyard, drew out his feathered pen, and stroked the quill thoughtfully before taking a seat at the desk to finalize his proposition.

Greetings:
Mr. Charles Collins
Mr. Carl Ebbers
Mr. Benjamin Paulie

I write this with urgency as I have been informed of an engagement I must attend in St. Louis, just a half-day's journey to your establishment. I would most welcome the opportunity to pay a visit. It would be pleasant to spend some time at your facility and get acquainted with Benjamin's training routine, and I believe it would be a benefit to build a familiarity as we progress into his future training structure here at my stables.

As a young lad, it might be less disruptive to his comforts if we are able to meet once more in his home environment before we embark on this new adventure.

I will plan to arrive next Thursday unless I hear otherwise and look forward to our meeting again.

Good day gentlemen,
Arthur F. Davies

*　　　*　　　*

Paul brought up the last harvest of cucumber and squash, unlatched the pull-behind, and noticed a family walking up to the market. The man wore trousers, a shabby button-down shirt, and worn-out boots. The woman beside him tugged at his arm, pointing at Claire and Gladys as they worked to set up bakery shelves through the window. The two children looked around and whispered to each other as they observed Paul separating damaged produce from the haul. Paul felt their eyes on him as he sorted and met their glances a few times. They looked to be about six and eight years of age. The girl wore a dress that looked about two sizes too big, and the boy had a few holes in his britches. He noticed the boy pull at his mother's dress skirt and whispered into her ear. She turned her head and looked at Paul as he tossed a split cucumber in the bucket to discard. He kept his head down and continued sorting when he heard a soft voice say, "Excuse me, sir."

The woman stood at his side, looking over at the small bucket; the two children followed behind her.

"Hello, ma'am, can I help you?" Paul asked, noticing the children slowly walking over and the man looking around when he realized they were no longer next to him.

"We're from Madison County, sir, we heard about this market that's close to opening. Many others in our parts have heard about it too."

"We're fixin' to be ready next week; you folks traveled a good ways to get here—didn't expect word to reach that far."

"We live in a community of displaced families. My husband was let go from his job and folks are just trying to get by. Times are tough in most places with the coal mines and refineries cutting back."

"Haven't heard much of it—we tend to keep to this area," Paul said, watching her eyes settle on the bucket of scrapped vegetables.

"How much are you asking for those?" she asked.

Looking at the bucket, he grimaced. "Those are ruined, mostly picked over by beetles and squash bugs. They ain't good eatin' I'm afraid."

The woman pulled out two coins from her skirt pocket. "Would you accept a nickel for four of the cucumbers and two squash? I can cut around the flesh."

Looking at the faces of the children, he noticed them staring at the bucket intently. The man stood behind them with his hands in his pockets and held out a few pennies. "I can add this to our offer, mister, but it's all I got today."

Paul waved at Elliot who was whistling across the lot with two empty baskets and a lemon meringue pie.

Elliot noticed the family, assuming they were one of the eager beavers anxiously awaiting the opening day. When he got closer, he could sense their desperation and timidness. "Howdy folks! What can I do ya for boss?"

"Can I take those off your hands?" Paul asked, pointing to the baskets.

Elliot handed him the baskets, nodded, then walked off, lifting the pie to his nose. Before he reached the door to the store, he turned back to the family, watching Paul set the bucket aside and fill the baskets with vegetables from the pull-behind. After he filled the baskets, the woman hid her face in her hands, then wrapped her arms around his neck. When she backed away, picking up one of the baskets, the man grabbed Paul's shoulder and shook his hand. Paul handed a basket to the older boy and waved as they walked away. Elliot soon realized what Paul had done and looked down at the pie, then looked over to the family.

As they approached their wagon, Elliot sniffed the pie one last time.

Paul continued sorting and was looking out over the lot, when he saw Elliot by the wagon giving the little girl his lemon pie. He watched Elliot wave goodbye, then stuffed his hands into his trousers and scuffed his boot along the ground.

"I bet that was hard," Paul chuckled. "You best be talkin' up Gladys to make you another one."

Elliot took off his hat and scratched his head, looking over at the market. "It ain't easy—them pies come with strings attached."

"What strings? They trying to trade for paint?"

"Not exactly. It's more like extortion without the threat of arms."

Paul cocked his head, but figured it was none of his business. "Say, you see more folks coming in with those government vouchers lately?"

Elliot nodded, kicking at the dirt and watching the wagon pull away. "Had to empty last month's collection to make room for more. I put 'em in a folder in the safe for the next deposit run. Why?"

"That family that just left, they said they come from Madison. The woman said something about folks being out of work—they looked to be hungry, too, and boy did she hug me tight," he said, rubbing the back of his neck. "She offered money for the throwaways."

Elliot stopped sulking about the pie and took notice of some of the folks loitering around the lot. "You might have timed this just right. If times are gettin' lean, fruits and vegetables will start outpacin' pork and beef. Darn good thing you planted when you did. The Holy Spirit must have been nudgin' ya!"

Paul rolled his eyes, but as he thought about what had happened on the roof, Elliot's ramblings over the years, about the spiritual realm and angels and such, began to make sense for the first time.

47

ELIZABETH TAPPED THE DRIVER ON the shoulder when they reached the corner of Eighth Avenue and Fortieth Street. "This is good, Leo. I would like to walk the rest of the way."

Leo pulled over and opened her door. "Shall I pick you up at the normal time and place?"

"Yes, that would be fine, but let's delay it an hour. I think I would like to walk in the park for a bit, it is a glorious day today."

He watched her cross the street, her long legs taking brisk strides across the crosswalk. Her high-waisted dress clung to her small frame as she sashayed along the sidewalk, eventually fading into the foot traffic. He always got a kick at the fellas that would turn to watch her breeze past, surprised like they had just seen a unicorn, and he quietly chuckled when the women would frown upon their obvious distraction. It still dumbfounded him how oblivious to the attention she was.

Elizabeth walked along the gates of Madison Square Garden, peeking through the archway at the very spot where she had met Paul. She could remember him clearly, pacing and checking his watch. She stopped to say hello to the sweet lady peddling freshly cut flowers; it was the same lady that he purchased her rose from. She walked away with a yellow one, rolling it under her nose and smiling when the image of his blushing face came to her memory. Every step reminded her of something. She saw him in front of the hotel next to Freddie's sausage cart, under the Italian bakery awning holding up the shirt she bought him, passing the theatre poster where their hands brushed each other's for the first time. She lingered at the window of the pizzeria, looking at the table where they had sat, and waved to her brother Tony. Continuing along her walk, she gazed at the flower while waiting for the crossing guard to signal. When she looked up, she saw two young boys hurrying inside FAO Schwarz. In all her years walking these streets, the only memories that filled her mind now were recent—Paul was everywhere.

"Good afternoon, Miss Rockwood," Scotty said, "we're almost done with the counter tile! Is Jack and Ben with you?"

Elizabeth shook her head. "Unfortunately, they are not. Jack is still in school and Ben has returned to Iowa."

"Iowa! That's a ways away. You think he'll be back to visit?"

"I sure hope so Scotty, that would be wonderful," she said, walking over to the window to admire the tailored window treatments. Her eyes caught the embrace of two lovers passing by, the man rubbing the woman's hand against his cheek and softly kissing her ring finger. Her inclination to turn away and busy herself was surprisingly not her first reflex. Instead, she smiled and drew the rose under her chin, remembering the kiss Paul had pressed to her lips.

"Miss Rockwood," Scotty called, clutching a wired dress mold by the base, waiting for her to respond. "Miss Rockwood," he called again.

Turning around, she found him standing in front of her. "Apologies Scotty, I was lost for a moment."

"That's alright, it's not heavy. Where would you like this one? We put one by the side door."

"Right there would be fine," she said, pointing to an open space at the center of the window. "I can model it to suit the season."

Looking over the progress, it was just as she had envisioned. The floor-length mirrors surrounded a measuring platform with plush cream carpet. The sitting areas were fragrant with flower blossoms, and crown molding with picture-frame wood floors accented the walls. It was beautiful, bright, and elegant—everything she had hoped it would be. And yet, the most powerful emotion she felt was from two strangers on the street who were so obviously smitten with each other.

Scotty positioned the form at the center of the window as Elizabeth walked out the door, figuring she was going to the window to guide it center. He stepped away to gauge its distance from the window, looking for Miss Elizabeth. He stepped up to the glass, looking right to left, but she wasn't there. He looked to the street and saw her crossing the walk toward the park and train station.

Elizabeth sat cross-legged on a bench at the train terminal, watching people come and go. Couples hugged and women waved as their men boarded while they coddled children. Families gathered luggage as they walked the platform. She watched the ticketer punch the boarding passes for a woman and her son, when a wonderful idea came upon her. She uncrossed her legs, placed her hands on her knees, and tapped her heels, then got up and went into the vestibule.

"Good day, miss, can I help you?"

Elizabeth looked up at the trip scroll and then to the man behind the counter. "Yes, could you tell me the next train scheduled for Iowa would be?"

The man opened a large black binder, licking his finger as he flipped page after page. The more he flipped, the less brazen she felt.

"Iowa," the man repeated. "We don't see many passengers heading out west these days, especially from the city," he said, continuing to thumb through the pages.

Elizabeth exhaled, thinking what a foolish idea this was in the first place. "That's alright, sir, I was only curious." She turned to walk away when the man tapped his finger on a page. "Here we have it. It isn't soon, but we have a train leaving out on Monday. That would get you there by Wednesday mid-morning."

"Wednesday," she whispered to herself. "Wednesday!"

The man checked the schedule again. "Yes ma'am, says right here in bold print, 'Wednesday arrival.'"

She smiled. "That is the day of the grand opening! That's perfect! I'll take two tickets please."

The man tipped his hat, stamped two tickets, and slid them under the counter. "Glad it worked out for you, miss."

"Thank you so much, sir, I appreciate it very much!"

She walked away holding the tickets close, feeling unsure and certain all at the same time, playing out the scenario several times as she strolled through the park. After arguing with herself for a few minutes, she sighed. *What is the harm.* She had the tickets if she decided to surprise him and would travel back the next day so they wouldn't be a burden. She and Jack could stay at the quaint inn on the outskirts of town and be there to show their support. The more she thought about it, the more delighted she felt. She glided along the curved path, listening to birds sing, and crossed over the bridge just as Leo pulled the car around.

48

GLADYS UNTIED HER APRON, PULLED it overhead, and took a moment to appreciate the work they put in. "My lands, we have ourselves a sweet little nook here."

Claire placed a lid over the last cake stand, smoothed the doily, and backed away, admiring the baker's racks and taking Gladys's hand into hers. "We really have, haven't we. Oh, this is so exciting! I can't believe we are just days away from being working women! Just imagine all the fun we're going to have baking cookies, pies, scones, breads... and we can make seasonal items, too. In the fall we can bake pumpkin pies, cinnamon rolls, molasses pecan pie, and sweet potato pie!"

"Lord help me," Gladys said, patting her hips.

"You ladies need anything before I lock up for the day?" Elliot asked, poking his head inside the door.

"About six inches off this caboose—how's that for a request?" Gladys leaned over to Claire, holding her hand to her ear. "'Cause he sure isn't good for gossip," she whispered.

"*Whoo-wee*, you ladies are ready to roll, literally!" he said, stepping inside to look around. Rolling pins, spatulas, sifting boxes, and all types of baking accessories were organized in baskets with colored ribbons.

"I just thought of something," Claire said, "we can decorate the baskets for the seasons! Orange and brown for autumn, white for winter, yellows and greens for spring, and red and blue for summer."

Elliot reached for a sifter, turned the handle, and watched the bars turn against the wire screen. "This could work right well for gold panning."

"You know what else it's good for?" Gladys asked.

Elliot could feel a zinger coming and slowly set it back down. "What's that, Miss Gladys," he said uneasily.

"My lemon meringue pie crust."

Claire put a finger to her lip and giggled under her breath.

Elliot knew he'd walked right into the trap and resorted to his only fail-safe escape tactic. He walked over and kissed them both on the cheek, thanking them for their hard work in making everything so beautiful and inviting, then walked out the door, tipping his floppy hat to them as he ambled past the window.

Claire fanned her eyes to dry the tears that started to pool as she looked at him adoringly.

"I think we just got bamboozled," Gladys said, flapping her hand in a wave with the other over her heart.

*   *   *

Elliot yanked the store's door open, noticed Paul was still in the office, and tapped on the doorframe. "I'm fixin' to head home and grab my pole and tackle. Want to join me for some night fishin'?"

Paul put his pencil down, pushed the chair back, and stood up to stretch. "Not tonight. I got a few more things to wrap up here."

Elliot nodded. "I'll see you in the mornin'."

Paul watched Elliot load his truck, feeling a little bad for not going with him. He waited until Claire and Gladys locked up and the lot was clear, then grabbed his toolbox and headed for the shed. Daniel and Denny had unloaded a truck full of timber and stacked it neatly in three lengths. He set the toolbox down and took a seat on top of a stump, reaching into his pocket and pulling out the velvet box. In his mind, he couldn't make sense of how the ring ended up in the box, and how in the world he found it on the ladder. Having thought on it all day, he wasn't any closer to finding an answer, but he knew it was too strange to ignore. *Maybe someone or something was giving him a message*, he thought. He sat for a moment, watching the shade creep across the grass as the sun started to settle, then grabbed the tape measure before it got too dark to work.

*　　*　　*

Elliot made his supper while he waited for dusk. Once the crickets started chirping, he gathered his pole and checked his tackle. With only a foot of twine left on the spool, he grabbed the store key and loaded his gear. On his way to the store, his mind wandered—from the family who had shown up at the store, to what Paul planned to do with the timber, before finally settling on which end of the creek to drop his line. Pulling into the lot, he noticed Paul's truck in the same place, then saw him carrying a plank just off the backside of Bernie's place. He approached the door, holding the key to the lock, watching Paul in the distance. He entered and walked to the storage room, taking a roll of twine from the shelf. As he passed the office, he saw a large sheet of paper spread over the desk. There was a ruler and several boxes with measurements and foundation markers. The shape of the larger square looked to be a sketch, and the more he scanned the diagram, the clearer it became. He looked out the window and held up the drawing. "That's Bernie's place alright," he said to himself, "that bugger is buildin'."

*　　*　　*

Paul pulled the saw blade across a plank, the rasping sound of wood being cut filling his ears, drowning out the sound of Elliot's footsteps.

Elliot recognized the pattern of the stake markers—it matched the drawing from the paper. Paul used twine to create a border with double lines to mark windows, which explained why there was none left on the peg board. Realizing Paul had no idea he was there, he had a seat on the stump so he wouldn't startle him when he turned around. Twirling the end of twine around his finger, he looked down and saw the small velvet box sitting on top of the toolbox. He looked at the wood, the stakes, the box, and suddenly it all came together. He slowly dropped his arm, picked up the box, and held it in his palm. Leaning over the stump and keeping his hand low beside him, he flipped the top open with his thumb. His jaw dropped as he brought it closer to his face, turning it slowly to watch the diamond sparkle. He was so surprised and captivated by the sparkling jewel he didn't notice the saw blade cease cutting. He snapped the lid closed and looked up to find Paul leaning on the handle of a shovel, his chin resting in the crook of his elbow as he stared at him.

Elliot flinched and bumbled, stuttered, and fumbled the ring box in his hand before setting it back on the toolbox. Avoiding Paul's glare, he gave his knees a slap and stood up. "Looks like you're busy, so I'll just be on my way to the—"

"Oh no you don't, you ain't slinkin' away nowhere," Paul said, pointing to the stump. "You best sit your ass back down."

Elliot sat down, trying to hide his grin under the brim of his hat.

"And take off that ridiculous hat."

He pulled off his hat, letting it dangle loosely over his knees as he waited for a scolding, only to be surprised when Paul flipped a bucket over and sat down across from him.

They sat quietly for several minutes. When Paul stretched out his legs and folded his arms, Elliot relaxed. "You think she'll say yes?"

Paul dropped his chin to his chest and shook his head. "I wouldn't be asking if I thought she wouldn't. But I know if I don't, I'll be kicking myself for being a coward."

"You got some big plans here," Elliot said, looking around at the lumber. "You're gonna need some more hammers."

Paul looked over his shoulder. "It ain't close to what she's accustomed to in the city, but I can do what I can."

"I seen the way you two looked at each other. If you can keep from bumblin' your words, I think you stand a good chance, but if I ever met a lady as purdy as Miss Elizabeth, my tongue would be tied up, too."

Paul looked at the box and blew out a deep breath. "Sure can't put it into words, that's for sure; darn near used up one of those timbers in wasted paper trying."

"Make it quick, brother, Miss Gladys has been squeezin' me like teats on a momma goat," he said, pulling on his waistband. "Trousers are gettin' tight. Better play that hand quick—a fine lady like Miss Elizabeth ain't gonna be walkin' 'round unescorted for long." Flipping his hat back onto his head, he picked up the ring box and handed it to Paul. "We best be callin' on the guys; we got some buildin' to do."

As Paul watched Elliot walk away, he pulled the shovel from the ground and drove it back into the dirt, deciding to join him for some night fishing.

49

Jack sat hunched over his paper at his desk, writing his letter to Ben, when Elizabeth tapped softly on his door. "Hello, Mother, I'm writing to Ben. Oliver said he's not gonna play outfield no more, so I need to know when he's coming back, because Tommy can't catch anything."

Elizabeth walked over to open the window to let the night air cool his room. "Sounds like rain is coming—do you hear the frogs?" She looked out the window, then turned to Jack who had turned the page over and was now writing with fervor on the backside.

"How do you spell 'marshmallow'?"

Elizabeth giggled and sat on the edge of the bed. "Why do you ask?"

"Me and Ben and Lucas want to have a campfire and we're picking our jobs. Ben is bringing the marshmallows, but I want to spell it right, even though he won't know if I get it wrong."

"Jack," she said, fanning the tickets in her hand. "How would you feel about going on a little trip?"

"To where, Mother? I don't want to go back to Italy again; it's too far and the water smells funny."

"Not Italy. I was thinking someplace that would be ideal for a good campfire."

Jack dropped his pencil and spun around in the chair, looking at the tickets she held in her hand. "Are those for us? You and me?!"

"I was thinking we could pay a visit. Not a long one, but we could make it in time for the grand opening of the market."

Jack jumped out of his chair. "Yes! I can't wait to tell Ben; he probably won't read this before we get there, but I'll hurry and finish it tonight to mail in the morning!"

They laughed together as Jack wrapped his arms around her waist and looked up with a grin. "Thanks, Mother. This is going to be the best time ever!"

"Don't stay up too late. After you finish your letter, go straight to bed."

"I will, Mother, I promise!"

Returning to her bedroom, she lit a candle, placed it at the corner of her vanity, and plucked the rose from the vase. The edges had started to wither but the scent was still fragrant. Sitting in front of the mirror, she reflected on darker days when she'd avoided them. Sliding the tickets beneath the vase, she studied her reflection; her skin had a pink glow, and her eyes seemed brighter. The emptiness inside her was gone and she felt happiness and joy in her heart. Warming a dollop of lotion in her hands, she massaged it over her skin, looking at her bare ring finger. She brushed her hair, changed into her sleeping gown, and pulled the duvet back. When she finally fell asleep, she dreamt she was standing on a small wooden bridge surrounded by marigolds. In the distance, she heard a voice calling to her. Looking out over a pond, she saw a large white house nestled among large trees sprouting creamy yellow blossoms. There was a man in the yard looking out into the sky and a thunderous rumble overhead.

She walked faster, her bare feet catching dandelions between her toes. When she reached the man, he pulled her close, wrapping his arms around her. Her belly was large, so large he could barely clasp his hands around her navel. The rumble grew louder, and a large shadow passed over them. The man held a letter; she couldn't see it, but it was there, and she could feel a sadness as he began reading. His voice soothed her as he rubbed her growing belly. She could see Jack walking down the driveway along a white picket fence carrying a sack over his shoulder. She called for him over and over, but he couldn't hear her voice. Another boy joined him carrying the same sack over his shoulder. She walked toward them, but the closer she got, the further away they seemed, until they stopped just over a hill, calling to her and waving their hands. She could hear their laughter fade into the distance as she called over and over, her calls muted against the roar of a plane's engine.

"Jack… Paul, where did they go, Paul," she murmured. "Where did they go—the boys."

"Mother," Jack whispered, "wake up, Mother."

"Jack, where did you go, Jack… Paul," she called quietly.

Jack put his hand on her shoulder, "Mother, I'm right here. Open your eyes, you're dreaming."

Elizabeth awoke, immediately sat up, and glanced around, touching Jack on the arm.

"We have to hurry, Mother; I'm going to be late for the trolley and I need to mail Ben's letter."

"Good heavens," she said, putting her hand over her chest. "I'll be right down."

Jack ran to the mail post, then sat on the porch steps.

Elizabeth closed the door behind her and tapped him on the back. "Here we go, we're on our way now."

Jack listened to the quick clack of her heels, happy he had a mother that could spring out of bed and four minutes later look like she could be on a magazine cover. She was humming, which meant she was either processing something or wanted to divert any and all attention from herself. He knew her tactics and wasn't falling for it.

"You must have been dreaming good, Mother; I heard you talking from my room!"

"I can't remember the last time I had such a strange dream. I must have had oodles on my mind last night."

"We did talk about our trip last night," Jack said, waiting for a reaction.

"That's right, we do have that to look forward to."

"And you did mention the opening of Mr. Paul's market store." He gave her an extra minute to reply, but when she started humming again, he knew she wasn't going to say much.

"Do you have all your school supplies, sweetie?"

"You know I do, Mother; this isn't my first day."

When the trolley pulled up, he grabbed his school bag and held it over his shoulder.

Elizabeth looked at him, tilting her head. Even though she saw him off to school each morning, something about him standing there today felt especially familiar.

"I heard you say Mr. Paul's name when you woke up. I like him, Mother—don't worry about that part."

She grinned and shook her head, looking at him sweetly and blowing him a kiss. She was never as surprised at his spontaneous observations as she was at that moment.

50

Charles walked onto the porch, cupping his mug in both hands. He inhaled deeply, watching the steam rise, and savored the thought of cooler mornings ahead. He looked out over the property, comforted by the stillness and thankful he wasn't in the hustle and bustle of the city. Closing his eyes, he listened to the birds and the gentle breeze through the treetops. He heard the side door open and shut, the sound of running feet over gravel gradually fading, figuring it was Ben on his way to the barn.

Claire opened the door and stood next to him, warming herself in the sun. "Ben sure did talk a lot about Mr. Davies this morning—he had three buttered rolls before he so much as took a breath."

"Arthur is a good fit for him. I think they will do right well together."

"He told me about the medal. That must have been very touching to Carl; it isn't easy to let go."

Charles took a sip of coffee and chuckled when he saw Carl's truck coming over the hill.

"Look, here comes Oscar!" Claire said. "I'm so glad I didn't scare him off. After my exuberant display during his last delivery, I was worried he wouldn't return."

"Good morning, Mr. and Mrs. Collins. I have a letter here stamped for expedited delivery."

"Does that mean you have to peddle faster?" Charles joked.

"This came by airmail, Mr. Charles. We don't see that very much—it must be really important."

"Thank you, Oscar, I appreciate your expediency."

Charles glanced at the letter. "It's from Arthur."

Claire watched his expression change, his eyebrows lifting in surprise as he finished reading. He folded it up and tucked it into his shirt pocket.

"Well?" Claire asked, pressing her hands together. "What did he say?"

"Mr. Davies will be paying us a visit next week."

"How exciting! This is quite an honor to welcome him to our home. Why, Ben went on and on about his travels and how well known he is. I should get busy planning for this. Did he mention which day next week?"

Charles opened the letter again. "Says here he plans to arrive on Thursday."

"Wonderful! The grand opening is Wednesday, so this is good timing!"

*　　*　　*

Ben bridled Juniper and fastened the saddle straps. As he began walking, he felt a lump in his jacket pocket and pulled out the apple he had taken from Arthur's apple tree. "Look boy, I forgot all about this."

Charles waited by the fence holding the letter. To his right, he watched Ben push off into the saddle—young, vibrant, and brimming with energy. He seemed ready to take the world by storm, with his whole life ahead of him, filled with victories to claim and challenges to conquer. To his left, he watched Carl hobble up the path with a cane and his notepad tucked under his arm; an old man who had lived a heroic life in many ways.

"What's that in your hand?" Charles asked. "You said pigs would fly before you used one of them sticks."

"Pigs did fly this mornin', after getting singed with bacon grease. What do ya have there?"

Charles handed him the letter. "It's from Arthur—he's coming for a visit."

Carl scanned the letter. "I got a good feelin' about him. I feel it in these fallin' apart bones, and I know you feel the same. And what's more than that, the kid does too."

51

The Angels

AFTER BACK-TO-BACK LOSING HANDS, JOSHUA'S interest in the card game waned and Jacob was already nodding off. Gabe was the only one still enjoying himself, mostly by belittling them, but even he was starting to struggle to come up with new insults.

"I see four empty bowls of cheese sauce; you sharks devoured it before I could dip a chip, so the cleanup is on you. I'm going to bed," Sarah said, pulling the band from her hair and giving it a shake.

Joshua drummed his fingers on the table, looking at the cheese blob oozing down the front of Gabe's shirt.

"Don't look at me," Gabe said, "I had to clean up after you toddlers had your picnic."

Sarah washed her face and braided her hair. She looked out the window at the glow of the fire from across the field and thought about the stories she'd overheard, then laid down in bed. She thought about reading the last chapter of *War of the Worlds*, but she was feeling a little sleepy and her eyes were getting heavy. She drifted in and out of sleep, turning on her side to feel the breeze coming through the window. The edge of the tree line was dimly lit from the light of the fire, and she rested quietly, watching the leaves flutter. The scenery was blanketed by a gray mist that hung just above the ground, and slowly, images began to take shape before her eyes. She saw a large building with many windows on every side and tall columns supporting the overhang of the grand entrance. The roofline was bordered by spindled framework that wrapped around the building. A wide, circular driveway with decorative edges curled around lush greenery, manicured trees, and rosebushes. The scene narrowed to a window at the very top of the west corner; inside she could hear voices. At first, they were loud, as if talking over each other, but gradually they softened to whispers. There was a man in a suit, appearing to be in command, shaking out a newspaper while a group of men sat around a long rectangular table. He was shouting at them, wagging his finger and demanding more censorship to curtail the incitement of panic among the people, insisting something was frivolous speculation. One man rose from his chair clasping his jacket lapels, standing in defiance before leaving the room.

The room grew dark, and three men followed the directive of the man in charge to follow him across a hallway and through a door, then through another, each time bolting the doors shut. There was a large desk at the center of the oval-shaped room with picture windows and several flags on each side. The men gathered around the desk, looking at the headlines covering the surface as the man shuffled among them, pulling out paper after paper and dropping them one over another. The headlines were grim: "Market Crash Cripples America," "America in Economic Turmoil," "The Fall of Free Economy," "America in Poverty."

The leader pulled out more papers from under the heap, all with the same ominous, desperate message. He pushed the papers aside, some falling off the corners of the desk, and reached into a drawer, taking a document out and placing it in front of the men. She heard the words "Federal Bank," "Reserve," and "Credit System." The private, secretive chatter between them felt mysterious and deceptive. As the vision faded, the lamplight in the room grew dark and she began moving away from the building. Watching it get farther away, she noticed shadows, like the one Gabe described, hovering in the air around the corners of the window before disappearing.

The scenery bled into a rolling scroll of countryside, mountains, and cities. It was just like her dream before, only clearer. She saw people begging in the streets, homeless encampments, and widespread poverty reaching from coast to coast. Suicides, underground fighting rings, and dealings in dark places festered.

The sharp sound of a shattering bowl startled her out of the vision, and she sat up, feeling a chill creeping through her bones. She closed the window, splashed water on her face, and left her room.

"Way to go, butterfingers," Gabe said, looking down at the floor.

"It wasn't my fault!" Jacob said. "You're the one that bumped into me with your ape arms."

"Jealousy is a sin, is it not?"

"You might want to use that peanut-brain of yours and read the Bible. Galatians 5:19–21. It's actually envy, knucklehead."

Joshua was entertained by their bickering and let them continue their volley of smack talk before interjecting. "Not entirely so. James 3:16: 'For where jealousy and selfish ambition exist, there will be disorder and every vile practice.'"

"Oh sure, take his side again," Jacob said as he swept pieces of the bowl into a dustpan. "Selfish ambition, vile practices—that pretty much sums it up," he said, giving Gabe a scowl.

Sarah came around the corner, looking down at the mess, pulling a towel over her neck and drying her face.

"Why are you all… sweaty?" Gabe asked, crinkling his nose. "Might want to use soap next time."

"I didn't take a shower, princess. I had a vision. We need to have a talk."

"I'm not sitting next to her," Gabe said as they followed her to the table. "Do we need lagers for this?"

"Oh yes, and more than one for me."

As soon as they got comfortable and leaned in to listen, they heard a knock on the door. "Why now?" Gabe grumbled as he walked to the door. "It's always during story time."

Abram, Zelach, and Caleb stood at the door. Gabe stifled a laugh staring at Caleb's curly mustache; he was never quite sure what look he was going for, but he sure got it wrong. "You run out of weenies?"

Caleb walked past him with an unamused look on his face and rolled the edges of his moustache, waiting for him to crack a joke about it.

Abram discreetly nudged Gabe with his elbow. "Not now," he whispered, "he's not in a good mood."

Gabe closed the door behind them with a thud. With humor off the table, he was stuck listening to their lackluster conversations.

"Pardon the intrusion," Caleb said, "but we have something to speak about."

"Yeah, well… pull up a chair, so does Sarah," Gabe said. "We can all have one big happy circle time."

Gabe carried an armful of lagers, sliding them to the center of the table, then pulled out one of the chairs on the end. "Who's gonna start us off?"

Caleb looked at the faces around the table. "We believe we are on the precipice of something that will require us to work together, and after hearing what we are about to share, we expect your agreement."

Gabe lifted his hands, counting on his fingers. "One, two, three, four, five, six, seven," he said, holding up seven fingers.

"Oh good, you can count. Everyone, raise your beers for a toast!" Joshua said.

"Where are the other two wallflowers?" Gabe asked.

Caleb looked at Abram, then over to Zelach. "They are on assignment… on earth."

"What's so heavy about that?" Jacob asked. "We're all here for assignments. We do our job, then wait for the next. What's so important about theirs?"

Caleb folded his hands on the table. "There's a shift taking place and a dark undercurrent brewing. Men in high places are summoning things from below; they're plotting and scheming hidden agendas. They are building a foundation of depravity and greed, looking to gain for themselves while others suffer from their misdoings. Their souls are lost; they lack compassion, are consumed by arrogance, and love only themselves. Money and power are their gods."

Gabe rolled his eyes and reached for a bottle, sliding it across the table to Caleb. "Please, drink that—might help lighten your mood."

"Arrogance and love of themselves," Joshua repeated. "Maybe we got Gabe by mistake?"

"Quit it you two! You been at each other all night!" Sarah scolded. "Be grown-ups for a change—this is serious!"

Gabe held his hands out to his side in compliance. "Fine… geez, just trying to survive this tea party we have here."

"I had a vision," Sarah said, "just a short while ago in my room. I saw people suffering, living in tent shelters, destitute… Men had no means to support their families, industries closed, and businesses boarded up. The market crash left many penniless with no place to turn; children wore tattered clothes, hungry and scared."

Caleb nodded. "Yes, it is coming, and it will leave many broken. It will come upon them in waves and rumblings as the resources are scavenged and hoarded by the ones unscathed."

"All this doom and gloom wasn't a thing until she overheard you talking about it by the fire the other night," Gabe said. "Now we have black apparitions, depressing dinner conversation, and the heebie-jeebies. I'm waiting for the devil himself to manifest in the middle of our beers right here! Didn't you see anything good, or was it all a poop show?"

Sarah reached for another bottle. "I did see some people making a difference. They were growing, planting, harvesting, and helping others. They were the ones that people sought out for help. They created jobs, new ideas, new inventions, and kept their faith, refusing to lose hope. But they were the few, not the many."

"Well, why didn't you mention that instead of all the famine and destruction? Give us something that doesn't make us want to crawl under our beds," Jacob said.

Abram chuckled. "It wasn't our intent to share this prematurely. Zelach has been hunting them, 'the apparitions' as you call them, for quite some time. We wanted to be certain we had good cause before bringing this to the table."

Joshua pinched the bridge of his nose. "So let me get this straight. We, meaning the four of us, have been playing around with horses, fires, storms, pandemics, and some guy that thinks roofs and rain make a good pairing, while you three and the other two are off hunting demons and in-the-know about approaching earthly calamity. Is that what I'm piecing together?"

Caleb, Abram, and Zelach all nodded their heads.

Gabe slouched against his chair, leaned his head back, and stared up at the ceiling, shaking his head. "Guys… guys. We have got to do better."

"Hey, don't include me in your mediocrity," Sarah said. "I'm the only one getting visions in our little dysfunctional family."

"So what is the point here?" Joshua asked. "What do we all need to agree on?"

Caleb pushed his chair back and buttoned up his coat. "We need to stay close to each other; when one of us is sent, we all need to know about it. If one of us has a vision, we all need to know about it. When Asher and Amos return, they will tell us what they saw, and we will in turn tell you. I feel our time being here among each other, yet separate, is coming to an end. We will need to become one family; we were assembled to be united and that is what we shall be."

Gabe raised his bottle over the table. "Should we all sing 'Kumbaya' to seal the deal?" He watched as everyone got up from the table. "Guess not… Seemed like the right call to me."

"I got one more question for the group," Joshua said. "With all of us together, what do you think the last one will be able to do?"

Caleb nodded slowly. "You mean the tenth angel, the last of our tribe—the one we are all waiting for." Caleb took a deep breath and exhaled slowly. "He is the catalyst—our leader. His power will be unmatched, possessing strength beyond measure. Nations and leaders will crumble in his shadow and his sword will be a searing blade of fire. He carries the keys that will unleash the dark powers. The ones we will triumph over; the ones Jesus will send to the lake of burning hot fire. He will lead us into a great battle someday. Until then… we wait."

"Whoa! Did you hear that Gabe? You best be lifting bigger logs tomorrow morning buddy, sounds like you got some competition coming your way!" Joshua joked, slapping him on the back.

"Don't get too excited," Sarah said. "Can you imagine two of them!"

52

Gladys and Claire handed off trays and baskets packed with scones, muffins, cookies, and bread loaves, while Charles, Elliot, and Ben packed them into the cars, filling every crevice available.

Denny held a corner post in place, waiting for Paul to line up the nail. He wiped the sweat from his brow, seeing a line of cars, trucks, and wagons in the distance. "You seein' what I'm seein', or is it the sawdust in my eyes."

Paul drove the nail, then dropped the hammer into his tool belt and stepped out from the framework.

"If I was you, I'd be puttin' on a clean shirt, or at least shakin' off those shavings. We'll keep movin' while you shake hands and make the women swoon, but you better get to gettin'."

Paul hopped around tools, sanders, and a murky bucket of water on his way to the bedroom. He batted at the tarp keeping the dust down, grabbed the shirt Elizabeth had given him from a box, and quickly buttoned, rolling up the sleeves to his elbows. He tucked the shirt into his waistband and stepped in front of a mirror wrapped in packaging material. Even though his reflection was muted by a layer of thick plastic, he frowned and pulled the shirt out, letting it hang freely over the pockets of his jeans. He licked his hands, spitting out the residue of stone dust, and ran them through his hair. Looking down at his boots covered in the thick white dust, he untied the laces and pulled on the city boots before hurrying for the door, narrowly avoiding a full paint tray. He walked along the edge of the porch's foundation, jumping over a leveling rake and staying clear from the cobblestone walkway JT was busy setting.

Walking beside the stone pavers, he imagined walking hand in hand with Elizabeth. Seeing the long line of cars and wagons approaching, he snapped off a marigold stem, plucking the petals to ease his nerves. He was never one for crowds and small talk. The tension subsided when he saw Elliot's truck, followed by Charles and Gladys. Chuck Grover and Fred Comer were parking, and Reggie and Cecelia were getting the children out of the car. Carl, Earl, Frank, and Millie were walking around admiring the storefront. By the time he got there, the lot was filling up, and more kept coming.

"Dear, isn't this wonderful! The day has finally arrived!" Claire said, rubbing Paul's arm. "Look at all the people!"

"Get in here," Gladys said, wrapping her thick arms around him. "Oh, I know, you hate this yucky love stuff, but you got this coming whether you like it or not. Now then, we need to man our posts, but first, you strappin' strong men are going to help us feeble old women carry in the goods."

Elliot and Ben hung a sign for the grand opening, tossed a few more corn husks into the vegetable bin, and emptied a bucket of snap peas into a large basket.

"Can I help out at the store today, Mr. Elliot?"

"Darn tootin'!" Elliot said, hanging an arm around Ben's shoulder. "We'll have us a good ole time! We might well be runnin' 'round like headless chickens, but we'll find some time for throwin'."

"Lucas said he was coming by to help, too, so we got one more chicken."

Claire and Gladys tied their aprons, welcoming folks with bright smiles as they came into the market. Gladys quickly cut a dozen scones into sample sizes and placed them on the bakery counter only to watch them vanish before her eyes. "If I keep doing that, we'll be out of business faster than my hair turns gray," she whispered.

Claire peeked around two women deciding between the blueberry or apple scones and noticed Gretta Grover holding a compact up to her face and applying a thick coat of red lipstick. Her dress was a bit showy for a day trip to the market and the neckline left nothing to the imagination. "Don't look now, guess who just sauntered through the door."

"Hello ladies!" Gretta said rather loudly, drawing attention to herself.

Gladys smiled politely and waved. "As if we couldn't see her; that dress is redder than Satan's tail."

*   *   *

Paul enjoyed watching people fill their baskets with his vegetables, the sight of their satisfaction making the endless hours of laborious planning, planting, and tending the crops feel well worth the effort. He spent most of the morning answering questions about their technique, the equipment they used, seed saving, and what they expected to yield in the fall. After a while, he felt like one of the traffic cops he'd seen in Manhattan, directing people as they walked from the market to the store, through the corn paths, and into the orchard for berry picking. Carl looked to be enjoying himself, seated on the tractor and pulling a hay wagon full of kids, each one snacking on handfuls of Claire's caramel-coated popcorn balls.

At the store, Elliot and Ben were busy with customers. Ben handed out the last sales receipt and hurried to the office before the next customer reached the counter. He opened the desk drawer, picking up a small velvet box that was sitting on top of the slips when he heard Elliot calling him. In a rush, he grabbed the slips and closed the door.

Elliot started another pot of coffee and looked out the window. "I ain't too sure, Ben, looks like there's more roamin' about than before. We might not get to catch today."

"That's alright, Mr. Elliot, we can play tomorrow."

"You got that order from Mr. Crampton? I wanna get that to him before he leaves."

"Got it right here in my pocket," he said, pulling out the piece of paper and the small box along with it. "Here you are Mr. Elliot."

Elliot reached for the paper, then looked at the ring box on the counter. Feeling somewhat baffled and having a loss for words, all he could do was point to it.

"I don't know what that is, Mr. Elliot, it was on top of the sales slips. I shut the door before putting it back. Do you know what's in it?"

"You didn't open it?"

Ben shook his head.

Elliot relaxed and slid it across the counter, dropped it into his shirt pocket, and whistled as he stepped outside.

*　　*　　*

"Congratulations, Paul, this is quite a success," Chuck said, blowing out a puff of pipe smoke as he admired the engine of a Ford Model AA. "Pretty soon, you'll be able to buy five of these beauties!"

"Thank you, Mr. Grover, sure did surprise me. Never expected this turnout."

Chuck looked over the crowd, pointing his pipe toward the market. "Speaking of beauties, here comes mine now."

Gretta shook a yellow scarf in their direction. Paul could feel her eyes peel him like a banana and quickly looked around for an escape. Luckily, he saw Elliot from across the lot and abruptly excused himself.

"Boy, you showed up in the nick of time," Paul said.

"Yeah buddy, she locked eyes on you like a hawk over a muskrat, must be that purdy shirt you're wearin'."

"Did you need something?" Paul asked, checking over his shoulder. "I was gonna see if Denny needed a hand."

Reaching into his pocket, Elliot pulled out the ring box. "Better keep this close to the vest—seems to be turnin' up in unexpected places."

"Thanks, forgot I left it there," Paul said, stuffing it into his pocket.

"I'm startin' to get a little hungry. What'd ya say we sneak one of them blueberry muffins?" Elliot said, his words muffled as he opened a bag of sunflower seeds with his teeth. When he didn't hear Paul answer, he looked up and saw him slowly walking away, his body moving like he was in some kind of trance. "Wait up!" Elliot called, looking into the crowd to see what grabbed his attention. When he found the answer, he stopped, spat out a seed, and stared across the field.

*　　*　　*

"Look over here, Mother, there's a pond and a bridge like the ones in the park, only smaller. I bet there's frogs in it! And look at all the people… I wonder if Ben got my letter in time? If he didn't, boy is he gonna be surprised!"

"That does resemble the park bridges—and look at all the lovely marigold trees! They smell wonderful."

JT held a paver in his hand, brushing at the sand for a level set, when he saw an exquisite looking lady wearing a wide-brimmed hat with lace trim and a form-fitting blue dress that flared just below her knees. He wrenched his neck watching her pass, accidently setting the paver crooked.

As they walked along the marigolds, Elizabeth admired their rich color. "Feels a bit familiar," she said, "but I have no idea why."

Jack reached over, bending a flower until it broke free from the branch, and tapped her on the shoulder. "It matches your hair, Mother. Maybe you can stick it in your hat."

"Thank you darling, that is very sweet," she said, smiling at him. "Although, we might want to be careful about taking other people's flowers, that might be frowned upon."

Jack looked at the marigolds all around them. "I think they got plenty, Mother—they won't even notice."

Elizabeth walked with her head down, spinning the flower between her fingers.

Jack slowed, reaching for her hand. "Mother."

Deep in her thoughts on why the flowers resonated with her so, she was blissfully unaware of his plea for her attention.

"Mother!" Jack said again, this time pulling on her hand and pointing in front of them, his face lit with excitement. "You might want to look up, Mother."

Jack grinned and waved at Paul, pretending not to notice the googly-eyed look on their faces.

Paul closed the gap between them, still in disbelief.

"You sure do like that shirt, Mr. Paul."

Paul laughed. "It's the only one I got that isn't covered in paint."

"We thought it would be nice to celebrate the day with you and everyone else. I know this means so much to you; we just wanted to be a part of it," Elizabeth said. "I hope our arrival isn't a disturbance—it wasn't meant to be."

Paul shook his head. "Not at all. In fact, I can't think of anything better than this."

"Is Ben here, Mr. Paul?" Jack asked, looking around at the crowds of people.

"He is, Elliot put him to work in the store. He'll sure be glad to see you."

"Can I go see him, Mother?"

"Yes, you can go see him," Elizabeth said, watching him run across the field. "He was so excited about this that he barely slept on the train. I was going to write you a letter, but I doubt it would have arrived before we did. I have never done anything so spontaneous before, and I talked myself out of it at least a dozen times."

Paul took a few more steps closer, his eyes focused on her lips.

She felt rather flustered seeing him approach so intently, causing her to blunder and fidget. "We are only in for the day and evening," she said in an awkward manner as he came closer. "We're staying at that quaint inn, just outside of town," she continued, acutely aware of her breathless rambling. "I met the lady that keeps it up during my travels to town," she said, almost in a whisper as he stood just inches away, feeling his breath against her cheek. "I do hope our presence isn't a distraction."

Paul reached for her hand, breathing her in. "You *are* a distraction, Miss Elizabeth Rockwood, whether you're here or not. And I should know your middle name."

Elizabeth brushed a thick strand of her hair from her face and tucked it behind her ear, revealing a smile. "Emily," she said and squeezed his hand. She could feel him move even closer when she noticed familiar faces gathering behind them. "I have pulled you away long enough."

Paul inhaled her scent, bewitched by her beauty. Reluctantly, he took a step back, turning to find Elliot and Charles loitering under the market awning, pretending to be looking elsewhere. "I should apologize in advance for their lack of subtlety."

*   *   *

Gladys fetched the last two trays from the baker's rack when she spotted Charles and Elliot out the corner window, finding it rather peculiar to see them not doing much of anything. When she followed their gazes onto the edge of the roadside, Gladys nearly dropped her tray. "Oh my word, would you look at that!" she said, turning around and waving at Claire. "Claire, come look! Come look here!"

Claire hurried around the corner, peeking over Gladys's shoulder. "What is it? What do you see?"

"Over there!" she said, bouncing on her toes. "My bottom dollar says that's our mystery woman! And my oh my, she is beautiful! Come, let's say hello!"

"I don't know, Gladys. We don't want to appear meddlesome."

"Nonsense, we aren't fooling nobody—we're old women, that's what we do."

Elliot turned, loosening a seed skin from between his teeth just as the women closed the door behind them, whispering with their hands clasped together like giddy schoolgirls. Elliot leaned over to Charles and asked, "Does Mrs. C make a good lemon meringue pie?"

*   *   *

"I *am* looking forward to meeting everyone. I feel like I already know them from reading your letters," Elizabeth said, leaning into his shoulder. "I see Mr. Collins, and the woman wearing the yellow apron, standing next to him, is likely Claire, and I'm guessing the woman to her right would be Gladys."

"Beautiful *and* perceptive."

"Not exactly. You are just a descriptive writer."

Paul scoffed, remembering the last time he tried putting his feelings down on paper. "I got a full wastebasket that says otherwise."

*   *   *

It wasn't long before they were encircled. Charles and Elliot blushed four different shades of red and Claire and Gladys did their best to contain their eagerness to make her acquaintance, but they soon walked off with their arms around her, calling over a few ladies for introductions. Margie waved excitedly, dropping a handful of tomatoes back in the bin to join them.

"She's quite a lady," Charles said, watching the women huddle around her. "To make that trip for you… that's something special alright. You best not let her get away."

Elliot shoved his hands in his pockets and anxiously rolled back and forth on his heels, noticing Paul's hand movements inside his jeans pocket, and knowing darn well what he was thinking.

Paul couldn't take his eyes off her, but even so, he was quite aware of some not-so-subtle glances from men in her direction. He certainly couldn't fault them for their admiration. Watching her from a distance, he started to understand this feeling of security. She was either not aware of her striking presence or simply didn't pay any mind. Either way, it made him more certain of his attraction. During his conversations, he kept his eye on her as she mingled, feeling a surge of electricity run through his body whenever their eyes met. Her mannerisms were politely reserved yet outwardly expressive and inviting. Young girls and women approached her to marvel at her dress, and she drew people in effortlessly. Even though she stood out among the crowd and looked somewhat out of place with her style and elegance, she fit perfectly—there was no pretense of her privilege. She was modest and humble, yet spontaneous and interesting, and he found that positively thrilling.

"You got it bad brother," Elliot said, shaking out a handful of seeds. "Ain't seen you wooing like this since we sighted in that twelve-point last spring."

"I reckon you're right about that."

Elliot gave him a smack on the back as they watched Carl pull the tractor around. "I'm gonna see if the old man needs a break and leave you here to fancy."

"You just want a turn driving it around."

Elliot nodded, tossing a handful of seeds in his mouth. "Gonna get me one of them popcorn balls, too!"

*   *   *

After finishing his work for the time being, Paul spotted Elizabeth and meandered toward her, stopping to greet the family that came by last week along the way. The man shook his hand, thanking him again for his generosity. He saw many unfamiliar faces—folks whose wagons were loaded with household items and covered in canvas—and overheard two men talking about traveling west in search of work. Looking around, it was obvious some were on the move, coming from three or four counties over. He thought about the increase in vouchers they were seeing and couldn't help but feel something was happening that he didn't quite understand. Hearing familiar laughter, he turned to see Ben, Jack, and Lucas bobbing and weaving a path through the crowd running alongside the tractor. They waved their hands over their heads, calling out to Elizabeth, inviting her to join them on the adventure. He chuckled to himself, thinking there was no way she would accept the invitation to climb into a rickety old wagon filled with hay.

"I adore that woman," Gladys said, wrapping her arm around his. "She's my kinda people."

Elizabeth took hold of Jack's hand and Carl and Elliot guided her up to the platform. Paul never loved her more than he did in that moment.

Little by little, the lot began to clear. People loaded up their produce and the last group of berry pickers weighed their baskets. Elliot took the wagon on one final lap through the field while Claire, Gladys, and Elizabeth packed, cleaned, and straightened the market for the following morning. Elizabeth was entertained by the women's stories; they shared memories of Paul as a youngster that he would never think to tell her. Claire doted on him, complimenting his strength, courage, and business smarts, and confessing his tendency toward solitude and how she often fretted over it.

"Don't let that sob story fool you," Gladys said, hanging her apron on a wall hook. "Many have tried to lasso that stallion, but none caught him yet. Although I must say, he's turned every shade of red over you."

Elizabeth giggled and looked out the window, watching Paul jump in on a game of marbles with the boys.

"He's one in a million, sugar," Gladys said, leaning over Elizabeth's shoulder. "The Lord don't make 'em any better than that."

*   *   *

The boys' eyes boggled as Paul took out three of their marbles in one shot, huddling around the circle for a closer look.

"That was incredible!" Jack said, "the odds of hitting out three is almost impossible!"

"Lucky shot," Paul said, then walked over to the fence and threw a bag of seed over his shoulder.

"Ask him now," Jack whispered, "he will say yes after that shot."

Paul heard some whispering and footsteps coming up behind him.

"Mr. Paul," Ben said with a hint of apprehension.

He turned around and waited, watching them gesture and hand signal each other as if selecting one of them to speak on the group's behalf. Dropping the sack of seed, he crossed his arms, amused by the way they hemmed and hawed, giving each other the side-eye and scuffing their shoes along the dirt.

Ben took the lead, glancing over at Jack. "We know the last campfire we had didn't turn out so good…"

"Yeah," Lucas added, jabbing Jack in the arm.

"But we were hoping… if maybe… we could have one tonight?"

Paul waved over Elliot and Charles, waiting for them before giving the boys an answer. "How y'all feel about letting these young men have another crack at a campfire?"

"We got enough buckets for that?" Elliot joked.

Charles scratched his chin. "I'll let Patrick know to be ready with the hose," he said with a wink.

Paul chuckled and picked up the seed sack. "There's wood by that pond over yonder you can use."

"Thanks, Mr. Paul!" they shouted, running off as they high-fived each other.

*   *   *

The ladies closed up the market and walked along the fence, watching the boys run across the field.

"Paul's been working day and night over there. It sure is going to be something when he's finished," Gladys said.

"And the yard is going to be incredible!" Claire said. "The bridge was a bugger though. They toiled over that for a week—Charles said something about the center posts giving them a fit—and then we had all that dreadful rain… gave them a terrible time."

Elizabeth listened as they commented on the yard, pointing out the cobblestone, the beginning framework of a pergola, and the antique sitting benches. "Is that Paul's home?" she asked.

"He calls it Swiss cheese. The man doesn't have walls yet—and not much flooring either." Gladys said. "They've been working so hard, cutting, sawing, and hammering for days on end."

"That was Bernie's place," Claire said, "he left it to Paul."

Gladys lovingly rubbed Claire's arm. "I was wondering when he was going to move out of that tiny place he was in; it was so small, the poor thing had to stand on his head to sleep."

*   *   *

Paul and Charles waited for the ladies as they walked and talked. "What'd you suppose they talk about when they're off on their own?" Charles asked.

"Probably not huntin' or fishin'."

Claire leaned into Charles as he wrapped her in a hug, giving her a kiss on top of her head as she snuggled into him.

"I'm putting these bones to bed," Gladys said, squeezing Paul's chin and giving him a wink. "I'll see y'all in the morning."

Elliot sputtered over, cutting the engine. "How's about I load up the bandits and give 'em a ride through the woods to the campfire. We need the tractor by the paddock in the morning, anyways."

"We'll be right behind you," Paul said.

Waving goodbye, they watched the cars pull away and listened as the tractor's engine sputtered off across the field. Paul reached for her hand and removed her hat, pulling a piece of hay from a strand of her hair. He lifted her hand to his lips, gave it a soft kiss, and wrapped his arm around her waist, pulling her against him. "Thank you for coming today," he whispered, then lowered his head to hers and kissed her.

She lingered in the warmth of his breath against her lips. Leaning into him, she put her hand over his heart, feeling his chest rise and fall. He tilted her chin and passionately kissed her again. As their lips separated, he stepped back, and they both stared deeply into each other's eyes.

"I want you to know how much you and Jack mean to me. You've made me want something so desperately that I never even believed existed. I want you both, I want us to be a family—more than I ever wanted anything or anyone. I want to be the man who makes you smile every day. The man you lean on in times of trouble, and the man you laugh with in times of joy. I want to be your provider and protector, always. I don't want to be without you, Miss Elizabeth Emily Rockwood." Paul reached in his pocket, his sweaty palm clutching the velvet box.

Elizabeth put her hands to her mouth as he pulled his hand from his pocket, held the ring box, and kneeled in front of her on a bent knee. He looked up, staring into her eyes with such admiration and desire it took her breath away.

"Elizabeth Emily Rockwood, will you marry me?"

Elizabeth pressed her hands over her eyes to wipe the tears of joy streaming down her cheeks. "Yes! Yes, I will marry you!" she cried, throwing her arms around his neck as he lifted her off the ground and spun her around in a circle, both laughing and holding each other tightly.

He set her down, taking the ring from the box and sliding it onto her finger.

"It's beautiful, thank you. I love it and I love you Paul."

"I love you, too, Elizabeth. You have made me the happiest man in the world, and I will honor and cherish you both, every minute for the rest of my life."

Elizabeth touched his face, glanced around curiously, and then turned back to him in utter amazement. "Paul, look at where we are standing. Do you remember this spot?"

Paul thought back to the day they stopped at the store to say goodbye. He remembered being so tongue-tied he couldn't get his words out. He remembered Jack giving him the watch and Elizabeth handing him the candy bar with her address.

"Wait!" she said with a giggle, opening the clasp of her handbag and pulling out a Nutty Bar.

Paul shook his head and laughed as she unwrapped the shiny blue wrapper and broke it in half.

"This spot right here Elizabeth, when you came to say goodbye… That was the moment I fell in love with you."

She looked around, taking in the store and the market. Her eyes moved to the orchard and then the sky before taking his hand. "This would be the perfect spot for a wedding."

*   *   *

Elliot and the boys rode through the woods singing the baseball song and counting the stars overhead. They rode down the dirt path, waving at Carl as he ended his day. When they climbed out of the wagon, there were three packages of marshmallows sitting on top of some hay bales next to the paddock. Elliot helped them set up camp and stack the wood, showing them the proper way to build a fire. After getting the fire started, he looked out over the field. That's when he saw Paul walking hand in hand with Elizabeth by his side—and he knew.

Paul smiled and squeezed Elizabeth's hand when he heard a loud shout and saw Elliot waving his hat in the air.

*   *   *

Ben, Jack, and Lucas stuffed themselves full of marshmallows, laughing and telling jokes. They played a game of tag to burn off the sugar rush, then collapsed over the hay bales to catch their breath. They teased Lucas, retelling the story of when he ran from the tree line, convinced he'd heard a monster. Jack stared out into the woods, remembering a time when he wished for nothing more than a happy family and good buddies to sit around a campfire with. And now he had them.

"We should be cowboys when we grow up!" Jack said. "We can have campfires every night!"

"Or we can have a horse farm!" Ben said, "just like the one Mr. Davies has!"

Lucas looked up at the sky. "I want to fly planes! War planes, like the Aeromarine 40 or the Curtiss H-12, or the Dunne AH-7—did you know they can land on water?"

Jack and Ben listened as Lucas told them all kinds of stories that he'd heard from his father about military aircraft. They were engrossed as he talked about Navy boats and submarines. He showed them a picture of the USS *Holland* and they stared at it over the light of the fire.

"Maybe me and Ben can join the Navy and be on a ship, and you can fly around over our heads and wave to us. Wouldn't that be neat!" Jack said.

"My brother is in the Navy and he likes it a lot!" Ben said. "He doesn't get to come back a lot, but his uniform is neat, and he writes to me about all the places he gets to see."

Lucas leaned across the hay bale and stuck his hand out. "Let's make a pact that whatever we do, we do it together."

53

The Angels

JACOB, JOSHUA, AND SARAH STARED into the glow of the fire, listening to the crackle and pops of spitting embers as they shot into the night sky. Gabe turned a stick over the rim, watching it smolder. They listened as small voices echoed through the flames, whimsical and free-spirited.

Sarah followed a dancing ember as it drifted above the tops of the trees. Looking into the dark sky, she had a vision of planes swooping low with trails of smoke rolling behind them. Sounds of thunderous booms rumbled and flashes of light flickered and dimmed.

Jacob and Joshua leaned over the fire listening to the voices. In the middle of the flames, they saw ships pulling away from port, slicing through rough seas as white-capped explosions swallowed the bow, sending the hulls careening into dark waters.

Rolling the stick through the hot ash, Gabe heard laughter, and a sparkle caught the corner of his eye. The scent of marigolds drifted under his nose, and he lifted his head. He watched a white haze circle above him, and through the misty center, he saw a vision: The moon and stars illuminated fields of stone and white walls lining hills and valleys. He felt the sting of a hot ember hit his chest and it felt like a smoldering rod pierced his flesh.

One by one, they left the soft glow and warmth of the fire and disappeared into the woods.

Acknowledgments

As a first-time author, without a long list of accolades to shout about yet, this page will be short and to the point. To be honest, I wasn't planning to include this section—unless I am thanking the heap of dirty laundry in my mudroom for providing a cushion to sit on so I wouldn't wake my household with late-night typing; but then it came to me.

My friend from church, Rachel Dowling, a very talented artist who provided the first sketch that inspired the book cover.

My two sons, Griffin and Wyatt, were culinary casualties enduring more than a few nights of bad takeout because I was pushing myself to write "just one more page."

My friends and coworkers, who listened to me talk endlessly about the scene I had just finished at four o'clock in the morning.

And to all the readers out there who love a great story—the fantastic possibility to inspire and entertain through the written word gave me the motivation to dream, and this book was written for them.

About the Author

First-time author **Kim Koontz** hopes to give readers an inspiring story with *The Catalyst*. Through the years, she has been encouraged by others to write, but with an active life and two teenage sons and two jobs, finding the time was difficult. Four years ago, she made time. *The Catalyst, Book One: The Waiting*, is the first book in the three-book series to be launched. This novel is her debut as a writer; and her intention was to write a good story that will entertain and inspire readers as they experience memorable characters and a pivotal era in our nation's history. She resides in Michigan.

Author photograph: Corbin Boone, on Instagram @boone.corbin.photo